The Odd Fellows Society

By C.G. Barrett

The Odd Fellows Society

Copyright © 2015 by C.G. Barrett

www.cgbarrett.com

All rights reserved. No part of this book may be used or reproduced in any manner whatsoever without written permission except in the case of brief quotations in critical articles and reviews. Printed in the United States of America by Ink & Image Media II.

ISBN 978-0-9884419-3-4

This is a work of fiction. Names, characters, places, and incidents are either the product of the author's imagination or are used fictitiously. The author's use of names of historical figures, places, or events is not intended to change the entirely fictional character of the work. In all other respects, any resemblance to persons living or dead is entirely coincidental.

Cover design by Emma and Ruth Smith

Ink & Image Media II, LLC
10314 Seabridge Way
Tampa, FL 33626
E-mail: info@inkandimagemedia.com

For Maria

…and the Jesuits who made me a better person.

Brendan Lally
Dan Ruff
René Molenkamp
Ollie Morgan
Bill Sneck
Lucien Longtin

Also by C. G. Barrett

A Mouse's First Christmas: A Holiday Tail

...a children's novel

Chapter 1: Georgetown, Washington, D.C., April 1953

There was no point in screaming. Philip Cannon was a dead man.

He dashed past Healy Hall and through Georgetown University's iron gates. Behind him footsteps splattered a hollow echo across the cobblestones.

If he returned home, they'd kill him there – his wife and daughter too.

He fled past Holy Trinity Church. That's what broke him – the promise he couldn't keep: Philip clasping his baby above Trinity's baptismal font, the tumbling water, her startled wail, his vow as he pressed his lips against her wet forehead. *Hush now, Susan, for I shall keep you safe forever.*

His heel caught a cobblestone. He flew forward, his head cracking off the curbstone at the top of the stairs to Canal Road.

With a desperate moan, he staggered to his feet. He glanced down the steps, aglow with the full moon. Betrayal fused with fear.

His pursuer seized his jacket, shook him violently. "Where are they?" he hissed.

Philip wept. "Someone else will find them and you'll be finished."

He shook him again. "Tell me or die!"

Philip trembled. "You're going to kill me anyway."

A thin smile split the other man's face. Philip felt a punch to the stomach, an icicle sliding up behind his ribcage.

"You always were the brightest in the class, Philip."

Philip Cannon died staring his best friend in the eyes.

Chapter 2: Washington, D.C., February 2016

Santiago Torres clutched the string. He glanced at the white hen at its end, pecking at the sidewalk, and looked around the intersection. Where could that crazy, old woman have gone?

"I'd really like to help, but I'm terribly sorry," he'd told her. "I have a dinner appointment in two minutes."

The Chinese woman ignored him. She prattled on in Mandarin, pressed the string into his hand and even patted it to seal the deal.

He was sure she meant she'd be back in a moment. He looked at his cell phone. That was forty-five minutes ago.

And where the hell was Jasper?

His eyes flickered to the sky. A February cold front was arcing in from the northwest, promising either five inches of snow or torrential rain by nightfall. He sniffed the air. Wet asphalt. By tomorrow morning, the battleship gray sky would meld with all the granite and marble between the Capitol and the Lincoln Memorial, giving Washington the appearance of wet chalk.

Santiago avoided an amused glance of a young woman rushing down the street. Above the smile, her eyes raked him from his toes to his jet-black hair. They stopped at his angular face, the color of his abuelo's café con leche. As far back as college, his smile and light accent seemed to make all the girls from the small towns in the Northeast melt. He reddened at the attention.

Santiago looked away toward the enormous Chinese gate at the intersection of Seventh and H in Northwest D.C. He scratched under his clerical collar, struggled to appear nonchalant. The hen clucked and the woman suppressed a laugh. Santi felt ridiculous. Now in his late thirties, the respected headmaster of one of the capital's prep schools had suddenly become the opening line of a politically incorrect ethnic joke. "So this Puerto Rican priest was standing on a corner in Chinatown with a chicken on a leash..."

A horn wailed. A silver BMW swept erratically toward the curve, lurched to a stop. Bellows of laughter tumbled upon the sidewalk.

"Hey, Father Torres, you want some fries with that?"

He gave a wry smile, raised the string, and offered a pathetic shrug. The boys laughed like hyenas, darted into traffic again, nearly colliding with a cab.

Lacrosse practice was already out. Santiago checked his cell phone again.

What could be delaying Jasper?

Santiago turned, searched the intersection again. Parent conferences would begin back at Gonzaga in forty minutes. How could someone be so obsessive about everything in life except a clock? "I'll be on time," Jasper swore.

"Siéntate a esperar!" Santiago muttered.

A man shuffled past.

"Alex?"

"Father Santiago!" The grizzled, bearded man smiled in recognition, the teeth in his jaw notched with gaps.

Santiago's eyes flickered to the homeless man's feet. Frayed, filthy socks poked out of the fronts of battered work boots. Lashed with duct tape to keep them shut, the tops still flopped open and closed with each step.

He was about to ask Alex what he had done with the pair of shoes he had given him just last week but Santiago already knew.

He checked the time again. The six blocks back to the school would take fifteen minutes. No time for dinner. Typical Jasper. All worked up and excited. For the last month, it was either a new clue he'd put together for his annual history scavenger hunt or his insistence they sit down so he could reveal his latest thesis discoveries in excruciating detail.

Santiago simply hadn't had time.

"This will blow your mind," Jasper said over the phone, his voice falling to a whisper. "We need to meet. I need to give you something. Something important."

At first he thought Jasper wanted to test the difficulty of his scavenger hunt clues on him again, then Santiago caught the strained hitch in his friend's voice.

"Are you worried about something?"

A stressed laugh. "What's the last doctoral thesis in history that became a best seller and sparked an international uproar?"

"Why don't you just tell me what it is?"

"Meet me at the Friendship Arch at five-thirty," he said. "We'll grab dinner."

Then – typical Jasper – he simply doesn't show up. Lost in time, his nose buried again in Georgetown's archives.

"Whatcha doin' with that chicken, Father?"

"I," Santiago stuttered a fib. "I'm watching it for a friend."

"I could watch it for you."

The way Alex was leering at the bird, he'd be watching it over a campfire.

Santiago glanced at the chicken. It finally dawned on him. Even if Jasper showed up, he couldn't just walk into a Chinese restaurant with a live chicken on a string.

A cold rain began falling.

With conference night over, Santiago Torres ducked back into the headmaster's office to retrieve his cell phone from his desk. He passed through the small office of his secretary, Pearl, now gone home, and slid into his own. He crossed the room, glided around the desk and fell into the large chair.

No messages. The anxious fluttering that passed through his stomach echoed the urgent downpour pelting against the window glass. Was it just his evening's presentation, the parents' scattered, reluctant laughter, that unsettled him? Or was it Jasper? He usually lost track of time, but within an hour or two a harried, apologetic message dropped into voicemail.

He tapped Jasper's number again and someone rapped at his office door.

Santiago looked up. Abigail.

He gestured for her to enter.

Abigail Byrne smiled and crossed to the chair beside his desk. Eighteen years had passed since Santi had first been captivated by Abby's laughter. Her green eyes, pale skin, cinnamon freckles and hair the color of chestnuts still made his chest ache at times. Until he caught himself and purposefully flipped thoughts, imploring God, lurking about somewhere, to fill the ache with something more possible.

Jasper's phone rang.

Santiago's hiring Abby as foreign language chair was the smartest thing he had done as headmaster. It was also his greatest challenge. Now thirty-eight, she was as beautiful, kind and funny as when they met eighteen years back. Yet still unmarried.

Abby plopped into a chair and picked up one of the metal brainteaser puzzles strewn across his desk. As she fumbled to unhitch the two pieces of metal, Santi stole glances at her blue dress. He willed himself not to look at her breasts and hung up before the phone flipped to Jasper's voicemail.

"Brother Sinclair is going to kill you, Santi."

He leaned over and took the puzzle from her. He eyed it. With a flip of his wrist, the two pieces parted and he deposited them into her hand. "No. I was smart. Instead of just giving Alex my shoes this time, I made him trade his for mine. He won't sell them again or he'll wind up barefoot."

She dropped the pieces onto his desk. "You have the puzzle's directions."

Santiago smiled. "There were no directions."

"Brother Sinclair is definitely going to kill you," she repeated. "Probably with his fancy, new vacuum cleaner."

Santiago smiled. "He won't kill me. His face will just turn red. And he'll dash off to his room to print off another message on his official stationary." Santiago picked a piece of paper from his desk and changed his voice as if he were reading it aloud. "'Dearest Santiago: For the fourth time in recent memory, I find myself imploring you to not remove your shoes at any time whilst in public. Under any circumstances. Not even in the bathtub. Thank you for responsibly husbanding our Jesuit community's resources.'"

Santiago slapped the paper above his thick eyebrows. "And then he'll staple it to my forehead."

Abby struggled not to smile. "That's the third pair you've given away just this month. Do you know how you looked, crossing the gym floor and greeting the parents, rocking back and forth in your fancy, duct-taped construction boots? Your toes were sticking out the fronts!" She waved her hand through the air. "I can smell them from here!"

"Ah," Santiago waved his hand. "It's the boots, not my feet. I'm sure no one noticed."

She scoffed. "Yes. And no one also noticed the loud flopping sounds your new clown shoes made as you walked past." She shook her head. "You should have been a Franciscan, Santi."

"A Franciscan? Then I wouldn't have any nice shoes to give away. When I signed up, I did the smart thing, Abby. I joined the Jesuits, a wealthy religious order that only pretends it's poor."

The large file cabinet in the corner rattled. Abby's eyebrows rose. It shook again and she looked back at Santiago. "The ghost of Henry Prosser move in?"

"Despite what Dr. Stephens says, no Gonzaga student ever hanged himself from the lights in the theater. At least no one named Henry Prosser."

Santi was sure of it. On a fifty dollar bet with Stephens, who invoked the spirit of Henry Prosser on the opening night of every school play, he had talked Jasper into combing through the school's records with him last summer. Of the thousands of students who had attended the school over two centuries, not one had the name.

The file cabinet shook again.

"If it's not Henry Prosser, then you must have locked Pearl in there." Abby stood.

"Could you blame me?"

Abby started to laugh while looking at the cabinet warily. "Are you going to open it?"

"Me? I'm terrified of ghosts. But be my guest."

Santiago's school thrived on its traditions and legends. Its students — even many of its faculty — placed far greater faith in them than any theological point he could offer. They were a superstitious lot, taking great care not to step on the school seal in the main hallway. Any student who did, it was said, wouldn't graduate. Santi could force everyone in the school to study the school attendance records, but Henry Prosser's ghost would still be blamed for every theft, every practical joke.

The wind and rain rattled the windows. The cabinet shook again, a strangling noise coming from it. Abby edged over.

"Too chicken?" Santi asked.

Abby shot him a look and stepped over to the file cabinet. She pulled open the lowest drawer with a tug. A white feather floated upward and the hen's head popped upward.

Abby gasped and burst into laughter. "You've lost your damn mind."

Santiago's laughter was interrupted by his cell phone. He looked at the phone, cocked his head. "It's my brother. He hasn't called in two months." He reddened when he realized his tone conveyed annoyance. What could Nicolas want now?

Knowing he might regret it, Santi answered. His brother's greeting was perfunctory, the voice formal and chilly. When Nico finally uttered the words, when he had awkwardly dumped the terrible news into his lap, Santiago's face turned to ash.

"I'm at Georgetown now. I'll wait for you," his brother said in Spanish.

Santiago could no longer hold his phone and it slid to his desk.

"What is it?" Abby said.

"Jasper is dead."

Chapter 3: The Fall

Thirty minutes later Santi pulled off Canal Road and into the parking garage that sat on the southwestern corner of Georgetown's campus. He and Abby had passed the drive to the university in stunned silence.

He had met Jasper years before at Georgetown, though Jasper was a few years ahead. Their friendship was truly cemented during Santi's stint at the Jesuit School of Theology at Berkeley. Jasper belonged to the San Francisco province of the Jesuit order. He had grown up there, the son of an Anglo father and Chinese-American mother. It explained Jasper's love for Washington's Chinatown, despite it being an underwhelming, block-long imitation of San Francisco's. He loved visiting its restaurants, ducking into the kitchens to keep up his Mandarin. In his spare time, he even worked with the men and women in the neighborhood's stores and restaurants, teaching informal English classes, helping to sort out their legal status.

Santiago was thrilled when Jasper called him three years back, announcing he was returning to Georgetown the same summer Abby came back to town. Jasper came east to complete a doctorate in history, his thesis focusing on the early years of the Maryland Province of the Society of Jesus – the Jesuit order of Catholic priests and brothers to which they both belonged. Santi was thrilled when Jasper and Abby hit it off and the trio became fast friends.

Santiago wove through the garage and slid quietly into an open spot. What his brother insisted was impossible.

Tucking themselves under a large black umbrella that threatened to buckle in the wind, Santi and Abby splashed past Village C. They hustled across the patio toward the 10-story residence hall in which Jasper lived. Santiago's shoes flopped loudly and he grimaced at the ache pulsing from his cold, wet feet. To the dorm's northeast lay a small cemetery, holding hundreds of Jesuits who served the university over the years. Santiago knew he'd find Jasper and his brother Nicolas between them.

But why would Nico be involved?

A small crowd of students was beginning to gather on the patio, huddling beneath umbrellas that were not keeping them dry. Santiago pushed through them toward Harbin Hall. The beams of two flashlights danced to the right of the building, glancing off the grave markers. Santi shivered in the cold. Two D.C. policemen, standing in a yellow rain slickers just inside a line of plastic tape, held up their hands to stop him.

"I'm Father Santiago Torres. I'm a close friend of Father Willoughs."

The police officers looked at each other. One shook his head. "I'm afraid you're too late for last rites. It's currently being treated as a crime scene, Father. I'm sorry."

Santi tried looking over their shoulders but could make little out in the feeble light. Another group of people seemed to be milling about behind the dorm. "My brother Nicolas Torres is FBI. He's over there somewhere. He called—"

Nico stepped into the courtyard light and Santi fell silent. One glance at them and the D.C. officers would know Santiago was the FBI agent's brother. They had the same angular features, light brown complexion and thick, black hair. There the similarities fell away. While Santiago had brains, Nico possessed brawn. And while Santiago was gentle and personable, Nico was prickly and aloof, *el hijo del lechero*.

Nicolas nodded to the policemen. "I'd be grateful if you could let them through." He didn't wait for the officers' answer. He lifted the tape, nodded at Santiago and Abby to follow.

Nico looked over his shoulder at them as they walked toward the dark cemetery. "You really want to see your friend?"

His tone made clear they didn't.

"Of course we want to see him." Santi hooked his arm through Abby's and pulled her forward. Truth was, he didn't want to see Jasper alone. It's not that he hadn't seen dead people. He'd seen people in their last moments, seen them breathe their last. Yet not a friend. Not like this.

The thought of branding an image of Jasper's dead, damaged face onto his brain made Santi hesitate. Even Abby pulled back as if her shoes were cast of lead. Yet Santiago pressed forward, passing two other officers and an agent huddled against the rain. He'd need Abby to buffer him from Jasper – like she was doing from Nico.

The flopping noise caused Nico to look back. He grunted a disdainful laugh and turned around.

"What really happened? What you said can't be true." Santi steadied the umbrella, which a gust threatened to tear from his hand.

Nico said nothing. Instead they came upon Jasper's broken body, lying prone on the sidewalk between Harbin and the Jesuit cemetery. His bloodied, rain-splattered face looked upward, his eyes and jaw open, giving Jasper a look of perplexed shock. Santi sucked in a breath and felt his belly rise. He handed Abby the umbrella and moved forward to touch his friend. Nico's arm quickly extended, pressed against his chest. "You can't do that."

A wave of grief rolled across Santiago and he shuddered, blinking the rain out of his eyes. His grief and shock exploded in anger and he pushed his brother's arm away. "How did this happen?"

Nico's face held the warmth of a statue. "I called you because I hoped you might know."

"How could I possibly know?"

"You were the last phone call made from his cell. What did he say before he jumped?"

The blood rushed to Santi's face. "Jasper didn't jump!" He looked at Abby for backup. "Dios mío, why would he have jumped?"

Her full lips were a thin line.

Nico continued speaking in an emotionless drone barely audible over the downpour. "Cálmate, Santi. No friend ever expects this. I just need you to think back over the past few weeks. What was he upset about?"

Images from the past month flooded Santi's mind. Jasper's excitement over his annual scavenger hunt. Jasper like a child at Christmas at some mysterious Dahlgren discovery. His hurried, happy calls between dives into the university's archives. Jasper's love of stringing Santi along, adding drama and intrigue to his otherwise mundane thesis work. Then, more recently, the anxiety and stress that had crept into his voice, his hushed whispers. *This will blow your mind. Meet me at the Friendship Arch at five-thirty.*

"He wasn't upset. Nothing that would make him kill himself. He was excited, putting together clues for a big citywide scavenger hunt he does every year. Also about some discovery he made, something that forced him to rewrite his doctoral thesis. We were going to grab dinner and talk about it. And he said he was going to give me something. I thought he just wanted me to run over the hunt with him." Santiago omitted mentioning of the stress in Jasper's voice over the thesis issue. Nico would only misconstrue it. He studied his brother's face. Something wasn't right. "Why is the FBI here?"

"What was he going to give you?"

"I don't know."

"You didn't go to meet him?"

Santiago was growing frustrated. "Of course I went. He never showed up."

Nico squinted. "Where did you go after that? Did you visit campus here at any point this evening?"

There it was. Every conversation with his brother eventually took a turn into snide putdowns and insinuations. Nico had the ability to flip a switch, turning Santi into a person he always later regretted becoming. Santi glared. "Vete pa'l carajo. You can go to hell."

"Settle down, your holiness. I'm just saving the D.C. cops a visit to your office tomorrow morning."

Santiago's voice rose. "You call me down here to look at the dead body of one of my best friends just so you can suggest that I killed him? Estás tripeando!"

"Get over yourself, Santi. Anyone in your place would be asked the same question. It's how this is done."

Abby looked disgusted. "If you really think Santiago needs an alibi, three hundred people can vouch for him. We had parent conferences at school."

"Now it's your turn to answer my question," Santi shot at him. "If it's a suspected suicide, why did the FBI sent a bunch of amateurs to puzzle it out?"

Nico shrugged. "A favor." He offered Abby a forced smile. "For my boss. He got a call. That's all."

"A call from whom?" Santi demanded.

A figure silhouetted by the dormitory's lights spliced away from a group of police. An older man, dressed in black, his trembling hands clasped together, approached. From the gestures, Santi knew who it was before the dim light illuminated the man's face.

"Father Donnelly," Abby said.

Donnelly's eyes were red. His hands fluttered about, effeminate gestures punctuating his precise pronunciation. "Oh, Abigail! And Father Torres, Santiago!"

Donnelly had called one of his FBI contacts. As director of Georgetown's alumni office, Donnelly knew nearly everyone in official Washington, or knew someone who knew them. Nico was here because Donnelly had called in a favor.

"Quien a buen árbol se arrima, buena sombra lo cobija." Santi looked at Nico. "You're here to protect Georgetown."

"Oh, no, Santiago." Donnelly's hands took flight. "Jasper deserves the full respect of the D.C. police. To ensure he receives it, I called Bill Sampson at the Bureau and asked that he send a man."

Santiago rolled his eyes at Sampson's name. Not just any FBI contact. The head of the FBI.

"Everyone's on their best behavior that way," Donnelly continued. I didn't want Channel Twelve here, filming away, turning this tragedy into a circus. Nothing more."

Nico gestured with his chin to Harbin Hall. "I need you to come to his room."

"And just leave Jasper out here like this?" Santiago glared at Donnelly. "Is that the respect you expected from the Bureau?"

Nico walked past them in the direction of the dorm entrance. "Your girlfriend's quite a hothead," he muttered to Abby.

Abby shot Santiago a warning look.

Santiago furiously removed his coat. He began to cross to his friend, but Nico rushed back. "I told you not to touch him." Nico's wet face was just inches away from his. "I said I need you to come to his room."

Soaked by the cold rain, Santiago stood toe to toe to let his brother know he wasn't intimidated. "I heard you the first time." He broke off and fumed all the way to Harbin Hall's entrance. He blew past the monitor, gossiping with two girls in the hallway, and pounded the elevator button. Respect. What did his brother know of respect? And Donnelly? There was no Channel Twelve filming but you could be damn sure he'd be quoted in the *D.C. Post* in the morning.

The others caught up. They rode the elevator to the eighth floor. Outside Jasper's room stood another cop. Jasper lived in the dorm as its chaplain. He loved campus life, especially the room's proximity to his office in the library.

Nico spoke to the officer. "You guys wrapping up in there?"

"Yeah. It's been released. Seems pretty clear where this one's going." He reached over, pulled down the crime scene tape, stepped aside to let the others through.

They entered to find another cop preparing to leave. The room looked like Santi last saw it. Like it looked all the time. While Jasper couldn't keep time, he was fastidious about his living space. Everything had its space, right down to the ten perfectly sharpened pencils in the San Francisco coffee mug on his desk. Nico crossed to the desk, picked up a piece of paper inside a plastic bag and handed it to Santiago.

I'm sorry.
I'll say it again: I'm sorry.
This is no one's fault. No one missed anything because I made certain there was nothing to miss. Some who loved me may be tempted to spend many

miserable hours pondering why I did this. I could write for hours. For anyone but I, the words still would not logically add up to the decision I've made. It simply makes sense to me. I was in turmoil. And now I'm at peace.

Mom and Dad, you have given me the world and I could not have been blessed with more wonderful, loving parents. This is not your fault. You have always wanted me to be happy. And now I am.

I trust I will find God as merciful and loving as the wonderful friends I have been privileged to have. Please forgive me.

Be at peace. I love you all.

Jasper

Santi pressed his eyes shut and exhaled.

Nico spoke first. "Father Donnelly says it appears to be Jasper's handwriting."

Donnelly was right. Jasper's signature was perfect. Profoundly confused, Santiago opened his eyes to look at Abby. She was standing by Jasper's long bookshelves, which sat below a perfectly empty wall.

Santi blinked, stepped forward. He could see them, four tiny holes made by the old tacks, delineating the four corners of a very large rectangle. He stepped closer, rubbed his fingers over a strange, faint oval on the otherwise perfectly clean paint.

"Did the police take anything from this room?" Santi asked.

"No."

"Aquí hay gato encerrado." Santiago turned to his brother. "That note is a forgery."

Chapter 4: The Package

"Pearl, what do chickens eat?"

Pearl stared over the top of her glasses through the door to his office, where Santiago was kneeling on the floor. Santiago recognized it. It was her come-to-Jesus look. It kept her grandsons on the straight and narrow. It even kept her bosses in line.

"Chicken feed."

Pearl was a no-nonsense, church-going, sixty-year-old, black D.C. native. She raised four kids and was now raising one of her daughter's two teenage sons. Present a problem and Pearl Freeman had a simple, straightforward answer. She didn't spare the rod with her own boys but was the first to lecture Santiago about his heartlessness when he expelled a student. She confounded him.

Santiago shook the large cardboard cylinder he was holding and the large rolled map he had purchased that morning slid out into his hand.

"Okay, what exactly is chicken feed?"

Pearl pulled her hands away from her computer keyboard. "Father Torres, this girl grew up in Shaw before moving to P.G. County. I don't live with farm animals. I simply buy them at the supermarket and eat them."

She turned back to her computer screen. "It's beginning to stink in there."

Santiago looked at the hen. It was tied to the file cabinet and standing on an old, laminated map of Europe Santiago had dug out of the history office's closet. The chicken was ignoring the

Styrofoam plate from the cafeteria. "I don't think it likes cheeseburgers."

Santiago unrolled the large map of the world across the rug in his office, tacking down its four corners with books.

Pearl's keyboard rattled. "There is this newfangled miracle thing called the Internet. It's even available on your desk if you happen to sit behind it sometime." She leaned into her screen, tapped her glasses up the bridge of her nose and read: "Chickens may be fed mealie-pap, bread and vegetables. To produce strong, healthy eggs and chicks, hens must have calcium from such things as limestone grit, oyster shells or small quantities of bonemeal."

She shook her head. "Just give it a multivitamin." Her keyboard began clicking again. "Better yet, wring its neck and throw it on the grill."

Santiago scratched his head. "That's just it. I can't kill it."

Pearl didn't look up. "What did you eat for dinner last night?"

"Chicken." Santiago smiled. "This is different. I personally know this one."

"So it's your policy to only eat strangers?"

"Pearl, if I asked you what mealie-pap is, would you kill me?"

"Right after I get my paycheck on Friday."

Santiago turned his attention back to the world map he had unfurled across the floor. It was a perfect copy, straight from the gift shop of the National Geographic Society. It was identical to one he had given Jasper for his birthday a year ago. Jasper, who loved maps, immediately hung it on the wall right above his bookshelves, from where it was now conspicuously missing.

"Let me get this straight," his brother had mocked him last night. "You know the suicide note is fake because a map is missing from the wall?"

"It's not just that the map is missing. It's the way it was removed." Santiago pointed to the markings that remained on the wall. "Look at that oval. Jasper circled something repeatedly on that map. He circled it so much, the ink leaked through and you can still see it faintly here on the wall."

Nico laughed. "What's wrong with the way it was removed? He just took it down just like everyone else would."

"Exactly! The pinholes are still there. And the oval."

Nico offered an impatient, make-your-point gesture.

"Everyone else might leave them there. Not Jasper."

Even Donnelly's eyebrows rose.

Santi shook his hands in frustration. "You people clearly don't know Jasper. He was obsessive-compulsive, a complete perfectionist. Those holes would have driven him absolutely crazy. He would have patched them immediately after pulling down that map. Not left them like that."

Nico shook his head. "If your friend was jumping off a roof, why would he give a damn about patching the wall? It's not like he'd be coming back to look at it."

"You're right! He wouldn't have patched it for himself. He would have felt so bad about the holes he would have patched them so the next person to use the room wouldn't have to look at them!"

Santiago looked at Abby. "Am I right?"

Abby bit her lip.

Santiago pointed at the faint oval. "In fact, after Jasper patched the holes, he would have felt compelled to touch up the paint. Then, because it wasn't a perfect match, he'd have to paint the whole room again."

"That's ridiculous," Nico said.

"That was Jasper!" Santiago shook his head. "Jasper didn't kill himself. If he did, he would have planned it meticulously. This wall would be perfect. And all his books – all of his belongings – would have been boxed and donated. This room would be completely empty, perfect, ready for move-in." Santiago crossed the room and jammed the suicide note back into his brother's hand. "This note is a fake. And the person who faked it killed Jasper and took that map for some reason. And I'd bet it's tied to his thesis."

Yet no one seemed persuaded. Jack Donnelly and the D.C. cop politely excused themselves. Even Abby looked to be on the fence. To calm him, Nico finally agreed to take a closer look at the hard drive on Jasper's laptop, which contained nothing that looked like Jasper was rewriting his thesis.

But the image of the faint oval on the wall ate at Santiago all night. That morning, after school began, he slipped out to buy the map. With it now open before him, he took out a piece of paper containing measurements he'd made the night before with a ruler he'd borrowed from Jasper's desk.

He measured twice to be sure and inked the same, small oval on the new map. He sat back on his haunches and looked up at Pearl.

"Israel."

"You're sending the chicken to Israel?" Pearl was staring at him over her glasses.

"No. My friend Jasper circled Israel on a map on his wall." Santi shook his head. "But that makes absolutely no sense. His focus was American History, his thesis about the Maryland Province of Jesuits."

She eyed the chicken. "And you are suddenly an expert on what makes sense?" Her eyes narrowed, a sign she was setting him up for another scolding. "I can smell your boots from here. When are you getting a respectable pair of shoes?"

"You probably should buy some air freshener. It might be a while."

"And why might that be?"

"Because—"

"Because," Pearl interrupted, "That's the third pair of your own shoes you've given away this month and you've spent your entire monthly community allowance on replacements."

"My mother used to do that."

"Do what?"

"Ask questions she already knew the answers to."

Pearl offered a self-satisfied nod. "It instills a healthy sense of shame in those who lack it." She tsked at him. "Father Torres, you have the responsibility to represent this school in a professional way. That's not accomplished by looking like some hobo dragged in off the street. You need to go upstairs to Brother Sinclair right now and tell him you need to purchase a respectable pair of shoes."

"Can't do that."

"Why not?"

"He'd definitely kill me."

Pearl harrumphed and disappeared behind her desk. She crossed to him and dropped a box on top of the map. "Ms. Byrne went shopping too, during her free period and lunch. Apparently that's what all the school staff do instead of actual teaching. They go shopping."

Santiago flipped off the lid to reveal a beautiful pair of new shoes. He grinned up at her.

"Those were an expensive gift," Pearl lectured. "If you give them away, it would be a terrible insult to the giver."

Santiago raised his hand in an oath. "Te prometo. I will not give these away."

A knock sounded at Pearl's door and the FedEx man's pudgy brown face appeared. "I've got a package for the headmaster, Miss Pearl." He gave her a big smile to ward off any possible grumpiness. "Don't you look beautiful today?"

She jabbed her thumb over her shoulder towards Santiago and walked back to her desk. "Farmer Brown will sign for it."

The driver crossed the room and extended the electronic clipboard for Santiago's signature. He looked over Santiago's shoulder and whistled. "Nice chicken."

Santiago signed and handed it back. "Yesterday I was standing on a street corner in Chinatown, waiting for a friend and an old lady came up to me and told me to hold onto it for her."

"You stole an old woman's chicken, Father?"

Santiago could hear Pearl stifle a laugh. Even the FedEx man was mocking him now.

"No, I think she just asked me to hold onto it for a moment. I couldn't really understand her. She spoke Chinese."

"Mandarin," corrected Pearl.

"Mandarin," repeated Santiago. "But I had to return to school for parent conferences before she came back for it. So I didn't really steal the woman's chicken. The chicken was legally abandoned."

The man handed him the package and turned to leave. He looked at Pearl and spoke loudly enough for Santiago to hear. "You just can't trust anyone these days."

Pearl waved him away and her keyboard rattled some more. "In South Africa, mealies are corn," she called into Santiago's office.

Santiago tore open the cardboard envelope and stared at an ancient looking parchment stroked with neat calligraphy. He glanced at the empty return address label, leapt over the map on the floor and dashed into the hallway. "Who sent this package?" he shouted.

The startled FedEx man turned around. He picked up the electronic keyboard and poked at it. "For some reason it's not linked to any FedEx account in here. You'll have to call FedEx with the package number. Is there a problem?"

Santiago looked at the materials in his shaking hands, shook his head and rushed back to his office. "Hold my calls, Pearl. Unless it's Ms. Byrne, I'm not here."

Pearl tsk-tsked her disapproval and his office door closed with a click.

Chapter 5: The Odd Fellows Society

Santiago slid into his desk chair. He turned the stiff, light brown paper over before examining the writing on its front again. The words were scrawled in quill and ink in handwriting reminiscent of the country's founding documents.

Santiago's eyes drifted to the signature on the note: The Odd Fellows Society of Historical Bounty Hunters.

His mouth ran dry. It was Jasper's secret society, a Georgetown club of hardcore history and trivia geeks his friend founded. Other than gathering once a month in Jasper's dormitory room to talk historiography and blitz obscene quantities of pizza ("Watch the crumbs, Odd Fellows! Watch the crumbs!"), the group's major annual undertaking was a weeklong scavenger hunt. Each March Jasper's skull-numbing clues sent his club members skittering across important sites and monuments from Washington, D.C. out through the capital's suburbs. The scavenge culminated in a formal dinner where the winner was named president of the Odd Fellow Society. The following month the students quietly returned to gorging on pizza and watching the crumbs.

Santiago questioned whether he was holding a real clue from the Odd Fellows Society. Yet its words were scrawled across the same ancient-looking parchment Jasper distributed each spring.

My fellow Odd Fellow,

If you seek the Truth

Discover the Past in the Euture:

22-20, 56-11, 99-6, 65-16; 42-2, 73-7, 1-28, 36-6, 84-6; 35-3, 8-7, 47-13; 105-11, 28-9, 61-3, 90-29, 12-9; 71-4, 3-4, 57-1; 32-12, 88-14; 69-27; 34-15, 78-2; 16-3, 45-19, 6-11, 38-27, 20-1, 93-7; 32-1, 53-21, 75-22, 55-30; 10-5, 70-2; 103-1, 50-13, 25-14; 41-22, 80-12, 19-27, 48-1; 67-7, 97-1; 17-15, 52-3, 86-25, 9-25, 82-3, 98-25; 5-24, 62-21, 94-11, 29-20, 37-9, 77-17, 39-18, 14-6.

Your obedient servants,

The Odd Fellows Society of Historical Bounty Hunters

    Jasper always ran the scavenger hunt's clues by Santiago before he used them each year. He did it to test their difficulty, but not like this. Santiago saw them over e-mail. If Santiago, with his own broad knowledge of history and the U.S. capital, cracked a clue within a half hour, Jasper rejected it as too easy. He shook the thick paper. Santiago had never before seen the clue he was holding.

    So why and how did it wind up being overnighted to him?

    He leaned forward and ran a finger across the final word of the message's second line: *Discover the Past in the Euture.*

    Euture.

    Santiago half-smiled. Jasper had actually misspelled a word.

    His brow furrowed. Jasper? A misspelling?

    The odds of the U.S. Congress unanimously passing the federal budget were far better.

    Santiago's spine straightened and he glanced at the map on his office floor. He was sure of it. This wasn't some random clue merely intended for future use. This was specifically sent to him, sent to reveal the truth about Jasper's death.

    Santi's brain crackled. The parchment's numbered pairs had no apparent pattern. The strange word "Euture" was undoubtedly a clue to the key. Without it, no one could crack the numerical code.

    Euture.

His mind tumbled through possibilities. Santiago seized one of the brainteaser puzzles on his desk and began working it. He flipped through its solution quickly, twisted it around to confuse himself and worked it again.

Euture.

The metal pieces dropped apart in his hand again.

The word ate at him. An image of Jasper sitting in a chair on the other side of the desk laughing at him flittered through his head.

Euture.

Where had he seen it before?

He slapped the puzzle onto his desk in frustration.

He closed his eyes, pushed back into his chair and breathed deeply. Jasper was there again, chuckling. "You know it, Santi. Of course you know it. Your frustration is just getting in the way of your seeing it."

Each of its letters floated separately through his mind, twirling and flipping before reassembling again.

Euture.

The hen clucked.

Santiago opened his eyes and they fell upon the framed Matthew Brady photograph of Abraham Lincoln hanging above his office's mantel. Old Abe's melancholy face stared down at him, the president's bushy eyebrows arched, amused that a century and a half after his death, anyone even still bothered to remember him.

"Por supuesto!" Santiago flew out of his chair, seized his coat and threw open his office door.

"Pearl! I'll return in an hour!"

Chapter 6: The Sage of Little Mountain

Santiago passed between the enormous Doric columns and stepped into the dim interior of the memorial, patterned after a Greek religious temple. When they reached the top of its steps, nearly all visitors' voices fell to a reverent hush.

"Look at his hands." A mother pointed her young son's attention upward. "The sculptor carved them in American sign language for his initials, A and L."

Santiago smiled. He knew the legend wasn't true. Nor was the story that Robert E. Lee's face was carved into the back of the statue's head.

Santiago considered Daniel Chester French's nineteen-foot statue of Abraham Lincoln one of the capital's greatest works of art. The carving sparked reverence and awe: Lincoln the mighty giant. Yet the statue's open coat, its tousled hair and contemplative face invited the most timid children to approach. It looked like Lincoln would lean over, gently lift them upon his lap and read them a story.

Santiago turned toward the north chamber of the Lincoln Memorial, where he knew he'd find his second inaugural address.

He stood before the three chiseled panels holding the speech. Above them the Angel of Truth stood between the Union and Confederate leaders, urging them toward reunification. The address, given just a month before the Civil War's end, famously evoked national healing – with malice toward none and charity for all. No president since Thomas Jefferson could turn a poetic phrase like Lincoln. No politician since had grasped the power of brevity. The speech wasn't even seven hundred words.

Santiago studied the first panel, his eyes drifting to the end of the first paragraph: WITH HIGH HOPE FOR THE FUTURE...

If you looked closely, you could still see it: the sculptor's small error.

The boy and his mother were now beside Santiago. He couldn't resist. "Look at that line right there, halfway down the panel, the line that ends in future."

"I see it," the boy said.

His mother's eyes rose in surprise.

"The sculptor made an error while carving."

The boy nodded, pointing. "He made an E instead of an F, but they filled in the bottom part to hide it."

Santiago nodded. "Someone can make a mistake and still inspire awe."

The boy and his mother began discussing the find. Santiago stepped back and pulled the parchment and a pen from his pocket. He looked at the first line of paired numbers. *22-20, 56-11, 99-6, 65-16.*

He glanced back at the panel and counted the lines – one hundred five in all. He peered at the parchment. The highest number was just that: one hundred five.

Santiago's heart thudded. He studied the pairs and the panel again. "No estoy por la luna! You can stop laughing, Jasper. The first number of each pair is the line of a letter, the second number is its position of letters on the line."

Santiago began puzzling the pairs out. Forty minutes later, he had the clue decoded. He pocketed his pen and read over the entire message.

Pier under the north end of a meridian sunk by the Sage of Little Mountain.

Thirty minutes later he was standing beside the school seal in the main hallway floor as the bell marking the end of Gonzaga's school day rang. Abby sidled up, still reading the text message he had sent.

"Thank you for the shoes."

She smiled. "You're welcome."

"I'm really not scared of Sinclair, you know."

"Yes, you are. Where is this super secret important clue you mentioned?"

He pulled it out and she peered at the parchment where Santiago had scribbled the clue's words. Santiago began bidding the students a good evening on their way home.

"This makes no sense," Abby said.

"Tell me about it."

She scrunched her nose. "Meridian?"

Santiago nodded to a junior. "Have a good night, Jack. Get that homework done." He lowered his voice, speaking again to Abby. "That word's particularly odd. You can't sink or bury a meridian. It's an imaginary line on a map."

She pointed at the first word. "What about this misspelling?"

"You think he misspelled pier? This is Jasper we're talking about."

Abby nodded and they said the words together: "That's no misspelling."

A freshman passed and Santiago addressed him. "How did exams go for you, Nathan?"

The boy flashed a smile. "I did great, Father Torres."

"Good job! Good job!"

"What about this?"

"The Sage of Little Mountain?" Santiago shrugged. "I even broke down and did an Internet search. I got a flower farm, a bike trail and a winery. I can't think of any American in history ever called The Sage of Little Mountain."

"How about just the Sage then."

Santiago thought it over and teased a freshman tottering beneath an enormous backpack. "Date prisa, Tomás! Estas más lento que una caravana de cojos!"

Thomas smiled back. "No entiendo!"

"I said you're walking slower than a caravan of wobbly, old people."

Thomas laughed and tottered past.

Santiago turned to Abby. "Technically the real translation is 'You're slower than a caravan of lame people,' but making fun of the disabled is a little less politically correct here than it was in my parents' house." Santiago tapped the clue and thought some more. "John Adams referred to Thomas Jefferson as a sage but he called him The Sage of Monti—"

His eyes widened.

"What is it?"

"Qué tonto soy! The Sage of Monticello! Jefferson called his plantation Monticello, which is Italian for Little Mountain!" He grinned broadly. "Grab your coat while I find a shovel."

"A shovel?"

"Hurry!"

"Santi, I have to moderate Key Club in fifteen minutes."

"Good idea! They can help. Grab the keys to the school van and meet me in half an hour." Santiago dashed down the hallway.

"Meet you where?" Abby called.

"The Washington Monument!"

Chapter 7: Digging History

Santiago whistled. Across the vast lawn, Abby and ten Gonzaga boys turned. "Echa pa' ca!" He gestured and they began to walk. He gestured more fervently and the boys broke into a jog.

Abby and the boys arrived laughing a moment later. "What have you dragged the Key Club out here for?"

Santiago gestured up the incline to the great obelisk in the center of the National Mall. "As we say in Spanish, *obfuscación*."

"Obfuscation?" one of the boys asked.

Santiago pulled the small garden trowel out of his winter coat. "A person can't go around just digging up the National Mall, so the Gonzaga Eagles Key Club is going to stand between me and that park ranger walking around the Washington Monument up there to keep their beloved headmaster from getting arrested."

The prospect of breaking the law with the school headmaster got the boys chattering.

"What does the Washington Monument have to do with Thomas Jefferson?" Abby asked.

"Nothing at all," Santiago responded. "But this does." He gestured to a three-foot-high stone protruding from the ground behind him. "It's called the Jefferson Pier."

The boys fell silent and stared at the square stone, two and a half feet on each side. One finally spoke up. "A pier? It looks like a grave stone."

"Stephen," Santiago explained. "A pier is a sturdy surveying stone sunk into the ground. Most of this pier lies beneath the grass. You're just seeing its top."

"Thomas Jefferson put it there?" another asked.

"Not personally." Santiago pointed northward across the Ellipse toward the White House. "But when he was president and lived there, he had a surveyor determine a line running perfectly north and south through the center of the White House. Jefferson believed the new nation should have its own meridian. Until the 1880's, there was great competition among map makers and countries regarding the location of the Prime Meridian, from which longitudinal lines and, now, time zones are calculated. This one was one of four meridians proposed within the U.S." Santiago pointed to the east. "The first meridian Jefferson proposed actually ran north-south through the U.S. Capitol, the house of the people." Santiago laughed. "But he changed his mind about the importance of the people when he became president."

One of the other boys walked fully around the stone. "But if it's a meridian, it's a line of longitude that runs all the way to the north and all the way to the south of here. Why'd they put this stone here instead of at the White House?"

"A very smart question, Matt." Santiago pointed to the east toward the U.S. Capitol. Another east-west survey line was shot right out the center of the western entrance to the capitol building and this is where the meridian intersects with it." He indicated the Washington Monument. "In the original plan for the federal district, an equestrian statue of George Washington was proposed for this very spot – the Jefferson Pier. But when they changed the proposed statue to a much heavier, giant obelisk, the engineers discovered the soil here wouldn't support it, so they shifted the Washington Memorial slightly to the east up the National Mall."

Santiago spun a full circle. "But you'll notice the layout of the entire mall pivots around the Jefferson Pier and the perpendicular cross that created it." He pointed out all the structures as he named them. "Due north is the White House. Due east is the Capitol. Due south, just across the Tidal Basin, lies the Jefferson Memorial. And due west sits the Lincoln Memorial. All on the lines originally shot by Jefferson's surveyor and marked by this stone."

"Cool," one of the boys said. "I've lived my whole life in D.C. and never knew this was here."

"Okay," Santiago said. "Ms. Byrne, if you would kindly line up the boys like you're taking a photo of them with the Washington Monument behind them. It'll block the ranger's view of me. Meanwhile," Santiago held up the trowel. "I'll dig."

Abby scooted the boys into position and held up her phone. Santiago began digging on the north side of the Jefferson Pier.

"What's he digging for?" Matthew asked.

Abby ignored the question. "Okay, smile, guys!"

Santiago dug deeper. "It must be here. This is the place the clue is directing us to. I'm sure of it."

"What clue?" Matthew said.

"Smile some more!" Abby called.

Santi kept digging.

"Are you really taking a picture, Ms. Byrne, or just pretending?" another student asked. "If you're just pretending, can I just pretend to smile?" He laughed at his own joke.

"Dork," a friend commented.

"How much longer, Father Torres?" Abby growled.

"Just keep smiling and don't move!" Santiago dug deeper.

The boy named Matt spoke up. "Um, I hate to break this to you, Father, but some guy in a uniform is walking over here."

Santiago looked up. "How can he even see me? You're blocking his view."

"We're not blocking the view of *that* guy." Matt pointed to the southwest. "He's walking from that ranger station over there."

Santiago glanced over. The guy was two hundred yards away, looking at him and speaking into a radio.

"Okay, not good," another student chimed in. "That ranger up at the monument is now walking down the hill. And he's walking kind of fast."

Santiago began digging furiously.

"Hurry up!" Abby urged.

Stephen spoke again, this time his voice a stressed squeak. "If I get arrested right before dinner, my dad is going to be *so* pissed."

"Angry," Abby corrected.

"Angry," Stephen agreed. "My dad's going to be *so* angry."

"The closest ranger's only thirty yards away, Father," Matt called.

The trowel blade struck something hard and Santiago froze a moment. Then he dug furiously, the hole now nearly a foot and half deep. He shoved the dirt aside, etching out the edges of a small metal box with his fingers. Frantically brushing the dirt off its top, Santi seized its metal handle and yanked.

Santiago whirled around towards Abby.

"Hey!" the closest ranger called out. "What do you think you're doing there?"

"Run!" Santiago hissed.

The boys shot off like antelopes.

Chapter 8: The Stewards

Santiago was back in his office a full hour, peering over the documents he discovered inside the box, before Abby had packed off her club members and returned.

"I knew it!" he said excitedly.

Abby peered over his shoulder into the metal box.

Santiago held up a paper. "It's the cover page to Jasper's rewritten thesis." He pointed to its scrawled title: *The Liquidation of the Maryland Province Plantation System and the Rise of the Georgetown Stewards.* "This proves there was something erased from Jasper's laptop."

"The Stewards?" Abby snorted. "You've got to be kidding me.

"Jasper wasn't. Part of his thesis is in here. But there are also copies of documents about the old Jesuit plantation system and the Stewards. You've obviously heard of them."

Abigail laughed. "Of course. One of Georgetown's supposedly secret societies. Cloak and Dagger, Crux Orbis, the Stewards."

"That's right."

"If they exist, Santi – and that's a ridiculous if – the Stewards are a running joke on campus." Abby cited Georgetown's student-run newspaper. "Every decade or so, the Hoya becomes obsessed with outing them, yet all they print are silly rumors."

Santiago shuffled through the documents in the metal box and Abby ticked off the campus newspaper's past charges against the secret group. "The Stewards are very conservative. They're patriarchal. They're Catholic students, all white guys, fighting to preserve the most sacred traditions of the university and church." She smiled. "If the Stewards really exist, they're about as influential as the Reformed Marxists Club. You remember them, Santi? The hairy guys that named the marijuana leaf as their official state plant and lobbied to have all classes in the School for International Studies taught in Esperanto?" Abby laughed at the recollection. "After we graduated, didn't the Stewards supposedly start that campus fight about keeping crucifixes in all the classrooms? Not exactly earth-shattering accomplishments."

"You're opposed to the Stewards working to preserve the university's Catholic identity?"

"Of course not. I just have a problem with guys who think good, old-fashioned virtues include keeping women in their place."

"Who did you know that was a Steward?"

"No one. It was all just silly talk."

Santiago tapped the title page of the thesis. "Jasper didn't think they were nonsense."

Abigail laughed.

"Mira los papeles, Abby! Whatever was found in Dahlgren Chapel two weeks ago turned Jasper's original thesis on its head. Look, I heard the same talk about the Stewards when I was at Georgetown. But these documents show that the Stewards are real and go back a lot farther than anyone thought. They weren't just some self-important secret fraternity. Based on Jasper's voice when we spoke the last time, he really thought they were dangerous."

Abby's voice lowered as if she was embarrassed to utter a heresy. "Then maybe he did lose it, Santi."

"No lo digas. Don't say that." Santiago took her by the arm. "Sit down and hear me out. Jasper's original thesis may not be widely known, but it's not groundbreaking by any stretch. But you can't understand all the stuff in this box without understanding the Jesuits' early history."

Abby sat, her face making clear her lingering doubts.

"In the 1700s and the 1800s, the center of the Maryland Province of the American Jesuits was the Middle Atlantic States, specifically Maryland."

"Of course. Because it was the only Catholic colony."

Santiago nodded. "It wasn't Catholic exactly, but it was founded by Catholics – Lord Baltimore and the Calvert family – and it was surrounded by other Protestant colonies that would have preferred to expel and even kill Jews and Catholics. While Maryland became a safe haven for Catholics, unlike the other colonies, it still allowed its residents to practice their different religions. By the 1800s, Maryland was also the northern-most slave state. And you'll never guess who was one of Maryland's biggest slave owners."

"The Calverts?"

Santiago shook his head. "The Jesuits."

Abigail's eyes rose in disbelief. "What?"

"Yes. The Catholic priests and brothers of the Jesuit order," said Santiago. "Specifically the Maryland Province. Jasper's and my order."

"No way." The suspicious look on Abby's face, however, told Santi to continue.

"What? You think the church isn't capable of evil, Abby? Have you ever read about the Inquisition or the Crusades?"

"That was five hundred, a thousand years ago, Santi. But American priests who actually owned slaves?" Her words trailed off.

"The Maryland Province wasn't the only group of American Jesuits who owned slaves. The ones in the Missouri Province did too." Santi crossed to one of his many bookshelves and opened up a history text. He leafed through it before placing it on Abby's lap. It was a drawing of Spanish conquistadors beheading Native Americans while a Catholic priest stood in the background. He pressed his finger against it. "In colonial Latin America, the church was one of the biggest landowners. Who do you think worked their land? The bishop?"

She closed the book. "You'd think by the 1800s—"

Santi interrupted. "Absolutely. It was inexcusable that the church's involvement in slavery lasted so long, but it did. My order owned four plantations in Maryland, beginning in 1650. Six if you throw in the two small ones on Eastern Shore." He dug into the metal box, pulled out some documents and pointed at the names. "They're in here. White Marsh, St. Thomas's Manor, Newtown and St. Inagoes."

"How many slaves?"

He tapped the papers. "Just under three hundred. The number varied with births and deaths. The wealth they created through their work actually paid for the establishment of Georgetown University, which didn't charge its students any tuition in its early years. Those plantations and slaves bankrolled the university for its first fifty years."

"Did you guys ever set them free?"

"About twenty years before the Civil War the Maryland Province was pressured by Rome – the pope himself. The province ran some numbers and decided they could run their plantations more profitably by leasing their land to farmers. So the Jesuits got out of the slave business in 1838."

"That's when you set the slaves free?"

Santi grimaced. "Unfortunately," he said. "That's when an embarrassing history becomes absolutely shameful."

"How so?"

"We sold the slaves down river, Abby. Three ships took them – all two hundred seventy-two men, women and children – and sold them to a planter in Louisiana. Rather than grant them their God-given freedom, the Jesuits sold them into the Deep South."

Abby looked at him. "That's horrible." She picked up the cover sheet to Jasper's thesis. "That's what he was writing about?"

"It's part of it," said Santiago. "But that part's actually been acknowledged for years. Jasper was doing something different. He was trying to figure out what was done with the huge amount of money that came from the slave sale."

Abigail's entire demeanor had changed. "What did he find out?"

"These documents, which I think were the ones recently discovered in Dalgren Chapel, suggest something shocking." Santiago dug through the papers and pulled a handful of other photocopies out. "The Articles of Incorporation for the Stewards. Look at the founding date."

"1866."

"These papers suggest there's some connection between the founding of the Stewards on that date and the funds that were earned from the slave sale thirty years before." He shuffled more paper. "The box held the first one hundred pages Jasper had managed to rewrite of his thesis and Stewards' documents that go up to around the mid-1950s. But none of his other research notes are here, so I can't figure out the connection he made or what he learned about the modern Stewards. But his thesis says the Stewards still exist."

Santi turned to another page. "Oíste! According to this, the Stewards were established to promote the goals and ideals of 'the true church.' Their goals were to expand their own power and influence and destroy the enemies of Catholicism."

Santi quoted the final sentence of the document. "The Stewards will righteously stand as a bulwark against the mongrelization of the world and the United States and defend those of the one true Roman Catholic faith against pernicious persecution in these United States and abroad."

"Whoa," Abby said, "Mongrelization?"

"The documents all point to the Stewards as white men who were very unhappy about the freedom and rights won by freed slaves during and after the Civil War. In that respect, they were like most American men in the South at the time – even an awful lot of Americans in the North. Today a lot of people believe that because the North supported an end to slavery, people living there also supported equal rights for former slaves. That wasn't the case at all. Most whites back then wanted separate societies. They strongly supported segregation and Jim Crow laws."

"If that was so common back then, why would the Stewards have been a secret? Why bother worrying about persecution from others?"

"Because there was also a lot of anti-Catholic prejudice in the U.S. in the nineteenth century. The first big wave of immigration to the U.S. after the American Revolution involved Germans and Irish. Many were Catholics and they triggered a lot of anti-immigrant sentiment. The Masons are one notorious example of an early, anti-Catholic group. Catholics were even pretty high up on the Ku Klux Klan's hate list well into the 1900s. As late as 1960, many Americans didn't trust John F. Kennedy, who was Catholic. They thought if he was elected, he'd be a puppet of the Vatican."

"If Jasper thought the Stewards were an organization of Catholic Georgetown alumni who stood together against Protestant American prejudices, how is that so shocking? You're saying they were typical men of their times."

Santi shook his head. "The documents suggest it goes way beyond that, Abby." He placed a second document in front of her. "In 1839, Pope Gregory issued an apostolic letter that made clear that the church clergy were to no longer be involved in the slave trade." He slid another paper in front of her. "Now look at this one. It's a list of the Stewards' initial investments. Look at these shipping companies and captains on this sheet, Abby. I looked them up online. They were all slave runners – their cargo was shackled human beings. Despite the end of slavery in the U.S. in the 1860s, the Stewards were involved in smuggling slaves into Latin America for decades after. Brazil and Cuba didn't ban slavery until the 1880s."

"And the Jesuits were involved?"

"No sé," he shrugged. "I don't know. A bunch of documents are missing." Santiago shook his head. "But this doesn't look good at all."

Santi pointed to the bottom of the paper listing the Stewards' early investments. "Look what happens when slavery ends in South America in the late 1880s. The Stewards shift their money elsewhere."

Abby looked at the bottom entries. "Railroads and mining."

"Foreign petroleum, guns and arms manufacturing," he added. "These guys were captains of industry. They got a toehold in the very first days of the industrial revolution."

"I'd sure like their bank account," said Abby. "If they still exist today, they'd be worth—"

"Billions." Santi placed another paper in front of her.

"What's this?"

"The names of early companies that Stewards invested in, but it only goes up to about 1950."

Abby read down list of companies. "Even if the Stewards really exist, and all this money too – what's it all used for now? It certainly didn't make my Georgetown tuition any cheaper when I was there."

"Someone – Jasper before he died or someone else – took the trouble to make sure I found these documents. There's something that connects this to what happened to Jasper. And that missing map from his room."

Santiago turned to his desk. "Mira! I bought this today, the exact same one that was on Jasper's wall, and I put the oval exactly where Jasper did."

"What does Israel have to do with this?"

"No clue. But if we can find the rest of these pages and figure out where all the Stewards' money is today, I'm sure we'll have hard proof that Jasper was murdered to keep the answer quiet." He gathered up the papers and slipped them back into the metal box he had unearthed. "Are you coming?"

"Where?"

"We're going back to Georgetown."

Chapter 9: The Dahlgren Lockbox

Before they left, Santiago held up a finger. "I need my brother to track the FedEx package for me. There's no return address on it."

Santiago sent an e-mail and then opened his office door. Pearl had gone for the day. He stepped forward and tripped. At his feet was a can of corn and a can opener. "Pearl's a teddy bear."

"Not to be contrary, but most teddy bears don't come with fangs," said Abigail.

Santiago opened the can with a smile and drained all the water into a coffee mug left on Pearl's desk. He scattered half the corn across the laminated map of Europe. The hen clucked.

"So you think Pearl is going to let you keep that thing in here the rest of the school year?"

He raised an eyebrow. "Is the National Zoo looking for donations of chickens?"

"To feed the tigers."

Santiago shuddered. "Why does everyone want to kill and eat the poor thing?"

She looked at the chicken in the corner on the laminated map. "It seems more humane than making him stand all day on France. Instead of torturing the poor thing, why not just set it free, Abe Lincoln?"

Santi pulled his office door shut behind them. "We're in downtown D.C., Abby. If I set that hen free, between the thousands of bloodthirsty lobbyists on Capitol Hill and the equal number of homeless men between here and Union Station, someone *will* kill and eat it."

"So you're gonna keep it tied up and locked away for its own safety?"

"Something like that."

"And you actually think you're an improvement on Jesuits from the 1800s?"

Santiago ignored the jibe and they walked down the hallway. He paused at the door of the school treasurer's office. White-haired, 70-year-old Father Vin Guilotti was still at his desk.

"Vin," he said. "Could you lock this inside your safe?" He held out the lockbox containing the papers and gestured to the large safe, as tall as a man's shoulders, built into the wall.

Guilotti rose. "Sure, Santi." He turned his attention to Abby. "So pretty as always today, Abigail."

Taking the metal box, he crossed to the safe and spun its large tumbler. "Royden tells me you're saying Jasper's memorial service tomorrow, Santiago."

Santiago nodded. "Are you going?"

"Of course. Of course." Guilotti pulled the heavy door open and put the box on the top shelf. He closed the safe and spun the tumbler again to secure it. "A terrible tragedy, Jasper's death. You knew him better than, I, for certain, Santi, but that whole matter took me by complete surprise."

Santiago threw Abby a told-you-so look and they bid Guilotti farewell.

Thirty minutes later, Santiago and Abby were fighting rush hour traffic on the Rockhurst Expressway when his cell phone warbled.

"Yeah?" he answered.

"I've traced the package sender." Nico said, "It was sent by a guy named Philip Cannon."

Santiago searched his brain but the name was unfamiliar.

"The address on the package is listed at 4354 P Street, Northwest."

"A Georgetown address," Santiago said. "Did you do a background search?"

"What kind of moron do you think I am?"

Santiago muttered at a cab that cut him off. "What did you find?"

"Philip Cannon died in 1953."

"Ay!"

"It gets better," Nico said. "He was murdered. Guess where they found the body?"

Santiago waited.

"Cannon was found on those steep steps that climb down from Prospect to Canal Road a few blocks from his home. The steps that Jesuit priest died on during *The Exorcist* movie."

Santiago's breath came out in a whoosh. "What could that mean?"

"Quién sabe? You're the guy he's sending love notes to from the grave."

"And you tell me you can't get the FBI involved in this? First, the map went missing from his room. Then, this morning I was able to figure out what he circled on it. You know what country it was?"

"I have a feeling you're gonna tell me."

"Israel. And now I have proof that Jasper's rewritten thesis was erased from his laptop."

"De veras?" Nico scoffed. "Really?"

"The FedEx package you just traced. It contained clues that led me to that and a bunch of other important documents."

Abby gestured and Santiago covered the phone. "What?"

"If you mention the Stewards, he's going to think you're a lunatic," she said.

Santiago returned to the phone. "I think the documents will help prove Jasper was murdered to keep him silent."

"What do they say?"

"They're locked in the school safe. You'll need to come see them."

Santiago abruptly ended the call. He smiled mischievously at Abby.

"Will he come?"

"Eventually."

Santiago finally pulled into the visitor's parking lot at the university. Walking with Abby through the clusters of students chatting in front of Dahlgren Chapel, he spotted a young couple kissing, the girl, tiptoed, looking into her boyfriend's eyes. His mind spun back eighteen years to the first kiss he'd received since leaving Puerto Rico. In that very spot, late one night, autumn leaves swirling about their feet. He was stomping to keep warm. A girl with red hair and hundreds of freckles, letting go of his hand, stepping forward, making him suck in a deep breath. He turned to Abby, smiled and squeezed her hand.

She smiled back "What was that for?"

Her hand lingered but Santi caught himself and pulled his away. "Just a good memory." He sped up and made a beeline for the Alumni Office. The receptionist was closing up when they arrived. "Has Father Jack Donnelly gone over to the Jesuit residence?"

"He's actually over in Carroll Parlor giving a tour of the art collection."

"Thanks!" Santiago and Abby headed toward Healy Hall, the oldest building on Georgetown's campus. They slipped inside and darted toward Carroll Parlor, named for Archbishop John Carroll, Georgetown's founder. The fussy Victorian parlor that held his name featured an elaborately gilded ceiling overlooking a handful of bronze, marble and wooden sculptures and even a pair of chairs belonging to Pope Pius X.

Santiago entered the room. For him, it felt crowded, its walls lined with ornate art-laden curio cabinets. Above these hung a number of paintings – a crew team sculling on the Potomac, a view of Georgetown from across the river in Rosslyn – all by early American artists. Carroll's portrait was featured prominently among them, acknowledging the man's role in founding the Catholic Church in Maryland.

Like any formal room filled with irreplaceable treasures, the place put him on edge. Donnelly was standing in front of the painting of Carroll. "This portrait is Archbishop John Carroll, who founded the university in 1789 when he acquired sixty acres of land on what was then a hilltop above Georgetown village," explained Donnelly. "Senator, this particular piece was painted by the great American painter Gilbert Stuart at a studio he briefly opened here in Washington."

Donnelly was speaking to two men and a woman. One of the men, standing behind the others, was a tall, gaunt man with a handsome face whose lines suggested he carefully rationed its smiles. The other was a thick man with a full head of salt and pepper hair and a pressed charcoal gray suit. The woman seemed glued to him. Two decades younger, she was a sculpted, starved blonde who nodded at Donnelly's every word. It wasn't until Santiago got a good look at the man's face that he finally recognized him. Senator Byron Bradwell of South Carolina, chair of the influential Senate Intelligence Committee. Donnelly spotted Santiago approaching and nodded in greeting. Santiago held back until Donnelly finished, then the old priest turned to him.

"Santiago!" he said. "So good to see you! Let me introduce you to Senator and Mrs. Bradwell and Ambassador Edward Cochran."

Santiago quickly introduced Abby and Donnelly continued. "Father Torres is headmaster of Gonzaga High School, not far from Capitol Hill."

The ambassador nodded politely but the senator seized Santiago's hand, nearly crushing it. "Good to meet you. Heard great things about your school. Great things."

Santiago studied the man's face. Bradwell had never heard of the place.

Mrs. Bradwell pressed her hand across her ample breasts. "Please, call me Heather."

"Are you alumni?" Santiago asked the trio.

The senator's laugh filled the room. "Ah, while Edward is, we are not! But I do have a son who is hoping to attend this fine institution next fall. So, with the good ambassador's assistance, I'm here today to twist the arms of some of the most important men in the city."

Donnelly laughed warmly in delight.

"No better school on the east coast," said Santiago.

Donnelly chortled again. Too loudly. By then, Abby had squirreled her way behind the men and looked back at Santiago, her face slightly elongated, her eyes comically expanding in an effort to make him laugh. Santiago had to look away. He felt ridiculous, part of a social charade, paying homage to one of the most powerful men in the United States. Bradwell's national recognition and popularity had recently skyrocketed with his investigations of intelligence leaks and the federal government's own spying on Americans. When his committee's hearings began, Bradwell's face ran above the fold in the *Post* for two straight weeks while his sound bites filled networks from CNN to Fox. "What are you men hiding?" he thundered at two representatives from the National Security Administration, who spoke with the abrupt, impatient edge of those raised in New York. Only the word came out *hahden*, which left the NSA spooks nonplussed. And that immediately made the senator believable to more than a hundred million Americans, who were regularly confused by New Yorkers.

What could Santiago say of significance to such a person?

"You've had a busy year," Santiago finally offered.

"Indeed," the senator agreed, "cleaning up Washington."

It came out *WASHenton*.

"And with me facing reelection just next year, it has been one wild ride."

Wile Rahd.

The senator must have concluded he had twisted enough arms. "Well, Father Torres, if you'll forgive me, we need to depart for a far less enjoyable cocktail party up the Hill. You need two things to get elected in this country. A handful of votes and a bushel barrel of fat cat donors."

Santiago nodded and stepped to Abby's side. Bradwell put his hand on Donnelly's shoulder and walked him to the parlor door, trailed by Bradwell's wife and Ambassador Cochran. Santiago kept a respectful distance as the two spoke quietly. Bradwell's arm finally shot out, seized Donnelly's hand and shook the man silly.

"Quien a buen árbol se arrima, buena sombra le cobija," Santiago whispered.

"Translation?"

"It's the island version of 'It's not what you know but who you know.'"

As Santiago spoke, the trio departed, Donnelly returned walking on his toes, almost giddy drunk. "A fine catch for Georgetown," Donnelly said. "Father Bob Stanley asked me to show the senator around."

Santiago wasted no more time. "Jack, before his death, Jasper was very excited about the historical documents found in the Dahlgren renovation. He told me you gave them to him to review, study and catalogue as part of the Georgetown Plantation Project."

Donnelly nodded. "The contractor called me over to the chapel a few days before Jasper—" The priest caught himself. "Before Jasper died. During renovations the workmen had to move the altar and under its foot was a small opening in the floor. At first they thought it was a time capsule of some sort but the space beneath the altar wasn't on any of the original drawings from 1893."

"What did the box look like?"

Donnelly thought. "Simple gray gunmetal, very dusty of course. Looked like it had been in there decades. It had a name and a date engraved, come to think of it."

"Do you recall them?"

"The name, no. But I think the year was 1953."

Santiago looked at Abby. "That date corresponds with the documents we found."

Donnelly's eyes rose, but Santiago returned to the questions. "What caused you to call Jasper?"

"When I quickly poked through them, most of the papers didn't make any sense to me. I spotted articles of incorporation but then some older documents with the names St. Inagoes, White Marsh, St. Thomas's Manor. The old Jesuit slave plantations. Since they were clearly related to the Georgetown Plantation Project, I called him to come down and have a look."

"What was his reaction?"

"He took one peek and uttered, 'Good Lord!'"

"Did you keep the documents, letting him make copies?"

Donnelly waved his hand. "He took the originals, of course. I asked him to make copies and return the documents to me in the lockbox"

"And you don't think it's odd that the documents and Jasper's new thesis based on them weren't found in his room?"

Jack Donnelly's eyebrows rose. "Not particularly."

"Not particularly?"

"No, Jasper gave me back the lockbox the day he died, Santiago."

Santiago's heart began pounding. "So you have it?"

"Yes." The priest corrected himself. "Well, not at the moment. Yesterday I decided to give the documents to another historian to determine their importance. But Jasper placed a padlock on it and didn't give me the key. So yesterday I dropped it off at the maintenance facility and asked Steve Grady to get it back to me the moment he opened it."

"You left it in the maintenance building?" Santiago didn't even hide his incredulity. He began pulling Donnelly toward the door. "We need to get that box."

Donnelly grew defensive. "Well, yes. Like me, I'm sure Steve just forgot. I've known Steve Grady for two decades, Santiago," said Donnelly. "He's a perfectly honest man, if you're worried about its contents."

Santiago rushed Donnelly across campus toward the maintenance facility, dodging a dozen attempts by Donnelly to find out why Santiago was so intent on seeing what was inside. In ten minutes, they blew into the maintenance building.

"Hello, Henry." Donnelly greeted one of the men in the front office. "Has Steve left for the day?"

The man nodded.

"I left a box with him. I'm just going to poke around in his office to see if he's gotten it opened for me."

"No problem, Father Donnelly."

The three of them entered Grady's office.

"See!" Donnelly exclaimed. "There it is. He's just busy and hasn't gotten around to it yet." He jiggled the padlock. "Hasn't even been opened."

Santiago ducked back into the main room. "Would you have a bolt cutter?"

"Sure." The man named Henry went over to a far wall, filled with hand tools. "We use it to pull the locks off the lockers at the gym at the end of each semester."

Santiago returned to Grady's office, grabbed the thinnest part of the padlock with the cutters and squeezed. The tool sliced through it with a click. Santiago dropped the cutters, held his breath and opened the lockbox.

"Jesus," Santiago whispered.

"What is it?" Donnelly said.

Santiago pointed to the inside of the lid where the original owner of the lockbox had engraved his name and a date. Philip Cannon, April 1953. "That's the same name used on the return address of the FedEx package."

"Do you know him?" Donnelly asked.

Santiago shook his head and rifled through the blank white paper that filled the box.

"Is there anything inside?" Donnelly said.

"Just blank paper in here. Look how new it looks. There's no way it's a half century old."

"So the original documents are gone?" said Donnelly "There's nothing else?"

Santiago reached into the bottom of the lockbox and he held up the only other item.

A crisp, new dollar bill.

Chapter 10: Confessor

Santiago wavered before the closed office door. His hand, raised to knock, felt like a stony weight. He read the nameplate on the door: Fr. Royden Taylor, S.J., Psychology.

Perhaps he could just call Roy on his cell and postpone their session until next week. The day ahead would be busy enough. Jasper's upcoming memorial service. Afterward, another possibly contentious conversation with Nico. The strange dollar clue that was confounding him.

Santiago exhaled. It had been a terrible night. His return alone to his room at the Gonzaga Jesuit residence after the lockbox discovery. Two hours staring alone at the strange dollar bill until his head spun. On the bottom frame of George Washington's portrait, someone had scrawled the initials JSTSJ. He was certain they stood for his full name, Jose Santiago Torres, followed by S.J. for the Society of Jesus. No Jesuit signed his name without adding the S.J. Jasper had scribbled the letters for him. But the clue was leading him nowhere. Its only other marking was a simple circle in yellow highlighter around Washington's head. As the night deepened, he became increasingly sure he would never figure out the clue. Grief as thick as a Chesapeake Bay fog washed over him as he thought of Jasper. He couldn't sleep. And Abby. Always that stubborn ache for Abby. Qué revolú!

He stood exhausted before Roy's office door. He pulled out his cell, thumbed through the contacts. Roy was Santiago's spiritual director and confessor, his biweekly trip to forgiveness after an inventory of his struggles, joys and failures. Yet Roy was a good and loyal friend too. Santi used to love these meetings with Roy. He'd leave emotionally spent yet filled with hope, emptied yet overflowing.

But now?

He felt a shredded ambivalence.

In the past year, as he spent more time with Abby, a stubborn doubt had trickled into his skull. While he wished otherwise, he found himself desiring less the life of a Jesuit priest. Instead his mind chased the fantasy of the life he abandoned the day he uttered his first vows. Now as he stood before the bathroom sink mirror, the what ifs and should haves of his life were etched in the corners of his sad eyes.

Adding to the struggle was a shift in his faith. As a young man entering the Jesuits, he happily accepted his calling and Catholic beliefs without question. Yet as he matured and studied his church's history and its teachings, it actually had a perverse effect: doubts crept in. He still believed in God's existence. And in the importance of living a life of love, charity and goodness. But in recent years Santiago increasingly stumbled over more specific points of dogma. Out of loyalty, his heart still wanted to believe. Santiago's brain, however, proved more stubborn.

He read the office door's nameplate again. Royden Taylor was as much responsible for Santiago's joining the Jesuits – for becoming a priest – as anyone. A Georgetown fixture for twenty-five years, Roy was Santiago's teacher his freshman year. After that, as Santi wrestled with the whole idea of the priesthood, Roy became his spiritual advisor and friend. No one made Santiago more certain that he wanted to be a priest. Yet no one else asked him more questions that caused him to ponder the depth of his commitment.

Santiago pulled in a breath and knocked.

Roy called out and Santiago entered his small, warm office, illuminated by lamps. He closed the door behind him.

"Hello, Santi! Come in! Come in!" Roy got up from behind his desk to give Santiago a hug. The sixty-five-year-old priest was shorter and plump. His cardigans smelled of sweet pipe tobacco and his round eyeglasses slid down his nose when he smiled. He gestured for Santiago to sit in a worn recliner and fell into an identical one across from it. Then he shook his head "A terrible week, Santi."

"Yes, Roy, it was." Santi sat on the recliner, draped with a plaid blanket. He sighed, bent his head forward and rubbed his hands through his thick hair.

"I'm looking forward to Jasper's memorial service tonight," Roy said.

The words hung in the room.

"Not me."

Roy looked at him in surprise and Santi gave a hopeless shrug. "I don't know what I'm going to say."

"You're his best friend in the world. What's behind your confusion?"

Santi's words burst out. "The police say he killed himself. Everyone is walking around talking about how surprised they are that Jasper committed suicide. He didn't kill himself, Roy. I'm sure of it."

The old priest shifted in his chair.

"See? You don't believe me either."

"So you think it was an accident?"

"For God's sake, Roy, of course not. Jasper was shoved or thrown off that roof because of what he discovered in the documents found last week in Dahlgren Chapel. He was going to expose all of it in his doctoral thesis. I've seen some of the documents he had before he was killed. They're sitting in the school safe. But anyone I try to talk to about it just thinks I'm crazy."

Roy was silent another moment. "So who do you think is responsible for Jasper's death?"

Santiago sighed. He knew the reaction he was going to get. He should have brought the papers to show Roy. "Maybe the Stewards."

Royden Taylor's eyebrows rose. "The Georgetown Stewards?"

"Yes. The Georgetown Stewards."

Roy's eyebrows narrowed quizzically as if he expected Santiago to burst into laughter at the joke. When the laughter didn't come, the look melted into concern. It sat on his face only temporarily before the trained psychologist in Roy replaced it with an expression devoid of judgment. Still he squinted a bit before reaching out and patting Santiago on his knee. "Listen, Santi, it's been a terrible week for you."

Santiago's frustration got the better of him. "Don't patronize me, Roy!"

Roy Taylor fell back into his chair, his hands held out helplessly. Santiago immediately regretted the words.

"It's been months now. When are you going to tell me what's going on, Santi?"

A powerful wave of grief suddenly caught Santiago off guard. "I'm sorry," he whispered. He fell silent, closing his eyes until it ebbed. Then he spoke in a whisper. "I just need you to believe me on this. I'm not losing my mind. I know it sounds crazy. But it is what it is."

Santiago swallowed. "So what do I say at the memorial service? Do I just announce that Jasper didn't kill himself and then politely wait to be escorted away by the men in white jackets? What do I tell his parents, for God's sake?"

Roy's eyes narrowed thoughtfully. "You tell them the truth."

"Ha!" said Santi, a half laugh, half sob. He waved his hand. He couldn't figure out the truth inside his own head half the time. And he was supposed to make sense of this damn mess?

Royden Taylor remained quiet a long time before speaking. "Santiago, when was the last time you prayed?"

"I said mass yesterday."

"No." Roy shook his head. "I didn't mean that. I meant found yourself a quiet place and privately prayed."

"This morning."

Roy smiled gently and pushed his eyeglasses back up his nose. "I suppose that's not the first time someone's lied during confession, but most tend to do it far more convincingly than that."

Santiago pressed his forehead into his open hand and pushed down the grief that was building again. Was his sadness about Jasper's death? Or the slow, twisted death of his own commitment to the priesthood? "I've hit a dry patch."

"That's normal. We all fall into those," said Roy. "For how long?" He eyed him a moment. "And risk the truth this time, Santi."

He braced himself for Roy's reaction. "Five months. Half a year. I don't know."

Roy leaned forward and peered at him over his glasses. "Half a year of meeting every other week and you only get around to mentioning it today? People can't hide from the truth, Santi. Those who try to do that quickly discover that it has a way of coming out crooked. It's better to face it, head on." He gestured with some frustration. "I could tell you've been struggling for months, yet you've kept me miles away."

Santiago remained quiet.

After a moment, Roy leaned back and tried another approach.

"Have I ever told you about my favorite philosopher?"

Santiago waited.

"He was a Greek fellow you've heard of. A little obsessed with simple machines like water screws and fulcrums. And for saying, 'Give me a long enough lever and a place to stand and I can change the world.'"

"Archimedes." Santiago said.

Roy nodded.

"I'm not following."

Roy scratched his chin. "What do nearly all older Jesuits say when people ask them why they became a Jesuit?" He raised his eyebrows before answering the rhetorical question. "'I entered for the wrong reasons and stayed for the right ones.'"

Santiago offered a wry smile. "I remember Mark Albright telling me exactly that four years before he left for good."

Roy chuckled, his eyebrows arching mischievously. "Oh, come now, Santi. You expect God to realistically compete with a twenty-seven-year old male dancer?"

Santi offered a pained smile and Roy waved his joke aside. "Mark Albright makes my point exactly. In my forty years beneath this collar, I've seen scores of Jesuits – and lay people alike – go through the same process. I'm convinced life has two stages, like a clay bowl being made by an artist."

"I thought you were explaining the man with the lever."

"Shouldn't mix metaphors, I suppose." Roy paused. "Let me see if I can tie the two together. The first thirty or forty years after we come into the world, we're on a quest to discover ourselves – like an artist discovering a bowl from the lump of clay spinning on her pottery wheel. In our teen years – while our brains host a great battle between cynicism and idealism – we're all convinced we were born to accomplish something great. We'll be a great scientist, inventor, leader, Hollywood star, famous singer or, perhaps if all those fail, your run-of-the-mill superhero." Roy smiled. "We don't doubt our ability to change the world."

Santi nodded.

"Yet so many of us never make it off the pottery wheel. We get stuck, going around and around. We never really discover our purpose." He held up a finger. "If I can return to my Archimedes metaphor for a moment, it comes down to this: we haven't found a place to stand. We simply go through the motions, reacting to what life throws our way instead of acting on it. Before long fatalism, regret and resentments seep in. We wake up someday in our 40s in an unfulfilling job, surrounded with all the external trappings of success, overwhelmed with family or work responsibilities and find ourselves saying, 'Is this it? Is this all there is?' We're filled with a profound ache for something more. Something to fill up that emptiness."

Roy leaned forward again. "Despite beautiful families or influential jobs and wealth others envy, we've not found our place to stand – or the lever we need to change the world."

He tapped Santiago on his knee. "But here's the rub, Santi. We were right when we were teens. We *were* born for something great. We were born to shift the world."

Santiago felt prickly. "So you're saying I've not discovered my purpose?"

Roy cocked his head. "No, no, no. That's not for me to say, Santi. But many women and men I've known – deeply good people – often find themselves stuck. Call it a mid-life crisis or something else, they're just like a partially formed clay bowl or pitcher that can't serve its true purpose. They can never pour out into the world what life has filled them with. With a profound sense of emptiness, many of them crash and burn in their mid-40s. Alcoholism. Prescription drug addiction. Financial disasters. Bizarre affairs that destroy their families.

"Some never recover. The lucky among them finally discover themselves through those terrible experiences. They emerge like a clay bowl from its firing – sturdy and ready to fulfill their purpose. These fortunate people have found their lever and their place to stand. Only then can they fill up the world and change it."

Roy gave a sigh, frustrated at his inability to explain himself clearly. "This will sound blunt, but for six months you've worn the grim smile of a man who wakes up in the morning and, instead of hitting his knees, greets the world with: Is this all there is?"

The old priest looked kindly at his friend. "Are you stuck, Santi? Are you stuck and merely spinning?"

Santiago remained silent.

"Here's a little irony. I keep in touch with Mark Albright. He's still with Stephen and he's never been happier and felt more fulfilled. And that's what's most important. That's what God wants for all of us."

Santiago felt profoundly uncomfortable. He'd never mentioned his feelings for Abby to anyone. He suddenly felt stripped naked and exposed and his embarrassment flared into anger. "So I should just leave the Jesuits?" he spat. "Are you suggesting I should just abandon my vocation?"

Roy sat back, shock playing across his face. His voice grew quiet. "That's not what I meant at all. I'm just wondering if Jasper's death is forcing you to confront some important truths. I don't know what they are, but among them may be the painful truth that you're still searching for your place to stand." He paused, his brow furrowing. "Whether you do that as a Jesuit or not, Santi, is your choice."

Santiago stood up. "I can't do this today, Roy. I'm sorry. I have to prepare my remarks for Jasper's service." He crossed to the door, turned the doorknob and suddenly felt overwhelmed with grief and guilt. Roy was one of his closest friends and he was storming out because he'd jabbed a finger into the truth?

Santiago stood for what seemed like an eternity, wondering whether to speak, whether to try to right the wrong.

He finally let the words tumble from his lips in a whisper. "I'm obsessed."

Roy waited a long time before speaking. "Obsessed with what?"

"Abby."

He heard Royden shift again. "Then let's begin there next time."

And Santiago was gone.

Chapter 11: Jasper's Service

Santiago closed the Book of the Gospels and pulled out his prepared remarks. He grasped the sides of the lectern, his knuckles skeletal white. His eyes flickered across the faces floating above St. Aloysius' oak pews. In 1857 the enormous, majestic church, a stone's throw from the capitol dome, had climbed brick by sensible brick above the dusty lanes of Swampoodle, a hard drinking Irish-immigrant shantytown even cops avoided.

Standing on its altar, Santiago now felt a temptation to brick up the truth.

Before the funeral, he had dressed silently in the sacristy, crowded with dozens of Jesuits from Georgetown, Gonzaga and Georgetown Prep, the other Jesuit high school just outside the Beltway. For Santi, the growing, murmuring throng became a sea of black. Their presence pressed on him, clawing at his chest and neck until they could pour down his throat and drown him.

To make his heart stop fluttering, Santiago stepped out into the empty vestibule. He found Jasper's parents trembling in the first pew, stoically repeating greetings to each arriving Jesuit. Before he could turn, Mrs. Willoughs spotted him. Her delicate face, like ancient, discolored lace, flickered and she gestured to him.

Santiago stepped off the altar and Mrs. Willoughs touched his wrist. "I have something for you." She opened her purse, pulled out a photograph of Jasper mugging with a number of Georgetown students in a restaurant. "I just want you to remember Jasper as happy."

"He was—" Grief closed Santiago's throat and he hugged her, unable to finish. "Thank you."

He fled back to the lectern, bending behind it, pretending to search for something hidden upon its shelves. He looked again at the photo, Jasper's broad, happy smile. Unable to bear it any longer, he jammed the photo into his pocket and pressed his forehead against the lectern's cold wood.

Didn't she deserve the truth?

The procession followed, the blessing of the casket with incense, the opening prayer, stolen glances at Jasper's parents, the readings, fidgeting, fumbling.

If not the truth, what could he say?

Should he simply go along with the story that Jasper killed himself? Or speak his doubts and be taken for a grief-stricken fool? An unstable priest, unfit for office. Unfit to serve as headmaster of nearly two-century-old Gonzaga High School.

Santiago peered over the dozens of Jesuits, robed before him, lining the front pews. Which one would one stand, walk up to the podium and put a hand on his arm. "Listen, Santi, it's been a terrible week for you."

Royden's other words echoed in his head: Di la verdad! Tell the truth!

The truth? Based upon a handful of documents that could be fakes? A secret society that was a running joke on Georgetown's campus?

Santiago looked out on the congregation. Abby was there. Pearl. Most of Georgetown's history department. A few dozen of Jasper's undergraduate students. His eyes flickered across the swath of empty pews behind them, settling on three dark figures seated in the back. One he recognized as Nico. Two other men in suits and raincoats sat on the other side of the aisle.

Santiago's heart rattled.

"Jasper Willoughs was my great friend."

Santi's voice boomed through the sound system, bouncing about the vast spaces of the great church. His fingers found the papers on the lectern and he began to read. "Eight years ago I traveled to Berkeley."

He glanced up, his eyes landing on Abby for reassurance. "I felt a great sense of adventure. A new chapter of my life was about to be written. Yet I felt great anxiety also. Terror even. I was in California, after all."

The church echoed the scattered, polite laughter. The attempt at a little humor had fallen flat. The two men had set him on edge. He wasn't preaching. He was reading.

Santiago took a deep breath. "I was there to begin my theological studies. Living in a whole new world, a completely foreign place where I knew no one. The first Friday I was there, I went to Chinatown alone for dinner. At the end of the meal, the waitress – a kind, old woman – presented me with a fortune cookie. 'This one,' she said, patting my hand, 'is especially for you.'"

He offered a dramatic pause, glancing at the entire congregation before continuing. "I opened that cookie and can still remember its fortune word for word. It read: Life is full of treasures, the greatest being friends; a wonderful, life-long treasure lies in your immediate future.'"

Santiago looked down at Jasper's mother and he nodded, his eyes welling up. "The next morning I met Jasper."

The edges of a smile pulled up the woman's trembling face and she wiped her eyes. Santiago felt fulfilled.

Unsure of what to say, he had added the fortune cookie story just that morning. It aptly captured the feeling of that first week in San Francisco – his good fortune of meeting Jasper.

Tell the truth.

Yes. Strictly speaking, it wasn't true. But, like many Old Testament tales, it was an effective story that captured the essence of the truth. Such stories were the difference between sermons that soared and sermons that snored.

And, for a moment, it blunted the sharp edge of an old mother's grief.

"Jasper was a great treasure. One I – and others here – were so very blessed to uncover in our lives. Yet like other treasures stolen from their owners, I never understood the true preciousness of your son until he was gone."

Santiago continued the homily, touching upon their ordinations, Jasper's bizarre quirks, Santiago's school adventures and Jasper's thesis roadblocks. Santiago's mind hummed as he looked over the congregation, his fellow Jesuits, lost in laughter and nostalgia for a lost son. A lost member of their company. La compañía.

The word caught in his throat, the nickname his fellow Jesuits used for their religious order: The Company.

Who were the two men watching him from the back of St. Al's Church?

Could Santiago even trust the Jesuits seated before him?

He pressed his lips together, eyeing the final paragraph of his homily, weighing whether to utter it aloud:

How do you grieve the loss of such a great treasure, of such a beloved friend? I've spent three days searching for that answer, Mr. and Mrs. Willoughs. It is this: Pursue the truth and proclaim it loudly to bear witness to what is right and just. And here is the truth: Your son, Jasper, did not kill himself. He was killed by someone who was afraid Jasper would tell the truth. And this afternoon, Mr. and Mrs. Willoughs, you have my solemn promise as Jasper's friend that I will work to uncover that truth so that his memory is paid the great love, respect and loyalty that it is due.

Santiago looked out at Abby, who smiled back at him.

Tell the truth.

One of the two men in the back shifted, leaning forward, staring intently at Santiago.

Santiago's heart galloped, nearly bursting from his chest. He placed the palm of his hand across the prepared text. He looked up at Roy Taylor, who cocked his head curiously at the long pause.

Santiago finally turned to address Mrs. Willoughs. "And so I arrive at the most difficult part of my remarks." He shook his head. "I wish I had answers that made sense. I wish I had a great and miraculous power to heal all that has gone wrong these past few days. But I do not. And so, left without answers, I leave you with Jasper's final words instead of my own."

Santiago closed his eyes, recalling the note they had found in Jasper's handwriting: "'Mom and Dad,'" he recited from memory. "'You have given me the world and I could not have been blessed with more wonderful, loving parents. This is not your fault. You have always wanted me to be happy. And now I am. I trust I will find God as merciful and loving as the wonderful friends I have been privileged to have. Please forgive me. Be at peace. I love you all. Jasper."

Santiago folded his homily and pushed it through his robes and into his pocket. He walked silently back to his chair and sat, batting away rising shame. He listened in silence, unsettled by the gentle sobbing of Jasper's mother.

No longer able to bear it, he shut his eyes, trying to utter a prayer. He struggled to work up the courage to beg God's forgiveness, but his mind kept leaping away to the image of Abby's freckled face.

He opened his eyes again.

The two men were gone.

Chapter 12: Cold Reception

With a reception back at the residence promising enough food and liquor to stun all living school alumni, the Jesuits and the congregation abandoned the church after singing the final hymn. Back in the empty sacristy Santiago shrugged off his chasuble and alb and stepped back into the church.

Despite the church's vastness, the scent of myrrh and frankincense from incensing Jasper's coffin still hung in the air. It stuck to the back of his throat, an acrid taste of mortality.

At the back Nico smirked and leaned against a confessional door. He shifted the laptop he was carrying to his other arm.

Santiago spoke in Spanish "Did you see the two men?" He gestured to the pew where they had been sitting.

Nico ignored the question, responding instead in English. "Do other priests lie during mass, Santiago?" He pushed himself off the door. "Or only the saints like you?"

"What would you do in my place?" The loud echo of his words made them sound too defensive and Santiago lowered his voice. "I need you to help me prove someone killed Jasper before anyone else will believe me."

His brother's smirk turned into a pinched smile. "I was talking about your ridiculous fortune cookie story."

Nico's comment brought Santiago up short. "I'm responsible for inspiring people to goodness. What good is it if I'm boring and ignored?"

Nico laughed. "Qué guillao! You even lie to yourself. You do it today for the same reason you told ridiculous stories as a kid,

Santiago. To be the center of attention." His eyes flashed resentment. "And yet you expect me to believe your story that your friend was killed? If you made up the beginning of your friendship, why not its end?"

Santiago refused to let his brother get him riled. He turned to walk back up the aisle. "You don't need to believe me. I'll prove it. Más claro no canta un gallo."

"As I suspected, your friend's laptop was completely clean." Nico's words stopped Santiago.

"What does that mean?"

"When the tech went in to reconstitute the hard drive, he found nothing but the existing files." Nico handed him the laptop. "You insisted we'd find erased copies of a thesis, the new version he was supposedly writing. It wasn't there." He paused, the smirk reappearing. "In short, it means you were wrong."

"There were no erased files?"

"None at all."

"That's ridiculous. Jasper's had that laptop two or three years."

Nico held up both hands. "It is what it is. Despite what you insist, there was no mysteriously erased thesis."

Santiago's frustration rose and he fell back into Spanish. "And you just left it at that?"

"The guy was using his time to do me a favor. You insisted there'd be erased files on that laptop and there weren't. If you're gonna prove your friend was killed, you need to find some evidence, not a lack of it."

"I am not going crazy."

"I didn't say you were. I just said you were wrong."

"The papers I have say otherwise." Santiago paused. "Think about it, Nico. Something I know for a fact existed vanishes and you don't find that suspicious? Someone killed Jasper and now, given those two men in the back of the church, you don't think someone might try to kill me?"

The final comment made Nico's smirk evaporate.

"I'm asking for a favor as your brother. No matter how bad of one I've been."

"You said you could prove that he killed himself."

Santiago nodded. "It's all in the school safe." He began walking up the aisle.

"That nonsense you mentioned about The Georgetown Stewards?"

"You need to look at it. It's not another story, Nico."

Nico shook his head and followed him through the sacristy. Santiago opened the door to the Jesuit rectory, whose first floor held the offices of Gonzaga's receptionist, treasurer and headmaster. Calmer now, his brain flipped back to English. "At least give me credit for being an accomplished liar. If I was going to concoct a story about Jasper being murdered, what Georgetown alum in his right mind would pin it on the Stewards?"

The comment wasn't lost on Nico, also a Georgetown graduate. A slight smile pressed across his face.

"Give me half an hour to show you the package I received," Santiago said. "If at the end you don't think something might be suspicious, I won't bother you about it again."

They entered the dimly lit, empty hallway. With the sun down, the light from the opened door of the treasurer's office spilled out into hallway, providing the only light.

Santiago nodded in its direction. "Vin is still working."

As Santiago reached the office door, goose bumps prickled his arms. He hadn't spotted Fr. Guilotti's face among the sea of Jesuits that had filled the front pews. Yet Vin never let work interfere with Jesuit community matters.

"Vin? You here?" Santiago pushed open the bottom half of the split door and stepped into the office. "Vin?"

A pair of legs was visible on the floor behind Fr. Guilotti's desk.

"Vin!"

Santiago rushed over to the fallen man. A small circle of blood was already coagulating beneath the old Jesuit's head. He shook the old man's shoulder before reaching for his phone.

Nico was already barking into his. "We need an ambulance."

Chapter 13: A Startling Revelation

As the paramedics lifted him onto a gurney for transport, Vin Guilotti regained a groggy, incoherent consciousness. He pointed to the opened safe and muttered, trying to sit up. Pushed aside when the men arrived, Santiago had already looked into the safe. The lockbox containing the Stewards' documents had vanished.

"Lie back now, Father." One of the paramedics placed a hand on Vin's shoulder and pressed him against the gurney. "Let's not move around until we get that head checked out."

As they wheeled the old priest out, D.C. police detectives and several other Jesuits, who came downstairs from the reception, crowded into the room.

"Father?" A detective approached Santiago. "You in charge here?"

Santiago nodded.

"Can you tell me what happened?"

Nico interrupted, flashing his FBI identification. "We didn't see the attack. We found the man, lying here behind the desk. It looks like a robbery."

The detective nodded to the open safe. "Any idea what was taken?"

Santiago walked over to the safe again and noted its open drawers. "Looks like the petty cash is gone. And likely the cafeteria receipts from this afternoon. About two thousand dollars, I would guess. Vin doesn't keep a lot of cash on hand. It's not the best neighborhood and he doesn't want to put the office staff at risk. He takes it to the bank every afternoon."

"But not today?" the detective said.

Santiago shook his head. "There was a memorial service for a friend in the church."

"What about the papers?" Nico encouraged Santiago. "If they're gone and they contained what you said they did, it could trigger the bureau's involvement."

Santiago remained silent.

The detective spoke up. "Are there important documents missing?"

Santiago looked back at the safe and then at his brother. He wracked his brain. Who besides Nico had he told about Jasper's package? Two more perhaps, but he trusted Nico the least. And all three could have mentioned it to someone else.

"No," Santiago said to the detective. "Nothing important."

Nico's eyebrows rose. Santiago's eyes met his. Nico clearly didn't trust his brother either.

"Detective, would you mind if I head over to the hospital to be with Fr. Guilotti? I'll get someone else down here to answer any other questions." The detective nodded and Santiago introduced him to Roger Draper, the school's dean of discipline. He turned to his brother. "I need you to drive me to the hospital."

Another lie. He could have driven himself. He simply wanted Nico there.

His brother's face looked like he'd been punched. He stepped stiffly into the hallway after Santiago. In the hallway, out of earshot, he let loose in Spanish. "What the fuck, Santi?"

"You saw that the Stewards' documents are gone."

"Then why not tell the detective? You expect me to believe your story and you pull this? Even if your story of those documents is true, you just lied again. This time to a cop investigating a crime. And now you want me to haul your ass to the hospital?"

"Yes," said Santiago. "We need to talk to Vin first."

"Drive yourself."

Santi held up three fingers and pressed them close to his brother's face. "Three people knew about the documents. You, Roy Taylor and Abby. Who do you think I trust the least?"

"And a dozen students you told me saw you pull that box from the ground." Nico pushed his hand away. "You're a jackass if you think I arranged this robbery."

"Then who did you tell?"

Nico offered a dismissive laugh and turned to walk away.

"Come with me to the hospital then."

Nico waved his hand and strode down the hallway.

"Nico, por favor." Santiago's voice fell. "If you won't believe me, if you won't help me, who will? Are you going to wait until I'm dead too?"

The words – the guilt trip – sounded exactly as if their mother had uttered them.

Nico slowly spun, his words colored with both annoyance and admiration at the manipulation. "Telling me the Stewards might kill you if I leave isn't exactly the best incentive to get me to stay."

Chapter 14: Nico Unconvinced

When Nico and Santiago entered his hospital room, Vin Guilotti was already propped up, his face flickering with tired recognition as they entered.

"Hello there, Santi," he said feebly.

"Vin, you okay?"

"Oh, sure." He raised a hand to his head. "A headache is all, I think. They're taking me for a scan in a few. They'll confirm for sure I've got rocks up here."

Santiago smiled and the old priest looked up at Nico. "Vin, this is my brother Nicolas. Have I ever introduced him before?"

Vin looked at Nico. "Could be." He extended his hand and Nico shook it.

"He works for the FBI."

Vin gave a laugh. "Is the bureau now investigating hold-ups of old Jesuits?"

Nico smiled at him. "Only the important ones, Father."

Vin seemed to enjoy this.

"Hey, Vin, you up for some questions?" Santiago pressed.

"Shoot," the old priest agreed. "It'll give me time to practice my answers before the D.C. cops interrogate me." He winked at Nico.

"That lockbox I gave you to put in the safe," Santiago began. "You didn't move it before the robbery, did you?"

Vin shook his head. "No, once I put it in the safe, I didn't touch it again. Did they take that too?"

Santiago nodded.

"I'm terribly sorry, Santi. Was it important?"

Santiago felt grave disappointment but waved his hand. "Not as important as your keeping your head, Vin."

Nico spoke up. "How many men came into the office, Father?"

"One is all I saw," said Vin. "There may have been more outside, I don't know."

"Can you describe him?"

Vin thought a moment, touching his head again. "It was cold outside. He was pretty bundled up in dark clothing. His face covered, of course. Kind of like a ski mask, but I couldn't even see his eyes. He had sunglasses on."

"Black, white or Hispanic?" Nico asked.

Vin shrugged. "I don't know."

"What did he sound like?" said Nico.

Vin shrugged again. "All he said was 'Open the safe.' He didn't sound like anything. He just sounded like he was in a hurry."

"So you can't tell me if he sounded black, white or Hispanic?" Nico looked as if he were ready to dismiss Vin Guilotti as a buffoon.

Vin could read it too. His face reddened. "Look, son, I'm no old fool. I've been working at Gonzaga for more than two decades. I've spoken to white boys with pants falling off their backsides and speaking like they grew up in the ghetto. And I've spoken to black boys who could pass for some billionaire blowhard from McLean, Virginia. I don't put much stock in speech for judging anything about a person, least of all his ethnicity. But I can tell you one thing. The gun that cracked me in the skull wasn't white or black. It was steel gray and it didn't say a damned thing."

Santiago watched his brother swallow.

"Excuse me." A young man stepped into the room. "We're here to take Father Guilotti for his head scan. You ready, Father?"

Vin nodded. He turned back to Santiago, his calm demeanor returning. "Don't wait here for me, Santi. You go back and sit with Jasper's parents and give them my condolences and apologies for missing his service. I'll be fine on my own. I'm sure to get swamped with visitors soon enough and it'll give me time to work on this headache." Vin rubbed his forehead and turned to

Nico. "It was nice meeting you, son. My apologies if I'm a little crabby. It's no excuse, but my head feels like the circus fat lady used it as a stool."

The men began wheeling Vin's bed out of the room. Passing Nico, he patted his arm. "I'm sorry I can't be of more help. The next time I get held up, I'll be sure to remember to study the guy."

Santiago and Nico left the room. "Live wire," Nico said.

"Vin's a great guy. You just made the mistake of speaking to him like he was stupid." Santiago let his brother brood until they were standing in the hospital's parking lot. He dropped into Spanish. "So, are you going to help me?"

"If you're asking me if I believe you," Nico said, "the old man confirmed you gave him the lockbox. But you're still asking me to trust you regarding its contents. What more have you got?"

Santiago pulled out his cell. "Graham Cooper."

Chapter 15: A Grilling at Old Ebbitt

Halfway through lunch, Graham Cooper shed his suitcoat and draped it over his chair. Since the arrival of Graham's third child and his recent promotion at the Treasury Department, Santiago had noticed the top button of all of his friend's suitcoats had begun to pucker. Rather than cut back on the fries, his college buddy simply started abandoning his suitcoat whenever they met for lunch at Old Ebbitt Grill.

With Nico looking increasingly impatient, Santiago finally broached the topic. "Coop, I recall you once telling me that you got tapped by the Stewards back at Georgetown." Santiago nodded at his brother. "Nico's working on something related."

Cooper shrugged into a more comfortable position beneath a painting of a chubby cherub on the wall. He looked from Santiago to Nico. "That's what? Almost two decades ago?"

Nico let slip an almost imperceptible sigh.

"They tapped me when I was a sophomore at Georgetown." He nodded at Nico. "Right after we both started working for Father Stanley in Georgetown's Office of Federal Relations. I was a sophomore, so you must have been a freshman."

Another Jesuit, Stanley worked the Capitol Hill cocktail circuit like a four-armed, glad-handing K Street lobbyist. He was famous for its ability to win congressional federal budget earmarks benefitting Georgetown. The Jesuit was incredibly popular with small coterie of students, but to Santi, he always seemed aloof and drank too much.

"So, I get a call from a guy who asks me to meet him in the lower quad," said Graham. "Wouldn't give me his name. Wouldn't even tell me why. 'You've been recommended for membership in an organization I represent,' he told me. So I went out of curiosity."

"What happened?"

"When I go down there to meet him, the guy's still elusive," said Cooper. "'What organization do you represent?' I ask. And he responds, trying to sound all important, 'I can't reveal that. But you can't speak of this to anyone. I can only tell you I represent an important organization that protects and benefits Georgetown and this great country.'"

Nico shook his head.

Graham eyed him. "Then he spends the next half hour trying to impress me by telling me absolutely nothing," said Graham. "Mr. Mystery Man."

"Did you ask him about what members of the group did?" Santiago asked.

"I asked a hundred questions he didn't answer. When I finally asked him point blank if he was from the Georgetown Stewards, he just laughed. 'I never said I was with the Stewards,' he said. 'That group doesn't exist.'"

"So what did you do?"

"Nothing," said Graham. "After I told him it was a little difficult deciding whether to join an organization I knew nothing about, he said, 'Just think about it. You can meet me back here next week, same time.'"

Nico checked his phone and finally spoke. "Did you go back?"

Graham laughed. "My mother made me swear not to. She said only perverts joined secret organizations."

Nico stared at Santiago. "How exactly does this help?"

"Look," said Graham. "I don't know if the guy was from the Stewards but he's certainly not that secret. I see him at The Tombs nearly every Thursday and Saturday nights."

"¡Viste!" Santiago gave his brother a triumphant look.

Unimpressed, Nico dropped thirty dollars and a business card on the table and stood. "Graham, it was good seeing you again. But if you really want to help, get me a photo of the guy and his name. Then I've got something to work with."

Nico walked away.

Graham's eyes followed him out the restaurant. "Your brother's still quite the charmer."

Santiago smiled. "Will you do it then, Coop?"

"For you, sure. I'm meeting the guys at The Tombs tonight." Graham pocketed Nico's card. "But why didn't Nico just tell you about the Stewards?"

"As far as Nico's concerned, they don't exist."

Graham Cooper folded his arms. "Your brother is shitting you, Santi. The Stewards tapped everyone who worked Federal Relations their sophomore year."

Chapter 16: The Tombs

Santiago shrank into his coat. In D.C. February was a gray wall of cold with all the warmth of a marble statue. Like a politician, the frigid air always lulled him into initially thinking it wasn't so bad. Then the icy wind, stabbing inland from the river, made his teeth ache. Georgetown's cobblestones sucked the warmth from his legs. And with every breath, the chill squeezed him like a giant constrictor.

A bitter wind blew him sideways down P Street toward The Tombs. He had ditched his collar, and instead dressed in regular civilian street clothes. Four days had passed since Jasper's memorial service and the attack on Vin; then on Thursday night, a dark photo appeared on Santiago's phone: a man sitting in a restaurant booth. Graham Cooper even finagled a name from a waiter: Pat Kelly.

"Should I send it to your brother?" Graham added.

Santiago stood, staring at his phone screen for fifteen minutes as his brain careened back and forth.

"No," he finally responded.

Santiago had avoided Abigail in the meantime, answering her phone calls just once. "I'm fine," he lied and felt immediately ridiculous doing so. "It's just this damn chicken. It's taking more time than you could imagine."

At Pearl's insistence, the chicken was banished from his office. So Santi had smuggled it up through the Jesuit residence and into his room. He tucked it under his coat, in part to hide it from Brother Sinclair. It was silly, really. He could have walked right into the commons room and announced, "After some prayerful reflection, I've decided to keep a live chicken in my room." The rest of the Jesuits would have been too preoccupied with preprandials – the society's official name for getting snookered before dinner – to hear. Old Father Breckinridge would have faintly nodded. No, Santiago smuggled the chicken upstairs simply because it was just too weird.

It now spent the day tethered to the top of the mini-fridge in his bedroom corner. It perched there until he returned and dropped a few more kernels of the canned corn at its talons. He later replaced the newspaper beneath it with another filched from the common room. Up there, at eye's height, the chicken stared back while he dropped the corn – as if it was expecting him to say something.

Unconsciously, Santiago began talking to the chicken.

Her name came to him later as they eyed each other. Perched there, the chicken reminded him of a children's story he'd once read his nephew James in English. "Your name is Penny," he said.

Chicken Little wouldn't do. The chicken on his fridge wasn't the one dashing around clucking the sky was falling. Santiago was handling that just fine. So if he was Chicken Little, what did that make the real chicken?

Henny Penny? At least that's what Santiago thought was the name of one of the other barnyard animals Chicken Little sent out of their minds with fear, flapping like chickens with their heads cut off.

The thought snatched an image from his memory. His grandmother, back in Puerto Rico, tying a chicken by its feet to a tree branch, seizing the chicken by its head and arcing a machete blade through its neck. It flapped convulsively, spraying little Santiago with blood.

"I told you to stand back, Santi." His abuelita laughed. "Now you look like Christ crucified."

Henny Penny. He was pretty sure that was a name from the folk tale, but he was fuzzy on the English ones. They weren't told to Puerto Rican kids. Instead it was all Juan Bobo.

Santiago pulled his collar closer against the frigid wind. He quickly typed a text – "You ready?" He pocketed the phone without awaiting a response, pattered down the steps and entered The Tombs.

A crash of dishes offered a raucous welcome. The Tombs was pure college rathskeller, a dark watering hole whose walls were speckled with sports prints. Dozens of oars sat like open fans on its wood walls, their spoons painted with the colors and names of Georgetown crew's rivals. The place offered decent, reasonably priced food and was popular with Georgetown students and faculty.

"Hi, I'm supposed to meet an old friend for dinner." Santiago pulled his phone out, showing the photo Graham sent him. "His name's Pat. He might already be seated."

"Oh, Mr. Kelly," she said. "He's already seated in his booth. Just go to the right, all the way back. He's with a lady."

Santiago thanked her, slid around a group of patrons by the bar, and headed to the right. Two wait staff in dress shirts and bow ties poked orders into a touch screen. Santiago hadn't considered that the Stewards' recruiter might be here with someone else. In Graham's photo Kelly was alone. Santiago spotted the beefy fellow, more fat than muscle, early fifties, with thick white hair above a ruddy face. He wore an expensive sweater and collared shirt that shouted weekend Chesapeake sailor.

Santiago stood a moment, his stomach lurching.

"Excuse me." A waiter hustled past.

Santiago's eyes locked onto the man and he walked over to his booth. The fellow's face pinched into a question mark. Santiago pushed into the booth on the lady's side and she emitted a startled squeak.

Santiago was sure they could hear his heart knocking against his ribcage.

Kelly offered the kind of exaggerated smile that slices the faces of office workers meeting the CEO at the company Christmas party. "Give me a minute!" Kelly's voice boomed. "I know that face. Give me a minute and my pickled brain will catch up."

Santiago turned to the woman. She was Kelly's age. Expensive clothing, lots of jewelry, no wedding band, too much perfume. A divorcee, perhaps. "Sorry to interrupt."

The woman glanced back and forth between Santiago and Kelly and burst into loud laughter. Drunk already. "My, my, you are popular tonight, Patrick."

Santiago nodded, playing along. "Mr. Kelly knows everyone important at Georgetown."

Kelly beamed. His eyes searched Santiago's face, still waiting for his brain to properly slide him into the proper name and context.

Santiago stared back at his best friend's possible killer. The capillaries in Pat Kelly's fleshy nose looked like a road map to the neighborhood's liquor stores. He found the glassy, smiling stupor of the man infuriating.

"Oh, yes, Patrick here gets around." Santiago said. "Just the other day he knocked an old priest over the head in order to steal something from the poor guy."

Kelly's mouth fell open. The clueless woman laughed again too loudly, thinking it all a joke. "Who is your friend, Pat? Are you going to introduce us?"

Santiago grew bolder. "Or did you have someone else do it for you?"

Kelly recovered. "I think you've mistaken me for someone else." He cocked his head to the side. "Have we met before, sir?"

"Although I suppose knocking priests over the head beats throwing them off dormitory roofs. Were you starting to feel guilty?" Santiago offered a steely smile. "Tell me, Pat. Am I next on your list? Will you kill me personally or will you have one of the guys you sent to Jasper Willough's funeral do it for you?"

The drunk woman finally realized there was no joke. She slid into the corner of the booth. Her hands began to tremble.

Santiago's mouth was dry, his heart thudding in his ears. He had never been so frightened. "I just dropped by to tell you to your face that you and your friends don't frighten me. And I will prove the truth about you and the Stewards."

"Excuse me?" Kelly sputtered a contrived laugh and made an exaggerated face at his lady friend. "Did you say the Stewards?

He actually believes the Georgetown Stewards exist!" He bellowed a laugh and looked around the restaurant for an audience.

Santiago's courage wavered. Kelly's ridiculous denial would have sparked suspicion in a gullible child.

He pressed forward. "I'm going to expose you and the Stewards if it's the last thing I do." Santiago then baited the trap with a lie. "You actually think you have Philip Cannon's papers? Do you think I was so stupid that I'd keep only a single copy of them in that safe?" He laughed. "Mr. Kelly, do you understand how the material I have will destroy the Stewards and send you to jail for a very long time?"

Kelly's face grew serious, his eyelids flickering. He glanced over Santiago's left shoulder and made a slight gesture with his head. A waiter approached behind Santiago. "Mr. Kelly, is there something I can get for you?"

The fake smile again. Kelly gestured to Santiago. "This gentleman has me confused with someone else. If you could escort him to his correct table, I would be most grateful."

"I'm not finished." Santiago's eyes bored into Kelly's skull.

Kelly nodded at the waiter, who placed his hand firmly on Santiago's shoulder. "Sir, if you could come with me…"

Santiago shoved the hand off his shoulder and turned to face the waiter down. His anger evaporated.

"Father Torres?" The waiter's face melted into a surprised smile. He extended his hand. "Matt Williams. I graduated from Gonzaga three years ago."

Kelly's face shifted.

"Sure, Matt! Of course I remember you!" Santiago feigned a smile. He stepped into the restaurant aisle and clapped the waiter on the shoulder. "I'm running late, Matt. We'll have to catch up sometime. Be sure to stop by and visit."

"Absolutely, Father!"

Santiago pushed past and rushed out of The Tombs. He climbed the steps two at a time and paused at the top.

The wind knifed through him and a bolt of fear turned his spine to ice. Up the block, a car's headlights flashed.

He dashed up the street and slid breathlessly into the car.

"Now what?" said Graham Cooper.

"Now we wait."

Chapter 17: The Black Mercedes

Within twenty minutes, Pat Kelly was standing at the top of the steps to The Tombs. Santiago watched as the man nervously looked around. Kelly poked at his cell phone and pressed it to his ear. He waited a moment before his head shook dramatically with a curse. Struggling to return his phone to his pocket, it clattered across the brick sidewalk.

"He's not happy," said Graham.

Kelly nearly fell over retrieving his phone. He took an unsteady few steps, turned in a complete circle and cursed again before wobbling up the street. "And in no condition to drive."

"Leave off your headlights, Coop. We should keep our distance."

Repeatedly checking his phone, Kelly weaved seven slow blocks away from campus. He finally stopped in front of a large, white Georgetown home and Santiago held up his hand to stop Graham. The home was surrounded by an imposing iron gate. In the flickering light thrown from the street's gas lamps, the property appeared expensive and immaculate.

Kelly checked his phone a final time before hauling himself up the stone steps. He looked around and rang the doorbell.

"Find a spot and pull over," Santiago said.

"How do you know it's not just a friend's house?"

"He just abandoned a tipsy date back at The Tombs. You really think he'd do that just to go meet a friend?"

The door of the home opened, a dim light spilling across the steps. Kelly stumbled through it.

Graham gave a nervous laugh after the door closed. He slipped into an empty parking spot on the street. They sat quietly for ten minutes, Graham's hands thrumming against the steering wheel.

"You going to tell your brother?"

Santiago thought a moment. "I don't know."

Graham nodded. "That's certainly one crazy ass story you've told me."

Santiago stared at the door that Kelly had disappeared behind. Graham sighed and resumed thrumming.

Twenty minutes later, a gate crossing the home's driveway rolled back.

Santiago leaned forward. "What time is it?"

"Just after eleven."

A large black Mercedes rolled to the end of the driveway. It paused before turning away from them and driving down the road.

Graham shifted for a better look. "Was Kelly inside?"

Santiago grunted. "Its damn windows were tinted."

Graham started his car and looked at Santiago. "Should we stay or follow?"

"I don't know." Santiago glanced back at the dark home and gave a frustrated grunt. "Let's follow!"

Graham backed up, threw the car in gear and lurched out of the spot. He gunned the car forward, throwing on the headlights at the intersection. The Mercedes rolled on, about a half block ahead, and stopped for a red light.

Graham hung back, repeatedly clearing his throat. Santiago looked over at him. Graham's hands were trembling on the steering wheel.

The traffic light changed and Graham gunned his car to catch up to the Mercedes. He kept tapping the wheel and finally spoke. "Look, Santi. I'm going to be uncharacteristically blunt for me."

Santiago waited.

"As I see it, after hearing about your friend Jasper and what you say he found out about the Stewards, there are really only two possibilities here."

Graham fell quiet.

"Spit it out, Coop."

His friend offered an awkward smile. "You're either bat shit crazy or you're fucking around with a group who've got no qualms about throwing people off roofs."

Santiago wondered what Graham would decide if he knew about the chicken in his bedroom.

"Coop—"

Graham's normally steady voice warbled. "You know Katie and I just had another baby."

Santiago's brain flashed with the wonderful memory of holding Lauren Cooper over the baptismal font. The way she looked up and cooed when Santiago smiled at her.

Santiago flushed with shame at his selfishness. "Stop it, Coop."

Graham fell silent, turned onto a side street behind the Mercedes and looked over at Santiago.

"No. I meant stop the car."

Graham Cooper slowed.

"We don't even know that Kelly's in that Mercedes."

"Santi, no, man. That's not what I meant. If you need me—"

"Graham, it's time for you to go home and kiss your kids goodnight."

Chapter 18: A True Steward

Pat Kelly hauled his thick body up the stone stairwell. He nervously checked his phone and rang the doorbell.

He waited a moment for the heavy door swung in. He nodded at the Latina maid and thumped across the parquet floor past dark antiques. The cloying scent of lavender and furniture polish clawed at his throat. He checked himself in an ornately carved mirror before parting the French doors.

His friend was reading the paper behind his desk. He gestured to a cold, leather chair whose cushion whooshed as Kelly dropped into it. "I appreciate your seeing me with such short notice."

His friend nodded.

Kelly leaned in. "The headmaster of Gonzaga, Father Torres, you know who he is?"

Another nod.

"I was at The Tombs last night and he damn near assaulted me."

His friend let the paper fall to the desk and peered at him over reading glasses.

"He accused me of killing Father Willoughs."

He removed his glasses and tapped them on his desk. "The young Jesuit who jumped off Harbin?" The icy voice sounded like a quivering bowstring.

Kelly nodded. "It's clear he thinks the Stewards did it."

His friend offered a disarming chuckle.

"That's not all. He mentioned someone's papers. A fellow named Cannon. He made it sound like someone had stolen them from him. But he said he has another copy."

His friend shifted in his chair. "It sounds like this Father Torres has a screw loose."

Kelly pointed a thick finger. "He said the papers would destroy the Stewards and put me in jail for a very long time."

His friend laughed again, a dry sound, like leaves in a gutter stirred by a passing car.

"What the hell is going on?" Kelly's voice boomed.

The man held up his hand. "Lower your voice, Patrick. What are you going to get arrested for? Putting Christ back into Georgetown?"

Kelly's face twitched. "Father Torres seemed very upset. He wasn't kidding around."

"Secret societies are forever getting blamed for other group's nonsense. Stupid people become paranoid very easily. Go home, enjoy your Sunday and put your mind at ease."

"You sure I'm not going to jail for anything?"

Another laugh. "Now you are growing paranoid. There's no crime in trying to keep the school the great place it was when we attended, is there?" He stood up and walked around the desk. "Why not drop by the marina next Friday night and join me for drinks on the boat? We're going to have quite the D.C. crowd aboard."

The invitation seemed to surprise Kelly, but it worked like a salve. The large man stood up, smiled and nodded. "Sounds great!"

The man ushered Kelly through the office doors and down the long hallway.

"Look, I'm really sorry for bothering you with this."

"Not a bother. None at all." He clapped Kelly on the back and he lumbered down the steps.

Back in his office he sat and rubbed his gaunt face. He fought the blooming fear in his gut. *He said he has another copy.* He cursed and leaned forward for the phone. It rang twice before it was picked up.

"Meet me in thirty minutes," he said. "I'm in need of a permanent solution to a growing problem."

Chapter 19: The Stewards React

Come Monday Santiago felt two sizes smaller sitting in his desk chair. He'd been useless all morning, his anxious brain swirling around the dollar clue when it wasn't replaying the dangerous confrontation with Kelly two days prior.

Saturday night, after Graham Cooper dropped him off at the Jesuit residence, he'd looked up the Georgetown home's address on the Web site of D.C.'s Recorder of Deeds. His heart fell when he read the owner's name: Marguerite Kelly.

Sunday morning, he called Ed Reardon, the Jesuit pastor of Holy Trinity.

"Would you happen to have a parishioner named Marguerite Kelly?" Santiago asked after greeting him.

"Certainly. Mrs. Kelly has been a parishioner of Holy Trinity for at least four decades."

"What can you tell me about her?"

"She's elderly and private. Keeps to herself. On the conservative side, I'd say."

"Any children or grandchildren?"

Ed thought a moment. "I don't think she has any grandkids. Only one son as far as I know."

"Pat Kelly?"

"Yes, that's it. They're quite close. He went to Georgetown, but lives out in Maryland now, I think. She worries a lot about him." Ed's voice dropped. "Between you and me, he's a bit of a drinker. Lost his license. His mother drives him everywhere now."

Santiago hung up and let his head hit the back of his chair. He'd put a big target on his back in exchange for the address of Pat Kelly's mother.

The rest of Sunday, paranoia and anxiety crept in. To calm himself, he tried reading in his room. Every creak in the old Jesuit rectory, every footstep outside his bedroom door, set him on edge. To escape the pressing walls, he drove down to the Gangplank Marina, a stone's throw from Memorial Bridge.

Whenever he walked among its docks, the gulls' accusatory cries calmed him. In the summer it reminded him of his grandfather's simple town back in Puerto Rico. His abuelo would nudge him before dawn and his abuela tucked cold empanadas and a thermos of café con leche into their hands. They'd eat silently, padding down to Fajardo Bay. There he'd help his grandfather drag his yola, one of the brightly painted fishing boats that lined the beaches, into the water.

Yet the February weather in D.C. was blustery. Even the gulls had the good sense to stay grounded, glumly pulling their necks into their bodies for warmth. It added to Santiago's sense of foreboding, of death tapping upon his shoulder. So Santiago abandoned D.C. and drove up I-95 to Baltimore, doubling back twice to ensure he wasn't being followed. Outside Ellicott City, he was so busy studying a black SUV in the rearview mirror, he almost drove under the back axle of a semi.

He walked Baltimore's Inner Harbor until dinnertime. He sat, folded into his coat like one of the gulls, and studied the tourists among the shops and restaurants. The way parents grasped their children's hands more tightly near the water's edge. The way young couples laughed and brushed against each other. The way older, exasperated men turned to reassure themselves their wives were not ducking into a new store. He envied them all. More, he regretted not calling Abigail and bringing her along.

Yet what good would that have done?

He came back late, slept fitfully, dragged himself into the office early. He locked the door behind him until he heard Pearl arrive. At ten-thirty he picked up the phone and called Roy Taylor.

When Roy answered, Santiago stayed quiet a moment, letting the gentleness of his voice seep through him. He finally spoke up. "It's Santi."

"Hey, there, Santiago."

"A quick question. You know a guy named Patrick Kelly?"

Roy collected his thoughts. "Sure. Pat Kelly's a Georgetown alum. A big supporter of the school."

"Anything else?"

Roy chuckled. "Oh, he's a bit on the conservative side, I suppose. He thinks Georgetown committed a grave wrong by accepting women. Personally, I think they've humanized my classes." Roy thought a bit more. "Other than that, I don't know much else about him. Except that he works in business in some way and he's pretty close to Bob Stanley. You could call Bob. He'd know more."

"Is Kelly a good guy?"

"Seems nice enough." Pause. "Why?"

"Didn't know what to make of him. I ran into him the other night."

Roy laughed again. "He's definitely a character."

"Thanks, Roy." Santiago went to hang up.

"Santi?" Roy's voice hung a moment, making clear he found the whole phone call abrupt and strange. "Let's try to schedule another sit-down. I think it would be good to talk."

"Absolutely." Santiago paused. "Look, Roy, I'm gonna have to call you back to schedule, though. A parent just walked in."

He hung up and shoved his rising guilt about lying to Roy into an obscure corner of his brain. Kelly was a friend of Bob Stanley. Powerful, wealthy, connected. No surprise there. But in The Tombs, he had come off like a buffoon.

Santiago shook his head. The guy was an obvious fool. If anything, his conversation with Kelly confirmed that a group called the Stewards actually existed. It also made clear that Kelly was a member. But what respectable group would have Kelly tapping its future members? Certainly not an organization with the wealth and power that Philip Cannon's papers suggested.

So little sense could be made of it all. Who sent the package with the thesis and documents? Why, if Jasper had done it before he died, weren't they complete? Where were his research notes? Then there was the map in his room and the perplexing dollar clue.

"Get out of here!" Pearl shouted. The sounds of a struggle grew in the next room.

A shot of fear and adrenaline surged through him and Santiago leapt to his feet. After the attack on Vin and his conversation with Graham, he'd let no other friend get hurt on his account. He dashed to his office door and threw it open.

"Stop it!" Pearl cried. She was fending off a young black man in a wool cap, parka and pants falling off his hips. As he struggled with Pearl, the man burst into laughter.

Santiago dashed around Pearl's desk, seized the man by the arm and spun him around.

"Father Torres!" Pearl cried.

Santiago shoved the man against the wall. The man's startled face triggered a flash of recognition. Santiago's mouth fell open. "Bradley?"

The man gave a laugh and straightened. "Sorry about that, Father. I just asked my mama for a kiss. That's all. She's getting all high and mighty on me." He pulled down his coat, pulled up his jeans and fell back into a chair with another laugh. "Won't kiss her oldest boy if he don't got no tie on."

"I told him to get right on out of here dressed like that," said Pearl. "What kind of mother does this fool make me look like?"

"Jus' business, mama," said Bradley, pulling off his wool cap. "Whaddya think, Father?"

Santiago looked confused. He took another look at the man, who smiled back at him. No doubt, it was Bradley Freeman, but he was almost unrecognizable. Pearl's oldest son had gone through Gonzaga, never once wearing anything but a buttoned down shirt and belted trousers that never sagged. Pearl would have it no other way. She would have slapped the back of his head had she found his pants sagging. Fifteen years ago Bradley had graduated second in his class and went on to Princeton, then MIT. Three years ago, he landed back in D.C. and opened his own IT security company, which major corporations hired to close their security holes. Pearl assured Santiago the company was growing like a weed.

"I get the boy through the Ivy Leagues and this is how I'm repaid." Pearl sat back down at her desk and rustled some papers to make clear her anger. "The fool calls himself G-Daddy."

"Just today." Bradley smiled at Santiago, his speech suddenly dropping the street dialect and slang, speaking again like his mother. "The G is for Gonzaga. I thought she'd appreciate that."

Pearl harrumphed.

"You scared the hell out of me," Santiago finally said.

"Now you know how I feel whenever he visits," Pearl growled.

Bradley rolled his eyes. "Mama, I've told you it's just for work."

"Is it Casual Monday?" Santiago joked.

Bradley smiled. "The best way to break into a company is to dress like this. They're less suspicious that way."

Santiago's thick eyebrows arched.

Bradley held out his hand and dropped a flash drive into Santiago's palm. "Triad Capital Funds," Santiago read its logo. "Largest investment firm in the D.C. area."

Bradley nodded. "Two weeks ago my company finished repairing breaches in their Internet security. I even threw in a three-day training of Triad's management and IT principals regarding internal security practices. Triad's gotten hammered by Web attacks originating in North Korea and China. We plugged their security holes and got them in tip-top shape."

"And all you got was this flash drive with their logo?"

Bradley gave a wry laugh. "I warned Triad's CEO that their internal security was still the company's weakest link. His Vice President of IT made the mistake of publicly scoffing at me in the meeting. He offered me a bet in front of the company principals that I couldn't personally compromise his network from inside."

"You bet a flash drive?"

"No. He bet me ten grand, which I'll collect at lunch today. This flash drive simply was simply my key."

"A key?"

"To the vice president's life." Bradley sat down in a chair opposite his mother. "I had to get inside Triad, but their human and external security was incredibly tight. The company VP even printed my business photo from my company's web site and circulated it to all the security guards. I saw it, sitting right there on the security guard's desk at the entrance. So while they were keeping an eye out for a guy in a business suit," Bradley gestured to himself. "G-Daddy dropped by."

"And you thought the guards would let you in dressed like that?" his mother said.

"No. Can you believe it, mama? They grabbed me and wouldn't let go of me. Not even when I shouted I was dating three of the secretaries in the building and they were violating my civil rights."

Pearl pursed her lips, unamused at his mockery.

"The point was, to get inside, I had to convince the guards they were doing their jobs and keeping all the bad guys out." Bradley continued with self-satisfaction. "Only then would they let their guard down. So while the security guards were feeling all important, collaring poor G-Daddy, picking him up by his saggy-ass pants to toss him out of Triad Capital Funds, I dropped a flash drive just like that one onto the guard station floor."

Santiago smiled. "So the security guard later found it, spotted the logo and thought someone in the company dropped it."

Bradley nodded. "It played out like a charm. He took it right over to desk of the young blonde I saw him flirting with all last week and asked her if she had dropped it. Wanting to impress her superiors, the woman popped the flash drive into her computer and opened all the files to figure out who the drive belonged to. Just to make sure she skipped the scan for viruses and malware, I slapped Triad's logo on it."

"It was that easy?"

"Getting in the front door was easy. Getting from there to the vice president's machine through the company's internal network was a bit more challenging."

"How can you even prove you got in?" Pearl challenged.

Bradley laughed. "I had two options. I could have printed off a couple of unsavory photos the Vice President of IT foolishly saved to his hard drive…" Bradley paused and searched through the bag he had looped around him.

"Or?" Pearl said.

"Or I could just hand him this copy of the user names and passwords to all his Web accounts, including an illegal tax-dodging investment account he keeps down in the Caymans and the Web site he frequents for married people looking for affairs." He waved the paper in the air. "Triad's head of IT Security kept all this stored in a folder named Important Stuff on his hard drive."

"You should have e-mailed his mother from his own account and attached all those pictures," Pearl said.

"You're ruthless, Mama. You really should work on Wall Street."

Santiago squinted at him. "Can I ask a favor?"

"Sure," Bradley said. "Since my mother likes you so much, I'll do anything for you, Father."

Pearl scoffed. Santiago gestured for Bradley to enter his office. He went around his desk and pulled Jasper's laptop out of one of its drawers. "A friend of mine owned this," Santiago said. "I'm nearly sure there were some important files erased from it but a guy who checked it says there are no erased files at all. But the laptop is at least three years old."

Bradley looked skeptical. He took the computer, sat in a chair beside the desk, pulled a handful of tools out of his bag and, in a moment, had the case of the machine opened. He poked around a moment. He pulled out his own mini laptop from his bag and his fingers tapped the keys. "You're right. The serial and model numbers of the laptop suggest it's just over three years old." He looked up. "This belonged to your friend who died?"

Santiago nodded. Clearly Pearl had mentioned Jasper and his suspicions he'd been murdered. He wondered if Pearl also confided in Bradley that she thought her boss was going crazy.

Bradley reached into the guts of the laptop, extracting a small box. More tapping. He reached into the bag, extracted a few more wires and hooked up the box to his own laptop. More tapping. He leaned over to study the screen and then looked up.

"According to the diagnostic S.M.A.R.T. feature on the drive's firmware, its total power on time is about three hours."

"I'm fluent in English and Spanish. I even know a little French. But I don't speak Geek."

"It's a measure of how long a computer's hard drive has been on. Factor in a few minutes for factory testing, maybe two hours to load the operating system and files. Throw in an hour or so for the other guy's review of the drive." Bradley shook his head. "This drive is completely new. Someone swapped out the original one. That's why he couldn't find any deleted files. Whoever checked this for you should have picked up on that." Bradley paused. "Or he's the guy that swapped the drives."

A knock on the doorframe of Pearl's office door caused them both to turn.

"Hello, Agent Torres," Pearl said. She pointed with her chin through the office door to Bradley. "I hope you're here to arrest my son. As the old saying goes, don't put off to tomorrow what can be done today."

"You're out of luck, Ms. Freeman. I left my cuffs at the office. Otherwise I'd be tempted to slap them on my brother."

Pearl looked over her eyeglasses. "Did he steal another old lady's chicken? Or was it a goat this time?"

Nico looked at Santiago for an explanation. Santiago stared back at his brother. Bradley looked back and forth at both of them, trying to puzzle out the chilly tension that had crept over the office. "Father, need anything else?" Bradley asked.

"No. Thank you, Bradley. I'm really grateful." Santiago shook his hand and Bradley handed the laptop back. Nico smiled wryly at the exchange.

"Anytime, Father. If you need anything else, just give me a call." He slipped Santiago a business card.

Nico waited for Bradley to exit and he shut Santiago's office door. He stood with his arms folded, a manila envelope in his hand.

"Where were you last night?"

Santiago eyed Nico. "I drove to Baltimore. Ate dinner at the harbor before coming back here late."

"Did anyone see you?"

"No, I made sure I wasn't followed."

"I meant here. Did anyone see you here late last night? Can any of your priest buddies vouch for you?"

"What are you accusing me of?"

His brother opened the envelope and threw its contents on Santi's desk – three garish photos of a man's body lying at the foot of a steep stone staircase. "Estiró la pata," Nico said. "A man named Patrick Kelly was found dead early this morning in Georgetown on the stairs that drop from Prospect Street to Canal Road. And the woman he's been dating happened to mention that you threatened him on Friday night at The Tombs."

Santiago's ears rang. He fell back into his desk chair, his eyes locked onto the vacant, unfocused eyes staring upward from the dead man's face. He knew the steps. They were a minor Georgetown landmark, famous for their appearance the final scene of the movie *The Exorcist*. The same place Nico had told him Philip Cannon had been murdered in 1953.

Santiago pointed to the photos. "I didn't do this."

Nico responded with a dry laugh. "I'm inclined to believe you," he said. "You may be a liar, but there's no way you're brave enough to kill someone."

Santiago sidestepped the insult. "I've been running around all weekend convinced the Stewards were going to kill me. This makes no sense." Santiago's hand covered the man's eyes with his hand and he shuddered. "My God, what if it's my fault they killed him?"

"You went to confront Kelly at The Tombs?"

Santiago blinked. "Yes."

"Because he was the guy that tapped Graham Cooper at Georgetown?"

Santiago turned to Nico. "If you've spoken to Coop already, why are you playing games with me?"

"I have to say, Cooper seemed a little nervous to me."

Santiago shook the photos. "Because he wants nothing to do with this."

"Your little meeting with Kelly didn't go well, did it?"

Santiago studied his brother's expressionless face. "Why do you have to assume the negative?"

"Déjate de estar pendejiando! Did Kelly tell you anything?"

Santiago shrugged. "He was useless. He was drinking. But when he denied the Stewards existed, it was obvious he was involved with them."

"Because you're a living, breathing polygraph machine?"

Santiago remained silent.

"What else did he say?"

"Nada."

"Nothing?" Nico grew annoyed. "Me tienes una teta incha y la otra en proceso!

"I tried to spook him by telling him I still had copies of the information they stole out of the safe. I hoped he would lead me to some other Stewards."

"And?"

"He went straight to his mother's home."

Nico burst into laughter. "A brilliant move if the Stewards are the murderous thugs you claim they are."

Santiago fumed. "You have some nerve coming in here and accusing me of being less than honest." He pointed to the laptop. "That's the one thing I asked your help with. And I just found out there were no erased files on there because it's a completely new hard drive. Why didn't your guy catch that?"

Nico bristled. "I asked my guy to locate any erased files, that's it."

"And you don't find the fact that a new drive was swapped in there suspicious?" Santiago decided to prod him. "Or maybe it was your guy who replaced it."

"My guy?" Nico grew incredulous. "More likely your friend Jasper recently replaced it!"

"Don't be ridiculous!"

"Ridiculous? You've never had a computer fixed? Are you aware hard drives break? Santiago, in court, I have to use proof not suspicion. Where's your proof? I'm still waiting to see anything!"

"Perhaps you'd see a lot if you actually made an effort to help instead of withholding information."

Nico folded his arms.

"Coop said everyone who worked in the Office of Federal Relations was tapped as a sophomore. You didn't think to mention that?"

"You heard Graham's story. Why repeat it?"

"I can't believe you never told me this before."

"When the hell were we ever talking?"

Santiago waited.

"I got a call from a guy who asks me to meet him in the lower quad. Wouldn't give me his name. At the time I thought maybe that's how the CIA picked people. Didn't want to miss out on my big break." Nico gave a wry laugh.

"When I finally figured out I wasn't getting an invitation to Langley, I asked him what the hell he wanted to do with a Puerto Rican if he was from the Georgetown Stewards. He just laughed as if I were a moron and said, 'That group doesn't exist.'"

"So what happened?"

"Nothing."

"So, you didn't speak to Kelly again?"

Nico made a face. "Kelly didn't tap me. It was some other guy."

"Who?"

A shrug. "I never saw him again. They must have sent the varsity squad to meet me."

"So you met him again?"

Nico laughed. "Why would I meet him again? A secret Georgetown organization? Even if it was the Stewards, what could they offer me, their token Spic? A super special secret handshake? Parties in the steam tunnels where they jerked each other off? Cut me a fuckin' break."

Santiago stood. "Look me in the eye and tell me you're not a Steward."

"Jesucristo!" Nico unfolded his arms and leaned over Santiago's desk. "I am not a Steward. But you, my friend, are out of your fucking mind."

The accusation troubled Santiago. He walked to his office window, overlooking the school's football field and stood silently a moment. "So are the D.C. cops going to be investigating me for murder?"

"He was found at the bottom of a steep flight of steps with cuts and contusions and a broken neck. As far as they're concerned, a well-known local drunk fell." Nico smirked. "But if you're correct, you just helped rub out the only lead that might have proved your friend was murdered."

"No." Santiago turned to Nico. "You're forgetting another lead."

Chapter 20: Mr. Lincoln Meets Huck Finn

"You have another Steward you'd like to get killed?" his brother said. "Perhaps you can tell me so we can put him into protective custody."

Santiago exhaled. Why did the Stewards kill Pat Kelly? It made no more sense than the Jefferson Pier lockbox holding some of the documents originally hidden by Philip Cannon in Dahlgren Chapel a half a century ago. At first it seemed clear Jasper had buried them at the pier and sent him the clue. But the more he thought about it, the more it seemed unlikely he had. Jasper would have sent the whole thing, carefully clipped at the top, paginated, annotated, and pressed with an iron. And why a second potential murder on the same steps in Georgetown? If nothing else, the Stewards were sending a clear warning to him to leave the matter alone.

He looked at Nico. "We should talk to Bob Stanley," he said. "Get a list of everyone who's worked in that office over the last two decades."

"Anda pa'l carajo! No jodas!" he cursed.

Santiago looked at his brother. Santiago viewed some Jesuits as personal heroes – Roy Taylor for one. Nico had put Bob Stanley on a similar pedestal long ago while working for him in Georgetown's Office of Federal Relations. Stanley had even gotten Nico hired by the FBI.

"Are you jealous of Stanley? Or is it me?" Nico switched entirely to Spanish and was now shouting. "Do you resent the fact that people actually like Stanley? That he's friends with influential, rich people? That they actually help him build Georgetown up?" His brother glared. "Or is this just your way of insulting me?"

Santiago held up a hand, trying to calm his brother. "Mira!" he said, "It's all I've got. And if I'm wrong, I'll write Stanley a personal apology."

Nico's eyes narrowed.

Santiago reverted to English. "About an hour ago, Roy Taylor told me Pat Kelly was closest to Stanley at Georgetown. It makes sense. The Stewards are supposedly archconservatives, old school Catholic, God bless America patriots. They're all in business. If there are Jesuits that are part of the group, Bob Stanley fits the mold." Santiago paused. "How long after you started at Federal Relations did you get tapped by the Stewards? Your sophomore year like Coop?"

Nico didn't respond.

"You think that was just coincidence?"

His brother's lips formed a thin line.

"Another thing we need to figure out is how the Stewards knew to steal the documents from the school safe. Only three people knew it was in the vault. You, Abby and Roy Taylor."

"And the old priest who got brained."

"Yes," said Santiago. "Vin Giulotti. That makes four."

"And all those students who saw you dig the documents up."

"They didn't know where I put them," Santiago protested.

"Would you stash them under your pillow? The school safe is the logical place to look. And then there's anyone else all of them happened to tell. As I've said before, you're on a wild goose chase, Santi. I've discussed your wild accusations with my superior while at least two other agents were present. Just imagine how many people the others may have told."

Nico gathered the photos from Santiago's desk and tucked them back into the envelope. "Don't confront Stanley like you did Kelly. I want to speak to him this time."

"If you're going to talk to him, I'm going to be there."

Nico's voice remained adamant. "I'll handle Stanley."

Santiago's desk phone beeped and Pearl's voice interrupted. "Father, Kevin Gaines and Marc Davis are here to see you."

Santiago wanted to press the argument, but his brother slipped out as two members of the English department strode in. Neither looked happy. Kevin Gaines, head of Gonzaga's English department was a fifty-year-old, still trim ex-Marine, particularly popular with the school's black students. African-American himself, Kevin had come up in the neighborhood adjacent to Gonzaga, where his childhood row house burned in the April 1968 riot. The quintessential, pull-yourself-up-by-your-bootstraps story, Gaines was a stern taskmaster whose sharp wit kept the boys in line.

Marc Davis was two decades younger yet a foot taller. Where Kevin favored sweater vests and ties, Marc was all open collars and hiking boots, straight out of a New England outdoorsman's magazine. He was easy-going, coached lacrosse and took his hiking club into the West Virginia mountains over long weekends. Marc's classes verged on chaos, but he inspired kids to write amazing things.

Davis handed Santiago the latest copy of his school newspaper, folded open. Photos of the two men stared back up at him, their headshots tucked beside opposing columns. The headline ran in black on white: Should Huckleberry Finn Be Banned?

Santiago looked up at the two men and offered an exaggerated, grim smile to defuse the tension. When that didn't work, he nodded to the seats in front of his desk. "Did you bust Marc plagiarizing again, Kevin?"

Both men sat and simply looked back at him.

Santiago cleared his throat and sat as well. "So, I take it there's some disagreement over the department's required reading list." He waited again for the two men to begin talking. He finally shook the newspaper. "Do you two care to explain or do I have to read this thing?"

Kevin broke the silence. "Marc is refusing to assign Huck Finn. All the junior boys purchased the book at the beginning of the year. And despite the department's decision to make it a required book, he's refusing to assign it." Gaines looked over his glasses at the younger teacher. The look made clear Marc Davis was guilty of insubordination.

"It's incendiary." Marc folded his arms.

"Incendiary?" Santiago repeated. It had been almost two decades since he'd last read Twain's novel in his graduate seminar, but incendiary wasn't an adjective he'd use.

"Look," Marc said. "Twenty percent of this school's student body is African American. And we're telling them they have to read a book that has the N-word in it over two hundred times."

Kevin's voice dripped with disdain. "The word you can't say is nigger."

Marc stiffened.

"I've been called it several times in my life. Are we going to pretend that for over 300 years it wasn't commonly used in this country to refer to black folk?"

"It's not used today."

Kevin chuckled. "If you actually believe that, you need to step out of Northwest D.C. occasionally."

Santiago held up his hand and addressed the younger teacher. "Marc, you know Twain was anti-slavery and the book is anti-slavery. It was even provocative in its day for its view on race."

"Father, I know that. In a perfect world, it could be taught without the historical baggage that surrounds the word. But I have a question for you. Would you let a teacher in Gonzaga's history department hang a Confederate battle flag or the flag of Nazi Germany in his classroom even though they have a significant place in history?"

"That's different," Kevin interrupted.

Santiago held up his hand. Emotionally, he had the same initial reaction as Gaines. The flags were different. The Rebel flag wasn't used to condemn slavery as had Twain's novel. But he was curious to hear Marc's argument. "I'd have a problem with the flags," he said. "They're needlessly provocative and could be misinterpreted." Santiago paused. "But more important, their significance as teaching tools would be pretty questionable."

"The n-word is also needlessly provocative. It's an explosive slur. When the word is used, for some young men, it blocks out everything else of value in the book. Meanwhile four-fifths of the classroom they're sitting in, studying the book, is all white. Are we saying there are no other great American novels that can serve as a substitute?" Marc shook his head. "As a white person, I'm just not comfortable teaching it."

Kevin's head turned to him. "What's that supposed to mean? That as a black person I should be more comfortable with it?"

"Kevin," Santiago gently interjected. "I don't think that's what Marc meant."

"Then what did he mean?"

Marc shot back. "You're clearly more comfortable using it than I."

Santiago raised his hand. "We're all aware that the word is used with greater license by blacks than it is whites. Let's move on."

"It shouldn't be used by either," Kevin retorted.

Marc slapped his knee. "Then why force these kids to read and discuss a book in which it's used two hundred times?"

Kevin's voice boomed in response. "So we should just pull Countee Cullen's poem *Incident* from the freshman reader? Who cares if it teaches the power and damage that words cause! Pull it from the damned book! Shall we pull *Uncle Tom's Cabin* from the junior history curriculum because the name is an insult blacks hurl at each other? Shall we sanitize all the curricula of any suggestion of race and pretend it hasn't been the great national obsession of the past four centuries?" He shook his copy of *Huckleberry Finn*. "For Christ's sake, Marc, it's how you teach it that matters!"

Kevin's voice dropped off and a strained silence followed.

Santiago tended to agree with Gaines, but the image of the Rebel flag hanging in Gonzaga classroom stuck in his head, despite his attempts to dislodge it. What if it didn't matter what was intended by assigning the book? What if Marc was right? That no matter what, what really mattered was the black students' perception that they were being forced, by a white teacher, to read a book with those words while surrounded by other white students?

Santiago nodded at Gaines. "I appreciate your passion, Kevin. And I hear you. I just think I need to think on this some more."

Anger blazed across the man's face again. "Fine."

Kevin stood and strode to the door. Then he turned and addressed Marc. "If we're going to sanitize race and all its historical contexts from our school, we'd better pass a rule banning hip hop from the boys' iPods. Perhaps you can organize the censor board."

He looked directly at Santiago, now offering him a challenge. "And, Father, every time I walk into the cafeteria, the black kids are largely sitting at one end of the room and the white boys are sitting everywhere else. It looks an awful lot like D.C. did when I was a kid in 1960. If we're going to pretend we're all one nation now and pretend race doesn't matter, maybe we ought to get around to integrating the tables."

The door slammed behind him.

Marc Davis awkwardly picked at some imaginary lint on his pants.

Santiago looked up at the portrait of Lincoln and sighed.

Chapter 21: A Matter of Prudence

Santiago stood beneath the yellow front porch light, an anxious, anticipatory flutter in his chest. He knew this wasn't wise. He knew that if he called Roy Taylor on his cell and told him what he was about to do, Royden would gently reply, "Given your state, Santiago, do you think it's prudent?"

It wasn't prudent. It was remarkably stupid. Still, with a thrilling rush building in his chest, Santiago simply didn't care. His heart pounding, his throat constricting, he raised his hand and rang the doorbell.

And immediately regretted it.

Abby had bought the Cleveland Park home – actually, her mother purchased it for her because no teacher could have afforded the place – when she returned to D.C. four years earlier. Abby returned to D.C. because of her mother's declining health.

While Gonzaga sat a mere three blocks from Union Station, Cleveland Park graced a low hill six miles to the northwest. The rise snagged the passing breeze, helping residents forget Washington was carved out of a breathless bog. Abby's neighborhood had gained its name from President Grover Cleveland, who built a home there to escape the city's epidemics of yellow fever – and its feverishly corrupt Congressmen.

The refurbished Queen Anne-style home, built in 1896 on the edge of the original capital city, sat on a side street called Highland Place. Abby loved its prim look, its broad windows and its wrap-around porch. Everything about it reminded her of her childhood dollhouse. From spring through fall, whenever Santiago dropped by with Jasper, they discovered her rocking in its broad porch swing. She'd be cradling a book, sunlight filtering through the giant maples, dappling the home's gables like the freckles playing across Abby's face.

And now he was here alone, ringing her doorbell.

When he pulled his finger from the bell, he nearly ran away. Then he simply hoped she wouldn't be home.

But Abby's hand pulled back the curtain of the door window. The light behind her illuminated a look of happy surprise. She unbolted and opened the door.

"Santi! What a surprise! Are you all right?"

Even Abigail knew his showing up like this, on a weekday night, was odd.

"Um, I'm actually okay." He paused. "It's just..." he began but then waved his hand in apology. "It's okay, Abby. I should go."

He bent to pick up his bags.

"What do you mean you should go? Come in! Come in! You just got here." The fact that he had two bags with him suddenly registered on Abby's face. She cocked her head.

"I need somewhere safe to stay," Santiago stuttered, rising without the bags. "I'm not sure I'm safe any longer living at the Jesuit residence."

"Then you're not leaving," Abby insisted. "But keep in mind," she teased, "unlike that prissy part of the inner city you call home, this is highly dangerous Northwest D.C. You might choke on an organic bagel."

Santiago smiled. He bent to pick his bags off the porch but she seized the smaller one first, a bowling ball bag. "You brought a bowling ball?" she said. "Was that in danger too?" Abby raised and lowered the bowling ball bag to gauge its weight, the smile slipping from her face. "This isn't a bowling ball."

"I was going to explain that before you grabbed it—"

"It's that damn chicken."

Santiago offered an exaggerated smile. "I couldn't just leave it. Father O'Brien's been looking at it with lust in his heart. He would have eaten it for sure."

"You expect me to let a chicken in my house?"

"It's only acceptable if it's plucked and in the freezer?"

"I can't have a chicken in my house, Santiago! I have cats!"

Santiago scoffed and pushed past her. "You don't have cats." He took the bowling ball bag from her and stepped into her hallway. "You hate all cute animals."

"I'm buying one tomorrow. A bobcat."

"I'll put the chicken in the bathtub." Santiago walked down the hallway toward the bathroom tucked beneath the stairs.

"That's a half bath, Santi!"

"The sink then." He unzipped the bowling bag, turned it over and dumped the squawking bird into the bathroom sink. As it flapped and protested furiously, Santiago leapt out of the bathroom and slammed the door. He turned to Abby and brushed the feathers off his coat. "I really appreciate this. Really."

"If the Stewards don't kill you, I will."

"Don't say that. Something terrible has happened." Santiago quickly broke the news about Pat Kelly.

Abby's face whitened with shock and she forgot her annoyance at the chicken. "I'm sorry, Santi. That's awful." When Santiago remained silent, she read the self-incrimination on his face. "No, Santi. You didn't kill Pat Kelly. You were trying to help Jasper. For all you know, the D.C. cops are right. He could have fallen."

"I feel responsible."

"Come on," Abby pulled his arm. "I was going to make some tea before you rang." She tugged him toward the kitchen and stopped before the stove.

"With Bradley Freeman's help, I figured out why there are no erased files on Jasper's laptop."

Abby removed some teabags from a steeping pot and filled two mugs. "Did you find anything useful?"

"No. But whoever killed him simply swapped out the hard drive."

"How about that dollar clue? Any luck?"

Santiago shook his head and extracted it from his wallet. "Look at the year on the bill. It's 2006. That lockbox was hidden beneath the Dahlgren Chapel in the early 1950s. It had to be Jasper who put the bill in there." Studying the dollar, Abby walked over to the kitchen table and sat.

Santiago found the impenetrable clue infuriating. It was a regular one-dollar bill. Other than his initials written in tiny print, the only other marking on the bill was a big circle in yellow highlighter around the portrait of George Washington.

"Jasper had to have kept backups of his work and documents."

Santiago nodded. "He always kept three copies."

"He must be telling you where the originals of his thesis and all the documents from the lockbox are. He circled George. Maybe he means Georgetown."

"If he does, given how big the campus is, it's a useless clue. It must mean something more specific."

"Some historical reference?"

"It must be. If I wanted to give Jasper a clue that wasn't obvious to others, that's how I'd do it. We're both historians. Half the time, it's all we ever talked about."

"What about Georgetown's library? Maybe he put something in one of their books on Washington."

Santiago shook his head. "That's still way too general for Jasper. Georgetown's stacks would take weeks to comb through to check every Washington reference. You know Jasper. Everything had its place. Nothing was random. This is a reference to a specific thing. A thing he believed I would immediately think of."

He sipped his tea and shrugged. "I can't think of any connection whatsoever between Georgetown and George Washington. The university and neighborhood weren't even named after him."

"They weren't?" Abby gave an embarrassed laugh.

"No one even knows for sure who Georgetown's named for. It's either King George II or two guys named George who owned the land the town was founded on."

Abigail put the dollar bill on the table between them.

"I'm completely stuck," said Santiago. "And I have no idea how to get unstuck."

Abby tried to be encouraging. "It's late and we have school tomorrow. Maybe with fresher minds we'll figure it out." She got up from the table, crossed to a drawer and pulled out an envelope. "I meant to surprise you with this for your birthday. But with

Jasper's death, I completely forgot it until I saw it reviewed in the *Post* this morning."

She put two tickets on the kitchen table for a play called *The Rivalry* at Ford's Theatre. "It's that play about the Lincoln Douglas debates. Tomorrow night at seven-thirty. I bought a ticket for Jasper too and gave it to him the week before he died. If you don't have plans and still want to go..." Abby paused awkwardly. "But it would be just the two of us, I guess."

Santiago picked up the tickets. "This is great! Right up a history nerd's alley!"

She smiled again, rose and put her mug in the sink. "Don't lose hope, Santi. If there's anyone who can figure that clue out, it's you." She pointed with her thumb upstairs. "I'll go get you some blankets. I'm sorry I have nothing better to offer than the sofa. I should have kept the second bedroom a guest room, but I got tired of seeing my fitness equipment in my living room."

"The sofa's fine."

Forty minutes later, Santiago was showered and lying on the sofa in Abby's living room, images and snippets of conversation from the day swirling in his head. Bradley and the computer. Nico's anger and the photos of Kelly. George Washington floating in his golden corona. The stormy argument between Marc Davis and Kevin Gaines. Abby's freckled face. *I meant to surprise you with this for your birthday.*

Santiago shifted on the sofa. The furnace came on, pulsing steam into the radiator across the room. His mind soared back in time, back across the Atlantic, back to Puerto Rico, a yard in Caguas, beside an overgrown field where coquis chirped at sunset. The line between consciousness and sleep grew attenuated and he began to dream.

Santiago's head snapped back and his right cheek burned, the penalty for glancing down.

Nico circled, menacing a left but pulling the punch. Santiago flinched and stepped backward. His brother barked a mocking laugh. The sun's dying light reflected off the flame tree. A fiery orange light blazed across Nico's sweaty chest.

Santi's hands perspired in the hot leather. His father yelled from his chair from the back veranda. "Fool! Keep your hands raised to defend yourself!"

He shifted towards the voice. His father shouted again. His mother stooped to pick up the wrapping paper and the box that held the boxing gloves.

He turned to look at Nico again, but found himself looking at the dead face of Pat Kelly. Kelly's bloodshot eyes flew open. "Did you say the Stewards?" He shot a mocking laugh toward the veranda. "He actually believes the Georgetown Stewards exist!"

Santi looked over. His father, mother, his sister Maritere, Nico – all laughing in derision. Then their faces became Pat Kelly's dead face and still they laughed.

Santiago woke with a gasp.

The steam from the radiator hissed back.

Chapter 22: A Coward Speaks Out

Santiago turned over Jasper's mysterious dollar clue in his head for the thousandth time. At last the car radio's warbling pulled him back to the present. *"And outside the workplace the situation is even bleaker in that there is almost no significant interaction between us. On Saturdays and Sundays modern America sadly does not, in some ways, differ significantly from the country that existed some fifty years ago."*

He pulled into his parking spot and watched as students crossed the campus, entering Gonzaga's grounds, preparing for a new school day. They walked in clumps, friends joking and jostling. Clumps of white kids. Clumps of black kids. His hand paused before tapping the radio knob off. National Public Radio was still dissecting the U.S. Attorney General's speech on race and Black History Month. The last sound clip kept Santi's hand hovering above the knob and he watched the attorney general's description unfold before him in the parking lot.

"Given all that we as a nation went through during the civil rights struggle, it is hard for me to accept that the result of those efforts was to create an America that is more prosperous, more positively race conscious and yet is voluntarily socially segregated."

For Santiago's students, the attorney general's words played out in their classrooms daily. The boys tended to sit in self-segregated clumps. Black beans and white rice, surely belonging together but never mixed. Served up on separate plates.

What did it say about Santiago as an educator and principal that he'd never thought to challenge it?

One comment in the attorney general's speech had triggered great controversy. It stuck in Santiago's head the moment he first heard it on the news – the very night Kevin Gaines and Marc Davis had argued heatedly about *Huckleberry Finn* in his office.

"Though this nation has proudly thought of itself as an ethnic melting pot, in things racial we have always been and continue to be, in too many ways, essentially a nation of cowards."

The words detonated the political talking heads in the town. Now, as Santiago sat listening in the car, Kevin Gaines' angry words flashed through his brain. "Every time I walk into the cafeteria, the black kids are sitting at one end of the room and the white boys are sitting everywhere else. It looks just like D.C. did when I was a kid in 1960. If we're going to pretend we're all one nation now and pretend race doesn't matter, maybe we ought to get around to integrating the tables."

Santiago had dismissed Kevin's challenge as ridiculous. In 1960, D.C.'s black students weren't allowed in most white schools let alone their cafeterias. But Santiago knew Kevin. The man wasn't joking. If Gaines were headmaster, he would do it without a second thought.

"In things racial we have always been and continue to be, in too many ways, essentially a nation of cowards."

Santiago tapped off the radio. He yanked his phone from his pocket and called the office number for Gonzaga's Dean of Academics.

"Hey, Roger, it's Santiago."

"Hey, there."

"I know it's last minute, but I need a brief assembly in the morning. Can we use one of the abbreviated class schedules? I need twenty minutes, tops."

He could hear Draper shuffling some papers. "I've got six teachers on the testing schedule today. Mademoiselle Babineaux is going to curse me in French. She'll demand someone's head on a platter."

"Offer her mine," Santiago said. "Some things are more important than the pluperfect subjunctive."

An hour later, all seven hundred fifty students and fifty faculty members were seated before him in St. Al's Church. Other members of the staff were sprinkled in the back, curious about the last minute assembly. Pearl stood among them.

"I need you at this morning's assembly," Santiago had told her.

"And why, pray tell, do I need to hear you talk more?"

"Please just be there."

Santiago was usually comfortable speaking before a big crowd. He loved watching their facial expressions change as he drew them in. But this morning his heart thumped in his chest. The entire student body sat before him, a mass of white flesh intermingled with pools of brown and black faces, clustered at the pews' edges. The students, waiting the assembly's start, all chattered at the same time, their noise rising and expanding, echoes folding over, doubling the cacophony in the space.

"Good morning," Santiago boomed over the microphone.

The roar sliced in half.

"This week the attorney general of the United States gave a very important speech that discussed race and race relations in both our country," Santiago paused, "And, by extension, here at Gonzaga."

Dead silence.

"How many of you heard or read out about it?"

A third of the students raised their hands. He looked back at the faculty and nearly all the hands in the back slowly rose.

"He offered some challenging, controversial words that have stirred some angry debate. One quote of his, in particular, has gnawed at me the last few days. And I heard it again on the radio this morning."

Santiago held up his hand. "He said, 'In things racial we have always been and continue to be, in too many ways, essentially a nation of cowards.'" He paused and tapped his fingers over his heart. "I've concluded the attorney general was talking about me."

He glanced at the faces of the seniors sitting in the front row. Normally slouched and studying their hands, the collection of seventeen and eighteen-year-olds had become immobile, their eyes locked on him.

"I'm a coward." He gestured across the student body. "But perhaps I'm not alone in that respect. Look to your left and right, gentlemen. You chose your seats this morning. How many of you chose to sit beside a student of a different race?"

A moment passed before a scattering of hands rose along the edges, where the white and black faces met.

"Of those with their hands raised," he continued, "was it really a choice? Or was it happenstance?"

The hands wavered in the air. He pressed them again. "Those who made the choice to sit by a friend of a different race, keep your hands up."

All but one of them drifted down. A hand of one of the seniors seated ten rows back from the front stayed aloft. He was seated beside a black student, who nudged him with his elbow and whispered. The white student smiled and lowered his arm.

Santiago knew them. He knew the names of all his students. Each day in the hall beside the school seal, he shook hands with all the freshmen until he had their faces and names committed to memory.

"Kyle, why did you put your hand down?"

The boy's face reddened. "Albert told me to put my hand down because—" he looked at his friend beside him. The other boy was shaking with suppressed laughter. Kyle's friend scratched his chin in feigned nonchalance and looked up at the church ceiling. Kyle finished, an embarrassed grin across his face. "He said he didn't even know my sorry name."

Laughter filled the church. Boys in the far corners began craning their necks.

Santiago chuckled. "For those curious who's speaking, it happens to be Kyle Stodges, who is speaking about his fellow football co-captain, Albert Bender."

More laughter.

Santiago knew the two were friendly. He frequently saw them together on campus. "So, Albert, you two aren't really friends?"

Albert turned to Kyle, then looked back at Santiago. "I'm sorry, Father. I didn't recognize Ky at first cause he's always running *behind* me at practice."

The seniors exploded in laughter.

Santiago raised his hand until the boys' laughter trickled into scratchy echoes. "If you'll let me, I'm going to embarrass you two some more." He smiled to reassure them. "I actually want to commend both of you because, joking aside, I think you guys do break the mold. You two are friends. But if I may ask, how often do you two travel together off school grounds?"

Kyle squirmed slightly before Albert answered. "You're right, Father. We're friends. But Ky lives way down in Mount Vernon and I'm up north in P.G. County."

"I feel like I'm unfairly picking on you two," Santiago apologized. "It's simply to offer an example of the attorney general's point. Most of you are likely sitting there, grateful I haven't called attention to you and your choices of friends. Rather than acknowledge the awkwardness of the issues I'm raising, it's easier to avoid talking about them completely." Santiago waved his hand through the air. "To pretend they're not really there. That they don't particularly matter. To use humor to defuse the tension of the moment, until safer talk of sports or the weather takes the floor."

Santiago's voice rose. It boomed through the church. "But are we all to remain cowards?"

Santiago spotted Kevin Gaines' face in the junior section. The English teacher's chin was jutting outward, his brow pinched in rapt curiosity.

"Thousands of Americans, both white and black, fought against segregation in this country. Yet almost three-quarters of a century on, we – as a nation and even as our own small, school community – remain voluntarily separate. Frequently separate as we walk into school. At times separate as congregate in the hallways. Often separate as we sit in the cafeteria."

Santiago shook his head. "Of course, no one can control your individual behavior or your personal choices every moment." He held up a finger and shook it. "But I can – with courage – challenge you. I, for one, can stop being a coward and firmly encourage a change in your behavior."

Kevin Gaines broke into a victorious grin.

The entire church had fallen silent. The random coughing had ceased. The cavernous space had emptied of sound, yet Santiago could sense a coiled, muffled tension.

"As long as we are seated in any Gonzaga seat, we are to be separated no longer," he announced. "We are one community and it is time we acted like it. Those common areas in which we mingle should reflect this truth." Santiago held up a hand. "This morning I have great faith that you will respect these wishes. However, as our country's history shows us, change in racial matters does not often come easily." He looked around the church until he spotted the school's Dean of Discipline, Mike Loughney. "I trust, if necessary, Dean Loughney will step forward and help remind everyone to rise to the challenge."

Loughney's eyebrows rose in surprise.

"I thank everyone for listening this morning, particularly those teachers who were inconvenienced by this last-minute assembly. I hope you all have a great weekend. Dean Loughney will now dismiss you by class."

Santiago stepped aside and let the dean take over crowd control. As the students in the back began exiting the church, they were far quieter than usual. Santiago rolled back and forth on the balls of his feet. It was an awkward topic. It would take some adjustment, but it would be for the better.

He stood on the three steps leading to the altar until the seniors in the front began filing out. Then he walked to the back, where Pearl was waiting for him. She looked at Santiago over the rims of her glasses.

"What did you think?" he asked her. "I need an honest opinion and I knew you'd give it to me."

Pearl's lips pursed and she nodded brusquely. "I think I'll be coming into the office late on Monday. Probably noonish."

"Why?"

"So you can answer your own phone."

Chapter 23: A Sordid Family History

"Why do you and Nico hate each other?"

Santiago fiddled with the radio in the front passenger seat of Abigail's car. "We don't hate each other."

"Okay, then, why do you dislike each other?"

Santi shrugged. "In every big family, there are siblings that probably wouldn't have much to do with each other if they weren't related. Chalk it up to different personalities." He paused. "Just because you don't like them doesn't mean you don't love them."

"You dodged the question."

Santiago gave an exasperated laugh.

"You know, I was just thinking the other day that I've known you for almost twenty years and you've never told me why you guys don't get along."

"We get along."

It was Abigail's turn to laugh. "Why don't you want to tell me?"

Santiago shook his head and offered a wry smile. "It's sordid in the way that Latin American families are uniquely sordid. You probably wouldn't believe it anyway."

"Try me."

Santiago turned and looked across the seat at her, then held up a hand. "Don't say I didn't warn you."

Abby laughed while Santiago wondered where to begin. Then he just said it. "Nico really isn't my brother."

"Get out!"

Santiago laughed. "Don't jump to conclusions. Nico's my half brother."

Abigail was confused. "But you have the same last name and were raised by the same parents."

"Yes."

"So your mom had you before she met your dad? Did he adopt you?"

"No. That would have been far too normal and tame for my family."

Abigail glanced sideways at him. He could see her perplexed expression in the flashes of passing streetlights.

"You gonna keep guessing?"

She mulled over what Santiago had just revealed.

Santiago finally interrupted the silence. "My father had two families at the same time."

Abigail's voice fell to a near whisper. "No way."

"Adultery is one of the four national obsessions of Puerto Rico. We're obsessed with the Miss Universe Pageant, our Olympic team, our relationship with the United States and our mistresses. Usually in that order."

Santiago smiled. "If adultery were an Olympic sport, I'm fairly sure the Puerto Rican team would medal."

Abigail chuckled. "You know, if a white guy said that, you'd be all over him."

"What are you talking about?" He pointed to himself. "I'm a white guy."

"Like hell, Mr. Social Justice. You're Hispanic."

Santiago scoffed. "Hispanic isn't a race. It's a linguistic group. You go to Puerto Rico and you'll find white Puerto Ricans, black Puerto Ricans and brown Puerto Ricans. All different races that happen to be Hispanic."

"So why does the biggest Hispanic organization in the U.S. call themselves La Raza?" Abigail challenged. "Which I believe means The Race."

"Ah, those Hispanics have been hanging around you crazy Americans too long. This country is obsessed with race and they probably felt left out." Santiago paused. "Anyway, I thought we were talking about adultery."

"Actually we were talking about your sordid family."

"Yes, that," Santiago said, getting the story back on track. "As far as adultery, the really heavy hitters, like my dad, have their public family and their private families. My father's public family was me, my older sister and my mom. His private one was Nico, another boy who died very young, and Nico's biological mother."

"And you knew all this when you were a kid?"

"Hell, no. Until I was nine, I had no idea Nico or the others even existed."

"You guys were the public family?" Abigail shot a glance over to him "What exactly determines which one's public and which is private?"

"Your actual marriage is the public one – the one you acknowledge in the professional world. The one whose photos hang in your office. The private family, on the other hand, is the result of an affair. The big secret that's not so very secret. The politely overlooked elephant taking a dump in the public family's living room." Santiago thought some more. "On the island, the whole public and private thing is also often a function of status, education and race. There are a lot of exceptions, of course, but the public wives of wealthy, successful men like my father usually come from upper class Puerto Rican families. They're well educated and often lighter skinned. But their mistresses often come from the barrio. They're poorer and often darker skinned. Women willing to play second fiddle in the hope that the man will help them improve their situation."

"But Nico looks just like you. He's not darker."

Santiago agreed. "His mom was. Nico inherited our father's skin color. He took great pride in pointing this out to me when we were kids. We'd have an argument, and he'd angrily point to his arm. 'You think you're better than me, Santi, but don't you forget I'm just as light as you.'"

"So you met him when you were nine? How'd you find out?"

"Nico's mother died." Santiago said. "To my father's credit, he didn't pawn him off to one of her poor relatives or abandon him. Papi just showed up for dinner late one night. He walked in with Nico while my mom, sister and I were eating. I remember the whole scene with perfect clarity. He came in pretty late when we were already sitting at the table. In the middle of dinner he walks in with this little boy I've never seen before. About my age."

Santiago paused a moment, the emotion of the memory tripping him up. "A frozen feeling descended in the kitchen. I could feel the cold tiles of the floor through my socks. My spine turned to ice and my stomach to stone. No one said a word, but I knew something terrible was about to happen. I looked up at my mom. Her eyes quivered then narrowed. There were only four chairs and plates set, enough for the family. 'Don't you dare,' she whispered. My father ignored her. 'Get him a plate,' he ordered." Santiago gave a pained laugh. "Papi pulled a chair from the living room up to the table. He sat Nico, who was eight, on top of it. Then he looked at Maritere and me. 'This is your brother,' he said. 'His name is Nicolas.'"

Santiago fell silent. The memory triggered an unexpected spasm of sadness that tightened his throat.

"Yikes," Abigail said. "Your dad was Mr. Smooth."

"That whole moment is seared into my brain," said Santiago. "The smell of my mother's fricasse de pollo. The sound of the coquis – those little Puerto Rican frogs – chirping off the back patio. The loud laughter from my neighbor's house that drifted over the backyard wall as my mom, trembling with rage, rose from the table to get another plate." Santiago swallowed. "I still feel like I'm going to throw up when I think of it."

Santiago rubbed his forehead. "Nico began to cry quietly. Maritere and I said nothing. And my mom, who must have known about the affair and the other children all along, couldn't bring herself to show Nico – the product of my father's betrayal – any compassion whatsoever. A fierce and silent anger had blanketed her. She clattered the plate and silverware in front of Nico and silently returned to her chair. Nico just sat, his lip trembling, the tears silently flowing down his cheeks. Even my father ignored him.

"Then, out of the blue, Papi just turned and asked me how my day was, pretending that it was all perfectly normal. Perfectly normal for a father to arrive home one night and announce to his son he has a brother the same age and he'll be sharing his room with him going forward."

Santi shook his head. "You know the worst part of it, Abby? The part I feel most ashamed about? When my father asked me how my day was while Nico was crying, I actually remember thinking that someone should go over and help Nico, but I couldn't bring myself to do it. Even though I had no idea about my father's affair, I knew that if I did anything of the sort, I would betray my mother. So I did nothing."

Abigail reached over and gave Santiago's hand a quick squeeze.

"What a damned mess." Santiago took a deep breath. "So why don't Nico and I get along? My guess is it all starts with that bizarre game of loyalty and affection. It played out for the next ten years before I came to Georgetown. With me trying to keep my mother happy, trying to make her feel like I wasn't choosing Nico or my father over her. With Nico trying like hell to win my mother's affection or at least some shred of acceptance."

Santi shrugged. "She just couldn't do it. So Nico was left with my father, who was so resentful of my mother's inability to accept Nico or forgive him, that he perpetually acted as if Nico was his favorite.

"The spot where Nico and I stand today," said Santi, "is the result of that mess. Our strained relationship, our different politics, even our different religious beliefs. My mother is an Independista. She wants the U.S. out of Puerto Rico. She believes the island will never solve its problems or stand on its own until it is forced to do so. She is also deeply religious and raised Maritere and me to be as well. My mother wanted a priest above all else. So her first born, loyal son has played the part well, don't you think?"

Abigail glanced over at him. "You regret the choice?"

Santiago waved his hand dismissively. He waited a fraction too long before responding. "Of course not," he said.

"And you still support Puerto Rican independence?"

Santiago smiled. "It's easy to support independence when you know it'll never happen. Then it becomes just an experiment in wishful, patriotic thinking." Santiago rubbed his chin. "It's complicated. I'm not as fierce a supporter of independence as my mother is."

He shifted in his seat so he could look at the side of Abby's face. "I suppose many would see my life as hypocritical. A guy who wants his nation's independence from the U.S. deciding to go to school here and ultimately calling the nation's capital his home."

He traced his finger along the radio buttons. "Life is just a whole lot easier here. There are more opportunities. Best of all, most of the crazy people who are related to me are a safe, three hour plane-ride away."

"So your father and Nico were close?"

"Nico is my father's twin. Papi – Nico's hero – strongly supports statehood. He is a real patriot who refuses to attend mass. He thinks all the Spanish priests that have worked at my mother's parish are subversives." Santiago chuckled at the recollection. "Papi is an attorney who has worked up to become the chief federal prosecutor on the island, busting all the corrupt politicians. It's been full-time work for two decades. Even then he has hardly scratched the surface." Santiago shrugged. "When you think about it, it all makes sense. I enter the seminary after college. Nico joins the military, and when he doesn't win a position with his beloved CIA, settles for the FBI. All of it winding back to that icy moment my father orders my mother to put another plate on the table."

He gently slapped the seat divider, shifting his tone back to cheery. "So there you have it. Why I allegedly dislike my brother. I actually don't, of course. If anything, I still feel great sympathy for him. And I think that pisses him off." Santiago shifted gears, no longer willing to wallow in the past. "Anyway, you've said nothing about this morning's assembly."

It was Abigail's turn to offer a laugh. "Kevin Gaines seemed thrilled."

"I'm not interested in what Gaines thought. I'm interested in what you thought."

Abby dodged the question again. "I thought," she said with smile, "that Kevin Gaines seemed thrilled."

"Do you practice infuriating people or does it just come naturally."

She merely smiled again.

Santiago's cell phone rang. He looked at the number and didn't recognize it.

Abby couldn't suppress a little giggle. "Is it Kevin Gaines, calling to demand you integrate your underwear drawer?"

Santiago answered the phone to annoy her.

"Father Torres?" the caller said. "Is this Father Santiago Torres?"

Santi's heart jumped when he didn't recognize the voice. Perhaps the police finally figured out he had confronted Kelly at The Tombs the night before he was killed.

"This is Regina Reynolds. I'm a reporter for the *Post*."

Santiago could hear his own heart beating in his ears. "Yes, Ms. Reynolds?"

"I've been contacted by several Gonzaga parents who claim you are forcibly desegregating the lunch tables at your school." She paused. "Can you confirm that is your intent?"

"Forcibly?" Santiago couldn't hide his shock. "Gonzaga parents have called you?"

"Yes," she said. "About this morning's school assembly."

"You've got to be kidding me."

Santiago heard the clicking of a computer keyboard and he grimaced. Poor choice of words. It was now a quote in the story.

"If I could begin again, Ms. Reynolds. Your call is rather unexpected and I wouldn't want my first, thoughtless words to appear in the paper and possibly offend anyone who called you to express their genuine concerns."

"Who is it?" Abigail whispered too loudly.

"Can you confirm that you are forcibly integrating the cafeteria tables?" the reporter pressed.

"Who is it?" Abigail now hissed.

He tried to cover the phone. "It's the *Post*."

"Hang up!" She tried to grab the phone from his hand.

"Father Torres?" said Reynolds.

"Hang up!" Abigail lunged for the phone again and swerved toward an oncoming cab.

"Jesus Christ!" Santiago's phone tumbled to the floor. He seized the steering wheel and straightened the car. "Are you trying to kill us! Just drive, for God's sake!"

He grabbed for the phone near his toes and banged his forehead off the dashboard. "¡Me cago en na'!" he cursed, nursing his smarting head and pressing the phone back to his ear.

"Hello?" he cried.

"Father Torres?"

"Hang up!" Abigail said again. She tried reaching for the phone but Santiago pushed away her hand and pressed himself against the car door.

"Yes, I'm here," Santiago said calmly. He fought his growing dread. What could the reporter possibly be thinking? The headmaster of Gonzaga had gone off the deep end? "I'm sorry, Ms. Reynolds. I'm traveling by car to a theater show and my friend, the driver, nearly just got us both killed."

"Father Torres," the reporter said again. "I spoke this afternoon with two of your black students as well as the boys' parents. They insist that you are forcibly integrating the cafeteria tables at your high school. In fact, the boys said that if they sit with their friends, they could be given detention, which they called..." Santi could hear the reporter paging through her notes. "Jug, they called it. Can you confirm this?"

"Forcibly? Ms. Reynolds, my talk before all students this morning simply challenged the racial status quo. The racial status quo in both our country and in the Gonzaga community, where we come together every day but very often choose to stay apart. It was inspired, in part, by the attorney general's black history speech this week."

The reporter spat questions like a machine gun. "So you agree with the attorney general that we're a nation of cowards? Do you view your students as cowards?"

An uncomfortable laugh escaped Santi's lips. "I think one can agree with the intent of a speech without agreeing with every syllable uttered in it."

"But you largely agree with the attorney general's speech?"

"I would say it appropriately challenged me to think in new ways. And to think about how the school community should address its issues of racial separation, which mirror the nation's."

"So you believe there is a racial problem at your school?"

"No, Ms. Reynolds, I think you're twisting my words. I said the school has issues of racial separation, the same kind of separation we see in any large group of people, where blacks and whites tend to sit and congregate separately."

"But, Father, you said the school suffers from racial separation. Isn't that a racial problem?"

"If it's a problem in your view, than our entire nation has a racial problem."

"And it's a big enough problem at Gonzaga that you think it needs to be addressed?"

"I think there's always room for a person to grow, no matter how far they've come in addressing past challenges."

Abigail hissed again. "Hang up! Don't play her game!"

"And you think the best solution is to put your black students in detention for wanting to sit with their friends."

"Hold on! Isn't the issue really bigger than that?" Santiago countered.

"Wasn't the Civil War fought and the fourteenth amendment passed to give black Americans the freedom to make their own choices?"

The implied insult took Santi by surprised. "Excuse me, Ms. Reynolds?"

"Do you think a white or Hispanic man should be telling black people where to sit and eat lunch?"

Santiago's voice rose. "Ms. Reynolds?"

"Just hang up," Abigail said.

"Father Torres?" Reynolds pressed. "I'll ask it again? Do you think a white or Hispanic man should be telling a black man where to sit and eat his lunch?"

Santiago's temper boiled over. "Are you calling me a racist? You know what, Ms. Reynolds? You sound far more like a prosecuting attorney than an objective reporter. It's beginning to sound like you're far more bothered by my morning assembly than the parents are. Perhaps you have some sort of guilt complex you're trying to resolve through this story."

"No!" said Abigail, reaching for the phone. "Don't say that."

Santiago pushed her hand away. "Ms. Reynolds, how dare you twist my challenge to all my students into some patriarchal, racist act like something that occurred during Jim Crow. I may wear black and white, but you apparently only see the world that way."

"Shut up now!" Abigail hissed.

But Santiago was on a roll. He let his words fly. "If you want a quote, ma'am, then write this down. What's perfectly clear, Ms. Reynolds, is that you had no intent to seek the truth before you called me tonight. What you planned was a media lynching. So you just write whatever the hell you want, because that was your intention all along. This conversation is over. Good night."

Santiago ended the call and flung the phone onto the dashboard.

They sat in silence for three city blocks before Abigail finally spoke. She shook her head. "You shouldn't have hung up."

Chapter 24: A Night at the Theater

Santiago spoke louder, so Abigail could hear him over the intermission crowd. "'Hang up!' you tell me. Thirty seconds later, you're screaming, 'Don't hang up!'" Santiago shook his head. "It amazes me more men don't opt for a life of celibacy. It's far less confusing."

The lights dimmed slightly three times, signaling the start of the second act. They entered the theater again and weaved back to their seats. Santiago had barely paid attention to the play's first act. Instead, the phone call with reporter kept anxiously playing through his head.

Abigail rolled her eyes. "I didn't scream anything. I cajoled. Maybe you'd be less grouchy if you had another drink."

"Do your students find you as confusing as I do?"

"There is a simple solution, you know," said Abigail.

"What's that?"

"Don't read the newspaper."

Santiago heaved a sigh and they slid into their seats. He regretted losing his temper. God only knew what would be in the *Post* in the morning. He could imagine the calls from the school president, the board of trustees, Roy Taylor. Roy would raise the issue casually, as if a photo of Santiago with his quilting group had appeared in the social section. "Saw you in the *Post*," he'd chirp.

Santiago sighed again.

Abigail giggled. She changed her voice to sound like Santiago's. "Let me make one thing clear, Ms. Reynolds. I may wear black and white, but you apparently only see the world that way."

"I'm glad you're enjoying this."

Abigail put her hand on his arm and her face had a look of surprise. The touch sent a shiver down his spine. "Are you really that worried about this?"

"Wouldn't you be?" Santiago said. "Don't you think the board of directors would consider removing me?"

"Don't be ridiculous," she said. "Who would want your job? Everyone else is terrified of Pearl."

A tap on his shoulder interrupted them. Santiago turned to the aisle, where one of the volunteer ushers stood smiling through perfect dentures. Her eyes gravitated to his white collar. "Father, I'm terribly sorry to interrupt. But someone insisted you dropped your program." She pressed a playbill into his hands.

Santiago glanced back and saw the back of a young woman head out the door. "No, ma'am," Santi held up his program. "I have mine right here."

The old woman shook her head. "No, Father," she said. "She insisted you should have this." She pressed the playbill into his hands and walked back up the aisle to the theater's entrance.

"What is it?" asked Abigail.

Santiago shrugged. "The usher thought I dropped my playbill."

The lights in the theater dimmed and Santiago reached back to adjust his coat. The second playbill fell open on his lap and a piece of yellowed parchment slid to the floor.

He recognized it immediately. The lights on the stage came up, spilling across the theater seats. Santiago reached down and seized the parchment. He looked at Abigail, who was already engrossed with the play.

Santiago looked back at the theater door. It was closed. The usher was gone.

He glanced at the parchment.

My fellow Odd Fellow,

Dig the undug from Digges

*Atop a rebel plantation hill
whose plan sprawls
In quadrants and circles
In repose.*

Your obedient servants,

The Odd Fellows Society of Historical Bounty Hunters

Santiago's heart thudded in his ears. The undug from Digges?

The mental puzzle of his memory clicked and whirred. Where had he seen the name before?

He struggled not to seize Abby by the arm and drag her from the theater.

Quadrants and circles in repose? A rebel plantation hill in D.C.? That was a dead end. D.C. was never captured by the Confederates.

The play's second act passed in a blur, his mind preoccupied with the parchment's words. For most, the clues would be perplexing gibberish. For Santiago, each word twirled a tumbler in his brain, throwing down walls in the maze, beating a path to a possible solution. He never understood why his brain worked the way it did, but it locked onto inane details, etching obscure trivia upon the inside of his skull. As a child, he could recite the entire batting order and performance stats of the Atlanta Braves, whose games the local Puerto Rican cable station broadcast.

A plan of quadrants and circles?

In school, his brain swept aside baseball like an umpire cleaning home plate and locked on to the mundane matter of schoolbooks. When his middle school friends found his memory freakish, he'd force himself to answer several questions wrong to avoid a string of perfect scores. Later in college, no one would play his roommate's Trivial Pursuit game against him after the first semester, let alone bet beer on the outcome. After he single-handedly played against eight other Georgetown students and won the $100 bet, they refused.

"You've memorized all the cards!" one accused.

He was taken back at the accusation of cheating. "Not on purpose!"

He waited until the applause peaked at curtain call. "Let's go!" he yanked Abby's arm.

She looked at him in surprise. "Did you like the play?"

"I loved it!" He nodded. "But we need to go."

The flicker of disappointment on her face evaporated when he held up the parchment. "How?"

"It was in my program. Let's just go!"

They dodged theater patrons gathering their coats and purses and were soon in Abby's car.

"Do you understand it?" Abby asked.

Santiago shook his head and spread the parchment on the console. She leaned forward and read it out loud. Meanwhile he pulled out his phone and did a quick Internet search of the name Digges.

Abby read it again. "These things make me feel like an idiot."

Santiago's cursory search produced nothing useful. "They're not supposed to come easy. The scavenge clues are designed to slow you down and puzzle you." Santiago said. "You start driving. Let's just brainstorm. Throw out any idea you have, no matter how ridiculous."

Abby drove north on Twelfth Street NW and Santiago read the entire clue again aloud. He paraphrased the last part. "A plan of quadrants and circles in repose."

"Could it have something to do with geometry?" asked Abby.

Nothing clicked in Santiago's mind. "What about architecture?" Santiago suggested. "Can you think of any buildings or monuments with quadrants and circles?"

"Are pillars circles?"

"Jasper would probably have said no."

Abby turned west on Massachusetts Avenue.

"What about Digges? Does that ring a bell?" she asked.

"I feel like I've seen it somewhere before but I can't place it. And nothing useful appears in the top Internet links." He read the clue silently again with a grunt. They reached the intersection of Vermont Avenue and 14th Street and Abby's car descended beneath Thomas Circle. In frustration, Santiago pointed at its statue. "That's George Henry Thomas, a Union general in the Civil War."

Abby snorted a laugh.

"How is it I can tell you the identity of every statue in every stupid traffic circle in the U.S. capital, but I can't remember a reference to name like...," Santi trailed off and twirled around in his seat.

"What?"

As Abby cleared the tunnel beneath the circle, its statue reappeared in the car's back window.

The tumblers in Santiago's mind clicked and fell into place. "That's it!" Santiago cried.

"George Henry Thomas?"

"No! Traffic circles!" Santiago shook the clue. "Quadrants and circles in repose. The clue is referring to the layout of Washington!"

"Quadrants in repose?"

"What does nearly every D.C. street name end with, Abby?"

"A direction." Abby said. "Northeast, Northwest, Southeast—"

"Quadrants!" Santiago said.

"Then it's talking about L'Enfant's plan for the city!"

Santiago gave a deep, satisfied laugh.

"Is he talking about L'Enfant Plaza? How could that possibly tie into a rebel plantation?"

"It doesn't." Santiago smiled at her. "Because it's not talking about L'Enfant Plaza."

"Now you're being infuriating."

"Turn around," he said. "We need to head back toward Memorial Bridge."

Abby turned and drove back into the city. She was driving west on Constitution toward the bridge over the Potomac when it finally clicked for her. "Arlington Cemetery!" she said, naming the national landmark just across the Memorial Bridge from the

Lincoln Memorial. "Arlington Cemetery was Confederate General Robert E. Lee's plantation! It's on a hill overlooking D.C.!"

"Now you've got it!"

She gunned the car into traffic and headed across the bridge. "But what's the tie in between L'Enfant and Arlington? He had to have been dead by the time the cemetery was designed."

"He was. He died a pauper and was initially buried where he was living at the time, Digges Farm."

"But now he's buried at Arlington?"

Santiago nodded. "I couldn't place the name Digges at first until I realized this clue is about L'Enfant." Santiago nodded. "L'Enfant was later disinterred from Digges Farm and reburied at Arlington." Santiago paused. "Wait till you see his grave."

Twenty-five minutes later Santiago told her to pull over to the side of McNair Road, which swept past the back of the cemetery. He checked their location on his cell. "Arlington's closed, but it's better this way. We're less likely to be spotted digging. We'll hoof it from here."

Abby eyed the woods behind the cemetery through the fence along the road. "Jasper's sole goal is to get me arrested digging up every national monument in the country," said Abby. "You really think this is wise?"

He reached into the glove box, pulled Abby's flashlight out of the car, and stepped out of the car. "When did you suddenly worry about appearing wise?"

Abby popped the trunk of her car and walked back to it. "I know I'm going to regret this." She reached in and pulled out a small shovel.

Santiago started laughing. Abby was the only person he knew that actually had in her trunk all the things safety manuals advise people to keep there. A blanket, a first aid kit, flairs, a can of spray foam to instantly fix flats, a small toolkit – even though she had no idea how to actually fix a car.

She shoved it against his chest. "My mother bought it for me after I got stuck in the snow on Foxhall Road last winter."

He eyed the trunk. "Wouldn't it be easier just to keep a mechanic in there?"

She kicked her high heels off and dropped them into the trunk. She pulled out a pair of running shoes and began lacing them.

Santiago laughed harder.

"I am not hiking through a cemetery in high heels. If I need to run away again, I'm going to make sure they catch you first." She gave him a little push when she was finished and they strode off the road. They passed into the tree line where the cemetery fence was. He tossed the shovel over and scaled the fence, dropping to the other side. He turned to help Abby but she jumped to the ground beside him immediately. He smiled. Abby was athletic and strong. It was what had attracted him to her back in college. They walked through the woods at the back of the cemetery, Santiago checked the map app on his smartphone. He held up his finger over his lips and they silently threaded their way between the maintenance buildings to their left and the ranger station to the right.

"L'Enfant is buried near the front of Arlington House on the hill," Santiago whispered, referring to Robert E. Lee's former plantation home. They spent ten minutes more walking and climbing the incline, keeping their eye out for the cemetery's night staff. Soon they emerged from the trees, rounded Arlington House to the left and he pulled her to a stop at the crest of the hill.

She gasped. "I had no idea this was here."

On the hill before them was an eleven by seven foot, two-tiered monument that rose to knee height, its based carved with a four-foot long broadsword that gave the stone the hint of a crusader's tomb. Beyond the burial site sprawled the Potomac River and all of D.C. The Washington Monument and U.S. Capitol Building glowed white in the distance.

Santiago approached the east end of the tomb and rubbed his fingers across a circle two and a half feet in diameter.

"L'Enfant's plan for the city," Abby whispered.

Santiago nodded, gesturing to the city sprawled on the other side of the Potomac. It's not quite how L'Enfant planned it. In his plan, the Washington Monument wasn't an obelisk. And the Capitol steps facing the mall were supposed to be a large, flowing fountain, like a waterfall. But it's close enough."

He put the small shovel to the earth closest to L'Enfant's city plan.

"Santiago," Abby hissed. "Someone's coming."

He reached back and grabbed her, pulling her out of the light spilling over L'Enfant's tomb from Arlington House. He crouched with her in the shadow of the tree beside the grave. A ranger approached on a nearby path, pausing to glance up at the old plantation home and looking around.

"He knows someone's here," Abby whispered.

Santiago held up a finger and shook his head.

The ranger glanced around again before lifting a pack of cigarettes from his shirt pocket, easing one out and lighting it. He inhaled deeply and breathed out a cloud of smoke. He stood, looking out over the Potomac and the city beyond, puffing.

The ranger was standing so close Santiago could smell the smoke. His heart raced. He only hoped the ranger was standing close enough to Arlington House that the floodlights illuminating the structure also limited the ranger's sight.

A radio crackled. "Yeah, I'm here." The ranger stubbed the cigarette out against his shoe, pocketed the butt and walked back in the direction of the rangers' station.

Santiago waited a moment, his finger still raised.

"Normal single women spend their Friday nights in bars and dance clubs," muttered Abby. "But I get to hang out in cemeteries with tomb-raiding Jesuits."

"Not everyone is cut out for a life of thrilling adventure." Santiago lifted the shovel and stepped into the light again. "If you'd prefer I drop you off at the Senior Center for Bingo, just say the word."

"They'd disqualify me. The undersides of my arms don't flap enough yet."

Santiago pressed the shovel's blade into the grass by L'Enfant's Tomb. Despite the thick grass, the larger shovel made it far easier digging than it had been by the Jefferson Pier. In a moment, he gave a little cry of triumph. He handed a sealed plastic bag containing documents back to Abby and quickly refilled the hole.

"Let's get out of here."

Chapter 25: The Steward's Confession

     Back at Abby's Santiago sat back on the couch and looked at the pages again once she had gone off to bed. One was another piece of parchment, another clue from the Odd Fellows Society. The others, he was sure, were a handful of the pages that were written in Jasper's own hand and torn from his friend's private journal. It made sense – no one could locate it in his room after his death. The torn out sheets constituted a single entry dated three days before Jasper's death. It recounted a meeting in a confessional. Which one, Jasper didn't say. When he had first read the journal entry's title, Santiago's chest filled with both excitement and dread. It was clear from Jasper's scribbled comments preceding the entry that he never intended it to be seen by anyone else – never intended to violate the sacred seal of confession. His friend had simply transposed it from a secret recording made with his phone – along with his private thoughts scribbled in parentheses – to help himself piece out the truth.

The Steward's Confession

     "I want you to hear my confession." (The voice belonged to a man, clear, confident and young – a mid-range, hesitant baritone.)
     "Certainly."
     "Bless me, Father, for I have sinned. It's been two weeks since my last confession."
     (My heart was pounding. I waited for him to begin. His silence stretched an awkward span.) "Would you prefer we just

talked? Similar to a conversation?" I finally asked. "Some find it more natural that way."

"I'm sorry."

(A flicker of emotion in his voice softened my own fear.) "That's okay. Confessing can be a very difficult thing."

"I was sent here to deliver a message."

"I thought you were making a confession."

His breathing made the ragged sound of paper tearing. "They will kill you if you don't hand over all of Cannon's documents."

"Did the Stewards send you?"

"If you even talk to anyone else about the Stewards or what you've discovered, they will kill you."

"I can tell by your voice you don't agree with them."

"That's irrelevant."

"How so?"

"Once in, there's only one out."

"So they will kill you if you try to leave?"

Wry laughter. "If mine were the only death, I could live with it. I am simply here to deliver a message. If you don't turn over the documents, you're a dead man."

"You have children, don't you? You're trying to protect them. Just help me a little. I beg of you."

(A long silence.) "Those documents you have – the ones you found in Dahlgren Chapel? They belonged to a man named Philip Cannon."

"I know that."

"Philip Cannon is me, more than a half century ago."

"I don't understand."

"Cannon was recruited by the Stewards just before graduating Georgetown in the 1940s. He was close to the upper echelons of the organization. But over a decade he..." (the man gave an awkward, dry laugh and searched for the right word) "he grew uncomfortable with their direction."

"So he tried to betray them."

"When he decided to stand up for what he believed was right, they crushed him. I won't make the same mistake. Even if I spend an eternity in hell, I will live to see my children grow up."

"I need your help. Come with me to the police or the media."

(A raised voice.) "Are you listening to me? They'll kill me and likely my family."

"We can get them protection."

(The man laughed.) "You don't understand."

"Then just tell me more. Why did Cannon want to leave?"

"Figure it out from his papers."

"Please."

"You're asking me to risk..." (He exhaled a jagged, resigned sigh. Then he relented and began the tale.) "When Cannon was a young man, in the early years after World War II, a lot of leaders in the U.S. government became worried that the defense industries – all the corporations that had grown wealthy from World War II spending – were becoming far too powerful. Just like President Eisenhower warned in his farewell speech..."

Santiago knew the speech well from the years he taught history. Ike, the general most responsible for winning World War II for America, had warned that the military industrial complex was growing in power and influence. He warned that if its power remained unchecked, it could undermine U.S. democracy.

"...By the fifties, defense companies owned by the Stewards fanned the fervent anti-communism that helped produce McCarthyism, the Cold War and all its proxy wars, from Korea and Vietnam to Cuba and Latin America. Meanwhile the Stewards' companies raked in hundreds of millions of dollars. They built factories abroad, using virtual slave labor in them. At home they used their profits to fund campaigns of all the most hawkish politicians."

"But what you're describing is just the modern corporate lobbying industry. That couldn't be the sole reason Cannon decided to betray them."

"You're right. He finally balked when the organization set up its own espionage network. They began spying on Americans, specifically Congressmen and Senators, blackmailing them to support causes that would both enrich them and promote the Stewards' worldview."

"Which was?"

"The destruction of anyone who didn't look like them, talk like them, think like them." (A long pause.) "You've been warned. I need to go."

"You need to help me. You need to help me fill the gaps."

"I have to go."

"If I withhold absolution, you will remain in the state of sin. Answer me this then. Why did you agree to join them if you find them so horrible?"

(The man laughed with embarrassment.) "Because I once believed they stood for what was right. But their methods..."

"What exactly is so troubling? What terrible thing are they planning? I can hear it in your voice."

"I've helped you. Now help me. They will expect me to come back with information. What was in Cannon's lockbox?"

(I hesitated, then decided to risk the truth, hoping to gain the man's trust.) "I'm still trying to make sense of it all. Portions of what appears to be Cannon's journal and the organization's ledgers. Cannon traced the horde of cash that came out of the Maryland Province's sale of slaves back in the 1830s. His numbers and description show that by the late 1940s and early 1950s, the Stewards' money was behind the most powerful military defense contractors."

"Then his material would have proven that President Eisenhower's warning was real. It would have destroyed those corporations and the Stewards. It would have ended their most important work and dismantled the early espionage network."

"So how did they find out Cannon wasn't loyal?"

"How do the Stewards find out everything? He trusted the wrong person. Maybe someone in the government. Maybe someone in the media. I don't know. The Stewards are well placed in a lot of powerful positions. But they killed Cannon only after they were sure he hadn't yet passed the documents on to anyone. They were certain they'd find the materials once he was dead. They upended his home, everything he touched. They never found them."

"Because Cannon had hidden them in Dahlgren Chapel during a renovation of the altar space."

"Right under their noses. For six decades those documents have hung like a guillotine blade over the Stewards' necks."

"There's nothing in the papers about the Stewards' espionage organization. What is its name? Where can I find it?"

"Grant me absolution. I need to go, Father. Follow the corporate trail Cannon spelled out. It's all there. It's why they're so worried."

"Wait. You tell me if I don't hand over the documents and my thesis, they'll kill me. Yet part of you wants the Stewards destroyed. What do you want me to do?"

(The man suddenly sobbed, startling me.) "What I want is irrelevant. You'll figure it all out?"

"Figure what out?"

"*Athenasisu contra mundum.* And the sacrificial lamb. Your death can save all of us – hopeless idiots like me, tens of millions of others. It has to happen this way."

"Then if I'm to die, give me a name! What is the name of their network?"

(The red light indicating someone was on the kneeler went dark.)

"Wait!"

(The light came back on.) "Don't press me more. You have all I will give. I swore an oath to remain silent and I've already broken it."

"Swearing in God's name is a sin. If you can tell me the history of the Stewards, you can certainly tell me this."

"I will say no more. I have sworn an oath on the Bible. I need a penance and absolution, Father."

"You want a penance? Help me reveal the complete truth to someone else!"

"You can't ask that of me. I will remain in a state of grave sin."

"Wait!"

(But the light indicating weight on the kneeler in the adjacent box went off. I heard his confessional door open. I rose quickly to catch him only to find the door on my side of the confessional jammed shut. By the time I freed myself, he was gone.)

At the end of Jasper's journal entry, Jasper had again scribbled the Latin phrase the man had called him.

Athanasisu contra mundum.

Latin for Athanasius against the world.

From his years studying theology, Santiago recognized the phrase. St. Athanasius was a bishop of Alexandria, exiled from his homeland five times by Roman emperors and condemned by his fellow bishops and even a pope. All because of his defense of church orthodoxy and the trinity against the first great threat to the church's unity – a heresy called Arianism. Arianism had swept the early Christian world, posing as great a threat to early church unity as the Protestant Reformation did to it one thousand years later. Arians believed that the Son of God, because he was created by God the Father, was a lesser being. They questioned Christ's very divinity. Rather than give in to the politically popular movement, Athanasius fought it, paying a dear price. At one point, as an elderly man, he survived only by hiding in his father's tomb for months. Years later, he was named a saint for standing up for truth – even when the prices for doing so were so costly.

Jasper against the world. Santiago felt overwhelmed with sympathy for his friend, so beleaguered in the days before his death. Why didn't he tell someone? *Why didn't he tell me?*

Because Jasper wished to protect him.

Yet now he was neck-deep in the mystery that had stolen his friend's life.

Santiago turned to the more helpful part of the documents found at L'Enfant's Tomb, the parchment holding a new message from the Odd Fellows Society.

My fellow Odd Fellow,

A clue amid
One hundred strong
Past but present perched
Frozen upon Jenkins Hill in New Troy:
A commodore's namesake, a copperhead killer
A Razorback esquire, a defender of union
Old Bullion, the schoolboy thief
The pugilistic progressive, a badger for reform
And the Green Mountain conqueror of Ticonderoga
By and by, dear Esther, a caretaker of orphans
A father of a Bluegrass law, a physician felled by his appendix

A traitor and loser: Sic Semper Tyrannis!

Your obedient servants,

The Odd Fellows Society of Historical Bounty Hunters

Santiago lay back on the couch, closed his eyes and began to think.

Chapter 26: Jenkins Hill

Santiago called up the stairs for the third time. "Are you coming?"

Abby clattered down them. "You don't have to shout."

"I wasn't shouting."

"You had a tone."

"I didn't have a tone."

She threw him a look.

"How did I have a tone? I hear this all the time when women come to me for marital advice: Whenever my husband talks to me, he has *this tone*."

"People come to you for marital advice?"

He ignored the jibe. "Men can be talking at a perfectly normal volume, and yet we still get accused of having a tone – usually by a woman whose voice is raised."

"You're doing it again."

Santiago gave up and opened the door.

"Where are we going?"

"Jenkins Hill."

She held out her hand. "May I see the clue again, Mr. Know It All?"

"Only if you watch your tone." He handed the clue to Abby. She read through it again as they climbed into the car and Santiago headed south.

"I've never heard of or been to New Troy," she said.

"Yes, you have."

"Or Jenkins Hill."

"You've actually stood on it. I'll give you a hint. New Troy's name was changed in 1791."

Abby changed directions. "Okay, then, who was Jenkins?"

"They don't know for certain. He might have been a guy who pastured his cows near the hill."

"Okay, smarty pants, why don't you just tell me where we're going, then?"

"Because I'm worried I'll do it with a tone."

Abby punched him in the arm.

Santi gave a satisfied laugh. "When Pierre L'Enfant was laying out the new capital city, he began by looking at parcels of land that were then named New Troy. Specifically he was interested in putting the grand new legislative building on a wooded hill there."

"Capitol Hill is Jenkins Hill?"

"Exactly."

She pointed to the parchment. "He mentions one hundred strong. Is he talking about the Senate?"

"There weren't that many senators during L'Enfant's lifetime." Santiago pointed to the clue's final eight lines. "I'm sure these lines must be talking about individual people, some of the one hundred strong the clue says are frozen on Capitol Hill."

"Frozen?"

"I have a hunch. I'm willing to bet all these frozen people have been turned to stone."

Thirty minutes later they were walking into the southern side of the Capitol Building, where the House of Representatives meet. It was still early on a Saturday before the tourist crowds gathered to gawk. Santiago led her through the dimly lit marble hallways, echoing with their footsteps, until they stepped into a large circular room filled with dozens of statues.

"One hundred strong, past but present perched, frozen upon Jenkins Hill in New Troy," Abby said aloud.

Santiago nodded. "Welcome to National Statuary Hall, where every state in the union has contributed statues of two of its historically notable residents."

They stood in a two story semi-circular rotunda with elaborate marble pillars. The area was interspersed with dozens of statues, over whose heads hung an elaborate burgundy drapery. Like the drapery, the rotunda's soaring white ceiling was beautifully trimmed in gold. "The House of Representatives actually met in this room during the first half of the 1800s," Santi explained.

Abby eyed the room. "But we must be wrong. There's nowhere near one hundred statues here."

Santi nodded. "They wouldn't all fit. Plus, the the hall's floor couldn't support all the weight of the stone."

"Then where are the rest?"

Santiago pointed to a nearby information sign. "Distributed throughout the capitol and the visitors' center. But this is as good a place to start as any." He tapped the clue. "I'm fairly sure I know three of the people hinted at here. Others I'm less certain about."

"If the statues are scattered, figuring it out is going to take a long time."

Santiago shook his head. "I didn't come down here to see the statues. I came down here to find a person who's a lot less frozen." Santi nodded at an elderly security guard just entering the hall. "We need someone just dying to share everything he's learned from decades of doing his job."

Sure enough, the guard crossed with a smile. "Can I help you?"

"I hope so." Santiago introduced Abby and himself. "We're looking for the capitol's expert on Statuary Hall."

"Well, not sure this old Virginian is much of an expert about anything, but I've worked on Capitol Hill now forty years, so I know a fair amount about these folks. My name's Cal." He shook their hands and offered a kind smile. "I love my friends in Statuary Hall."

"Why's that?" Abby asked.

"They're good listeners, never interrupt, and never leave behind a mess."

They both laughed. "We're completing a kind of scavenger hunt and I think the primary clue points us here." Santiago handed Cal the parchment. "But there are eight additional clues that I think refer to the statues. I need your help with some of them."

Cal tapped the paper with a bent finger and read the first. "A commodore's namesake, a copperhead killer. Cal nodded. "I believe that's one of Indiana's statues, Oliver Hazard Perry Morton. He was an Indiana governor named after Commodore Perry, the hero of the 1812 War's big naval battle on Lake Erie. Morton was a strong ally of Lincoln and crushed Indiana's secessionists during the Civil War." Cal looked at Abby. "This clue isn't talking about copperhead snakes. It's talking about northerners who sympathized with the Southern cause."

"How about the second clue?"

"A Razorback esquire, a defender of union," Cal read. He scratched his chin. "Well, a Razorback would be from Arkansas. And there's only one in the collection who defended the union. Uriah Milton Rose, a lawyer from Little Rock. His law firm still exists," Cal said with a wink. "Someone you might know named Clinton once worked there."

Clearly enjoying himself, Cal continued. "Old Bullion," he read, "the schoolboy thief." Cal gave a laugh. "That's a good one!"

"That one's stumped me," said Santiago. "But I know the next two – the pugilistic progressive reformer from the Badger State is Bob LaFollette of Wisconsin."

Cal nodded. "Fightin' Bob, champion of the common working man."

"And the Green Mountain conqueror of Ticonderoga is Ethan Allen."

Call nodded in admiration. "Who was a Revolutionary War hero from Vermont. But those are the easy ones."

"What about Old Bullion?"

"Thomas Hart Benton of Missouri, kicked out of law school for stealing from his classmates," said Cal. "He injured Andrew Jackson in a duel and later killed a man named Charles Lucas in another. Benton was a big supporter of western expansion."

"What's his nickname refer to?" Abby asked.

"Old Bullion?" Cal responded. "Benton supported only using hard money – currency actually made of gold instead of paper currency – during the country's early arguments over monetary policy."

"Made the gold easier to steal." quipped Abby.

Cal smiled at her and read the next. "By and by, dear Esther, a caretaker of orphans," Cal continued. "The 'by and by' is a clever touch."

"How so?"

"Most state mottos are in English or Latin. A handful of other mottos are in other languages – Greek, French, Spanish. Only two use languages from their original inhabitants. Do you know which?"

"Hawaii," said Santiago.

Cal nodded. "And Washington state, whose motto is Chinook, Al-ki, which means by and by. Some translate it as 'hope for the future.' This clue refers to Mother Joseph, whose given name was Esther Pariseau. She established a school and served orphans and the homeless. Hers is one of less than a dozen statues representing women in the collection. Did you know the state of Washington celebrates her birthday as an official state holiday?"

"I didn't!" Santiago smiled in fascination.

"You guys really should be married," Abby said.

Cal laughed. "This next one mentions Bluegrass—"

"The father of the Kentucky constitution," agreed Santiago.

Cal tapped the side of his head. "That would be Ephraim McDowell, an early settler of Kentucky. One of America's brilliant early physicians. The first doctor to ever successfully remove an ovarian tumor. If he had been able to remove his own appendix, he might have lived longer."

"The last clue is one I think I know," said Santiago.

Cal read it aloud. "A traitor and loser: Sic Semper Tyrannis!" He looked at Santiago. "Well, this one's pretty clear, given the state motto, which means—'"

"Thus, always to tyrants," said Abby with a triumphant smile. "The state motto of Virginia, which John Wilkes Booth shouted after he had shot Lincoln and jumped down to the stage of Ford's Theatre."

"Well done!" said Cal, who held up a finger. "The full quote from which Virginia's state motto is taken is actually *sic semper evello mortem tyrannis*."

"Thus always I eradicate tyrants' lives," translated Santiago.

"That narrows it down to Virginia's two statues," said Abby.

"George Washington and Robert E. Lee," said Santiago.

Cal nodded. "The clue points to the statue of the one that is a traitor and a loser." Cal cocked his head. "Depending upon one's perspective, both were traitors who rose up against their countries."

"But only one of them lost," said Abby.

Cal nodded again. "Confederate General Lee."

Santiago nodded. "That's all eight. Cal, can you think of anything all of them have in common?"

Cal rubbed his chin and surveyed the room. "They don't appear in the same part of the capitol. They're from different parts of history. They share different points of view." He turned to them. "If they have something in common, it's escaping this old, gray head."

Santiago pumped the old man's hand. "Thanks so much, Cal. You've been a huge help!"

"I've enjoyed our visit."

Cal wandered over to a group of tourists that had just entered the room and Abby turned to Santiago. "Can you think of anything they have in common?"

Santiago shook his head, pulled out a pen and wrote all eight names on the back of the parchment in the order the clue mentioned them:

Oliver Hazard Perry Morton, Indiana
Uriah Milton Rose, Arkansas
Thomas Hart Benton, Missouri
Robert M. La Follette, Sr., Wisconsin
Ethan Allen, Vermont
Mother Joseph, Washington
Ephraim McDowell, Kentucky
Robert E. Lee, Virginia

The two of them studied the list and Santiago's face grew somber.

"What is it?" said Abby.

"It explains why Jasper circled Israel on his map."

Chapter 27: Mi'jo Goes Viral

Each February twenty-third began the same for Santiago, an early phone call, just after six in the morning. "Feliz cumpleaños, mi'jo."

Happy birthday, my son.

Mi'jo. Every relative of every guy raised in Puerto Rico – fathers, brothers or husbands –called the poor slobs mi'jos.

My sons.

Proud mothers pinched the cheeks of their real son mi'jos. Frustrated wives shook their fingers at their husband mi'jos. Doting, stubborn sisters named Maritere called early on cold winter mornings to wish their older brother mi'jos a happy birthday.

"Are you coming to dinner tonight, mi'jo?"

Santiago checked his watch and nearly gagged on the dregs of Abigail's weak coffee. Heavily doctored with five teaspoons of raw sugar and the watery, fat-free, organic milk she stored in the fridge, it was still a poor excuse for waking up. You had to go to Puerto Rico or Cuba for real coffee.

"I don't think I can tonight, Maritere."

"Ay bendito, your godson James will be so disappointed, Santi."

Santiago sighed. Maritere knew how to lay on the guilt as thick as a glacier – and it was equally slow to melt, a skill learned from their mother. If he could get frequent flier miles for his mother's and sister's guilt trips, Santi could fly to Saturn for free. "I'm not James' godfather, Maritere. Nico is. I'm just the priest who baptized him."

The correction just launched the verbal bulldozing into high gear. "Ay, that's just like a godfather, Santi. Even more important than a godfather. There really should be a special name for the priest who baptizes you." She paused as if she were going to invent a Spanglish one on the spot, but gave up. "So you're coming to dinner, right? I'll make you tres leches."

"I hate tres leches."

"Ah, that's Nico's favorite."

"I can't come to dinner tonight, Mari." Santiago put his coffee mug in the sink and flung open Abigail's pantry cabinet. He pulled out a can of corn. Tucking it beneath the electric can opener, he clicked the top off and drained the water.

"I saw you mentioned in the *Post* this weekend. Why do those parents hate you so much?"

"What?" Then he thought better of telling her he hadn't read it. She'd just read the entire article to him over the phone. "They don't hate me, Maritere."

Santiago checked his watch again and edged over to the bathroom door. He balanced the phone between his chin and shoulder and slid open the door with one hand. The chicken inside began flapping and squawking madly. He blocked its escape with his foot. "Get back in there! Get back!"

"What?" said Mariteri.

The chicken had lost all fear. It attacked the door like a famished tiger. Santiago flinched, spilling some of the corn down the front of his shirt and dropping his phone, which spun across the floor. "Anda pa'l carajo! Get in there!" Santiago lunged forward like a defensive lineman. "Stop it! Coño! Get back, you dumb bird!" The chicken relented, turning back into the small bathroom. Santiago scattered the wet corn across a plate in the middle of the newspaper on the floor and slammed the door.

"Pollo jediondo!" He dashed after his still spinning phone and could here Maritere calling his name.

"I'm here. I'm here."

"What is going on there?"

"My chicken attacked me."

"Have you lost your mind?"

"Santiago ignored the question, returning to convincing his sister she was misinformed. "They don't hate me. It's just a very sensitive issue." He crossed into the foyer and shrugged himself into his coat. "I'm sure once I have the chance to explain, things will be fine."

"Why don't you let those poor boys just sit where they want?"

"Is it too much to ask people to stretch themselves?"

"Who said anything about stretching? The boys just want to sit. Who are you going to punish if they don't sit together? The white boys or the black boys? And what about the Latinos? Does this crazy seating chart apply to them too?"

"It's not a seating chart. And who said anything about getting punished?" Santiago stepped out the front door of Abigail's home. "I have to go."

"James is going to be so disappointed." Maritere paused appropriately. "Feliz cumpleaños, mi'jo. I'll see you tonight for dinner. We'll have chicken."

"No, Maritere..."

She hung up and Santiago shook the phone.

He should have read the article. It appeared in the Sunday edition, of all days, just below the fold. There it was: Santiago Torres, Gonzaga Headmaster, on the front page of the *Post*. Right below an article on the growing territory controlled by ISIS in Iraq and another piece detailing pundits' predictions for the March presidential primaries.

On Sunday morning he'd read just the headline and its teaser. High School Headmaster Forcefully Desegregates Cafeteria Tables. The article's teaser piled on the drama: "Father Santiago Torres' new rules forcing mixed-race seating anger Gonzaga parents, some of whom are children of America's civil rights heroes."

He had stopped right there, refusing to read more. He simply tossed the first section under the sink with the recyclables. Then he shut off his cell phone until this morning. Instead, all day Sunday, he buried himself in the same Internet research he had tackled on Saturday after Abby and he returned from Statuary Hall.

"How do the eight names explain the fact that Israel was circled on Jasper's map?" Abby had asked.

He pointed to the first letter in each name down the list: O-U-T-R-E-M-E-R.

"Outremer?" said Abby. "I don't follow."

"It's not an English word. It's a French phrase. *Outremer*."

Abby's face brightened. "The lands across the sea!"

Santiago nodded. "The first crusade established four Crusader states in the Holy Land: the County of Edessa, the Principality of Antioch, the County of Tripoli and the Kingdom of Jerusalem. Outremer, which means overseas, was the French name for them.'"

"Which explains why Israel was circled."

Yet that was as far as the latest clue from the Odd Fellows Society had taken them. Despite hours spent on the Internet doing various searches on the phrase, Santiago uncovered nothing related between the old Crusader states and Georgetown. The phrase produced an endless list of hits focused on books. All dead ends.

On the off chance Outremer referred to a corporate name, he did a comprehensive search of all corporations in all fifty states and the District of Columbia, locating just a Caribbean telecom company that had recently been acquired and a Florida boat manufacturer, not exactly effective covers for the Stewards' espionage network.

"Maybe their spy network is located in Israel," Abby initially suggested, but the look on her face conveyed she thought that was as unlikely as he did. Later, when she finally managed to pull him away for dinner late Saturday night, she simply offered a resigned shrug. "Maybe it has something to do with the dollar clue."

So Santi threw that into the mix, exhausting several keyword combinations: George Washington and Outremer, George Washington and Georgetown University; the Stewards and dollar bill; The Crusades and the dollar bill, George Washington and sun; even George Washington and yellow.

He read every word on the sites, unwilling to risk missing a message that Jasper was sending.

Some of it was surprising. Some he already knew.

The town of Georgetown was founded in 1751 on land formerly owned by George Gordon and George Beall. People still argued whether it was named for them or for George II, the British king when the port town's land was bought by the colony of Maryland.

Georgetown, perched just below the fall line of the Potomac River, hadn't become part of the nation's capital until 1871, just nine years after Congress voted to ban slavery there and shut down its slave markets on M Street and Wisconsin Avenue.

What Santi learned about Georgetown University's founders, however, was more surprising. The university was founded in 1789 by the first American Catholic bishop, John Carroll, a former Jesuit whose statue sat at the school's entrance. The university, however, became a truly impressive place of learning under its unofficial second founder, a Jesuit priest named Patrick Francis Healy. Healy was honored for his accomplishments by having the largest building on campus – one he built – named in his honor. Healy Hall was the imposing High Victorian-Romanesque building with an impressive clock tower that peered over the gates of the university's entrance. It dwarfed Carroll's statue. When Healy died, he was even buried in the Jesuit cemetery on Georgetown University's campus, the cemetery Jasper's body was found beside.

Enter the irony, a truth about Healy that thoroughly shocked Santiago.

Under Georgia law Patrick Francis Healy, the man who made Georgetown great, was born a legal slave.

Even the school didn't admit the truth until 1960. It was an inconvenient fact for a major southern university in the heart of a city that forced whites and blacks to attend different public schools until 1954.

Father Healy was the son of a Georgia planter, George Healy, and George Healy's mixed-race slave, Eliza. While George Healy lived with Eliza as his common-law wife, the interracial marriage was illegal in Georgia. Eliza was George's slave, as were all of her children under state law. And under Georgia law, despite having three-quarters European heritage, Patrick Healy and his brothers and sisters were all deemed black. The family tried to lessen the stigma of his legal status by sending him to live in New York, where Healy passed as white with the help of his father's wealth and influence.

Patrick Healy nevertheless became the first African American to earn a doctoral degree. He was also the first to become a Jesuit, just twelve years after his religious order had sold two hundred seventy-two slaves downriver rather than set them free. And Healy was the first African American to head a major white university.

All impressive and shocking, a striking paradox given the founding and motivation of The Stewards. Santiago mulled it over for hours Sunday night, staring at Jasper's dollar bill clue. Jasper thrilled at such historical paradoxes. He loved the messy truths that frayed the patriotic ribbons Americans tied around their black and white boxes – neat boxes in which they liked stuffing people and their dirty little secrets. Yet Santi could see absolutely no connection between Healy and the dollar's highlighted George Washington.

All the research simply sent him off to school on a Monday morning bleary-eyed. He tapped his phone. Twenty-three messages. They likely stopped only when his voicemail had jammed full. What other messes waited for him in his office? Santiago regretted not reading the article. It would help him gauge what to expect.

Twenty minutes later, when he pulled onto campus, he realized nothing could have helped him predict the mess awaiting him.

His car weaved through scores of gawking students being barked at by Dean Loughney through a megaphone. A half dozen media trucks were jammed beside his reserved spot outside Forte Hall. CNN. NBC. FoxNews. ABC News and CBS. Even a few local affiliates. Santiago was close to throwing the car into reverse and driving away when nearby students began pointing. The reporters and camera crews swarmed the car, cameras banging into the windows, questions shouted through the glass.

Santiago sat stunned, gathering himself for the storm outside the car. Then it occurred to him. They were already filming him and sitting there simply would make him look like he was avoiding them. Santiago took a deep breath and pressed open his door. The assault was suffocating. *Smile. Remember to smile.* He struggled to rise from his seat to exit the car. He finally jammed himself upward, accidentally squashing himself against the breasts of a female ABC news reporter who was shouting at him. His face flushed. "I'm terribly sorry." Camera flashes exploded in his face.

A shouting voice: "Father Torres, why are you taking away your black students' freedom to sit where they please?"

Santiago abruptly stopped, tracking the voice through the crowd back to its face. A tall, thin man. Perfect teeth and thick, salt and pepper hair sitting above a smirk.

The tumult suddenly gave way to stillness. Santiago licked his lips and heard the whir of a dozen digital cameras. He gave a nervous chuckle. "I thought you were all here to wish me happy birthday."

No laughter. Just more stillness.

He looked up the steps to the doors of Forte Hall, his closest escape route. There on the top steps stood Roy Taylor.

Not a good sign.

Roy quickly held his finger across his lips and gestured for Santiago to follow him. He disappeared through Forte Hall's glass doors.

Santiago smiled again and held up a hand to silence the rising din of questions. "I've not had the opportunity to read the *Post's* Sunday coverage concerning the remarks I made to the student body on Friday. So I obviously can't yet comment on the matter. If you give me a few minutes to get settled, I'd be glad to discuss them with you. In the meantime, I'd ask you to respect the school's primary purpose, which is to conduct classes this morning."

The reporters' follow-up shouts raised another hellacious din. Santiago ignored them and pushed up the steps to Forte Hall. He slid through the glass doors and into the quiet hallway.

Roy Taylor was standing outside the office of the school president, Father Stan Quigley. Roy Taylor, his Jesuit confessor. The Roy Taylor, who was also the vice chair of the Gonzaga College High School Board of Directors – who had recommended to Gonzaga's board that they pluck Santiago from the classroom and name him headmaster four years prior.

Roy offered a wry smile. "If I'm not mangling it, I believe the saying goes: your story went viral, Santiago."

"It's that bad?"

"I tried calling you five times yesterday. Even left two messages."

"I turned my phone off. I decided not to read beyond the headline. The whole thing's been blown completely out of proportion, Roy, and I had to focus on something else this weekend."

Roy gave a kind of embarrassed shrug to take the edge of his words. "Would that have been your commitment to the priesthood?"

Santiago bristled. "What does that mean?"

"Stan's waiting. We need to really talk this time, Santi. No excuses." Roy opened Stan Quigley's office door. Miriam, Quigley's septuagenarian secretary, looked up with a polite smile. "Good morning, Father Torres."

Santiago nodded, passing in front of her desk. "Miriam, I apologize for the circus I've apparently caused."

Another smile. "Never you mind."

The Four Horses of the Apocalypse, Messrs. Plague, Famine, Pestilence and Death, could be hurtling fire through the streets of Northwest D.C. and Miriam DeGrasso would smile politely, bob her white, cotton candy hair, tap the save key on her PC and assure the dying masses, "Never you mind."

Roy pushed into Stan's office. Quigley hung up the phone, leapt to his feet and came around the desk. Without saying a word, he buried Santiago in a big, silent hug.

Santiago looked at Roy Taylor. "Now I know I'm screwed."

Chapter 28: The Hug of Death

El abrazo de muerto.
The Stan Quigley hug of death.
The two things a person had to avoid to survive in the world were kisses from men named Judas and hugs from Stan Quigley.

It was one of the old Jesuit's trademarks. Santiago actually liked Stan. He was personable and kind, the school's chief mythmaker and alumni pickpocket. For Stan, love of God came first. Love of family and friends was an excusable second. But, in Stan's mind, if you were an alumnus, love of Mother Gonzaga had damn well better place third or he just wasn't golfing enough with you.

Quigley wasn't a meddler or a micromanager. He was the school president and fundraiser extraordinaire. For Stan, that meant alumni relations, increasing the school's endowment and expanding student scholarship opportunities – all of which were best accomplished with a minimum of three rounds of golf per week.

And avoiding a horde of satellite trucks in the faculty parking lot.

While Stan was the overall head of the school, he made clear when Santiago was hired he had no intention on running the school's day-to-day affairs. He just wasn't interested in staff matters or academics. That was the headmaster's job. For Santiago, Stan was the perfect boss. Quigley gave him free reign and backed him in all he did. When Santi fired a faculty member or expelled a student, the terminated always exercised their rights to appeal to the school president. Quigley invited them into his office, repeatedly blessed them with sympathetic pastoral nods as they spoke and then he gave it to them.

The hug of death.

See you later. Sayonara. Adios. God bless you. And please don't let the door hit you in the ass.

The decision to invite Santi to plead his case was a mere formality.

Eventually Stan released him from his grasp and he gestured for Roy and Santi to sit. Stan dropped into a chair beside them. "We're just waiting for one more person."

Almost immediately the phone intercom sounded and Miriam DeGrasso's voice floated into the office. "Father Quigley, Mr. Stokes is here."

Alvin Stokes. President of the Gonzaga Board of Directors. A director on two dozen other major corporate boards. The owner of the largest African-American media outlet in the Northeast United States.

The three stood and Stokes entered, his charcoal business suit filling the doorframe. He crushed Santiago's hand.

The four dropped back into their chairs. Santi wondered whether he should speak first, but Quigley relieved him of that responsibility. "I suspect you know why we're all here."

"I actually haven't read it."

Quigley's face registered surprise. He tapped Santiago's knee and offered a laugh. "Well, at least you have that in common with only half of the country."

Stokes and Roy Taylor tossed in their chuckles.

"Was it that bad?"

Stokes' deep baritone explained. "It was a slow news weekend. A group of conservative bloggers picked up the *Post* piece on Saturday. By Sunday the story began being aired by other online media outlets. Links appeared on Drudge, CNN, Fox, NBC. Reporters began deluging the school and Jesuit residence switchboards. After your unique approach was briefly referred to by the talking heads on *Meet the Press* on Sunday morning, the gauntlet you ran through outside began to gather. Have you been answering your phone? The reporters all tell me you dropped off the planet."

"I turned off my cell. I was working on something this weekend. This is crazy."

"No," said Roy. "Crazy is scheduled for this afternoon when talk radio and the cable TV pundits roll out their lunatics. Both Bill O'Reilly and Rachel Maddow want you to appear tonight."

"You're the first person in the country to get those two to agree on something. Every single board member's phone is ringing off the hook," Stokes said. "There is real concern."

"If you read the article, you'd know that a number of our black parents feel very strongly about what you announced on Friday," Stan added.

Stokes nodded. "This goes to the heart of what they felt the civil rights movement fought to win."

"The right to sit where whites do?" asked Santi.

Stokes leaned his imposing body forward. "The right not to sit where white folks tell them to."

"Santi, I don't think anyone here feels you had bad intentions," said Roy. "And in a perfect world, a policy like the one you proposed wouldn't be even needed. But this poked a finger into an awkward sore that needed a gentler touch."

Santiago moved to speak in his defense, but Roy held up a hand, requesting he be allowed to finish.

"None of this was anticipated. But your own secretary, Pearl Freeman, has received seven death threats just this morning. Is this what you want for your staff and students?"

Santi heaved a frustrated sigh. "What is it with Americans? Why does race make all of you crazy?"

Stokes and Quigley exchanged glances before Stokes spoke up. "This policy has even prompted comments from the ACLU and NAACP."

Santi waved his hand. "They can't sue us. We're a private institution. They have no legal standing."

"I'm not sure that's a defense on which to proudly hang a hat," responded Stan. "Santi, a number of our black alumni are also very unhappy."

"Is that what this is about, Stan? Alumni donations?"

Stan pushed back, his words shaded with anger. "Do you want to tell some of our minority students – some of our at-risk kids – they've got to stay home? All because your new racial harmony policy has so offended some of our most generous alumni they want to pull the plug on their minority scholarship programs? Because that's what you're asking me to do."

Santi stared hard at him.

"This isn't just about dollars, Santiago. This is about keeping good, deserving kids in the school. Would we finally have perfect racial harmony if all of our minority students left in protest?"

"So you want me to rescind the challenge? To pretend everything is perfectly okay in our society and school? Even when one glance at the cafeteria still makes clear that we largely choose our friends and associates based on skin color?"

Alvin Stokes bristled. "I think this room makes clear that that just isn't true."

Roy Taylor held up a hand to encourage calm. "Santi, there are larger personal issues at stake here. Since Jasper's death–"

"I knew it," Santiago growled. "I'm amazed it took you so long to mention Jasper's murder, Roy."

Stan Quigley tossed a told-you-so look at Alvin Stokes, whose eyebrows scaled the top of his head in surprise.

"Yes, I said murder. And Roy believes I'm unhinged for thinking it."

Quigley nodded in silence. Santiago felt like the floor was sliding out from beneath him.

Roy's quiet voice broke the quiet. "What were you doing this weekend, Santi? Your room in the residence has been empty for days. Where have you been?"

"Abigail's house."

Quigley looked surprised. "Do you mean Abigail Byrne, one of our English teachers?"

Santiago reluctantly nodded.

Quigley's surprise escalated to incredulity. "Doesn't that strike you as wildly inappropriate?"

"It's not like that."

Roy shifted uncomfortably.

"Do we know if any journalists are aware of where you've been staying?" asked Stokes. "That would make a rather salacious sidebar."

Quigley's hand came down firmly on the arm of his chair. "Santi, it just kills me to do this—"

"Then don't," Santiago interrupted.

"Can you offer a workable alternative? I think, given the circumstances of your loss, anyone could understand taking a brief sabbatical. And that's what you're going to do through the end of the school year."

"So you're firing me."

Quigley held up a hand. "You're not hearing me. I said sabbatical. It will give you time to heal and time to consider your commitment to the religious life. As I said, I think everyone will understand given the circumstances."

Santiago felt hollowed out, a swirling mass of anger and sadness filling the gap in his chest.

"We can sit down at year's end and see if you feel up to returning as headmaster. In the meantime, your position will remain unfilled and I'll step in as I can." Stan Quigley paused. "I'm sorry, Santi. Really, I am."

His lips trembling, Santiago turned to look at Roy. His friend and mentor's eyes were closed, the tips of his fingers pressed together, his head pressed back against the chair. Santiago rose slowly, turned and walked out of Quigley's office.

Quigley's lowered voice trickled out after him as he passed Miriam DeGrasso's desk. "Alvin, you'll handle the media…"

Roy's voice stopped him before he stepped back into the hallway. "Santiago, if you'll permit me to ask, where are you going?" Roy was standing in the door between Quigley's and Miriam's offices.

Santiago turned and his eyes narrowed. "Where anyone would go in my situation, Roy."

Roy waited.

"To get my chicken."

Roy Taylor's forehead pinched in concern and Santiago departed satisfied.

Chapter 29: Stanley Interrogated

Santi's breath caught in his throat and the hallway narrowed. He needed to leave, to escape the school. For the first time in his adult life he felt acute shame, like he was once more standing before his father, face down, hearing what a disappointment he was.

He wasn't just a passing story beneath the Sunday fold of the *Post*. In the afternoon he would be bloodily dissected across scores of talk radio and TV programs, whose hosts would celebrate or scream in outrage. The shrill national debate on race had claimed another victim. The firestorm would burn through tomorrow's newspapers, which would gleefully announce his removal and the school's overturning of the policy.

Damn that Kevin Gaines.

Santiago's conscience pricked. That was certainly giving Gaines a lot of power. The controversial decision was his, not Kevin's. He stopped and pressed a hand against the old, rough plaster wall. What if Roy was right? What if he was letting his grief at losing Jasper – his desperation over the whole Stewards mystery – cloud his judgment?

Santiago's guilt also demanded he stop at his office to apologize to Pearl. He grimaced at the idea. Quigley said his position would remain unfilled. The vast majority of the work and bother would fall onto the shoulders of Gonzaga's Dean of Academics, Roger Draper, who would shrug it into Pearl's lap.

He just couldn't bring himself to step into the office. God knows how Pearl would react. He couldn't face one of her silent, I-told-you-so looks. Santi's stomach surged and he suppressed the urge to vomit. He veered toward the doorway leading to the Jesuit residence and rode the elevator to the third floor.

From the window of his bedroom he looked down at the media mess below. Alvin Stokes stood on the steps of Forte Hall, pointing to various reporters and gesturing as he responded to their questions.

He could predict Stokes' words. *Father Torres recently suffered a great loss with the death of a close friend. Both he and the school administration agree that he needs some time to grieve that loss. As the result he's voluntarily elected to take a brief sabbatical. In the meantime, the school policy he announced Friday will be suspended. It will give Father the time he needs to reflect on the wisdom of the policy and on other ways that can encourage our community to break down those small barriers – both racial and otherwise – that perhaps, at times keep us a bit apart. He's expressed great regret that his well-meaning attempt to improve our community has proven such a distraction for the school he loves.*

His head near to exploding, Santiago ripped off his clerical collar. He threw off his black shirt and pants, pulling on frayed jeans and a warm, plaid shirt from his closet. He willed himself miles distant from his job, his vocation, even the Catholic Church. He wished to soar back in time, drag his toes through the sand of Luquillo beach, lose himself in the green mist of the island's rainforest, shout with joy beneath its waterfalls. He'd fly even further back until he was a mere jibaro, a Puerto Rican peasant, staining his hands red picking coffee in the mountains, two thousand miles from the cold stone of Washington's memorials to the dead.

A storm of fury filled him. He needed to get as far away from the school as he could. He glanced out the window. Stokes was still on the steps, less than twenty feet from Santiago's car. He couldn't go out that way. Reporters would be guarding every exit, waiting for his face, demanding a comment about his removal.

He laced his sneakers and threw on an old leather bomber jacket he hadn't worn for a decade. His bedroom door whispered shut behind him and strode down the hall to the common room. He nodded at silent Father Breckinridge, whose sole responsibility was to turn ninety-six sometime in the summer. The liver-spotted

Jesuit, who only heard afternoon confessions anymore, had sunk entirely into his puffy recliner, watching *The View*. The man never uttered a word. Santiago wasn't even certain he even understood what was going on around him anymore. In that respect, he had a lot in common with Breckinridge.

Breckinridge's rheumy eyes tailed Santi as he crossed to a window three stories above the campus quadrangle. The area was bordered on three sides by school buildings, off limits to reporters. He pushed up the window and Breckinridge cleared his throat. The old man's southern drawl rasped like sandpaper across rusty screws. "Well, well, aren't you the shit-stirrer?"

Santiago's spine stiffened. Breckinridge's sagging face cleaved into a broad smile. "You ain't much of a zookeeper if you forget to rattle the cages now and again."

Santiago balanced on the windowsill, a startled, wry laugh rising from his chest. For the first time that day he felt like he had a genuine ally in the world, even if his only ally only had half his teeth. Santi crawled onto the fire escape, shutting the window and clanging down the steps. He stepped onto the ladder and it descended with a bang. A handful of nearby boys whirled at the noise, their mouths popping open. Santiago nodded in feigned nonchalance, jogged across the quad, and scaled the nine-foot iron gate.

He was headed toward Georgetown.

Santiago suppressed the nagging thought that it was a remarkably stupid idea.

He just didn't care. He was done with nice. The Stewards had killed his best friend and now a local news story about a D.C. high school principal just happened to go viral the weekend after Patrick Kelly's death?

The gloves were coming off.

For the first ten blocks he jogged down P Street, Santiago glanced over his shoulder, checking if some reporter had seen him slip away. He couldn't afford cameras now. The last thing he needed was a microphone shoved up his nose, a smirk interrogating him.

He cursed his stupidity, for playing into their hands. There was no conceivable way to conduct a reasonable discussion about race in America, especially with the media playing chief intermediary. It was like throwing hunks of raw meat into a cage of famished tigers and expecting the beasts to lick it politely. In America race made people prickly, defensive and hostile. Whisper "race" and rational discussion was ejected out of the top of most people's skulls. Past grievances, caricatures and suspicion rushed in to fill the vacuum.

Santiago struggled to clear his mind, to calm the turmoil roiling his brain and stomach: the aggressive *Post* reporter's twisting of his words, the mass of bloodthirsty media hounds waiting to ambush him outside the school, Stan Quigley's embrace of betrayal – all had sprouted from the same bloody ground upon which he'd found Jasper's broken body. It wasn't just anger that filled Santiago, making it hard to breathe. It was anger poisoned with a horrible desire for revenge.

It was rage.

Rattling cages? Old Charlie Breckinridge had seen nothing yet. Bob Stanley, the Jesuit priest who headed up the Office of Federal Relations was next. And he wasn't waiting around for Nico to arrange a polite meeting.

Santiago spat on the sidewalk and the blocks flashed by, the rough and tumble row houses of Shaw giving way to Dupont Circle. When Santiago heard a bus belching down the street, he hopped on.

At Wisconsin Avenue Santi pulled the cable and jumped off. He pounded across the cobblestones, covering the last blocks to the college campus.

He considered what he was going to say when he finally shook Stanley by the collar. He had nothing but contempt for such priests. Despite the vows of poverty, chastity and obedience, despite the fact that they were all called to live in community as equals, a pecking order of power and influence existed among Jesuits. Some dedicated their lives to serving the poor and downtrodden. Others only thrived in proximity to power and wealth, ministering, they insisted, to society's elites, prying open their hearts to Jesus and their wallets to Jesuit schools and missions.

Santiago's heart had been inspired by the former – Jesuits who were work-a-day high school teachers, university professors and pastors. Jesuits like Stanley were living, breathing throwbacks to the Jesuits who served kings in the Middle Ages. Stanley preferred exclusive golf courses, fifteen-year-old scotch bought on someone else's expense account and the company of senators.

Bob Stanley was nothing more than a professional K Street lobbyist in a clerical collar. And if he had to beat the snot out of the man to get the truth about Jasper, it would be well deserved.

How does a story about a private high school headmaster wind up on the front page of an internationally important newspaper?

It was because someone like Bob Stanley wanted it there – to fully discredit him.

And if there was anything that the university's beautiful, thriving campus made clear it was what Bob Stanley wanted, Bob Stanley got.

When Santiago finally arrived at the Federal Relations office on the third floor of Healy Hall, he blew right past Stanley's flustered secretary.

"Father Stanley is in an important meeting!" she shrieked.

He flung open the office door.

Stanley was reclining in a leather, high-backed desk chair, a phone tucked beneath his chin. His startled eyes looked over bifocals perched on the tip of his patrician nose. He shot up. "Excuse me, Congressman," he said into the receiver. "I apologize, but something's suddenly arisen here. I look forward to discussing the project next Tuesday."

Stanley replaced the receiver, not once taking his eyes of Santiago. His face wore suspicion, even a flicker of fear, as he considered the man at his door. "Can I help you?"

"Congratulations." Santiago shut the door, locking it behind him. "You won that round."

Stanley was a talented actor. He looked thoroughly confused.

"I'm sorry," he said. "This is the Office of Federal Relations. I'm Father Stanley. If you tell me who you're looking for, I'm sure we can sort it out."

"I'm looking for you, Bob. For Christ sake, you don't even recognize me. Santiago Torres, a fellow Jesuit."

Stanley's face reddened. "Of course! Of course! Santiago!" He stood up and offered his hand. "I know your brother Nicolas quite well!"

Stanley's extended hand floated in the air until he lowered it. He shifted his weight. "How can I help you? What brings you here?" He eyed his office door as if he hoped his secretary would rush in with a shotgun.

"Just a simple question, Bob. Did you kill Jasper or did you have someone else do your dirty work."

"What? Are you talking about Father Willoughs?"

"You know damn well I am. And after what you did to me over the weekend, you'll be lucky if I don't strangle you right here."

Stanley's face blanched. His Adam's apple rose and fell and he leapt for his phone.

Santiago threw himself over the desk and seized the receiver. The phone toppled to the floor. Santiago shoved Bob Stanley back into his desk chair and it crashed into the wall.

"Don't hurt me," he whimpered.

"Then tell me where it is."

His chin trembled. "Where what is?"

"The documents you stole from Jasper and the package you had stolen from my treasurer's office."

Stanley looked bewildered. "What documents and package?" He held his hands up in terror. "I don't know what you're talking about."

Santiago shook him again.

His eyes filled with fear, Stanley tried to calm him. "Look, Santiago, I saw the morning news. I know things aren't going so well right now. I know you're going through a terrible time, but I promise you. I have no idea what you're talking about."

Santiago shook him hard. "Tell me or, I swear, I'll kill you right here for what you've done."

Stanley brought his trembling hands in front of his face. "I swear to you. I don't know what you're talking about." Stanley's face cracked and he burst into terrified sobs. "I swear it!"

Stanley's tears suddenly broke Santiago's rage. He hadn't expected them. They didn't feel right. A feeling of dread seeped into his stomach.

He shook Stanley more lightly. "Then tell me about the Stewards."

Stanley's eyes flickered toward him, his whole face quaking. "What do you want to know?"

"Are you involved with them?"

"Yes! Yes!" He nodded. "I groom and recommend students from the office for membership. They meet monthly and I sometimes attend. I occasionally say Latin mass for them. But that is all. I used to leave the rest to Pat Kelly." Stanley looked confused. "But what does that have to Father Willough's death?"

"It has everything to do with Jasper's murder!" Santiago had tried to sound forceful, but his words had lost their force. He had frightened Bob Stanley, a man accustomed to bluster and power, to the point of crying.

"Murder? How can that be? I heard it was suicide." Stanley began to beg. "They're just a group of good, Catholic alumni. We work them for contacts. For alumni donations. They don't go around killing people. Why in God's name would they do that?"

The anxious dread spread in Santiago's stomach. "You organized them, you say?"

"Yes. After Pat Kelly came to me and suggested it, some twenty-five years ago. For years people had talked about there being a secret Georgetown group called the Stewards. So we thought it was a great idea to actually form one."

"Twenty-five years ago?"

"Yes. Why would you think the Stewards would kill Father Willoughs?"

Santiago recalled the date on the lockbox: 1953. More than three decades before Stanley founded his group. He straightened and stared at the face of the trembling man. Years of bending the truth had made Santiago a skilled spotter of liars. Stanley was speaking honestly.

Or at least what Stanley believed was the truth.

Santiago whirled around, seizing his head with both hands. For the first time, he felt like he was going off the deep end. He had just assaulted and threatened to kill a fellow Jesuit. Maybe he *was* going crazy.

Stanley straightened slowly. "I can help, Santiago," his voice quavered. "We can get you help."

"I don't need help!" He strode over to the door. "I need answers!" He turned to Stanley. "You think I'm crazy. But, Bob, here's what's actually crazy. You believe Pat Kelly's death was an accident. Two men fall to their deaths in Georgetown in less than a month and you think it's just a coincidence."

Stanley's door closed with a slam.

Chapter 30: The Stewards Tap Twice

"Agent Torres, this is Teresa Sullivan from the director's office. Director Sampson would like a moment to sit down with you."

Nico bolted upright in his desk chair and nearly dropped the phone. "Director Sampson?"

Ten minutes later he was standing before glass doors with black lettering: William J. Sampson, FBI Director.

He'd met Sampson several times. Everyone working for the agency did, even those in far-flung offices. The director flew into town, requested a brief meeting with agents, shook hands all around and departed until the following year. The Washington agents – at least those on his level – saw Sampson nearly as frequently. And after each brief cheerleading session, Nico understood he was largely invisible.

Now he'd been summoned by an individual he had been fairly sure didn't know his name.

Sullivan waved Nico past her desk and through the interior doors until he was standing just inside the FBI Director's office. The door shut and he waited for Sampson to look up. Nico shivered. Sampson kept the office ice cold. Nico struggled to place the room's faint antiseptic smell.

Sampson kept reading from a manila file folder and gestured for Nico to sit.

Nico crossed the carpet and lowered himself, his back straight as a flagpole, onto the edge of the indicated chair.

Sampson closed the folder and placed a large hand over it. The photo from Nico's security badge was paper-clipped to it. Sampson offered a smile that his eyes declined to join.

Nico started to shift in his chair but stopped himself.

"This Georgetown matter. I understand you've been following it."

"Yes, sir."

Sampson nodded, his full head of gray hair, combed to the side and tamed by some kind of gel, didn't move. "The loss of that Jesuit priest was a terrible thing, Agent Torres. Yet the accusations his friend, another Jesuit, has been privately making are quite serious. As a fellow alumnus, you can therefore understand my interest in this matter." Pause. "I understand he's your brother."

"Are you concerned it could hurt Georgetown, sir?"

Bill Sampson took off his glasses and rubbed his eyes. "While I certainly care for Georgetown, our first concern – my first concern – regards matters for more important than my alma mater."

Nico waited for a question.

"So what do you think, Nicolas?" He cocked his head to the side. "Do you think Father Willoughs took his own life?"

Nico studied his lined face. Sampson was testing him. His hands trembled and he pressed them against his legs to still them. He suddenly knew that the way he answered the question would indelibly shape his future.

"No."

A half smile. Sampson leaned back, the tips of his fingertips coming together. "So we've established you're not a fool."

Nico's eyes narrowed.

Sampson gestured with his chin to the folder. "I understand the FBI was not your first career choice."

"I had initially hoped to work at Langley, sir, but I'm quite happy here."

Sampson dropped long silences between his sentences. "You know, of course, what derailed that option?"

"I do not."

Sampson languidly pulled the file open again. "Your mother was a rather vocal supporter of independence for Puerto

Rico, I understand." His finger traced the length of a page. "Apparently not the only independentista in your family."

A surge of resentment filled Nico, but he responded calmly, measuring his words. "I was unaware I was ever seriously considered by the CIA. And I was certainly unaware that I'd been rejected because of *her*. Or because of my brother." His eyes flashed. "She was merely my stepmother, sir. I never have shared her politics. Or my brother's. I embraced my father's point of view."

Another half smile.

"I understand you were offered membership in another organization during your stay at Georgetown."

Nico's eyebrows rose. "I didn't take it seriously at the time."

Nico searched his brain and studied Sampson's face. The night of his tapping, the campus quad was quite dark. The Steward's face had been shadowed from the lamplight by a tree. Twenty years had passed, further clouding the memory, but Nico had long thought it possible.

"Did you ever regret your choice?"

"I was young, immature. I would likely decide differently today."

A full smile this time. "Your brother trusts you?"

"He's merely my half-brother, sir. He came to me, asking for my help."

"Nicolas, I have a particular task that may be suited for you. If you handle it well, it will open some significant doors. Through my contacts in Homeland Security, you could gain an enviable position at Langley. I could benefit greatly by having another man I trust there. And it would open other opportunities with another group of influential people as well."

Nico felt emboldened. "Might I ask whom, sir?"

"We can address that at the appropriate time."

Nico waited.

"I want you to keep track of your brother. He's looking for what we believe is the last copy of some important documents that could prove very dangerous. It's imperative that we see them before anyone else. Of course, all information you discover should run solely through me." Sampson leaned over and handed him a card. "This is my direct line. In the meantime, it would benefit everyone if he believes you continue to doubt his story."

Nico stood. "I'll need wiretaps. Permission to track his location through his mobile. A warrant to compel his cell carrier's cooperation."

"You'll have it in twenty-four hours." Sampson stood and extended his hand. "Of course, all of this must be kept in the strictest confidence."

Nico shook hand with a nod. "I won't disappoint you, sir."

He strode across the carpet, his heart beating ferociously. He walked out the doors, past Teresa Sullivan and let the glass door of the director's suite swing closed behind him.

Nicolas Torres allowed himself to smile.

He had played his cards shrewdly.

Chapter 31: Against the World

Santiago had to vanish before campus police arrived. He cursed his temper. If any of his fellow Jesuits had wondered whether Jasper's death had pushed him to a nervous breakdown, his behavior back in Stanley's office would confirm it.

He dashed out of Healy Hall and headed toward the campus gates. He hazarded a glance back. Two campus police officers were trotting into Healy.

How convenient – how brilliant, really – for the real Stewards to have another group misdirecting everyone's attention on campus away from them. Given Pat Kelly's death, he was likely an unfortunate go-between between the two.

And how stupid of Kelly and Stanley. Leave it to that pompous Stanley to establish an organization that already existed. Yet, Santiago thought, had he been any brighter, believing someone as shallow as Stanley could be part of a group like the one described in the Steward's confession?

Had Santi become so desperate that he'd tossed all judgment to the wind?

He jogged down the street, his mind whirring. He stopped to catch his breath and finally reached into his wallet and extracted a business card.

He dialed and waited for a voice on the other line. "Hey, it's Father Torres. I know this is going to come a bit out of the blue, but I'd like to take you up on your offer to help." He paused. "As soon as possible, if it's not asking too much."

Forty-five minutes later Bradley Freeman slid into a chair opposite him in a Georgetown deli. He set a laptop on the table. He was wearing jeans and a long-sleeved shirt, looking more like the young man Santiago was used to seeing.

"Thanks for coming."

"Anything, Father, you know that." Bradley nodded. "My mother told me this morning you were likely to call."

"She did? How'd she know that?"

Bradley shook his head. "I'm fairly sure she's sold her soul to the devil."

Santiago held up a hand. "Before I ask you anything. Before you say yes. You need to understand that helping me could put you in grave danger. The only reason I'm asking you is you don't have children. So think carefully before you agree."

Bradley smiled. "Father, you know why I'm so good at catching other guys? Because I've never gotten caught myself." He sat back. "Tell me what you want and I'll tell you if I'm in."

Santi reached into the pockets of his leather bomber jacket. He laid the yellow highlighted dollar bill, the sheets torn from Jasper's journal and all the parchment clues from the Fairly Odd Fellows Society in front of his former student. "I'm stuck. There has got to be something here I'm missing and you are the smartest person I've ever met, Bradley."

"I don't know about that."

"It needs fresh eyes. A clearer head."

It took twenty minutes for Santiago to run through the story. He hadn't even finished it when Bradley raised his hand. "I'm in."

"For how long?"

"Until it's done," he said. "They killed your friend."

"And you trust me? You don't think I'm crazy?" Santiago's voice cracked. "I just assaulted another Jesuit."

Bradley laughed. "We're all crazy. My mother trusts you and she doesn't trust me. That's good enough." He pressed his fingers against the documents. "Why don't you finish explaining all these?"

Santiago spent ten minutes wrapping up, making sure he'd covered everything from the moment he found the missing map in

Jasper's room to his interrogation of Stanley. "I'm sure there are two Stewards groups," he concluded. "One's a cover for the other and Pat Kelly was probably some kind of go between." He swung around the parchment with the word Outremer circled and the dollar bill clue. "This is all I have. I must be missing something."

"I can make copies?"

Santiago nodded.

Bradley took out his phone and snapped photos of the journal entries. He opened his laptop, connected to the Internet and began typing.

Santiago spent an hour pacing the shop, looking at its old black and white photos of Washington, D.C. and studying the people who walked in and out to grab coffee. Bradley tapped away, going back and forth among the Odd Fellows Society's clues and studying the dollar bill. Santiago bought a large cup of coffee for Bradley, who turned it light brown with half and half, and sent Santiago back for two more sugar packets.

He finally slid back into the seat across from Bradley and the young man shook his head.

Santiago's hope dimmed.

"I have some other people I trust working on the dollar clue and the Outremer reference and have offered a reward to anyone who cracks them."

"Who are they?"

He shrugged. "No one knows their real names."

"Why not?"

"It's how they protect themselves."

"And you trust them?"

"I only work with the good guys."

Santiago swallowed. "How much is the reward?"

"A thousand dollars. It's play money for them, but they work better when they're motivated."

Bradley picked up the pages torn from Jasper's journal and began reading them.

"It's a transcript of a Steward's confession," Santiago explained. "It mostly helps explain the organization."

Bradley traced some words with his finger. "*Athanasisu contra mundum*?" he read aloud.

"It's Latin phrase that means Athenasius against the world. He was a saint from Alexandria that stood alone against powerful forces that were corrupting the church. The Steward called Jasper the name."

"But another part of the confession suggests the Stewards opposed any liberal forces in the church."

"Well, yes, the early Stewards were opposed to the church's eventual condemnation of slavery and later its call for racial equality."

"But what if the Steward wasn't calling Father Willoughs Athanasius?"

"What do you mean?"

Bradley read the conclusion of the journal entry out loud. "Right here the Steward asks him, 'Haven't you figured it out?' and your friend responds, 'Figured what out?' The Steward then says, '*Athenasisu contra mundum.* And the sacrificial lamb. Your death can save all of us – hopeless idiots like me, tens of millions of others. It has to happen this way.'" Bradley turned the journal back to Santiago. "What if the Steward wasn't really referring to your friend as Athanasius against the world? What if he was just calling Father Willoughs the sacrificial lamb?"

Santiago gaped at him. "Then *Athenasisu contra mundum* refers to the Stewards themselves, fighting against modern heresies in the church!"

Bradley turned to his laptop and quickly began shooting messages to several people. He paused, tapping his screen.

"What is it?"

"We're waiting." Five minutes. Ten minutes. Bradley's laptop pinged and a broad smile creased his face. "Athenasius, Inc., registered in the Caymans."

"How do you have access to that?" Santiago asked. "I thought all the Cayman's corporate and banking records are confidential."

"Some things are better left for confession, Father."

"But how does knowing the name of their Cayman corporation get us anywhere?"

"Patience." Bradley held up a finger and began counting backwards from ten. When he hit zero, the computer pinged again.

"Athenasius, Inc., is the holding company for ACM, Inc., a lobbying firm located on…" he spun his computer around so that it faced Santiago.

"K Street. Two miles from Gonzaga." Santiago slapped Bradley on the back. "The Steward's confession mentioned they established an espionage network. You may have just found it!"

Bradley spun the laptop back toward himself and began typing again.

"What's next?"

Bradley looked at his laptop's clock. "Lunch would help." He hunched over again, his fingers flying across the keyboard.

Santiago sat a moment, afraid to interrupt. He finally stood, walked over to the counter and ordered two roast beef sandwiches on rye. He picked up an abandoned *Post* from one of the tables, and put the sandwiches on the table. Bradley inhaled his while working.

After eating, Santiago opened the paper. He picked up one of Bradley's pencils laid out on the table and finished the crossword puzzle. He looked up. Bradley was completely still, staring at his laptop. "Anything?"

Bradley held up a finger. "Patience."

Santiago forced himself to read the comics. Then he began coloring them in with the pencil.

"Ha!" Bradley clapped his broad hands together suddenly, making Santiago jump. "Hooked two fish."

Santiago swung around his chair so he could see the laptop's screen.

Bradley was scribbling two names onto the legal pad on the table. "I created a private group on a very popular online networking site."

"LinkedIn," Santiago said.

Bradley nodded. "All IT geeks have one thing in common. They're smart as hell and it causes them to become arrogant and careless. If this corporation is a front for the Stewards, their security is going to be top notch. I needed a way in."

"So how does the LinkedIn private group get you there?"

"It doesn't really. It just gives me a target." Bradley pointed to the screen. "ACM, the alleged K Street lobbying firm, has no obvious external way in. They have a web site, very professionally done, but it names none of the company's principles and it sits on server space in Toronto. Not even worth hacking. I did a thorough search of the company and came up with nothing identifying their employees, which is incredibly odd. So I needed someone to volunteer the information."

"So you created a private group for them to join."

Bradley nodded. "All these social networks have uncannily powerful algorithms that figure out links between people far better than people can. After lunch, everyone checks out their social networking sites, right? So I created a private group called ACM Internet Technology Leadership Group. In less than 20 minutes, two guys joined it. Then they backed out almost immediately when no one else joined."

"Red flag."

Bradley nodded and clicked on two browser tabs. "Here are their individual LinkedIn pages, but neither lists their actual employer as ACM." He looked at Santiago. "But you can bet a year's salary on the fact that's exactly where they work. While they list fake employers on their LinkedIn pages, the rest seems legit. Look where they both went to school."

"Georgetown."

"And they both live in the D.C. Metro area." Bradley opened Facebook and did a quick search. Soon they were staring at the Facebook wall of one of the men, a Jonathan Feeney. Bradley laughed and scrolled down Feeney's wall.

"How's an IT guy from a top secret company fail to restrict his security settings on Facebook?" said Santiago.

"As I said. Arrogant and careless. He's not posting anything work related or even where he lives, so what does he care? He's so smart and careful, he thinks he's harming no one."

Bradley browsed the wall images, stopping at a photo of a coffee cup perched beside a laptop inside a coffee shop.

"He certainly likes posting photos of his breakfast," observed Santiago.

Bradley pointed to the top of the photo. "Which he buys, every morning at exactly six forty-five in the morning when he checks in at the exact same Starbucks a couple blocks from his office." Bradley turned with a broad smile. "We just found our keyhole."

"How so?"

Bradley ignored the question. "Now we just have to convince Jonathan Feeney to let us stick the key inside."

"I'm not following."

Bradley slapped the laptop closed, grabbed his coat and jumped out of his chair. "Meet me at the Starbucks bright and early tomorrow at six-thirty. Oh," he added, eying him. "And dress normally. Not like a priest."

Santiago rocketed to his feet. "Where you going?"

"To work!" Bradley strode across the shop and flung open the door. "Thanks for lunch!"

Chapter 32: An Unforeseen Distraction

The next morning found Santiago shivering in street clothes under the overhang of a bus stop. His stomach in jitters, he glanced up and down Connecticut Avenue for Bradley. He pulled his phone out of his pocket and tapped it alive. Six-thirty.

"You're late, Bradley" he muttered.

"I'm never late," Bradley retorted from behind.

Santiago whirled. Bradley was dressed in a suit, tie and overcoat, a typical D.C. businessman carrying a laptop briefcase. He flashed a grin. "Have you spotted our mark, yet?"

Santiago shook his head. "Not anyone that looked like the Facebook profile picture."

Rush hour traffic whirred past them as the light changed. Santiago was about to ask him what he had planned when Bradley nodded at a man who was approaching the coffee shop. "IT geeks are too predictable. You ready, Father?"

"Not really. I have no idea what I'm supposed to be doing."

The light turned green and they began to cross the street. Bradley held up a flash drive. "He's going to order the same exact coffee and the same exact breakfast pastry he eats every morning and then he'll sit and open his laptop and pause to take a ridiculous photo of his coffee cup, because it's the most exciting thing that will happen to him all day." He indicated the flash drive. "Once we're in there, this needs forty-five seconds plugged into his laptop to do its dirty work. It's your job to keep him distracted for those forty-five seconds."

"How am I supposed to do that?"

"Follow my lead. Use your instincts. You'll catch on."

"That sounds like a very bad plan."

"It's a great plan. Trust me." Bradley pushed him forward. "But we shouldn't walk in together. You go ahead. Order some coffee, a newspaper and grab a table near him."

Santiago hesitated. "But how will I distract him?"

Bradley gave him an encouraging shove. "You're smart, Father. You got this."

Santiago stumbled forward and approached the counter. Jonathan Feeney was just ahead of him, walking away from the barista to claim an open table near the window.

"Café con leche," he muttered. Santiago's heart beat erratically. *You got this, Father.*

No, Santiago countered mentally. *El padre no tiene nada.*

Santiago looked up at the young man behind the counter. The swirl of a black tattoo – a diabolical bird of some sort – and the nickel-sized black gauges in his earlobes reminded him he was not standing in some San Juan panaderia.

"It's coffee with lots of milk. Half strong coffee, half milk."

The barista looked insulted. "But you knew that already," Santiago added. He picked up a *Post* and the coffee, paid and claimed the table behind Feeney.

He opened the paper and looked over at Bradley, who was ordering at the countertop, tapping his foot impatiently. A moment passed. Bradley swooped up his coffee and slid into the table in front of Feeney. Santiago peeked around the side of his paper and threw Bradley a look. Feeney had his phone out, centering its screen on his coffee cup. It emitted a fake shutter sound.

"What now?" he mouthed to Bradley.

Bradley offered an encouraging thumbs up.

"GET THE FUCK ON THE FLOOR!"

A woman perched on a stool in the corner looked up and screamed.

Santiago leapt to his feet, nearly spilling his coffee on himself. A bulky man in a puffy black winter coat and ski mask was whirling in front of the counter fifteen feet away.

Feeney cowered as if he were trying to hide behind his laptop.

"I SAID GET THE FUCK ON THE FLOOR!" A gun blasted twice into the ceiling. The gunman whirled toward Santiago and aimed. Santi instinctually flew forward, slamming into Feeney, toppling him to the floor to deny the gunman a convenient target.

The woman screamed again. The tattooed barista behind the counter started shouting. "Stay cool, man! Stay cool. Just take all the money. Here! There's no reason for anyone to get hurt."

Feeney struggled beneath him, as if he were trying to escape out the back wall.

"Stay still or you'll get us both killed," growled Santiago.

He turned. Bradley was also lying nearby, hands clutched over his head. *Damn it*, thought Santiago.

"HURRY THE FUCK UP!" the gunman screamed.

"Here! Here! Take it! Take it and go!"

"COME OUT FROM BEHIND THE COUNTER! GET ON THE FLOOR!"

The coffee shop employees skittered around the countertop and sprawled across the floor beside them.

"YOU!"

Santiago looked up and found himself looking into the barrel of a gun. "COUNT BACKWARDS FROM THIRTY. AND IF YOU WANT TO STAY ALIVE, YOU'D BETTER COUNT LOUD! NO ONE GETS UP UNTIL HE'S DONE! WHOEVER I CATCH MOVING BEFORE HE FINISHES DIES!"

Santiago began counting.

"LOUDER!"

Santiago shouted the numbers, his heart pounding. When he reached twenty, he thought he heard the coffee shop door, and risked a peek.

"Keep counting!" Feeney screamed, quivering beneath him.

Santiago resumed counting, waiting five more seconds after finishing before pulling himself off Feeney and looking around.

"You all right?" the barista asked.

His mouth dry with fright, Santiago nodded. He glanced at Bradley and pulled him off the floor. Bradley quickly drew a finger across his neck and headed straight for the door.

"Call the cops!" the barista ordered another worker and he went to check on the woman in the corner.

"I want to thank you." Jonathan Feeney turned Santiago around and seized his hand. He began pumping it. "I just froze there, I couldn't move. You saved my life."

Santiago nodded distractedly. The thought of appearing in the newspaper for the second time in a week made him shudder. He gestured to the door with his thumb. "I actually should go."

He pulled himself free from Feeney and blasted out the door. Bradley was just rounding the corner, walking at a clip. Sirens approached from two different directions. Santiago jogged around the corner. Bradley was sliding behind the wheel of a car parked thirty yards from the intersection.

Santiago ran to the car, threw open the passenger door and slid in. Bradley was rubbing his forehead with both hands. "Unbelievable!" Santiago gasped and held up his own hands. They were still quivering from fear. "Someday, if I ever teach a class on literature, I'm going to use this morning as a lesson in irony. You tell me to create a distraction in a coffee shop. Meanwhile another guy walks in and shoots up the place, making it impossible to create a proper distraction." He took a deep breath to calm himself. "What now? If Feeney sees me again, he's going to recognize me."

The first police car blasted into the intersection, skidding to a halt. Santiago shivered and realized his window was down. "Hey, start the car so I can put up my window. It's freezing."

Bradley didn't move.

An old woman pushing a grocery carrier shuffled by. Her hand flew up to the open window, causing Santiago to flinch. An envelope landed in his lap. The woman shuffled past.

Another police car roared up.

Santiago looked down at the cash spilling out of the old lady's envelope. Unable to contain himself, Santiago blasphemed as he suddenly realized what Bradley had done. "Jesucristo!"

Bradley donned latex surgical gloves and blew into a large manila envelope to open it. He seized the cash-filled envelope dropped by the old lady, stuffed it into the manila envelope and sealed it.

"What are you doing?" Santiago seized the manila envelope and held it away from him. "This is wrong!"

"Ooh." Bradley shook his head. "Your fingerprints are now on that envelope, Father." He reached out for the envelope, but Santiago held it higher. "I'm going to need that back, Father Torres. Otherwise, you're going to have to go to confession for stealing."

Santiago looked down at the writing scrawled across the envelope's front: Starbucks Manager. It was followed by the street address of the coffee shop.

Santiago was yelling now. "You tell me to create a distraction and you pull that stunt?"

Bradley plucked the envelope out of Santiago's hand and lowered his own window. A bicycle courier, whizzing past at thirty miles per hour, yanked it from Bradley's hand.

"You did a great job pinning Feeney to the floor." Bradley then sounded incredulous. "You didn't actually think that was a real hold-up, did you?"

"Hell, yes! You could have given someone a heart attack!"

Bradley scoffed. "That didn't even rank up there with a triple-shot espresso. No, that was just James. A nice kid. He works in my company's front office answering phones." He turned to Santiago. "Did I ever tell you that James holds the Maryland state high school track record in the hundred yard dash?"

Bradley's smug grin dared him to laugh. He started the car and carefully swung out of the space. "But that's not why I chose James. He was actually the only one in the office who owned a gun."

"Your mother would be so proud."

"Well, not a real gun. Just a starter pistol he stole from a ref he didn't particularly like back in high school." He paused. "Which is why there were no actual holes in the ceiling."

"I almost threw up on Jonathan Feeney."

"Just don't tell anyone James took the starter pistol, Father. I wouldn't want him to get busted for stealing." Bradley laughed out loud and gunned the car down the street.

"Just tell me you successfully inserted the damned smart drive into his computer," Santiago growled.

Bradley held it up. "We're in, Padre. We're in!"

Chapter 33: The Baptized Baby

Santiago asked Bradley to drop him off in Georgetown, where a walk would help him think. He wandered the cobblestone streets aimlessly for an hour, skirting the campus in case security was still on the lookout for him. He refused go to the nearest Metro stop and hop on the subway to Abby's house. Arriving before the end of the workday would be staring straight in the face the fact that he no longer had a job.

The night before, Abby had been quiet when she got back from school. She just scrunched up her freckled nose. "I'm so sorry, Santi."

She had waited, of course. Waited for him to start talking. He stood in silence, unwilling to discuss the morning for fear it would tumble into admitting he had later assaulted Bob Stanley.

Doing so would support the school whispers. *Something's changed. Something broke after his close friend's death. Father Torres has snapped!*

Abby stood beside the kitchen table until his silence became awkward. Then she climbed the steps and tucked into her bedroom, where she spent the evening grading papers.

Santiago shook his head at the awkwardness of the memory. He walked, his mind skittering over the jumble of clues he had uncovered regarding the Stewards, berating himself for the disastrous confrontation with Stanley and guessing at what Bradley Freeman had up his sleeve. Yet in the whirlpool of thoughts, one issue – a final, unlikely stone left unturned – bubbled repeatedly to the surface.

It brought him to P Street's intersection with Forthy-Third Street.

The street from which Cannon's papers and portions of Jasper's thesis had supposedly been mailed. When Nico had told him the address, it lodged in Santi's mind: 4354 P Street, Northwest.

Of course, Nico suggested it was likely just a fake address to cover the identity of the real sender. Yet whoever had been feeding him information had been doing a very good job of it. Like Jasper, perhaps random details weren't their habit.

Santiago strode past the Georgetown neighborhood's ornate row houses and homes. Halfway down the block, he halted before a stately, wide home with a brass placard engraved with 4354.

He paused at the bottom of its brick steps, his heart clattering in his chest. Had the last two days not been insane enough? Wouldn't ringing the bell drag another potentially innocent person into danger?

He studied the city block for anyone who could be following him. Its homes looked like prim ladies with parasols parading before a cotillion. Their painted brick facades and brass knockers, like colonial era homes in Charleston and Old Savannah, whispered wealth and history.

The wind was blowing inland and Santiago could smell the canal far down the hill. The town's early businessmen, owners of the shops, factories and warehouses down on the waterfront, had built Georgetown's houses. Up the hill from the stink, the rich men enjoyed their gardens, homes and sumptuous kitchens – all staffed by slaves.

Now the street's brick sidewalks were empty. At mid-day the street held but ten empty cars.

A compact auto staccatoed by on the cobblestones, two young college girls laughing inside.

Santiago felt remarkably uneasy.

The ringing of his cell phone startled him. Nico. His fifteenth call in less than a day. Bob Stanley had called his brother.

Santiago looked up from the phone to the door of the beautiful white home. He turned off his cell and slid it into his pocket. He seized the metal railing, yanking himself up the steps to the small porch. A high-backed rocker sat there, arms jutted outward, like an ancient woman with her hands on her hips. "What do you think you're doing here?" it seemed to inquire.

Neatly printed above the home's doorbell was the name Cannon.

The name caused Santiago to catch his breath. He screwed up the courage and rang it.

The deadbolt slowly slid back and the door creaked open six inches. A young, blonde-haired boy no older than seven stared up at him.

"Um, hello."

Silence.

"Is your mom home?"

"Nope."

Santiago smiled awkwardly.

A muffled but gentle scolding burbled down the hallway. "How many times have I told you to wait for me until you answer that door?"

In a moment the door opened wider and Santiago found himself looking at a woman in her late sixties. Her short silver hair framed an attractive, lined face, punctuated by eyes that were startlingly gray – like liquid steel. The woman was dressed in expensive but casual clothes.

Georgetown senior chic.

Santiago offered a friendly smile.

"May I help you?"

"Well," Santiago gave an awkward laugh. "I'm in town for the week and was just walking by and recognized this house as belonging to a friend I had a long time ago. When I saw the name on the bell, I just felt compelled to ring it."

The woman smiled. "What was your friend's name?"

"Philip Cannon."

The woman's jaw dropped.

"I'm Philip Cannon!" The little boy bounced excitedly.

Santiago looked down in shock. "You're Philip Cannon?"

"Uh huh," the boy nodded. "Philip Cannon Stevens! But I didn't know we were friends a long time ago. Did you go to Visitation Preschool too?"

"You couldn't be over forty." The woman face had taken on a taut, suspicious look, like canvas hastily stretched in preparation for a brush.

"The boy's father, perhaps?"

"My son's name is James Stevens and my husband, who's deceased, was David Stevens. How did you know Philip Cannon?"

"It was a long time ago."

"A long time ago indeed." Her arm wrapped around the boy and she pulled him back toward her. "I don't know what you're playing at, but my father died more than two decades before you were born, sir." She emphasized *sir* in a way that made clear she didn't think him worthy of the honorific.

Santiago pulled on his ear awkwardly. The conversation hadn't simply taken an awkward turn. It had plunged off the awkward cliff. "Ma'am, I apologize. If you'll permit me to begin again."

Her face showed little inclination for patience.

Santiago took out his wallet. "I wasn't entirely truthful. I'm not just in town this week." He held out his driver's license, whose photo showed him in a priest's collar. "My name is Father Santiago Torres. I'm a Jesuit priest from over at Gonzaga High School."

She squinted. "The one from Sunday's *Post*?"

An embarrassed laugh. "Not a bright, shining moment, I suppose."

"So you didn't know my father at all."

"If your father is Philip Cannon, no." He held up his hand and shot out the words like a machine gun to keep the door from slamming. "Last week a lockbox was found on Georgetown's campus inscribed with Philip Cannon, 1953. Afterwards, an important package was mailed to me and it listed this home as its return address."

The woman's lips pulled to one side and her chin trembled. She looked down and patted the boy's head. "Perhaps you should come in."

Santiago stepped inside the beautiful home, whose wood floors reflected the dappled sunlight filtering through the windows. The woman's house was enormous compared to most Georgetown row houses. Spotless and well maintained, its antique furniture – even the dust motes that floated through the hallway sunlight – reflected education and status.

"Philip, why don't you go put on the television so Father Torres and I can talk."

"But I already watched a show today, Nan."

She tousled his hair. "Today you get two."

The boy jumped excitedly and ran down the hallway.

The woman turned and extended a hand. "I'm Susan Stevens, formerly Susan Cannon. As I mentioned, Philip Cannon was my father. He bought this home." She nodded down the hallway in the direction the boy had gone. "My grandson was named for him."

She led Santiago to the back of the house to a large sunroom with a table and chairs. It sat off an impressive kitchen and overlooked a large, fenced yard whose garden lent an air of bucolic peace to the place.

"Can I offer you something to drink? Perhaps some tea?"

Santiago nodded and a moment later, the woman set two teacups onto the table and they sat.

"I'm sincerely sorry," Santiago began. "When I saw the name on the bell, I just rang it. Then I didn't know what to say."

She stared out the windows across the garden and let slip a light sigh. "I sent no package to you, Father Torres. That's just another strange occurrence to chalk up to the mystery surrounding my father's death, I suppose." She paused. "Or I prefer to say murder."

The woman's brave demeanor softened and her fingers crept up as if to still her trembling lips. "One doesn't discuss such things in polite company, but that's what it was. Even six decades on, it's difficult to say it aloud. My father was murdered in the spring of 1953. I was six years old at the time. He was found a few blocks from here, lying on the steep steps leading from Prospect Street down to Canal Road."

Santiago frowned. "I apologize for triggering such a bad memory. My stepbrother lost his mother when he was a young boy. I think the grief of losing a parent at so young an age uniquely marks a person."

The phantom of a grateful smile creased her cheeks and her eyes filled. "After sixty years, the memory still taps on my shoulder each time I see a little girl or little boy with his father, like Philip and my son. Everyone in the room may be smiling at the child's laughter, but there's this small ache right here." She placed her hand over her heart. "Not for me, mind you. I think I feel the ache more for my dad. For what he missed – what we missed together."

"Your son is very lucky."

"Yes. And little Philip." She offered a quiet laugh to lighten the mood. "And me. How fortunate and blessed I've been to see them both grow up."

She blew across her tea and took a cautious sip. "The lockbox you mentioned, Father Torres. Does it seem new, as if someone might be pulling a tasteless prank?"

Santiago shook his head. "I don't believe it was a joke. I think it belonged to a man named Philip Cannon, who hid it in Dahlgren Chapel in 1953."

Susan Steven's chin trembled again, her face a fraying knot of conflict. "May I ask what was in the box?"

"I wasn't the one who found it, so I'm not entirely sure." He paused. "This may sound like an odd question but have you heard of the Georgetown Stewards?"

A nod. "I'm told they're now thought of as a joke or legend on campus." She shook her head to convey her doubt. "I'm not quite as familiar with the campus as my son and husband were. The Jesuits wouldn't allow women to attend Georgetown's College of Arts and Sciences until 1969. I attended Wesleyan instead."

Santiago offered a sympathetic smile. "This whole month has been a lesson in how imperfect my religious order has been." He tilted his head. "Would you have gone to Georgetown if you could have?"

Susan smiled, her steel eyes dancing. "What sane woman would wish to consort with such ruffians?"

Santiago laughed.

"Of course I would have gone. Attending Georgetown is a long-time Cannon family tradition. It's a wonderful school! Fortunately they came to their senses and began admitting women after I had graduated." She sipped her tea. "But back to the Stewards."

"You know something about them?"

"I know my father was part of a group he refused to discuss with my mother. My mother once told me that in the early years of their marriage he was forever going out here or there. Business dealings, he insisted. She even suspected he was being unfaithful. Ultimately she had to make peace with the fact that while she wasn't sharing him with another woman, she would have to share him with this silly, secret society if they were to remain together. She never met them all, but was certain it was the same group. But if she had her druthers, he would have had nothing to do with them."

The recollection plucked another memory from the past, this one sparking a smile on Susan Cannon's face. "My late husband David was also a proud Georgetown alum. It made my mother immediately suspicious and she wanted me to have nothing to do with him."

A light laugh trickled from her lips. "I can still recall the first night she had us both over for dinner. The conversation was quite light and convivial. Then, out of the blue, she became agitated and announced, 'All this is well and good, David Stevens, but it's time we got down to brass tacks. I'm going to ask you a single question and if you lie to me, I'll know it outright and you'll be banned from this house for eternity. And, if you happen to give me the wrong answer, you'll still be banned for eternity.'

"Poor David turned white as a ghost. Meanwhile, I thought my heart would gallop out of my chest in panic. My mother was telling him the truth about her talent for catching liars. As a child, the moment I told a lie, my mother immediately called me out on it. David and I both thought she was going to ask us..." Susan paused, embarrassed. "Well, it was the sixties after all. Instead, she shook a spoon at him and growled, "Look me in the eye, Mr. Stevens, and tell me if you're a Steward.'

"I thought David's head was going to fall forward into his soup bowl in relief." Susan smiled. "But my mother was dead serious. After what had happened to my father, if she had concluded he was a Steward, she would have thrown him out of the house and that would have been the end of it."

"What exactly did your husband say in response?"

Susan's eyes danced. "He managed to stutter, 'I'm an Irish Catholic Democrat, ma'am. I hope that doesn't make me a Steward.' Poor David had no idea what she was talking about. So, fortunately, he wasn't banned for eternity."

Santiago laughed.

She traced the rim of her teacup with her finger and turned serious again. "While my mother often refused to speak of the Stewards, I've pieced some of it together over the years. She was certain my father was one. And she was certain that being a Steward is what got him killed."

"So she didn't believe the police's report that it was a mugging that had turned violent?"

Susan scoffed. "In Georgetown in the 1950s? He was found on the same steps they found that poor drunk man last weekend. Another Georgetown alumnus, apparently. Terrible tragedy."

Santiago looked at her grimly and remained silent. How could he even explain?

But she read his silence and her face turned ashen.

"How stupid of me! It never occurred to me until just now. It's tied to the appearance of that lockbox. That man was a Steward, wasn't he?"

"I'm not certain. I've learned there were actually two Stewards groups on campus. I think one was simply a front, a cover for the real group. Mr. Kelly may have been the go between."

Susan Stevens looked out over her garden. "So you believe my father's lockbox contained information about the Stewards?"

Santiago nodded. "I had a friend, Jasper Willoughs, another Jesuit priest. He was a historian. When the lockbox was found in Dalgren Chapel during its renovation, he was given the documents after the names of several Jesuit-owned plantations were spotted among them. Those plantations were the focus of Jasper's doctoral thesis. But there was more. What my friend discovered caused him to lock himself in his room and completely rewrite his doctoral dissertation. And I'm fairly sure it also got him killed."

Santiago continued, retelling the arrival of the package after Jasper's funeral and its theft from the school safe.

Susan sat in silence until he finished. "Whatever was in that box must be terribly important to cost the lives of two people." She gestured down the hallway. "They certainly turned this house upside down after my father's funeral to find it."

"They did?"

She nodded toward the beautifully landscaped garden in the backyard. "They even brought in a backhoe, dug down four or five feet everywhere out there."

"That didn't strike your mother as odd?"

"Odd? Quite to the contrary. She immediately knew something suspicious was going on. She just couldn't figure out what. One of my father's friends insisted that a group of wealthy and generous alumni who were very fond of my father had set up a charitable fund for the children. He told her they wanted to make a gift of fixing up the yard and home." Her steel gray eyes turned to liquid again. "The Stewards took away my father and, in exchange, gave us the most beautiful garden in Georgetown."

Santiago took a sip from his teacup to give the woman time to recover. "Do you have any memory of your father's friends, the men your mother suspected were Stewards?"

"I actually remember only one, one of my father's closest friends at Georgetown. He was the only one ever to come by the home after my father died. He supposedly represented the rest. For a number of years afterward, he came by, checking up on us, poking around. Then, one day, I heard my mother yelling at him. Afterwards he never came back."

"Do you recall his name?"

Susan searched her memory. "McGary? McCleary?" She shook her head. "I was so young at the time and it's been so long, I can't remember."

"It's a shame your mother isn't still alive," Santiago finished his tea. "I would have liked to have asked her."

Susan Stevens looked at him oddly. "What makes you think my mother has died? She's up in her bedroom, watching *Judge Judy*."

Santiago's teacup clattered onto its saucer.

Chapter 34: Old Friends

"I assumed you knew. It's why the name Cannon is still on the doorbell. This is actually her home." Susan Jordan gestured to the steps and they climbed to the second floor. "I just don't know what luck you'll have getting her to talk about the Stewards. She's stubbornly refused for years. It has to be two decades since I last tried."

Santiago followed her down a long hallway with dark wood floors covered by a thick, ornamental runner. The prattle of a television trickled down to him. A man and woman were bickering over a dog's destruction of an apartment, the judge interrupting to berate them for interrupting. Heavy paintings hung between the hall's bedroom doors. Their ornate gold frames propped up stern, nineteenth century faces, looking grimly convinced that modern America was populated by fools.

Susan pointed to a partially closed door.

Santiago stepped through. An old woman sipped air beside a humidifier that puffed clouds of mist. Her face, a wrinkled, fleshy peach, parted with a curious smile. The same strong, steel gray eyes as her daughter. Santiago felt a moment's intimidation, thawed by the ancient woman's own nervous act: she pulled a shawl closed across her well-pressed blouse. With a gnarled finger she muted the TV.

"Mom, I've brought a friend that wants to talk to you a little about Daddy."

The way Susan Stevens spoke of her father unsettled Santiago. It seemed he was intruding on a long, troubled life that had finally made peace with itself. "Maybe I should go. Perhaps another time."

A soft but insistent noise made him look back at Mrs. Cannon. "Sit." She patted the chair beside her. "No one asks me about Philip anymore."

"This is Father Santiago Torres. Over from Gonzaga. He found something that belonged to Daddy."

The old woman patted the chair more insistently. "What did you say your name was?"

"Santiago." His face reddened as the peach puckered its lips and studied him. She leaned over, her hand flapping among newspapers in the credenza beside her chair. She plucked out one. It disgorged a magnifying glass when she pressed it flat in her lap.

Sunday's front page.

Santiago gave an embarrassed sigh. "Yes. It's the same Santiago."

She ignored him and studied the article again while he squirmed.

He waited, clenching his toes inside his sneakers, until she spoke. "I knew a Jesuit from your school many years ago. A Charlie Breckinridge. I don't imagine he's still alive."

"Father Breckinridge?" The happy recollection of his exchange with the old priest caused Santiago to relax and he finally sat. "In fact he is. He's retired, of course, but he still lives at the school. In fact, Father Breckinridge may be my only ally left there."

"Ally? Only people with enemies talk of having allies." She slid the paper back into the credenza and her eyes narrowed. "Now, Susan said you found something belonging to my Philip?"

Santiago was grateful she had changed the topic. "It was a gray lockbox, actually, found in Dahlgren Chapel on campus. It had his name and the date, April 1953, on it."

A long wrinkled finger moved back and forth across her chin. "The month I lost Philip."

Santiago paused, unsure how to proceed.

"And you've lost its contents and have come here to find out what was inside."

Santiago's eyebrows rose. "How did you know?"

"If it contained all the answers you wanted, would you be sitting here?"

"I suppose not."

"Plus, it is how they operate." The old woman pinched the plural pronoun. "*They* have their fingers into everything in this city. If Philip's lockbox turned up, they knew of it before the sun set."

She appraised Santiago with a look that made him sit up straight. "Given your name and the lilt you give your sentences, I don't suspect you are. But I'll look you in the eye and ask anyway. Are you a Steward, Father Torres? And don't lie to me. I can tell the difference between a lie and the truth as sure as I can tell a rhinoceros from a giraffe."

Susan Stevens chuckled.

Santiago's words were firm. "It's my goal to have all the Stewards thrown in prison for the rest of their lives."

His anger made the woman pause, her chin tremble. "So now you're going to tell me that Philip's hiding that lockbox has caused someone else to be killed."

Santi felt torn between reassuring the woman and telling the truth. "I don't know if it's fair to put his death at the feet of your husband, Mrs. Cannon. Truth is, most days right now, I don't know what to think. But my friend, Jasper, knew what was in that box and now he's dead."

The old woman placed a gnarled hand on Santiago's knee. "I'm so terribly sorry."

"Jasper was a Jesuit priest like me."

"A Jesuit?" The woman seemed startled. "Really?"

Santiago examined the woman's face, flushed with emotion. "I'm guessing you don't know what your husband put in that lockbox? I was hoping you might have a copy of it somewhere."

She shook her head. "If the Stewards ever suspected I did, I would have been dead years ago. Philip kept so many secrets from me. 'For my own good,' he used to say." She pursed her lips. "The arrogance of youth. There was no good in it at all."

She leaned forward again and rapped her finger against Santiago's knee. "There's one thing I can tell you for sure. My Philip was a good man. And when he found he was a member of a group that was up to no good, he tried to put a stop to it. You can bet your bottom dollar that's what he aimed to do with that lockbox. And it cost him his life."

"Your daughter told me there was another man – a friend who may have been a Steward. He was around here quite a bit after your husband's murder."

"Paul McInerny, Philip's classmate and one of his two closest friends. For several years afterward, Paul kept coming around, checking up on us. He was all over the house after Philip's murder, insisting on helping to put his effects in order, tearing up rooms, renovating this and that." The old woman nodded to the back of the house. "He even oversaw the installation of the garden. All under the guise of gifts from classmates."

"Did you believe him?"

"No more then than I do now. It didn't take long before I grew suspicious. I finally told him not to knock on my door until he was willing to tell me the truth." She shrugged. "He never came back. I didn't know what Paul was searching for more than a half century ago but you can be sure it was that lockbox. It was hidden in Dahlgren Chapel, you say?"

"In a small space in the floor beneath the altar."

Old Mrs. Cannon gave a satisfied laugh. "That was Philip for you. He probably enjoyed the irony of sticking it right under their noses – right in a spot that would be stared at by hundreds of Georgetown students every week."

Santiago smiled at her giddiness. "Would you happen to know if Paul McInerny is still alive?"

She shook her head. "He died in the late 1970s. Of cancer."

"Would you have any other information about him?"

"Nothing really. Paul was quite private. He was married and had a family. His obituary in the *Post* told me that much. I do recall Phillip telling me he worked in the Treasury Department in the 50's. Later, I read he was named to the Federal Reserve Board. After his retirement from there, I lost track of him until I saw his death notice."

"You never met his wife or any of his children?"

Mrs. Cannon shook her head.

Santiago reached for his wallet and extracted the one dollar bill with the burst of yellow highlighter around George

Washington's head. "An odd question, but does the word Outremer or this bill have any meaning for you?"

She reached into the newspaper to retrieve her magnifying glass and studied the front of the bill before turning it over to examine its back.

"My friend, Jasper, took the contents out of the lockbox to work on his thesis. His thesis and the materials were removed from his room after his death. Copies of a portion of it were sent to me in a package that listed your house as its return address."

"Sent from here?" The elderly woman's voice rose with alarm. "I sent nothing!"

Santiago nodded. "I know. But I think the person who did wanted me to know about you."

Mrs. Cannon placed a crooked finger over her lips in thought.

"Unfortunately, someone broke into Gonzaga and stole the contents of the package I received, so all I'm left with is the Outremer reference and the dollar clue, the only thing Jasper left behind in the lockbox."

"Perhaps, like Philip, your friend hid the documents, knowing the Stewards would be looking for them. And he left the dollar bill as a clue to their location."

Santiago agreed. "He probably hoped I would know what he was referring to. Unfortunately I'm not as smart as Jasper thought."

Mrs. Cannon's arthritic hand returned the yellowed dollar bill to Santiago. "I'm sorry I'm not able to be more help," she said. "I certainly wish it was in my power to stop the Stewards."

"Thank you, Mrs. Cannon. I appreciate your talking to me." Santiago nodded to Susan Stevens and rose. The two crossed to the door. The old woman waited politely for them to pass through it before she turned the TV back on.

The judge had ruled in favor of the plaintiff and she and the defendant were being interviewed. "Are you still friends?" a voice asked them.

Santiago paused at the door and he turned to Mrs. Cannon, who muted the TV again. "Mrs. Cannon, you said Paul McInerny was one of your husband's two best friends. Do you mind me asking who the other was?"

"Not at all. Another Georgetown classmate." Mrs. Cannon's lips slashed a narrow line of old anger across her face. "Named Charlie Breckinridge."

Chapter 35: An Old Headmaster

It took Santiago ninety minutes to get back to the school and hop the back gate to the quadrangle again. The day was largely gone, the late winter sun slipping behind the dilapidated D.C. row houses that leaned into the streets behind Gonzaga.

He could still hear the old man's southern drawl hanging over the place from the day prior. *Well, well, aren't you the shit-stirrer?*

Shit-stirrer. A zookeeper, Breckinridge had called him. *You ain't much of a zookeeper if you forget to rattle the cages.*

The elevator to the Jesuit residence stopped with a shudder at the third floor. Santi pulled back the retractable cage-door, likely the same elevator cage Charlie Breckinridge had rattled open when he was Gonzaga headmaster.

The old man was a complete puzzle.

Santiago had lived with Breckinridge for half a decade yet their exchanged words wouldn't fill a single yellowed page in a brittle book. The old man, whose spine had been bent into a comma by the decades, was a silent statue in the community room. Wheeled in with a nod in greeting. Now nodding off. Wheeled out with a nod in departure.

Something about Breckinridge's ancient, impenetrable silence made Santiago uncomfortable. It was easier to pretend he was just an occasionally animated piece of furniture.

What perplexed him was that the man was discussed with reverence by Gonzaga staff. Breckinridge, the school's old-timers bragged, had bucked Washington, D.C.'s big shots in the fifties. Even Cardinal Thompson, who had the ear of the pope, had ordered Breckinridge, more than a half century prior, not to rock the boat, not to get ahead of himself.

Had he listened?

The old-timers loved retelling his story at the annual Alumni Smoker. Breckinridge, a native of Virginia just across the Shenandoah from Harpers Ferry, was the first born son of a cigar-chomping, hard-drinking owner of rolling hills of tobacco fields. The land was plucked clean each fall by a legion of lean, black sharecroppers, whose sparse wood and tin-roof shanties lined the dirt roads of his family's farm. Breckinridge's father and grandfather were even long-serving state senators, staunch defenders of the Southern way of life, a paradoxical stew of genteel charm and twisted racism. In their combined careers they had proudly erected the sturdy architecture of Jim Crow in the great commonwealth of Virginia.

Sic Semper Tyrranis: Death, always, to tyrants.

Unless they're the *proper* kind.

Breckinridge's drawl and callused hands were artifacts from a rural life that populated the Virginia-Maryland border for three centuries. His childhood was now paved over, populated by shopping malls, gas stations and chain restaurants – all feeding suburbs whose winding, circular roads lead nowhere.

Breckinridge and Santiago had a single conversation in the four years prior to Santiago's firing, just days after he was appointed Gonzaga's new headmaster. Santiago had come up to the residence that afternoon, leaned against a chair in the day room and stared out the window over the quadrangle. He was mulling over his first phone conversation with a furious parent when the unexpected voice startled him. "Hmm," Breckinridge flicked a finger toward the Channel Twelve news reporter, known for his exaggerated reenactments of mundane crimes and events. "Would ya look at that."

"Look at what?"

"That new Italian restaurant."

Santiago spotted the sign behind the reporter. "The Olive Garden?"

"Hmm," Breckinridge nodded. "You a historian?"

"Yes, sir."

"They're paving over where Jeb Stuart died for its parking lot." The old man coughed, waiting for the name to sink in. "Best cavalry officer in the Confederacy. Ain't timing everything? If old Jeb had been born just one hundred fifty years later, instead of getting his ass shot off his horse right there, he coulda ordered lasagna with one of them fancy Mexican drinks."

Breckinridge looked at him when he drawled *Mexican*.

Soy Puertoriqeño, pendejo, Santiago wanted to say, but it came out in English: "A margarita, you mean?"

A half laugh and a shake of the head. "My pappy and grandpappy are rollin' in their graves. Sometime after the war, the world just started movin' too fast for most people to keep up."

And that was it. Breckinridge fell completely silent for four years.

From the comments Santiago pegged the old priest as an old-school, southern racist – an image reinforced by the black and white photos of him standing on St. Aloysius' Church steps. Black cassock, severe crew cut and smile, standing with each graduating class from 1954 to 1965. The photos lined the walls of the administration building, each six inches distant from the next, ticking off the Roman Catholic history of the capital.

But after he'd made a remark about Breckinridge, Santiago had been set straight by Pearl.

"Hold that wagging tongue of yours before someone takes you for an idiot. That old man is no racist. He desegregated this school when he was headmaster. Alumni swore they wouldn't give another dime." Pearl shook her finger at him. "He did it anyway."

"Breckinridge?" Santiago was incredulous.

"Father Breckinridge," she corrected him. "Tell you what. He wasn't a high-fallutin, know-it-all like some of the priests who have sat in that office." She nodded at the headmaster's door.

Santiago smiled. "Present company excluded, I hope."

"Jury's still out."

Breckinridge wasn't just Gonzaga headmaster, Pearl continued. On Fridays and Saturdays he drove the bus for the football team all over town. "Took Marcus Samuels, the first black boy to play football for Gonzaga, to a championship game," she said. "Thirty boys were on the team. They worked hard all year to reach that goal and were undefeated," Pearl added. "Out of respect for Father Breckinridge, all the other private school teams they played – even the ones in North Virginia, which didn't desegregate until the end of the decade – looked the other way. They just ignored the fact that one of Gonzaga's best players wasn't white. Father Breckinridge didn't even have to ask. Until they got to that championship game, when the coach on a Virginia team insisted that both schools were still in a segregated division and that Marcus Samuels had no right to play."

Pearl tsked. "Gonzaga's coach at the time went over to Marcus and started apologizing to the boy, explaining he wouldn't be able to play in the game. But Breckinridge strode over, red-faced, and stopped him. Made the entire team stand up and they crossed the field to confront the opposing coach together."

Pearl's voice rose. "Breckinridge walked right up to the man, his nose not two inches from his face, his cassock whipping in the wind like some furious Moses come down from the mountaintop with God's law in hand. 'I will not have Gonzaga students play another team coached by a bigot and a fool,' he shouted."

Pearl sat back triumphantly.

"So the other coach gave in?"

"Not at all. Gonzaga forfeited the championship game on principle. 'We're a team,' Breckinridge said. 'We play together or we go home.'"

"How'd the other boys on the team take it?"

"Father instantly became their hero. As he turned to walk away, the other coach said, 'If you wanna consort with niggers, that's your prerogative, Father. But me, I'm just gonna take my pure white chalk and scratch this championship in the win column.'"

Santiago's eyebrows rose.

"Breckinridge stopped dead in his tracks. He reached up and pulled his white collar out of his cassock and handed it to Marcus. Then he turned around, right there, in front of all the students. With a single punch, he laid that coach out cold on the fifty yard line," Pearl smiled. "In the middle of a stadium completely filled with parents and students from the opposing school. Then he turned to the other team's kids and said, 'When your coach wakes up, tell him Charlie Breckinridge chalked this one up in his win column too."

Pearl gave a deep, satisfied laugh. "Don't get me wrong. I don't advocate violence. I was all about Martin Luther King. But sometimes, you just gotta poke a fool in the nose!" She quickly waved Santiago's smile away. "My point is Breckinridge's no racist, Father Torres. He's a great man. Mark my words."

Santiago grunted and yanked the elevator door closed behind him. The truth about Breckinridge, like America's past, probably wasn't as neatly black and white as Pearl thought. Mrs. Cannon's lined face expressed a profound antipathy toward the old priest. Clearly she blamed him for Philip Cannon's death.

Santiago walked down the hallway and reached into his pocket to finally turn on his cell phone. Twenty-six missed calls. Someone had given the media his cell number. He thumbed through the list and sighed. At the top, three calls from Nico alone in the last hour.

He dropped his cell phone back into his pocket and walked into the day room. Brother Sinclair, sitting in a far chair, looked over his reading glasses. "Ah, Santiago," he said, avoiding the most obvious topic. "The residence at Georgetown called, looking for the number planning to attend John DeMaio's sixtieth birthday. Are you planning to attend?"

Santi shook his head. "Not the best week for public appearances, Sinclair. I'm going to pass." Santi jerked a thumb at the empty chair that usually held Breckinridge. "Father Breckinridge?"

"I wheeled him down to the church to hear afternoon confessions. I have to go down in a minute to retrieve him."

Santiago held up a hand. "Don't trouble yourself. I'll go get him. I need to speak with him about an old friend."

Sinclair nodded cautiously and Santiago left before the brother could change his mind. A few minutes later, Santiago was back downstairs, passing through the administration building and the door that led to the church's sacristy. He strode across the altar, only remembering to genuflect when he spotted a man kneeling and completing his penance in the back of the church.

He walked down the center aisle and nodded. The man looked away, avoiding his gaze.

Santiago tried to brush off the snub, but the sting represented what life likely held for him in coming weeks: Father Santiago Torres, local celebrity. Not actually famous for anything notable, but notably notorious, the sacked headmaster of Gonzaga High School.

Santiago reached the confessionals and shelved the self-pity. He listened for any murmuring but could only hear the hissing traffic out on North Capitol Street, jockeying past the church's oak doors. He almost knocked on the compartment that held the old priest, then changed his mind.

He slipped into the opposite compartment, where parishioners knelt to whisper their sins. He shut the door and let his eyes adjust to the darkness. He lowered himself, his weight making the kneeler squeak. He waited a moment, staring at the opaque plastic window, drilled with pinholes to let voices pass while hiding the sinner's face.

A faint rustling came from the other side. "You may begin," Breckinridge's ancient, gravelly voice prompted.

Breckinridge waited a moment before speaking more loudly. "Go ahead."

"Actually," Santiago responded. "I'm hoping to hear a confession."

Chapter 36: A Soul Unburdened

A hollow laugh trickled through the pinholes in the confessional window. "Then you're smart enough to be headmaster, after all."

"I'm not sure how I should take that."

"It's what I call a compliment."

Silence.

Santi cut to the chase. "I had a long talk with Philip Cannon's wife today."

"Elizabeth?" The old priest didn't speak for a long time. Santi shifted, the kneeler creaking again. Breckinridge's voice softened and drifted, as if it were floating somewhere distant. "She was so beautiful. I lost her to Philip, you know, back at Georgetown. I met her at a dance and made the fatal mistake of introducing them. Philip proved the better man."

The sentence didn't sound resentful. It sounded like Breckinridge himself believed it.

"A confession you want? Then a confession you'll have," the old priest continued. "Bless me, Father, for I have sinned. While it is not a month since my last confession, I have sinned in omitting much in seven decades of visiting these small, dark rooms."

Santiago leaned closer to the plastic window to hear the soft voice. He said nothing, afraid it would prompt Breckinridge to stop.

"There are some dark moments upon which an entire life pivots." The old voice had turned ragged. "Some dark moments that are so terrible, they stand behind you, forever whispering, reminding you of your capacity for grave evil. They're there when you wake in the morning. They're there when you lay your head on a pillow at night. They're there in the past and in the present. And you can be certain they are patiently waiting for you in your future. You can even stumble through life completely drunk for five straight years and, when the fog parts, they'll be there like smirking old friends, waiting to embrace you.

"I tell you, Santiago, the last seventy years, I've lived every day fully expecting this very moment to be lying just around the next corner, fully expecting its revelation would expose me, destroy me. I hoped that if I lived a good and decent life, it could somehow balance out the bad." The old man stopped, the shadow of his hand steadying himself, pressing against the plastic window. Santiago heard a stifled sob.

The sound of the old man weeping cracked open the dry hull of Santiago's chest. Regardless of where Breckinridge's words would lead, Santiago, at the moment, felt a glimmer of pity. "Charlie, you should know people view you as a hero."

A doubting laugh stilled him. "I've actually spent years composing my confession, rewriting it, shading the truth to explain my actions, to justify my part, squirming and squealing like a pig who knows he's being yanked toward the slaughter house. The truth is, no matter how I polish it, it's unforgiveable."

"It concerns Philip Cannon?"

Through the opaque screen Breckinridge raised an ancient, bent hand. "Indulge me a moment. Whenever I rehearsed this speech, it always started when I was eight years old."

His fingers tapped on the ledge that held the plastic window, drumming up courage. "I suppose I'm deflecting blame, but it helps ease the conscience. When I was eight, one of the farmhands on my father's land, a black boy about eighteen or so – we called them negroes and worse back then – was accused of carrying on with my father's youngest sister."

"You don't believe he did?"

"Did or didn't, if you knew my aunt, saw the way she shamelessly flirted with all men, especially the colored ones when my father wasn't looking, she certainly wasn't innocent in the matter. That afternoon, my father came upon her affectionately touching the boy, and he flew into a rage. He dragged her back to the house, laid into her, gave her a brutal beating. She accused the boy of whistling, likely as not to save her own skin. She told my father she had stopped to scold him for propositioning her.

"That night my father gathered up some neighbors and hired hands. Despite my mother's protests, he seized me by the collar and dragged me along, saying I was old enough to understand how justice worked in the county. I was terrified. The men were riled up, drunk. I had never seen them like that. Like frenzied dogs that had caught scent of wild boar. Yet I was equally terrified of what would come my way if I pulled free of my father and took off home.

"After dark, the men surrounded the shanty of the boy's family. Demanded he be brought out. His father emerged first, tried to reason with my father. Begged and pleaded with him. He had worked for my father for more than thirty years. Yet they tied him to a tree and whipped him, simply for trying to save his son's life. Then I watched as my father ripped the cabin door off its hinges and slapped the boy's mother to the ground. That brought their son out of hiding. He shouted at them to stop, promised he would go with them if they simply promised not to kill his parents.

"I witnessed it all, plain as day. A full moon shone so brightly you could have read a book outside that night. My father and his men dragged him up to Eagle's Perch, a cliff overlooking the river. Tied him up, plied him with whiskey, slapping his face when he refused, until the boy was good and drunk. They hauled him to the ledge a hundred feet above the rocks of the river bank. I grabbed my father's arm and screamed for him to stop. With a curse, he backhanded me, telling me to shut up or I'd be next.

"He hit me so hard I fell backward. When I looked up, it was directly into that poor boy's eyes. He just looked down at me, resigned, a profound sadness in his eyes. Didn't fight back at all. Didn't utter a word. He just trembled, staring at me. They cut the ropes off him, lifted him up. He spread out his arms and let out a horrible gasp into the sky and they threw him off that ledge.

Beckenridge's hand pressed against the plastic confessional screen and, with a crack, he slapped the window ledge hard. "My father grabbed me by the hair and yanked me over the edge. Far below, lit by the moon, I could see the boy's body sprawled out on the rocks along the river's edge. 'Don't forget it, son,' he said proudly. 'That's what justice looks like.'

"The men gave a triumphant cheer that sent a shiver of fear through my body. One of them, Mr. Stuckey, the general store owner in town, put on a mocking, sad face, 'Musta fallen!' he said with a laugh. 'That's right!' my father shouted. 'Eagle's Perch is no place for a drunk man to go wandering at night. Just a tragedy waitin' to happen!' My father roared with laughter, his rage completely evaporated."

Breckinridge paused a long time before he gave a sad grunt. "You know that was the only time in my life I ever saw my father genuinely happy."

The old priest suppressed a brief coughing fit. "For some people, a death stops the world a moment. A bleak, tragic punctuation mark at the end of a life. It leaves them wondering why the rest of the world just keeps speeding by, without pausing out of respect for their loved ones. In contrast, in the world I grew up in, murder was a county fair." His fingers were back on the window sill, tapping. "That fall, despite everyone in the county knowing what really happened, my father was reelected in a landslide and I watched down in Richmond as he was sworn back into the state senate."

The story seemed to suck all the air out of Santiago's compartment. The image of Jasper's face, a look of sad, hopeless resignation, at the edge of Harbin Hall's roof flickered through his mind. Santiago took a deep breath to shake the nauseating image. His thighs ached from kneeling for so long. He put one hand on the floor and shifted, sitting on the kneeler. His hands covered his face and he let the back of his head fall against the plastic screen.

"You probably wonder what all this has to do with Philip Cannon. It's this: the image of that boy's face is an inextricable part of everything that played out afterward."

"When you were at Georgetown."

"When I returned to Georgetown as a Jesuit priest, yes. When I was pastor at Holy Trinity, the Jesuit parish near the university. I served there prior to being named headmaster here."

More clicking on the sill. "The Stewards rushed into my life the first time I lived in Georgetown, during my sophomore year at the university. They made me feel something I had never felt growing up – a sense of safety, of family. It was wonderful. For the first time, I felt like I belonged, that I was part of something important that would guarantee I would never have to set foot in Harpers Ferry ever again. Through the group, I became close friends with two of my classmates, Philip Cannon and Paul McInerny."

Breckinridge exhaled deeply. "Mine is the typical, trite tale about how good, well-intentioned people lose themselves. The Stewards recruited students like Philip, Paul and me. Bright kids from broken, messy families, who showed great promise. We were all pliant, obedient and insecure, without exception, all somehow alienated from our fathers, still pathetically seeking, as young adults, the approval of some powerful man. And the men in the Stewards gave it to us, gave us someone and something concrete to finally believe in."

"You make it sound like a high-end street gang."

"In many ways, that's exactly how they operated. They exploited the same un-tethered neediness inner city gangs still do. They took kids like us, cajoling and bending us, culling future leaders in banking, in industry, in government, even the church." He uttered a laugh. "Although my choice to join the Jesuits instead of the traditional church hierarchy deeply upset them. They wanted a bishop. A cardinal."

Santiago uncovered his face in surprise. "They were opposed to you joining the Jesuits?"

"Of course. The Stewards had stolen millions from the religious order, after all. By that point, the Jesuits were the enemy, weren't to be trusted at all."

Santiago sat up straight. "Hold on. What do you mean, 'stolen'?"

"I mean the Stewards stole the money. Because of the Civil War and Healy."

Santiago's head swam. Breckinridge's words were upending everything he had assumed about the close ties he suspected some of his fellow Jesuits had to the Stewards. "When you say Healy, you mean the old president of Georgetown?"

"Yes. The Civil War wasn't over a year. Most of Georgetown's students had fought for the Confederacy. Yet the Jesuits hired the man as professor at the university. In a southern town where segregation was still the law of the land. Healy was a powerful personality and a finger in the eye of Jim Crow. Within seven years he'd become the university's president. Yet his mother was a Georgia slave. From the perspective of the pre-war South and the Stewards, so was Healy, no matter how white he looked. For the Stewards, the appointment was an abomination. It represented an unacceptable turn for the Jesuit order, who just over thirty years before had been dedicated slave-holders. For Stewards, the Jesuits quickly came to represent everything they viewed as wrong with the Catholic Church."

"So the Stewards have nothing to do with the Jesuit order today?"

"You mean besides working to destroy them?" Breckinridge offered a half laugh, half sigh. "The Stewards want nothing less than to destroy every progressive thinker in the Catholic Church. The Stewards are obsessed with four things, Santiago: money, power, breaking the lock on political and economic structures long held by American Protestants and reestablishing traditional morals and social structures that were part of this county in the 1800's. The Stewards believe the U.S. has been in steady decline since World War II. Yet since then, their money, their influence, has grown pervasive. In the U.S. and world banking system. In U.S. foreign policy. Look at the messes our country has recently mucked about in. The Great Recession. The occupation of Muslim countries. They've become obsessed with that part of the world. These men are experts at buying politicians, creating instability, achieving their goals while profiting handsomely from it."

"And the seed money that started it all was stolen from the Jesuits?" Santiago himself found it hard to believe.

"The men who founded the Stewards were Georgetown alumni, hired by the order after the liquidation of the slaves and the plantations to manage and invest the money. With the announcement of Healy's appointment, the men decided to undermine the Jesuits. They set up fraudulent, paper investments in railroad companies, which they then drove into bankruptcy, an elaborate shell game that allowed them to convince the Jesuits they had lost nearly all the money.

The Stewards' timing couldn't have been more perfect. At the beginning of the late nineteenth century, they sunk it into the beginnings of national corporations that were exploding in wealth and influence. With the documents Philip left behind, your friend, Jasper was able to trace the investments. He had pinpointed the Stewards' primary holding company."

"Athenasius, a company incorporated in The Caymans."

Breckinridge paused. "As your friend learned, that's a dangerous fact to know. Father Willoughs was hell bent on exposing its current board, men who control hundreds of billions of dollars. They own U.S. banks, brokerage houses, arms and weapons manufacturers. Companies that still deal in child labor and the illicit slave trade in Africa and Asia. That promote instability in the Middle East and then profit from U.S. intervention there."

"I saw some of Jasper's documents. They were mailed to me."

"Those documents, some of which Philip Cannon had hidden in Dalgren Chapel, were what got him killed. And nearly you too. The Gonzaga burglary succeeded, buying you time. Now they're hoping you will crack the remaining clue and lead them to the ones that remain out there. But if they find them first, they will kill you."

"How do you know all this?"

He could see the shadow of Breckinridge's hand rise in mild protest. "If you're thinking I'm still a Steward, I'm not. I broke with them soon after Philip's death."

"That's sixty years ago. If you're no longer involved, how do you know about Jasper and what he discovered? Even the Gonzaga theft?"

Breckinridge initially hesitated. "A year ago, a Gonzaga graduate, who went on to Georgetown, sought me out, here, on an afternoon like this. He had heard I was the only man who had successfully left the Stewards and remained alive. He wanted to do the same and asked me to help him. I heard his confession. When Philip's papers were found, I encouraged him to help Jasper as much as he could."

"You sent him to Jasper? Why didn't you encourage him to help me?"

"I did, but he told me you had a brother who works for the FBI."

"Why should that matter?"

Breckinridge laughed gently. "Can you name the head of the FBI?"

"Bill Sampson."

"A powerful man in a very powerful position. Do you know where he went to school?"

"Georgetown."

"And your brother?"

Santiago turned numb. The old man's earlier words echoed in his head: *Bright kids from broken, messy families...still pathetically seeking some powerful man's approval.*

Santiago felt like he was suffocating.

"In this game, Santiago, the survivors trust no one."

Chapter 37: Cherry Blossoms

Breckinridge's voice returned. The old priest offered a caution. "After ninety years, I don't pretend to know the truth for certain. And I certainly don't know who is at the top of the Stewards. I wasn't even trusted with that information in the 1950's. But I have learned to take my suspicions very seriously. You should too. It will keep you alive."

His gravel voice paused, then returned, heavy with hopelessness. "For more than six decades I've tried to figure out how to make things right – hoping that if I did, I could somehow slip the awful image of his face out of my mind. To let him and me make peace. To die in peace."

"The boy on Eagle's Perch?"

"The boy on the Canal Road steps."

Santiago was confused but he dared not speak. Breckinridge took two deep breaths and began his real confession.

"The week before he died, Philip had gone into hiding. At the time, I was unaware he had planned to expose the Stewards. I learned this later, but I don't blame him. Philip, as I said, was the better man. He was doing what was right.

"When he went missing, Paul McInerny and I were assigned to find him. I'm sure even others. Track him down, I was told. Simply bring him back to our superiors. A whole collection of sensitive documents identifying chief Stewards, the organization's holdings, documentation of political bribes, corporate malfeasance – all matters of illegal and immoral behavior – had gone missing.

Paul was relentless, insisting Philip intended to betray us all. Ruin us. Put us in prison a very long time.

"We searched unsuccessfully for days, traveling to all the places we had visited since we met back at school. I even asked Elizabeth to help me with something at the church one morning so Paul could break into their home when she wasn't there. He searched it top to bottom. I asked Elizabeth if she'd seen Philip. She insisted he was returning nightly after work and she'd have him call me. We knew it wasn't true. But I could tell from her face. She was terrified. And I terrified her. She didn't trust me at all.

"The next day Paul was in a frenzy. The Stewards had come down on him particularly hard, warning him that as one of Philip's closest friends, he'd be held responsible."

Breckinridge halted, working up the courage to continue. "It was I who eventually found Philip. I was on campus for dinner at the Jesuit residence and simply dropped by Dahlgren Chapel, which was then being renovated, to say my evening rosary. The place was usually empty at that hour. I don't think he expected anyone. I came across Philip sleeping in a pew. He admitted it all. He told me he had hidden the documents for safekeeping and was going to meet with a reporter from the *Post* in the morning. 'We have to stop this,' he begged me. He was weeping. 'This is torturing me. I can't even look at Elizabeth anymore.'

"I knew in my heart he was right and I told him so. I even told him I would help him the next morning, drive him to the newspaper's offices myself. He was incredibly grateful, throwing his arms around me and hugging me tightly. I meant it. At the time I really meant it."

Breckinridge had begun weeping. "But when I left, it was late. Near midnight. I was overcome with fear. I was terrified. I knew if I helped Philip, I was guaranteeing that Paul would kill us both. It was like I was back up standing on that ledge at Eagle's Perch, my father shaking me, forcing me to look down. Despite their insisting they just wanted to speak with him, I knew Philip was a dead man. He had betrayed them. And if I drove him to the newspaper, I was a dead man too.

"So I walked directly back to the rectory at Trinity. My hands trembling, I called Paul. I told him Philip was spending the night in the chapel and he said he still had the documents somewhere. Paul insisted he'd pick me up. That we'd go get Philip together. I refused. I lied, telling him I had a call from a parishioner who needed last rites. When I hung up, I got sick to my stomach. I began drinking and went for a long walk.

"Despite being drunk, I remember two things vividly from that night. It was April and there was a bright, full moon. The cherry blossoms were in bloom down along the Tidal Basin. How far is that from Georgetown? Four, five miles? I was on Canal Road, heading back to my residence at Trinity, feeling overwhelmed, empty and lost. I began dragging myself up that steep set of stairs that climbs the hillside between Canal and Prospect Street and I could smell them. The cherry blossoms, from all the way across town. I turned to look in the direction of the Tidal Basin. It was impossible, but I could smell their sweet scent. It sent a chill down my spine.

"Then, suddenly, they were both there. Philip falling and struggling to his feet at the top of the steps. He looked down and spotted me, twenty feet below, staring back up at him. That moment, when his eyes met mine, he just gave up. I could see it. He just stood on the ledge, on the very top of those steep steps, trembling. Then Paul was there, shaking him, lifting him up. 'Where are they?' he hissed.

"'Go to hell,' Philip said. 'You're going to kill me anyway.'

"And Paul did. Just like part of me knew he would. I was so terrified I didn't even try to stop it. Paul stabbed him. As he did, Philip turned his head and stared back down at me from that ledge. In the moonlight, from twenty feet below, I could actually see Philip's chin quiver. He looked at me, his best friend in the world, with the most hopeless, resigned look on his face. That's the second thing I remember most vividly about that night.

Breckinridge heaved a jagged sigh. "It was only then that Paul spotted me. He looked at me in utter disgust and hurled Philip's body down the steps. Philip landed in a heap at my feet. 'There's your parishioner, Father' Paul spat. 'He's ready for your last rites.'"

Breckinridge had stopped weeping. "It was on that step that the rest of my life pivoted."

Santiago felt overwhelmed, torn between his anger and suspicion toward Nico and his sympathy and sorrow for Charlie Breckinridge. "You quit the Stewards, Charlie. Why didn't they kill you?"

"I don't know. I fully expected them too. I suspect there were a number of reasons. Perhaps because they knew I was a coward. Perhaps because I had saved them from utter destruction. Because the murder of two close friends so close together would have raised suspicions. Maybe it was because I was empty-handed and they knew it. They had begun marginalizing me the moment I took my vows with the Jesuits. By that time, other than Philip and Paul, there were only a few other Stewards I even knew. Maybe, most of all, they didn't kill me because Paul McInerny was their chief assassin and he was a deeply superstitious man."

"How so?"

"After a month of not responding to any of the Stewards' calls, Paul simply showed up at Trinity. Confronted me in the sacristy. He told me the only reason I was alive is he wouldn't kill a priest, but if I said anything about Philip's death or the Stewards, he would make sure I would regret it."

"What did he mean?"

"He promised to kill Elizabeth and Susan Cannon if I said a word. And to this day, I've remained silent to protect them. But, I can assure you, the Stewards of my generation watched me closely for years until I outlived them all."

"But you've told me."

"I've told you under the seal of confession. Under church and God's law, you can tell no one else," he said. "Piece out what you have learned. I'm confident it will lead you to the truth. Now please, Santi, give this broken man his absolution and penance."

Santiago quietly said the closing prayer. "Charlie—" Santiago stopped and slowly said the words so the old man would know he meant it. "You are forgiven."

"And my penance?"

Santiago pressed his lips together. "Write down the names of all the Stewards you remember and give them to me. They are plotting something horrible – Jasper's journal suggests that millions of lives are at risk. You have to help me stop them."

"I have told you what I know. I can do no more. I will not do that and risk the lives of Elizabeth and Susan. They will know it came from me."

Santiago pleaded with him. "What if I get them protection?"

"Through the FBI?" Breckinridge laughed. "My whole confession, names included, has been written in my personal diary with directions that it remain under lock and key and only be read after Elizabeth and Susan Cannon are both gone."

"Then just answer me one more question."

"If it will not endanger the Cannons."

"Someone is leaving me clues signed by the Odd Fellows Society. Is it your Steward?"

"No. He could risk nothing like that."

Santi's cell phone buzzed, announcing the arrival of a text message. He pulled the phone from his pocket glanced down: "At Walter Reed Hosp. Come immediately. –A"

Breckinridge shifted. "May I have another penance?"

Santiago paused. "In seventy years, you've done penance enough, Charlie. Just pray for me. Pray that I make the right choices."

With that, Santi was gone.

Chapter 38: Extreme Unction

Santiago nearly dashed toward the hospital before remembering to open the trunk and grab the satchel that held the oil, holy water and prayer book he needed for extreme unction.

Last rites.

He was out of breath as he arrived at the visitors' desk. He raised the satchel, which had a white cross stitched into its top to make up for the fact that he wasn't dressed in his collar. "Father Torres for the Byrne family."

Two minutes later he stepped out of the elevator onto the sixth floor, which held the oncology patients. He jogged to the room, trying to recall the last time he had seen Abby's parents. It was two months prior, at their well-starched Christmas party, a gathering Abby insisted he attend every year – at least in between men she was dating – so she wouldn't be bored out of her mind. From this vantage point, Santi had witnessed lung cancer hollowing Mrs. Byrne. It had seized a beautiful, older woman with the same red hair as her daughter and carved out a skeleton that looked like the skin of a larger person had been carelessly draped over it. The previous December she looked ill, certainly, but very much alive. Yet her husband crossed the room, touching her shoulder every twenty minutes. "Are you okay? Can I get you anything? Let me get you a drink."

"No. No." She'd shoo him off. As he kissed her cheek and turned to go, her smile would too.

He recalled the last time he had seen Abby's mom appearing in good health. It was early on, just after her diagnosis.

She attended a school play that Abby was directing. During the first act on opening night, one of the painted set pieces behind the lead actor had toppled halfway through his soliloquy. The clueless senior looked out at the audience in confusion when they collectively screamed and pointed at him.

He woke up an hour later under the bright lights of an emergency room.

At the hospital Abby's mom had kept her arm tightly around her daughter, squeezing and repeating, "I don't care what you say. I'm still proud of you."

A video of the incident later received over a million hits on YouTube. The same student who posted it, the best friend of the lead actor, also generously offered it to all local TV newscasts. "Local actor hits the big time," intoned one of the perky, perfectly white-toothed anchors in the newscast tease. "Or rather," she smirked, "he gets *hit* big time."

"Great," Abby had muttered the next day. "The first play I direct and my lead actor becomes famous only because I almost killed him with a two-dimensional Tuscan village."

Santiago pondered when he had first met the Byrnes. He recalled an image of Abby standing happily with her parents at graduation.

Or perhaps he was just remembering a photo he had spotted on an end table in Abby's house.

But he must have been there. Maybe even taken the photo. He distinctly remembered them as very reserved and quiet, yet remarkably proud of Abby. Abby's father was always working. And Abby's mother's life revolved around her only child.

Abby was always with them, visiting, going to dinner, traveling, talking about them. "You want to find a guy?" Santi would lecture her. "Cut the cord."

She'd dismiss him – like her legion of suitors – with a wave of her hand.

Despite Santi's seeing them only occasionally, just from speaking to Abby, her parents seemed like familiar if formal friends. He stood at the door a moment, bracing himself for what he might see. He tapped and stuck his head into the dim room. Abby looked exhausted, taut, yet still managed a flicker of a smile.

"You okay?"

Abby nodded. His eyes fell to her mother, lying in the bed, her red hair gone. In its place was short-cropped, wispy, completely white hair, brushed back from her face. He could mark its length to eight months ago when she insisted they stop all treatments. Abby had fought her, but she was insistent.

Abby crossed to him, squeezed his arm. "I feel selfish dragging you here after the awful week you've had."

"Don't be ridiculous."

"I just wanted it to be you." She nodded at his satchel.

"I know."

"It should be you. Not someone we don't know." She gestured to the other side of the bed. "Santi, you remember my dad?"

Santi hadn't seen him at first, hidden by the privacy curtain. Santi extended his hand. "Mr. Byrne, I know the last few months have been very, very difficult for Mrs. Byrne and you."

Abby's father's eyes were red, his face like a drawn shade. Santi was suddenly struck by Abby's similarity to him. While her red hair and freckles came from her mom, Abby's fine features could be traced to her father's bleak, handsome face. Mr. Byrne began to speak and stopped. His face reddened with embarrassment and he gestured to his wife.

"Of course," said Santi. "Of course."

Abby hooked her arm through his and tugged him to the side of the bed opposite her father. "Mama," she said quietly. "Santi's come to say some prayers."

Her mother's eyes were barely open, her bottom lip moved slightly.

Santiago opened the satchel and unfolded the white alb, kissing the cross in its center before draping it around his neck so it hung down his chest. He opened the small, plastic bottle of holy water, squeezed a few drops on his fingers and sprinkled everyone. Passing quickly through the penitential act, he opened his bible. Out of habit, he turned to James, in the New Testament's collection of letters written by the apostles. "Are any among you sick?" he read.

Santi's hands trembled. The moment he finished the sentence, the image of his brother arriving at the dinner table so long ago, skittered into his mind. He looked up at Abby, her father, and suddenly felt overwhelmed. A surge of love rose in his chest. These people standing before him had come to mean so much more to him than his own family.

Santi blinked back tears and switched directions, opening his bible to Romans instead. He began reading part of the eighth chapter. "And not only that: we too, who have the first-fruits of the Spirit, even we are groaning inside ourselves, waiting with eagerness for our bodies to be set free. In hope, we already have salvation."

Santi's fingers traced the words that followed. He picked up farther on. "We are well aware that God works with those who love him, those who have been called in accordance with his purpose, and turns everything to their good." Santiago finished the verse and looked up at Abby's family, uttering the last line from heart. "If God is for us, who can be against us?"

He closed the book. "I don't think I can improve upon those words. But I do want all of you to know how grateful I am, how privileged I feel, that you have let me be part of this moment, part of all of your lives." He glanced toward Abby, hoping what he'd say would bring her, above all else, some comfort. "There are two things we are all required to do in life completely alone – come into this world and leave it. While others may be present, we have to walk both paths alone. It can seem so terribly frightening to think of it let alone experience it. I suspect, when we are born, that is why our first instinct is to cry out when we emerge into the light. Yet our fear is quickly eased. We are held, celebrated and warmed by those who love us so profoundly." Santiago offered Abby a sad smile. "Our faith tells us that in the same way, when we die, while we experience that same fear here, we will experience the same warmth, light and love there."

Abby reached for her mother's hand and grasped it tightly. Santiago prayed the brief litany and opened the bottle of oil for the anointing. He placed the chrism on his finger and leaned over Mrs. Byrne, tracing the sign of the cross on her forehead. "Through this holy anointing, may the Lord in his love and mercy help you with the grace of the Holy Spirit."

Santi took the woman's left hand, tracing another cross, then lifted Abby's, which still held her mother's other hand. Together, Santiago and Abby cradled her mother's palm as he traced a glistening cross on its surface. "May the Lord who frees you from sin save you and raise you up."

He could feel Abby's hand, her whole body, trembling. "Amen," she whispered.

Santiago nodded, indicating he was finished. Abby sat on the edge of the bed, pressing the palm of her mother's hand against her own cheek while stroking her head. Santiago looked at her, wondering if he should go or stay. She saw the question in his face. "I want you to stay." She looked at her father. "Santi can stay?"

Walter Byrne nodded.

Santiago closed his satchel. To offer some privacy, he walked over to the hospital room's window, where the night sky framed the buildings that lined the busy road below. Late commuters were rushing by to get home, get on with their lives, oblivious to the final breaths men and women in the hospital were taking beside others who loved them dearly, others who willed them to breathe more. Santiago's chest ached. His mind flickered through a frenetic frame of images. Breckinridge, an old man, awaiting death before a television set. Breckinridge, a boy, looking into death's face on Eagle's Perch. Himself, just nine years old, witnessing the death of the family he knew – in the middle of dinner, late at night, when his father arrived with a stranger. Santiago's spine turned to ice, his heart to stone. *This is your brother.*

Santiago pressed his forehead against the frozen window. He swallowed to keep the anger from consuming him.

The light sound of Abby's weeping rose up and dragged him back to the room.

Chapter 39: Charlie's Penance

Charlie Breckinridge set the pen down, squinted to study the ancient scratching that passed for his handwriting these days. Before closing the worn leather cover of the diary, he blew across the page. He caught himself pondering what had cracked open an old crevasse of his brain, dusting off an old writing reflex no longer necessary, one he'd last done more than three-quarters of century ago when ink had to be blown upon to dry.

He pressed it closed, rubbed a bent, soft hand against the rough cover. He'd filled many journals since making his vows. He'd documented his life, his thoughts, mundane and transcendental. None but this, the oldest, the one kept hidden, risked the hard truths – The Accounting, he called it – the failings Charlie had finally whispered under seal of confession.

He picked up the block of bright yellow sticky notes on his desk, one of a million marvelous, miraculous items he had witnessed in a century of marvelous, miraculous inventions. They were reminders you could slap anywhere, like a mother's nudging voice when you've shirked your morning chores: "Have you fed the chickens yet, Charlie! Mind your responsibilities before the sun sets!"

He picked up the pen again. "Upon my death, please deliver this to Santiago Torres, SJ, as it is his rightful property."

The sum of any Jesuit's personal property: his own thoughts.

He signed it simply: Charlie.

He peeled the note from the block, pressed it against the journal. He pushed himself to his feet, arms quaking from the effort, and avoided the night table where the rest of his personal writings were stored. Instead, he tottered to the room's large bookshelf. Its mementoes offered a sketch of his life – two framed and faded black and white photos, an etched glass award, a bronze eagle, cheap religious tourist items purchased in Rome, Greece and the Holy Land.

On the middle shelf sat eight Gonzaga yearbooks from the 1950s. He pulled the center one and tucked the journal into its hollow binding. He closed the yearbook's hardcover and slipped it neatly back in place. Charlie smiled. You'd never know it was anything but an old Gonzaga yearbook.

He hobbled to his bed. With great effort, Charlie lowered himself to his knees. He had given up kneeling for prayer three years ago, afraid he wouldn't be able to stand up on his own. But tonight he would kneel.

Charlie passed through his spiritual examination, recited a decade of the rosary and brought his prayers to their end. He wondered the appropriate thing to say to God under such circumstances. What could he possibly add that wasn't already known? Charlie felt his eyes well up. "My God, my touchstone, my friend. My final prayer tonight is for my friend, Santiago. Help and guide him, Lord, to make the right choices."

Charlie struggled a long time to stand up again. He found himself gasping with the effort. He turned down his bed, draped his robe across the foot of his bed, extinguished the lamp, and laid his head upon his pillow.

Charlie Breckinridge waited two hours, staring into the darkness, breathing steadily.

A sound ticked from the fire escape. A shadow flickered across the window. Charlie listened as the window edged open.

In a moment he was standing over Charlie.

"I've been waiting for you."

"Then why didn't you scream?"

Charlie looked into his ice blue eyes. "On account of you?" he said. "You flatter yourself."

Chapter 40: The Fall

Abigail fell against him, her body shuddering. He held her up, held her from falling over in despair until the first wave of grief was spent and she was too exhausted to sob more.

He could think of nothing to say that could ease her loss, so he began pushing her hair back behind her ear like he had seen her do herself thousands of times.

Santiago risked a glance at her father, seated on the bed's other side. He looked stunned, his eyes blisters of red, his lips pressing and easing, his hand still stroking his dead wife's white hair.

When Abby finally fell silent, Walter Byrne spoke for the first time that night. "Could you take her home, Santiago?"

"No, Daddy."

"No, Abby. Please. I'll be fine. There's no need to stay any longer. I'll take care of it."

"But you'll be alone."

"And that will be all right." He held up a hand. "Please. I need just a few hours. I want to take a walk to clear my brain. If you come home and stay with me, I'll worry about you all night. If you go with Santiago, I know you'll be all right. Do this for me."

Walter Byrne nodded at Santi. "Get her something to eat. She's eaten nothing all day. And then take her to her home. It's a brighter place in the morning than her old bedroom at my home. Take her there and let her sleep." He looked back at his daughter. "I will be all right."

Santiago stood, pulled Abigail to her feet. "He's right. Let me help now."

Abby leaned over and kissed her mother, pressing their cheeks together. Her body shuddered again.

Santiago gently pulled her arm. "Come, Abby. Your mom's not here anymore. She wouldn't want you doing this."

They drove to Abby's in near silence, stopping at a Chinese take-out place on the way. She finally spoke as they pulled up in front of her home. "She's free from all this now, isn't she? No more trouble. No more pain."

Santiago squeezed her hand. "No more pain."

"I'm going to miss her so much, Santi." Her face crumpled like a tissue and she fell against him again. Santiago hugged her, blinked his own tears into her hair.

It was like that for the next two hours before she went off to bed. Silence and quiet, sitting at the table devouring the lo mein and the spicy kung pao chicken that she loved. Santiago uncorked a bottle of wine he found in the kitchen. They ate and drank, the wine warming them, unraveling memories. Abby even laughed. "My mother hated Chinese food. Absolutely despised it." She looked at him, her eyes dancing again in that way that made Santi ache with longing. "But it's *sooo* good."

She sat up a while longer, leaning against him, too closely Santiago knew, but between the wine and the last few days, he couldn't care. They sat together on the kitchen window seat that overlooked her dark backyard. "Mom says I should plant a garden back here."

Santiago remembered the beautiful backyard garden at the Cannon's house – a refuge in the middle of the city. "That's a great idea. When spring comes, I'll help you with it."

She turned to look. "Really?"

"Of course."

She smiled and laid her head over his heart.

Santiago ached.

"You know, I miss Jasper."

He was grateful for the words, how they inserted their proper old friend between them, reminding Santiago who he was supposed to be.

"Me too," he said.

"I'm sorry about what happened this week. I haven't asked you at all about what happened in Quigley's office."

Santiago shook his head. "It will take care of itself."

It was after two in the morning. The wine was gone. Abigail finally stood up, confused.

"You should go to bed."

She smiled, the extended pause making Santiago hope and then feel guilty for doing so. "Yeah." She stepped toward the front of the house, toward the staircase. "Thanks for helping me tonight, Santi. You know you're my best friend in the world."

She climbed the stairs and the ache dug deeper into Santiago's chest. He sat a long time, listening to her pad down the hallway, the shower water running.

Santiago stood, cleared the clutter from the dinner. He reached under the kitchen sink for an old newspaper and opened and drained another can of corn. He walked down the hallway to the half bathroom tucked beneath the staircase.

He cracked the door and spotted the chicken perched on the back of the toilet tank. It cocked her head, looking at him suspiciously.

"Stay!" He stepped quickly inside, shutting the door behind them. The movement startled the bird, which began flapping wildly. "Cut it out!" The space was entirely too small for either of them to feel comfortable but he dared not open the door and risk the chicken dashing down the hallway. He gathered up the old newspapers on the floor, changed the water in the bowl and dumped the fresh corn into the bowl beside it. The bird cocked its head and pumped its wings slowly. "Don't even think about it." Santiago was sure it was preparing to swoop down to peck out his eyes. "We ate chicken for dinner."

If there was anything that absolutely confirmed he was crazy, it was this stupid chicken. No. Not a chicken, really. An albatross around his neck. A never ending, ridiculous commitment he wished would simply go away. "Tomorrow you find a real home," he said and slid back out the door.

Santiago listened. The shower water wasn't running and Abby was back in her room. He threw out the old papers and went to the corner of the living room where he had stashed his bag. He got his things, climbed the steps to the bathroom. He willed himself not to look at her closed bedroom door. It was open a slight crack. An invitation, he thought suddenly, and batted the thought away. Only a man would think that. Her mother had just died, for Christ's sake. She likely slept every night with the door open a crack.

He showered, threw on a pair of shorts and returned downstairs quickly before the crack in the door split his skull open.

He fell on the sofa with a sigh, stuffed a couch pillow under his head and wrapped himself in the comforter that was still folded neatly in its corner.

He fell asleep with the image of the chicken's cocked head staring down at him.

Forty minutes later he woke with a start. He lay perfectly still, listening intently, his heart pounding. A sound woke him? Or had he dreamed it? Across the room, near the front door, a floorboard gave slightly. Santiago held his breath. He turned his head slowly. A shadow crossed the living room's sheer curtains, back lit by the street light.

The shadow loomed over him on the sofa and Santiago exhaled. "You scared the hell out of me."

In the dim light cast by the yellow street lights, he could see Abby standing above him, her sheer robe open, the light reflecting off her pale skin. She pulled back the comforter where Santiago lay in just his shorts. Santi said nothing. In the dim light, she only had to look down to see his reaction to her naked breasts.

Abby placed her hand softly on his chest. "Your heart is pounding," she whispered.

He nodded, unable to retrieve words.

Abby's words caught in her throat. "I needed to try, one more time. One more time just to know."

Santiago kissed her and they melted together.

Chapter 41: A Clue in the Collar

Santiago's night crawled with unsettling recurrent dreams.

"Hoy tienes nueve anos. ¡Ya es hora de que aprendas a ser un hombre!"

Today you turn nine. It's time to learn to be a man!

The birthday gift paper torn, he lifted the lid. A pair of boxing gloves!

No, he shuddered. Two pair.

Nico shrieked with joy, tearing off his shirt. A knot of fear, like clotting blood, rose in Santiago's windpipe.

"Fight!" his father cried.

The sun, setting in the hills, burst through a thunderhead, raising a hot vapor from the grass and it thickened in his throat. Its dying light reflected off the sweet blooms of the flame tree, shining off Nico's sweaty, copper chest, transforming him into a rippling, orange inferno that promised to turn him to cinder.

He circled Santiago threateningly, gloves held high, gloves from the big box their father had insisted Santiago open first.

Nico lunged. Santiago dodged and fell back. He glanced down, afraid he would trip on the big rock in the back yard. Nico lunged again.

Santiago's right cheek burned, the penalty for glancing down.

Nico circled, menacing a feigned left. Santi grimaced, stepped backward. Nico coughed a derisive laugh.

Santi's hands perspired in the hot leather. His father waved an arm, yelled from his chair on the back veranda, staccato Spanish mingling with the chorus of catcalling frogs from the overgrown field.

Nico brazenly dropped an arm, turned his face to their father. "¡Mira! ¡Tiene miedo!"

He's scared.

Santi rushed.

Nico whirled, his right fist exploding against Santi's nose.

Vertebrae clicking, his head snapping, his legs now pinwheeling, falling, the back of his head cracking against the rock in the middle of the yard.

Santi heard its dull popping as it struck. Brilliant sparks of white light shot across the yard, like the raindrops clinging to the grass, precious jewels in the setting sun. His eyes rolled toward the emerald mountains in the distance, urging him upwards, daring him to scale the translucent blue sky.

"¡Que bruto! ¡Sube las manos para defenderte!"

Fool! Keep your hands raised to defend yourself!

He shifted towards the voice. Disappointment creased his father's face. His sister, Maritere, perched on his lap, licked cake icing from her fingers. His mother, picking up the wrapping paper and the box that held the boxing gloves, cried out.

Nico stooped, his leering face jutting into view. "¡Siempre estaré de aquí para tumbarte! ¡Para siempre!"

I will always be here to knock you down. Always.

Santiago gasped for air and awoke. It took him a moment to place himself: He was lying in Abby's bed.

Were it not for her warm presence, he might have dismissed last night as a different, more pleasant dream: sex without guilt, his vows still intact. But he hadn't dreamt it. Unmuddled by sleep or wine, Santi's brain and heart were now at war, interrupting, wrestling to seize the last twenty-four hours from the other.

In just forty-eight hours he had been dismissed from a job he loved and broken one of the three sacred vows that defined him as a Jesuit.

Chastity, poverty and obedience.

Santi grappled with the puzzle of emotion: shame shaded by elation, joy at a chance to start over, to redefine himself, to actually embrace the woman who made him ache whenever she smiled. All tempered by terror that he had just tossed away what he most treasured – the priesthood, his integrity, his very identity – simply to possess someone else.

He turned to Abby. In was two decades since he had last woken up beside her. On the very spring morning he had broken her heart, stuttering that he had decided to enter spiritual formation as a Jesuit novice after graduation.

She had sat, her hands folded, struggling so hard to pretend to be happy for him. He had left feeling he had profoundly failed her, broken something he might never fix.

Her sleeping face was beautiful, peaceful. She would wake soon, a glimmer of light slipping through her eyelids, prying them open to a cold, sunny morning in a beautiful, terrible life where her mother had blinked out of existence.

What impossible contradictions the spinning world wove.

Why did people so fear death when it was no more than a permanent version of sleep's peaceful escape? A respite from the struggle and stress of living? Of teasing out all its contradictions and taming the battle between head and heart?

He turned away, slipped to the edge of the bed. Abby breathed deeply and stirred. He remained still, hoping he hadn't woken her. He hoped to sneak downstairs, prepare breakfast: to give himself time to think. He'd return with her breakfast on a tray so she'd wake to a friendly, loving world, not a bleak, empty one.

Her warm hand lightly pressed against the small of his back. He looked to the ceiling and closed his eyes, weighing the two: the excitement at her touch or the embarrassment of his failure.

"Do you regret it, Santi?"

He turned. She was so incredibly beautiful. The sad smile on her face nearly broke him in two. "No," he said. "How could I ever regret you?"

She took his hand and squeezed it, yet her smile tightened. She didn't quite believe him.

"Do you?" he asked.

She didn't hesitate. "Never. I have always wanted you to be happy. But – it's selfish, I know – I've always wanted to be with you more." Her voice fell. "I guess that makes me a terrible person."

"No. Just terribly human." He leaned over and kissed her. "Wait here. I'll bring us up some breakfast."

Downstairs, he crossed to his bags and shrugged on a sweatshirt and jeans and a thick pair of socks. He started some coffee, wrestling at first with the grinder until he figured it out. He poked into the fridge and cupboards, pulled out eggs, flour, sugar, a half dozen other ingredients before busying himself with flipping pancakes, frying bacon, scrambling eggs. Santi lost himself in the work, listening to the bacon pop, watching the hotcakes bubble on the griddle, the smell of the brewing coffee warming him. It filled him with a sense of home, a feeling the chafing dishes and commercial, metallic coffee pouches back in the Jesuit residence's dining hall would never conjure.

Santi was in the middle of flipping a lightly browned pancake when he suddenly could name what he was feeling.

It was joy.

It was nearly unrecognizable, so much time had passed since he'd stumbled across it.

This is what newly married couples did. They slept together. Made coffee. Read the paper. In their flour-dusted sweatshirts, their socks sliding around the kitchen floor while the bacon popped.

Together, just the two of them. The rest of the world be damned.

He hadn't felt such happiness for two, maybe three years. He piled the food and two giant, steaming mugs of coffee onto a tray and climbed the stairs, sliding down the hallway to Abigail's room. Its door was wide open.

He stood in the doorway, watched her staring out the window at the sunlight. The dust motes he stirred drifted into the sunbeam that trickled down onto the bed pillows and shimmered off her beautiful red hair.

A tear rolled down his cheek. "I'm happy."

Her tired face, still traced with grief, trembled into a smile. "Me too. I know I shouldn't be. I feel guilty even saying it. But me too."

He brought the tray of food and coffee over to the bed and they ate in the sunshine of Abby's bedroom. Santiago's mind slipped out of the present, pondered his future. His gut fluttered.

Abby broke the silence. "This is delicious. If you promise to keep cooking, I may just ask you to stay."

Santi smiled at the tease but voiced his anxiety. "If I leave the Jesuits, what could I possibly do? Sell used cars? I have a history degree and a master's in theology, a handful of educational administration credits for a degree I was supposed to finish this coming summer. I'm not exactly what you'd call in high demand."

"You can do whatever you want. You can even do nothing if you want."

"I was hoping for something more realistic."

Abby touched his arm. "It is realistic, Santi. You know my parents have money. My mom inherited her father's estate and spent none of it in her life. My father's own work has made them so wealthy, she told me she was leaving me her family's money."

"So you're leaving teaching?"

"Santi, if I didn't want to teach, I could have left long ago. I do it because I love it. Because I believe it's one of the most important things I can do. My mom's money has nothing to do with it. All I'm saying is you don't have to worry about money. You could go back to school. You could simply crawl through some library's archives and write. Volunteer. Whatever you want."

The thought of being a kept man unsettled Santiago and flickered across his face.

"Oh, don't do that, Santi."

"I come from a pretty traditional Puerto Rican family, Abby. A guy doesn't usually live off his wife's money where I come from."

"Then get a job selling used cars if it soothes your Puerto Rican machismo."

Santi put down his coffee mug and looked at her in surprise. "Ouch."

She shook a piece of bacon at him. "Santi, we're not exactly taking the traditional, typical route here. I'm an English teacher who just slept with her boss, who happens to be a priest."

Santi laughed. "I suppose you'll demand a raise now."

She suppressed a smile and punched him in the arm.

Still laughing, he got up and stretched, walked to the window. "Maybe I could finish that educational administration degree as a start."

When he turned to reassure her, he noticed a frame covered in brown paper and propped against her desk beneath the windows. "What's this? New art for your room?"

"Actually very old." she said. "My mom gave it to me the day before we took her to the hospital. It's an old family portrait that I've always loved. But it's pretty valuable. It might look odd hanging in my house. Like putting a Renoir in Ikea."

He picked it up. "Is it a painting of your parents and you?"

"Open it," she said. "See if you can guess who painted it. It's Jacob and Julia Castle, two of my ancestors on my mother's side about five generations back. He migrated to the U.S. from England in the early 1770s and established my mother's family's fortune. It shows them and their children. It was painted in the early 1800s by an important American artist."

The frame was unwieldy and heavy so he took care peeling back the brown paper. He slid it off the back and found himself looking at a beautiful oil painting of the couple with their three children. He recognized it from the Byrnes' living room, where it had hung above the piano. Its colors, applied in broad, whimsical strokes, were cracked with age. Santiago was struck by Jacob and Julia Castle. Rather than the formal, posed, aristocratic look he had commonly seen in paintings of American families from the era, the two were painted looking at each other, touching their children affectionately. Playfully jumping up on the boy in the middle was the family dog.

"Are you sure this was painted in the early 1800s? It looks like a later style."

"You completely missed it, Mr. History Nerd!"

"Missed what?"

"Look at the dog."

Then Santiago saw it, in light strokes that he initially had mistaken as a design in the dog's gold collar: G. Stuart, 1804.

Santiago turned to her, startled. "My God!" he cried, "You've done it!"

Abby looked at him in alarm. "Done what?"

Santiago grinned wildly. "You've solved Jasper's dollar clue!"

Chapter 42: Letters and Numbers

"Whoa, slow down!"

Santiago felt in the back pocket of his jeans. "Hold on! It's downstairs!"

He laid the painting on the bed, flashed down the steps to retrieve his wallet from his bag and dashed back up.

Out of breath, he pulled out the one dollar bill with the yellow corona around George Washington's head. "Gilbert Stuart was an early American painter who specialized in portraits."

Abby pointed to the one on the bed. "I kinda knew that."

"You're missing my point." He held out the dollar bill and stabbed at Washington with his finger. "Stuart painted hundreds of different wealthy and important Americans from here to Boston. This is one of the most famous portraits he ever did. He made dozens of copies of it and sold them after George Washington died. A copy of one of them has been engraved on U.S. currency for the last hundred years."

Abby took the dollar bill and studied it. "But how does that solve Jasper's clue?"

"Think Georgetown."

Abby shrugged.

"That painting in Carroll Parlor inside Healy Hall."

"Santi, Carroll Parlor has a bunch of paintings."

"I'm talking about the painting of Archbishop John Carroll, who helped found Georgetown." Santiago pointed at Abby's painting, specifically the dog's collar. "Carroll's portrait was also painted in 1804. And you'll never guess who did it."

"Gilbert Stuart."

Santiago grinned. "Get dressed. We're going to Georgetown."

Thirty minutes later they were shooting across Northwest Washington to the old campus where they met. "We won't be an hour," Santiago reassured her as he drove. "Then I'll drop you off at your dad's house."

Abby waved the dollar bill she was still carrying. "Are you sure about this? You really think that yellow highlighter around George Washington really is a clue to check out a painting in Carroll Hall? Who in their right mind would think of such a thing?"

Santiago laughed. "Jasper would. He knew I'd eventually piece it together."

"So all history nerds think alike?"

"No," said Santiago. "I just know how a particular history nerd named Jasper thought. He understood the Stuart connection to Georgetown himself and probably thought he was being terribly clever, given how the artist's name sounded similar to the Stewards. Jasper needed to leave me a clue that would lead me to more information – a clue he felt I would figure out before the Stewards did."

"So you think Jasper's documents are hidden behind the painting?"

Santiago thought a moment. "Not likely. There are too many of them. My bet is he left more information somewhere near the painting." He looked at her. "You do understand how unusual your ancestor's portrait is, don't you?"

"You mean because it's actually signed by Gilbert Stuart?"

"Yes," said Santi. "He almost never signed his work. He used to brag that his style and talent alone was his signature."

"You don't know my family. The story was that Jacob Castle insisted Stuart sign it. He and Stuart supposedly got into an argument over it. Castle told him there was no way he was going to hand over two hundred fifty dollars for any painting unless everyone looking at it could see who painted it. And the last time the painting was appraised for insurance, Stuart's signature alone added twenty thousand to its value."

"What's it worth?"

Abby looked embarrassed. "Eighty thousand dollars. I just always liked it because of the dog."

Santiago chuckled and turned into the university parking lot. The clock tower bells chimed the nine o'clock hour as they crossed the campus to Healy Hall. Santi reached for the door and his phone rang.

He pressed a button to ignore the call and pocketed the phone.

"Who is it?"

"Nico."

"You're not going to tell him?"

"I don't think that's wise." He opened the door for Abby and measured how much he could share about Charlie Breckinridge's confession, given that he was bound to keep it confidential. Santi almost gave into the temptation to tell the whole thing, but he felt a loyalty to Breckinridge – a sympathy for the man – that made him respect the confessional seal.

Abby gave him a strange look. "You don't trust your brother?"

"I really can't go into details."

"What? You can sleep with me but not trust me?"

"It's not that. It's under seal of confession. Let's just say that yesterday I learned something significant from someone I trust. Among other things, he told me I'd better not trust anyone in the FBI."

Abby looked at him doubtfully. "Even Nico?"

"Especially my brother."

They walked through Healy Hall and passed into Carroll Parlor. Grateful to find the room empty, Santiago crossed to the Stuart portrait of Archbishop Carroll.

He examined the painting itself for some clue. He knew Jasper would never harm the painting, never alter it in any way – a sacrilege for anyone with a healthy respect for art and the past.

"What are we looking for exactly?"

"Anything." He stood on his tiptoes and studied the painting's frame. Nothing seemed out of the ordinary.

He reached forward and touched the painting, feeling like he was committing a sin. It moved slightly.

"Go stand by the door. Make sure no one is coming," he whispered.

Abigail put her hands on her hips. "You're not going to steal that."

"Of course not," Santiago said. "I just want to look behind it."

Abigail shot him a wary look.

Santi still couldn't believe she thought he'd actually steal the painting. "Do you think I'm crazy?" he whispered.

She gave him a long look: that's exactly what she thought he was.

His cell phone rang again. Its loud echo in the room made him cringe. He looked at the incoming caller. Nico again. Santiago hit ignore and returned the phone to his pocket.

Santiago gingerly pulled the painting of Archbishop Carroll away from the wall and peeked behind it. His heart nearly exploded with excitement. A small, jagged strip of masking tape held a small piece of paper to the back of its frame.

"Do you see anything?"

"Shh!" Santiago whispered. He peeled back the piece of paper. Printed in neat, block printing was a series of letters and numbers. Santiago carefully set the painting back against the wall.

He nearly danced across the parlor.

"What is it?"

He held out the paper for Abby. On the paper in block letters was written: JW: BX4705H372F65D7. "Jasper definitely put it there." Santi pointed to his friend's initials at the front of the sequence. "This is what he wanted me to find."

"So you know what it stands for?"

Santiago offered a sheepish smile. "Not quite."

She shook her head. "Another mystery. Even after he's gone he figures out a way to be infuriating. Why didn't he just come out and say where he put it?"

Santiago struggled to think like Jasper. "Because he didn't want just anyone to find it. He wanted *me* to find it."

Santiago's cell phone interrupted them again. "Damn," Santiago muttered, "My brother is relentless." He reached into his pocket to take his phone out to shut it off.

The name on the caller ID made him stop. He stared at the phone as it rang again in his hand.

"Who is it?"

"Pearl."

Santiago's tone made it clear. Pearl wouldn't call Santiago's cell unless the school was sliding into the Potomac. Santiago let the phone ring again. He hadn't spoken to Pearl since he was removed from his position. He was too embarrassed. Yet she also knew that and wouldn't call him unless it was urgent.

"Hello, Pearl."

"I'm sorry to bother you, Santiago."

"I'm the one who should apologize for not having called you."

"I have terrible news, Santi. Father Breckinridge died last night."

Santiago's heart fell into the pit of his belly. He had assured Brother Sinclair he would bring the old priest back up from confession. After receiving Abby's text, he had thoughtlessly rushed from the church to the hospital without returning Charlie to the residence.

"Pearl, please tell me he wasn't found in the church."

"Fr. Breckinridge died in his sleep, Santi. In his bedroom."

Santiago took deep breathe, yet even that seemed too much of a coincidence. "Is that what they're saying? Natural causes?"

"That's what the coroner suggested when he left. Father Breckinridge was so old, Santi. Why would anyone think otherwise?" She switched gears. "Your brother is also here. He's very agitated."

Santiago grimaced. "Nico's there? You're kidding me."

"He's waiting upstairs for you, inside of Breckinridge's room."

He cursed in silence. What possible reason could the FBI have for poking into Breckinridge's death?

He gave a sidelong glance at Abby, who was listening in. The suspicious look on her face made it clear she agreed.

"Pearl," Santiago said urgently. "I need you to go up to the Jesuit residence and keep track of everyone who goes in and out of his room. Make sure no one takes anything."

Chapter 43: A Confrontation With Nico

"I'll take you back and drop you at your dad's." With Breckinridge dead, the seal of confession seemed pointless, so Santiago shared what he had learned. "Yesterday Breckinridge told me he had written out his whole story. He was a Steward when he was young, Abby. And he promised he'd leave behind a document identifying all the Stewards he could remember. While he didn't want the information released until others he was protecting also died, if Nico is there, I need to find it first."

"I'm going with you," Abby insisted.

"But your dad?"

"I'm not going to let you confront Nico alone."

"I have no plans to confront Nico at all."

She looked doubtful. "Did you think you were going to jump Bob Stanley when you dropped by Georgetown?"

Santi's face reddened. Abby had learned of his behavior through the school gossip mill. "I don't need a babysitter."

She caught up and grabbed his arm. "Don't be ridiculous. Last night you made the decision. We're in this together now. You can drop me off at my dad's after we check Father Breckinridge's room."

Five minutes later, they were back in the car, speeding down Foxhall Road. Santi cheated a half dozen traffic lights on his way to Gonzaga.

Abby finally broke the silence. "If Father Breckinridge didn't want you to do anything with his journal until other people died, what are you going to do if you find it?"

"I'll decide that after I read it."

Abby had pressed her lips into a grim line. She wasn't one to play with a man's dying wishes. Santiago defended himself. "Jasper thought I'm as smart as he was and clearly I'm not. Look how long it took me to figure out the Gilbert Stuart clue, cracked by dumb luck. Now I'm just as stuck as I was before I looked at that painting."

"You'll figure it out."

Santiago's voice rose. "I don't know if I'll figure it out. Those damn numbers and letters mean nothing to me. I need Charlie Breckinridge's journal. It's the only sure thing."

"You'll figure it out." She pressed a hand on his leg to calm him.

Santiago fell silent and sped back to the Jesuit residence. When they arrived, he threw open the door to the residence and anxiously pressed the elevator button. What would he say to Nico, whom Breckinridge warned him not to trust?

They stepped out of the elevator. To their right several Jesuits were standing in the common room where Charlie Breckinridge usually sat in front of the TV. They were talking quietly but fell silent when Abigail stepped into view.

Santi strode the other way, pulling her down the hall.

Pearl was standing in front of an open bedroom door, fiddling nervously with a book and checking her watch. "This is no proper place for a woman," she scolded when he was close enough to hear. She looked at Abby. "Me or Ms. Byrne for that matter."

"Thank you, Pearl. I owe you one."

She looked as if she were ready to whack him with the book.

"Has anyone come or gone since we spoke?"

She shook her head.

"And before?"

"As far as I know, just Sinclair, the ambulance team and the coroner." She nodded through the door at Nico. "And your brother. But he hasn't left the room since he arrived."

The blinds on Charlie Breckinridge's bedroom windows were wide open, slanting shards of light into the hallway. Nico stood in front of one window, arms crossed. He turned when they entered. His eyebrows rose as Abigail stepped into view behind Santi.

"Why are you here?" Santi challenged.

"Why am I here?" Nico said incredulously. "After what you pulled in Stanley's office, the first thing you ask me is why I'm here?"

"If the coroner thinks Father Breckinridge died of natural causes, why are you here?"

"Because Brother Sinclair told me you were the last person to talk to him last night before abandoning him in the confessional. Have you noticed you have a habit of being the last person that talks to people before they die?" Nico smiled. "So, if you forgive me, if anyone should be asking where the other was last night, it's me."

Abby spoke firmly. "He was with me because my mother died."

"My condolences on your loss." He turned back to Santiago. "But I understand that happened at 10 o'clock. Where were you after that?"

Santiago's temper flared. "You don't have to worry about where I was. I have someone who can vouch for me all night."

Abby's face went scarlet.

Nico looked at Abby, then at his brother. A snide smile pulled at the corner of his mouth. "Perhaps you'd like to explain why you went to Georgetown the other day?"

"You know damn well why. To see Stanley."

Nico voice rose. "There's only one reason you weren't arrested for assaulting him."

"Because you intervened to save my hide?" Santiago's words dripped with sarcasm.

Nico nearly shouted. "Because I couldn't find you to turn you over to the D.C. cops myself!" Nico's face was brick red. "Bob Stanley's a better man than you are, Santiago. Once he calmed down, he's the one who convinced me he shouldn't press charges."

Nico's words stung but they were true. Santiago took a deep breath to calm himself. "I shouldn't have gone to see him."

Nico was relentless. "That's what I told you, didn't I?"

"Yes," Santiago ground the words through his teeth. "I shouldn't have gone without you, all right? I won't bother him again. He's got nothing to do with this."

"Nothing to do with what? Your complete fantasy? Your unwillingness to accept your friend killed himself? The fact that you've come so completely unhinged you've even lost your job?" Nico threw a triumphant glance at Abby. "Not to mention your self-respect?"

Santiago stepped forward but Abby caught his arm.

Pearl stepped between them. "Both of you roosters better calm down. You're no better than two sophomore hotheads in the school cafeteria."

Santiago seethed. "I'll ask you again. Why are you here?"

"Because you'd gone missing and weren't answering your phone. So I called Brother Sinclair this morning. When he mentioned the old priest died, I came here, figuring you'd finally show up."

Santiago remained silent. Nico turned to Pearl. "I'm sorry. Given how crazy my brother has been lately, after he beat up an old friend of mine, I thought he might have been overcome with actual remorse, gone over to the Ellington Bridge and tossed himself into Rocky Creek."

Nico grinned again. "But now I know why he was too busy to answer. I'll be going now."

Pearl looked at him with disapproval.

Santi studied him suspiciously. "That's it?"

"More or less," Nico said. "Just one question."

Santiago waited.

"Why are *you* here this morning?"

"I lent Charlie a book and need to get it back."

"No, you didn't. You think he was killed by the Stewards too, don't you?" Nico dropped into the desk chair, waving his arms around the room. "Go ahead! Have a look. Find your proof that the Stewards are killing all the Jesuits in town." Nico pointed to the nightstand by the bed. "All his journals are in there."

Santi decided, regardless of Breckinridge's warning, to prove his brother was a fool. "He wouldn't be that careless." He walked the room's perimeter, pulling out the clothes bureau to peek behind it, sliding his hands between the mattress and box spring, even looking under the bed. Finding nothing, he stood up and turned around.

Abigail slid over. "Maybe he hid it somewhere else, Santi."

"Where else would it be? Breckinridge couldn't take more than five steps without someone's help. Outside this room, he had no privacy to hide anything."

Santiago's attention fell on the shelf that held various mementoes of Charlie's life, photos, awards, inexpensive religious souvenirs. The Gonzaga yearbooks caught Santi's eye. He stepped toward them and Nico rose.

One of the yearbooks, tucked into the middle of the stack, seemed strangely thin, its floppy spine bulged slightly outward. His heart racing, Santi tucked the tip of his finger in its spine and pulled it out. The cover flopped open emptily. He turned it over. No pages. The interior of the yearbook was missing.

He peeled off a bent sticky note left behind inside the yearbook's cover and held it out to Nico defiantly. He read it out loud. "Upon my death, please deliver this to Santiago Torres, SJ, as it is his rightful property."

It was simply signed Charlie.

Chapter 44: Pearl to the Rescue

"Another dead end," said Abigail.

Santiago flashed a look of warning. He had no plans to let Nico know about the slip of paper they'd found in Carroll Parlor.

"Whatever Father Breckinridge kept in that yearbook was our last hope." Santiago sat on Charlie Breckinridge's bed in feigned hopelessness.

"I should go and talk to the coroner," Nico muttered.

Santiago stood. He couldn't let Nico leave without insuring he wasn't leaving with the journal. "I owe you an apology," Santiago said. "I shouldn't have gone to Stanley like I did. I'm sorry." He stepped forward and threw his arms around Nico in a bear hug.

He felt his brother's spine stiffen. Santiago couldn't remember a time they had shown any affection. Nico took an awkward step back, but Santiago held on, pressing his stomach against his brother to feel if he had tucked a small notebook or journal in his front waistband. "I'm truly sorry." He patted his brother twice on the back. As he let him go, Santiago ran his hands across the small of his brother's back, checking his back waistband and dragged his hands forward across his front pockets.

"What the f–?" Nico gave him a hard shove but, with a glance at Pearl, caught himself before finishing the word. A flustered twitch threw his red face into spasm and he glared at Santiago. "You have your head up your ass!" He stalked out of the room.

Pearl folded her arms. "Are you always that familiar with family members?"

"Very smooth, Santi." Abby's face wore an amused smile.

"If Nico has Breckinridge's journal, it's no longer on him."

Pearl still seemed unconvinced about Father Breckinridge. She gestured to a framed black and white photo on the bookshelf and her lips were pursed. "You really think the man was murdered?"

"Given that his journal about his involvement with the Stewards is gone, there's no question about it," said Santi. "However, I have one lead left. We found it his morning but I'm getting nowhere with it."

Pearl eyed them both. "Are you aiming to get someone else killed?"

Santiago reached into his pocket. "If anyone's next on the Stewards' list, Pearl, it's me."

"It's I," Pearl corrected him.

Santiago ignored her and looked over Jasper's scrawled handwriting again. JW: BX4705H372F65D7. He shook his head. "At least I might be among the Stewards' top ten biggest threats if I had the brain Jasper thought I did. We found this piece of paper on a painting in Healy Hall this morning. Jasper left it there for me to find. He thought I'd immediately understand it, but I can't make heads or tails of it."

Pearl took the paper.

"JW is Jasper's initials," Santiago pointed. "After that, I have no clue what the letters and numbers mean."

Pearl looked at them like they were a couple of dodo birds stuffed and mounted in a history museum. "And you two have the nerve to call yourselves educated?"

Nico Torres crossed the parking lot and slid into the driver's seat of a maroon SUV. He sat a moment, tapping on the steering wheel, growing impatient. "He's going to leave soon. Have you heard from the cell company?"

"The EID number from his phone just landed from their legal department," the tracking specialist said. "Give me a minute."

Nico listened to the woman tapping on her keyboard.

"Okay. His phone just pinged. I got him."
He turned. "Now make damn sure you don't lose him."

Chapter 45: Dreams of an Outcaste

"Would you believe me if I told you they were the winning bingo numbers at my church last Wednesday night?" Pearl said.

Santiago seized the paper and studied the numbers again. Pearl let tumble out a dry cackle. When he looked up, she was tapping on the small screen on her phone. "Shame on you!" she scolded. "Two alleged teachers at one of the nation's top high schools and you don't even recognize the Library of Congress Classification System."

"It's a book?" Abigail said incredulously.

Pearl took the book out from under her arm and pointed to the letters and numbers in the small white rectangle on its spine. "I'm taking a continuing education course over at Howard: African American Contributions to the Creation of the Federal District. This strange item in my hand, in case you're wondering, is called a book. It's part of my required reading. Perhaps you two might consider an occasional trip to a library to brush up on your basic literacy skills."

Santiago seized the book and examined its call letters. "My God, Pearl, I think you're right."

"Of course, I'm right." She continued poking at her phone's screen.

Santiago turned to Abigail. "What an idiot I've been. Half the books I borrowed to complete my theology degree had library call letters that began with BX."

Pearl held out her phone. Its screen displayed the search results from Georgetown's Lauinger Library. "It's a book by Albert

S. Foley called *Dreams of an Outcaste*," she announced. "It's about Patrick Healy, the first black president of Georgetown University."

"Pearl, I could kiss you!" Santiago threw her arms around her.

Abby took Pearl's phone and looked at the display. "So you think it's in Lauinger Library's stacks?"

Santiago thought a moment. "That's a bit of a risk, hiding it in the regular collection. Jasper wanted me to find this, not some random person. If an undergrad came across it researching a paper, he might not know the papers are significant and toss them in the trash." He shook his head. "Even if he tucked his papers inside a rarely used book, it could be requested by a faculty member from a completely different university using the interlibrary loan."

Santiago considered Jasper's peculiarities and perfections. "Jasper left nothing to chance. If I were Jasper and I were hiding something I wanted only one person to find, I'd pick a book that would rarely ever be picked up. One that wasn't allowed to leave its place. Ever."

"Like a Bible in a Jesuit's desk drawer?" Pearl said.

"Like a rare, non-circulating manuscript in a special collection that only nerds who recognize the Library of Congress Classification System would ever visit." He looked at Abby, who was reading a text message on her own phone. "Are you coming with me?"

She shook her head. "My father has an appointment with the funeral director at two o'clock. I should go with him."

Santiago nodded and turned to Pearl. "Thank you, Pearl. I mean it."

"So I may go downstairs and do my real job now?" she asked. "Or will you insist I tuck myself into a corner of the dayroom and take notes on the way Brother Sinclair slurps his soup?"

"Go already." Santi squeezed her arm as she passed. "Not a word to anyone about this, okay?"

"Don't be ridiculous." Pearl said and disappeared down the hallway.

Two hours later, after he'd dropped Abby off at her father's house, Santiago was back on Georgetown's campus. He climbed the stairs at the back of the campus, walking past Dahlgren Chapel and turned toward Lauinger Library. The library's dour, unadorned concrete – a 1970s reinterpretation of Healy Hall – reminded Santi of the swarms of public housing projects that peppered San Juan's poor neighborhoods. In contrast to the regality of Healy's clock tower, the library looked like it had been thrown up after the university had run short of money and aesthetic sense.

He entered Lauinger and stepped past a line of students waiting to check books out at the reference desk. The stomach of the man behind the desk puckered the fabric around his shirt buttons. He poked through the students' backpacks with a stick, looking as if he were worried a campus squirrel might take him by surprise.

Santiago turned right at the library stacks and walked the length of bookshelves. He slipped down the aisle holding books in the BX range and traced his fingers along their spines.

As he suspected, there was no such book. Jasper would never have risked hiding anything among the circulating volumes.

Santi headed back to the reference computers. Sliding into a chair, he pulled the slip out of his pocket and typed in the call number.

Santiago smiled. This was more like Jasper. It was a non-circulating volume, tucked onto a shelf within Riggs Library.

Santiago jumped up and strode toward the exit.

A young man with ice blue eyes dropped into the chair Santiago had vacated. He leaned forward, clicked the back button on the browser.

Riggs Library.

The man cracked his knuckles and departed.

Chapter 46: Cannon's Papers

Santiago knew the odds of Riggs Library being open were slim. Georgetown's main library for eighty years until it was replaced by Lauinger in 1970, Riggs was everything Lauinger wasn't. Riggs soared while squat and stocky Lauinger groveled. Lauinger was bleak utilitarianism while Riggs was light and air, inspiring visitors to catch their breath in awe – like a European cathedral of the Middle Ages.

While one of the nation's most beautiful libraries, Riggs wasn't a circulating library. No Hoya could blunder in and pluck books from its stacks. Its books were ancient treasures. Vellum scraped and delicately inked, the painstaking handiwork of thirteenth and fourteenth century monks. Its Latin, Greek and Arabic archives dated to early humanity's great philosophers and scientists, men who teased truth from fire, wind and water. They had to be special-ordered from Lauinger before library staff lifted them like delicate flowers from Riggs' iron shelves and delivered them to a special reading room on Lauinger's second floor.

If you wanted in to Riggs, you needed an invitation. The cathedral of books now served as a regal space for receptions, concerts and meetings of the university's board of directors. Its books, with their colorful palette of bindings, completed a painting of an architectural masterpiece. Riggs' four tiers of cast iron stacks delicately scaled the tower, its curved iron railings carving out alcoves, soaring heavenward around floor-to-ceiling cathedral windows. The bookshelves, which turned El Dorado gold when the sun poured through the windows, climbed like cathedral pillars, embossed with crosses and shields bearing coats of arms.

If a university held ancient secrets, they were hidden in a place like Riggs.

Santiago approached the library's entrance. The only chance of it being opened was if the university administration was honoring some dignitary or hosting a reception. But Santiago swore that he would not leave empty-handed.

He was thrilled to find a well-dressed woman standing at its door. A small reception was wrapping up and the university's catering staff was pulling down tables. The woman looked up from her clipboard.

"Can I help you?"

It was a polite way of saying: Where do you think you're going?

Santiago wasn't dressed nicely enough to fake his way inside as a guest returning to retrieve his coat or cell phone. So he reached for his wallet and pulled out his license. He had lost count of how many times the DMV photo on it – one that showed him in his clerical collar – had won him a free pass on speeding tickets on the beltway. "My apologies," he said. "I'm Father Torres." He pulled out the big guns, dropping the name of the Jesuit president of the university. "I'm here assisting with the planning for Father DeMaio's sixtieth birthday celebration tonight. While speaking with Father DeMaio at breakfast this morning, I mentioned I was looking into early church history. He insisted I should stop by Riggs to check on a point I've been researching."

The woman's face looked troubled.

"I won't be a minute," Santiago pulled the door open. "Don't let me interrupt you. You go ahead and finish up and I'll let myself out."

"I'm locking up in five minutes," she hesitated.

"I'll be long gone by then." Santiago waved his hand and ducked into the library. He strode over to the corner and began climbing the circular iron staircase. He glanced back at the woman, who had followed him into the library. Santiago was helped by a clumsy member of the catering staff, who collapsed a folding table too soon, sending a chafing dish clattering to the library floor.

The woman scolded the man and rushed over to help clean up the mess. She turned her back to the library's entrance and he tucked himself into a hidden alcove and waited.

After a few minutes, the library grew silent as the remaining catering staff departed. He waited for the woman to lock up. He heard her eventually call out. "Father?" She waited. "Father, are you still in here?"

Santiago stayed silent until she extinguished the lights. He heard the lock turn in the library door.

The afternoon sunlight, filtering in through the enormous windows, provided ample light for his search. Santiago crept forward to the railing and peeked over to the broad, square room below. Seeing the floor empty, he went to the circular staircase and climbed to the B section on the third level. It contained old manuscripts related to theology and ecclesiastical history.

His heart thumped with excitement. He ran his finger along the spines of the old collection. Volumes labeled BT gave way to BU, then BV.

An odd sound caused Santi's hand to freeze. He turned in the alcove, facing the large, central open area again and listened. It was an odd, iron creaking sound, as if someone were mounting the stairs. Santiago's breathing rate doubled.

He ducked low to stay concealed and edged out of the alcove. He scanned the stairs and the broad square floor below.

Empty.

He stayed there a moment, crouched, ready to spring, perfectly still and silent.

No movement. No sound.

Santiago smiled at his nerves. His room back at Gonzaga was always popping and creaking as the building joints expanded and contracted in the heating and cooling of the day. He ducked back into the alcove to complete his search.

BU, BV…

BX.

There! *Dreams of an Outcaste* by Albert S. Foley. Santiago's hand trembled. He reached out, pulled a large manuscript box from the shelf. Santiago still doubted his luck, still fully expected that the Stewards had beaten him there.

He loosened the flap on the box and raised its lid. A yellowed stack of typewritten papers was topped by a title page: *Dreams of an Outcaste : Patrick F. Healy, S.J. : The Story of the Slave-Born Georgian who Became the Second Founder of America's First Great Catholic University, Georgetown.*

Santiago gingerly lifted the brittle pages, typed a century earlier by a now dead Jesuit. His heart soared.

Below the manuscript was a collection of white paper. New white paper with computer print and Jasper's handwriting scrawled across the top: The Rise of the Society of Stewards of Georgetown University. Beneath it, a bundle of older papers, folded in half, bound by a rubber band.

Philip Cannon's papers!

Santiago nearly gave a shout of triumph. He tucked Jasper's thesis under his arm and pulled Philip Cannon's secrets out of the box. His trembling hand paused a moment before he pulled back the rubber band.

A shot of adrenaline made Santiago tense. A dark shape rushed the alcove.

Chapter 47: Rectitude

Bradley Freeman leaned into the laptop monitor. Eighteen straight hours. The last of his office staff had trickled out an hour prior. His lone head bobbed in the dark offices, lit by his solitary desk lamp.

He leaned in to his monitor, his fingers tracing the words across the screen. His heart thudded and he reread them again to be sure.

"Holy fuck!" he whispered.

He hurriedly clicked opened the last file and two paragraphs in the words confirmed his worst fears. His hand trembled as he flipped his browser to another site and did a quick mathematical calculation.

Bradley swallowed. The Stewards were constructing a nuclear weapon powerful enough to level a major city.

A rustling by the door.

He shaded the lamp glare with a hand to see across the open office space. "Bailey? You back?"

Silence.

He picked up his cell but it flipped to voicemail for the third time in an hour. "Father Torres, it's Bradley again. I've gotten in to their server. All last night – all today – I've gone down rabbit hole after rabbit hole. And it's all led to one seriously disturbing place. The Stewards store their most sensitive files, all encrypted, on a hidden partition of an NSA server. A server no one, certainly not the Stewards, should even know exists. And I don't think the

NSA even knows they're there. It's the most brilliant way I've ever seen of evading national security."

Bradley's mouth was dry from anxiety.

"A whole series of files on here are tagged the Outremer Project. We've seriously underestimated these guys. ACM isn't the only subsidiary of Athenasius. The Stewards own four companies that are the Pentagon's biggest contractors, including one hired to decommission outdated weapons from the U.S. military." Bradley swallowed. "Here's where the story gets really scary…"

The voicemail message timed out. Bradley tapped the phone in frustration and threw it to his desk.

He glanced back at the laptop monitor. The file transfer he had begun while studying the documents was finally complete. Now he had to back out without leaving a trace, carefully wipe his feet on the welcome mat and disappear into the ether.

No room for error. He had heard hackers speak of cyber brethren who had simply disappeared, never to stalk the internet again. Hackers who'd stumbled across toxic material, who'd hacked the wrong system, poked around the wrong server.

If Bailey left the slightest trace of his presence, the files he had discovered would get him killed.

Bradley had no doubt the files were authentic. They spelled out intricate safety protocols for lifting minute, undetectable quantities of bomb-grade plutonium from old, decommissioned nuclear missiles – missiles made obsolete by time and arms control treaties.

And, with the collected material, constructing a fully functional nuclear bomb.

A weapon, judging from the plan's specifications, that was less than two feet wide and just under five feet long. Based upon the documents' timetable, a fully functional weapon was now in the Stewards' hands.

The documents were as frustrating as they were frightening. They vaguely referred to a mission named Rectitude. Yet the Stewards were smart enough not to record all their secrets. The files offered no insight into their target, how they planned to deliver the weapon or what they even hoped to accomplish by detonating it.

Bradley's thoughts flickered back to one fact: Israel had been circled on Father Willough's map.

A trashcan toppled over in the corner across the room.

Bradley shot to his feet. He instinctively glanced at the light switches by the front entrance, closest to the front door.

Bradley's voice became guttural with fear. "Bailey, if that's you, you'd best stop screwing with me right now."

Silence.

Bradley's hand flashed to the desk lamp and extinguished the light.

The soft whirring sound of a person rushing toward his desk caused Bradley to dive away. He rolled across the ground and rushed like a panther to the opposite side of the company floor, twenty feet away.

He crouched, hands raised, listening for some clue to the intruder's location.

Silence.

The flash of a lighter at the end of a cigarette illuminated the gaunt, chalky face of a man with the bluest eyes Bradley had ever seen. He was sitting in a chair in front of Bradley's desk. "You know, Mr. Freeman, all IT specialists have one thing in common." A dry, mocking laugh slipped from his lips. "They're smart as hell and it causes them to become arrogant and careless." He reached across the desk and held up Bradley's cell phone. "I learned that from your blog."

The man continued. "When your breach was discovered this morning, our best man connected it all the way back to Jonathan Feeney's computer. Mr. Feeney, in turn, traced his own stupidity back to the private ACM social networking group you created.

"Yet you couldn't help yourself, could you, Mr. Freeman?" he continued. "You created the group under a fake e-mail account that featured the odd name, G Daddy. Which just happens to be the moniker of the author of a popular IT security blog. A blog whose profile is linked to your real e-mail address." The man clicked his tongue. "Sloppy, Mr. Freeman. Very sloppy."

Bradley began creeping toward the office's entrance.

"You'll find the doors chained."

The lighter flickered and darkness blanketed the room.

"Don't you want to know how this story ends, Mr. Freeman? Don't you want to learn about Rectitude before you die?"

Chapter 48: Checking Out in the Library

Santiago's reflexes exploded. He dropped the papers, grabbed a heavy book from the shelf, spun it wildly. Unopened for decades, it stayed shut, flew true. Its heavy spine thudded into his attacker's nose, spraying scarlet.

The man cursed, his eyes an icy blue fury, intent on murder. Santiago flashed backward into the alcove, pulling books, hurling them. Coiled like a lithe cat, his attacker slapped them away. Santiago eyed him. The two men were the same size but his attacker was a decade younger, wiry, undoubtedly stronger. Santiago's only advantage was weight – at least twenty pounds. He reached the back of the alcove. Trapped, Santiago had no option. A caged beast, he rushed, put all his weight behind his right fist, swung hard for the man's bloodied nose.

Like lighting, the Steward ducked, came up, slammed a fist hard into Santiago's stomach, another to his chin. Santiago reeled sideways, slammed into the cast-iron shelves.

Santiago was outmatched. It had been years since he had fought anyone.

To lose means to die.

Fear and adrenaline exploded in his chest. Years of fistfights with Nico and boxing matches with neighborhood friends swarmed back.

Think. Don't blindly swing.

The Steward lunged again, his right fist aimed for Santiago's face. Santiago waited, parried, ducked, the man's fist hammering the iron shelf behind his head. Santiago came up hard, his left shoulder crunched into the man's ribcage, lifted him off the floor.

With a guttural shout, Santiago rushed forward, pounding the man's spine into the back wall of the alcove. The Steward landed on all fours and wheezed for air. Santiago's right fist rose, plunged, smashed the man's face as he looked up.

He slumped.

Santiago wheeled, scooped up the manuscript and papers from the floor.

He reached the alcove's opening, but the Steward rushed forward, buried his shoulder into Santiago's back. They slammed into the metal railing. Papers rocketed out of Santiago's hands. The man shifted, aiming to hurl Santiago headfirst over the railing to the floor twenty-five feet below.

Santiago spun hard, his elbow aimed for the Steward's head. The man ducked, his head rocketed up against Santiago's chin. Santiago's own head rattled with the impact and his back curled over the iron railing. Mere inches from toppling over it, Santiago flailed with his right hand to grasp the railing.

His attacker grunted, pressed down. Santiago heard the click of an opening switchblade.

Santiago gasped, struggled to keep his feet on the floor. The man glared down, his eyes like cold, glass marbles. A hiss: "You lose."

Think.

One last lunge, Santiago twisted, freed his arm. The man countered, shoved him forward, up and off the floor. The Steward plunged the blade downward toward Santiago's throat.

Santiago gave a wild shout and bucked, shifting his weight over the iron banister. His attacker's murderous eyes flickered with startled fear. Thrown off balance by Santiago's unexpected move, the man's weight also shifted over the railing. He reached back to seize the railing and missed.

Fully over the banister, Santiago seized the Steward's coat just behind the back of his arms. He scissored his legs against the man's body and arched backward in a flip.

The two men peeled over the iron railing, cartwheeling through the air. A terrified shout.

His attacker smashed into the marble floor first. Santiago thumped hard on top of him, his attacker's body cushioning the impact. The blade clattered across the floor.

Santiago gasped for breath. He rose, half knelt, half stood, lifted the man by the front of his coat. No resistance. The man's face and arms were slack. His blue, glassy eyes slid toward Santiago's face, locked onto his eyes.

Santiago shook him. "You shoulda brought a gun."

The man's blue eyes fluttered, rolled back in his skull. Santiago dropped the man to the floor. He desperately glanced around the library to make sure no one else was poised to attack. He staggered to his feet, collected the scattered papers: Foley's transcript on Healy, Jasper's thesis and notes. Then he tucked Philip Cannon's papers in his waist, still bound in their rubber band and dropped his shirt over them.

His legs still quaking uncontrollably, Santiago shook his head to clear the lightheadedness. He'd been followed here. Somehow they knew where he was. He couldn't go back to his car.

Abby!

A flash of panic. If he'd been followed, Abby wasn't safe either.

He tore his cell from his pocket. She was likely finished at the funeral home and headed home. He punched in her cell number.

It rang hollowly.

"Answer!"

Abby's calm voicemail message clicked on.

Santiago jammed the phone back into his pocket, limped toward the library door and clicked the deadbolt. He threw off the ache in his leg and dashed down the hallway to the staircase.

The elevator door slid open to the third floor of Healy Hall. Nicolas Torres stepped out into the empty hallway. He glanced down the empty corridor in the direction of the fading, clattering footsteps coming from the far stairwell. He rushed over to the closing door of Riggs Library, stepped inside.

He uttered a surprised curse and an impressed smile creased his face.

Chapter 49: The Final Crusade

Bradley cursed himself silently. In leaping away from his desk in fear, he'd not only left his phone. He'd also left behind the thumb drive with the downloaded files still in the USB port of his laptop.

Bradley listened to movements coming from his desk. The man clicked the desk lamp on and sat back in the chair, illuminated in a circle of yellow light and cigarette smoke.

"I have all night, Mr. Freeman. Why don't you come over here and we can have a nice chat."

Bradley peered around the corner of the far cubicle. The laptop with the thumb drive still sat on his desk. If he was going to die, it would not be before he could hide that drive.

Bradley's hand searched the cubicle desk normally occupied by Bailey Hall. He picked up the phone receiver and slid it to his ear.

Dead.

Which meant the internet was also cut.

Bradley's fingers continued to search his friend's desk. A rabid Nats fan, Bailey kept three autographed baseballs perched beside his monitor. Bradley's fingers closed around one. He stood and hurled the ball as powerfully as he could against the far glass entrance doors.

It bounced harmlessly off its thick glass, ricocheted into a nearby cubicle, smashed a computer monitor.

The man laughed again.

Bradley breathed heavily. "I've already e-mailed all the incriminating files to a half dozen other people."

"No, Mr. Freeman, you haven't." He pulled his own phone out of his jacket pocket and waved it. "Mr. Feeney, who now controls your network, assures me of that."

Bradley grasped another of Bailey's baseballs and stood. He eyed the laptop on his desk.

"Ah, you've decided to be reasonable." He gestured to Bradley's desk chair. "Why don't you sit and we can discuss this like gentlemen."

Bradley kept the lower part of his body obscured by the cubicle walls and stepped closer to his desk. "I'm not sure actual gentlemen kill other people for a hobby."

"Hobby? I assure you I'm generously compensated. That, if I'm not mistaken, makes it my profession."

"And that is how you justify it?" A few steps closer.

"Don't be obtuse, Mr. Freeman. That was just my dry sense of humor percolating into the world to make it a happier place." He crossed his leg and snuffed his cigarette out on the bottom of his shoe. "You presume to judge me as a killer. Yet you applauded the death of Osama bin Laden, did you not?"

"That was justice for the deaths of thousands of Americans."

He waved his hand broadly. "So is my employ."

Bradley scoffed and took two more steps.

The man shrugged at Bradley's disbelief. "From my point of view you stand in the way of the annihilation of tens of thousands of soldiers of the growing Islamic state – men, women and children who would think nothing of wrapping themselves in an explosives belt and walking into a café where your mother is sitting, or your future wife and children to forge their new caliphate."

"Rectitude." Bradley slid closer.

"An apt word for our little project, don't you agree? I presume you know the word's meaning?"

"Supremely moral behavior. It's a word often used by the supremely self-righteous."

The Steward laughed.

"There are just two things I don't understand." Bradley took a step.

"Oh?"

"Just how you are going to kill tens of thousands of ISIS soldiers by detonating a nuclear weapon in Israel? And you'll have to explain to me how killing millions of innocent people is supremely moral."

The man cocked his head. "You really do see the world as a collection of ones and zeroes, don't you? That is the problem with your profession, Mr. Freeman. When your life largely consists of computer code, you eventually lose all imagination."

He took out another cigarette and his lighter flared, giving the impression of his face flush with flame. "I am a moral man just like you." He eyed Bradley. "I daresay, more so."

Bradley reached the last cubicle across from his own desk. "This I've got to hear."

"We live in a nation that has turned its back on the greatest threat it has ever faced. We have grown so weary with war, our memories of the brutal way we were attacked have so quickly faded, we are simply turning our backs on our enemy." The man grew animated. "In World War II, did we walk away?" He looked up at Bradley and shook his head. "Or did we press that battle until those who attacked us surrendered unconditionally and were hanging from the gallows?"

He pulled on his cigarette. "Meanwhile, we invite our enemies into this country, treating their false religion – whose leaders refuse to condemn violence and instead continue to incite it – as an equal to our own. We allow their imams to radicalize their youth under our very noses. Convincing them to kill the very people who have so warmly welcomed them. And to join their fight in Syria and Iraq."

He pointed to himself. "You think I'm the barbarian." He laughed. "You are a naïve fool, Mr. Freeman. The true barbarians are blowing themselves up on buses and murdering innocents in Parisian theaters and stadiums. They are dropping airplanes from the sky. They're beheading Christians on the internet. Every day they are plotting still. Yet what does our government do, applauded by its citizenry?"

Bradley stepped behind his desk, his fingers taut around the hidden baseball and stared at the man over his laptop. "We look away."

The man nodded.

"But Israel is not our enemy," Bradley said.

"No. Just the sacrificial lamb."

"You want to start a war."

"Not just any war. We want a war that annihilates the Middle East. To definitively end that threat. Not shock and awe. That pathetic effort failed. We want a scorched earth, from which the Middle East will never rise again. And we shall do this by leveling Tel Aviv. A new Holocaust. Do you happen to know what that word means?"

"It's one of history's most unforgiveable acts," Bradley challenged, his heart fluttering in his chest.

"It means 'sacrifice by fire.'" The man blew smoke across Bradley's desk.

"You actually think you will successfully smuggle a nuclear device past Israeli security?"

The man joined in. "Oh, I know we will." The man's icy, confident tone prompted Bradley to fall silent. "Do you understand Middle Eastern geopolitics, Mr. Freeman?"

"Well enough," Bradley said. He slid over, eyeing the desk lamp's plug into the outlet beneath his desk.

"Rectitude simply exploits its different hatreds. After the leveling of Tel Aviv, Israel will respond with its own nuclear weapons. The Stewards that we have sprinkled throughout the NSA, CIA and State Department will helpfully provide intelligence initially implicating Iran, which has been developing nuclear capabilities for years despite our worthless attempts to stop them."

He took a last pull on his cigarette and stubbed it out on his shoe. "Israel's attack on Iran will draw Iraq and Egypt into the fight. With the Stewards' help, Israel and the United States will later discover the initial intelligence implicating Iran was fabricated by Saudi Arabia to trick Israel into destroying the Saudi Kingdom's enemies. With proof of Saudi Arabia's complicity in the attack, the U.S. and Europe will be forced to break ties with the Saudi princes and go to war on the side of Israel."

He looked Bradley in the eye. "The Final Crusade. The purification of the Holy Land. You see? I'm not a barbarian, Mr. Freeman. I'm a savior." The assassin offered a cold smile. "And your death is therefore justified." The man reached inside his jacket and his hand emerged with a weapon.

"You have a gun!" Bradley grinned and kicked the lamp plug from its socket, sending the office into inky blackness. He pivoted, cocked his arm and rocketed the baseball directly at the spot where the man had been sitting. The killer cried out and Bradley seized the laptop, yanking the thumb drive free.

The man's knees thudded against the floor. Bradley flung the laptop in his direction and sprinted toward the office door. He took three steps and then leapt sideways into a cubicle. Two explosions, two flashes of light, bloomed from the gun muzzle. The bullets whizzed past and the chained glass entrance doors exploded into shards. Bradley leapt for the open space.

Another flash and explosion. A powerful punch to his back sent Bradley reeling. He straightened and kept running. Another bullet thudded into the wall above his head and he dashed out the door.

He turned right, dashing toward the street with the heaviest traffic. He turned to head north. He tried to pull in oxygen. A strange sucking sound made him look down. A hole in his chest sprayed crimson with each jagged breath. Bradley pressed his hand on the hole, took two more steps. His vision and balance tilted. Grunting, he spun, sprawling downward, splaying outward across the sidewalk, rolling onto his back. Bright flecks of light filled his eyes and black circles began constricting his vision.

His killer ran up. A grin crossed his face as he raised his weapon again. "Yes, Mr. Freeman. I have gun."

Bradley Freeman blacked out.

Chapter 50: Pursued

Santiago sprinted across Healy Lawn through the South Gatehouse. He headed east, past Holy Trinity, Charlie Breckinridge's old parish. Ten minutes later, he breathlessly reached Wisconsin Avenue and ducked into a sandwich shop on the corner.

"Welcome to Wally's," a young man called out.

Santiago ignored him, stared out the restaurant windows, studied the dark intersection and its pedestrians.

Santiago pressed his hands against his jeans. His legs were still quaking. He reached into his pocket, redialed Abby's number. He winced as the phone brushed his cheekbone. The right side of his face was swelling, probably turning eggplant purple.

"Come on, Abby! Just answer already!" he whispered.

"Welcome to Wally's!" the man called a little louder.

The call clicked to voicemail. Santiago turned his battered face and glared. The young man's eager smile collapsed. He seized a cloth and began wiping down the restaurant's very clean counter.

Santi turned to look back out the window but caught the eye of a middle-aged woman staring at him from a corner of the restaurant. She was eating a grilled chicken panini with a plastic fork and knife. She stared at him, frozen mid-chew, her hand poised above her purse.

Was she reaching in to offer him her wallet or to seize her pepper spray?

Georgetown, the land of the bohemian and the beautiful.

Santiago smiled at her and her hand crept closer to her purse.

Definitely the pepper spray.

Santiago eyed the guy at the counter again. Mr. Welcome-to-Wally's was gonna call the cops. They'd get here, flashing double-barreled, pump action shotguns in forty seconds flat.

Santiago needed to quickly get to a crowded Metro station. Georgetown, of course, made that impossible. The neighborhood's residents rallied to kill a subway stop when the system was built back in the 1970s.

To keep the non-panini-eating, purple-faced, Puerto Rican riffraff out of their silver-buckled, cobblestone-lined neighborhood.

A southbound black and yellow cab nearly ate a red light, skidded to a stop just across the street.

Santiago yanked open Wally's door, dashed across P Street against the traffic and ducked into the taxi.

"Where to, Bud?" The driver's eyes settled on him in the rearview mirror. "Whoa! You have an argument with your girlfriend?"

"My boyfriend," Santiago responded. "I don't think he was that into me."

That shut the cabbie up.

Santiago turned and studied the cars behind him, mentally clicking through his options. The light changed. "Take me to a Metro stop."

The driver hesitated. "Am I gonna get a visit from the cops?"

"Only if you don't start driving," Santiago growled.

The cab jetted into the intersection. "Foggy Bottom?" the cabbie said.

"Dupont Circle."

"Foggy Bottom's closer."

Santiago needed a big station. A bigger crowd.

"Dupont Circle."

The driver switched lanes too quickly and Santiago held the door. He hated D.C. cab drivers. The driver swerved again onto M. "You'll get a bigger tip if you use all four wheels."

He glanced out the back window again. The one benefit of an insane driver is that anyone following would stand out.

The driver flew down Pennsylvania, whipped around Washington Circle. He muttered at a sedan with an Iowa plate. "That idiot's been driving in the same damn circle since last Tuesday."

Santiago braced himself. The guy accelerated and cut off the Iowa driver, swung across two lanes of traffic before blasting onward. At the intersection of Q, the cabbie braked to turn right. Santiago dropped a twenty-dollar bill over the seat and jumped out.

He jogged the block east to Dupont Circle. At the top of the Metro entrance, he stepped onto the enormous escalator that descended into the Red Line. He pulled his cell out again and redialed Abby as he ran down the moving escalator.

Abby's recorded voice came on again and Santiago ended the call. Twenty steps down a tourist was standing beside his wife, blocking the left side. "Stay to the right!" Santiago called out. The man slid aside, stuttering an apology.

"They're always in such a hurry!" the woman whispered to her husband.

At the bottom of the escalator, Santi stuffed a ten-dollar bill into a tall machine and it spat out a rectangular fare card.

"Stop! Stop here!" she shouted.

Nico Torres hit the brakes too hard. Her shoulder popped against the seatbelt, the laptop sliding to the floor. She cursed. "He's stopped! He must have jumped out of the cab!"

"Where'd he go?" Nico shouted back.

"Here! Somewhere here! He's hardly moving!"

Nico craned his neck, his eyes flashing across the hundred faces milling around the intersection. He spotted the escalator sucking metro riders below the street. "Get out! Get down there!"

"We can't track him if he's down there!"

"Goddamn it! Get down there!" he shouted again. "North or south! I need a fucking direction!"

Rush hour was rapidly filling the station. Santiago slid the fare card into the turnstile and rode another short escalator down to the platform. He looked around. If someone were following him, he'd have no idea in such a huge place with hundreds of different faces.

The round, white lights lining the track flashed. The arriving southbound train, headed toward Metro Center, blasted air across the platform. Its door chime sounded and Santiago jostled on, pushing his way through the crowded car to the next door up. A woman, propped up against a pole in the train aisle, turned to glare at him. Spotting his swollen face, her eyes shot back to her e-book.

He waited until the door chime sounded again. The northbound train toward Shady Grove pulled into the station and began disgorging commuters. The moment the door began shutting, Santiago jumped back out and dashed across the platform. He leapt aboard the northbound train just before its doors closed.

She took the return escalator back up to the street at full sprint. "Stand right!" she screamed. She shouldered her way past, one hundred eighty-eight feet of escalator to the surface. She dashed to the SUV, leapt inside.

He gunned the engine. "Which way?"

"Towards Shady Grove," she could barely croak. "He went north!"

The SUV's tires smoked and he blew through the red light.

Nico Torres' face was ashen, tight-lipped. His brother was too damned predictable.

The subway train swallowed a handful of passengers at Woodley Park, mostly tourists returning from a day at the National Zoo. The door chimes sounded again.

The car blasted through the tunnel. Another car rocketed south on the opposite track, setting the train rocking. "Next stop, Cleveland Park," the driver marble-mouthed. The door's pneumatics hissed. Santiago bound off the train, rushed up the escalator. In a moment, he was street level again, glancing at the dark sky. He began running west toward Abby's house.

He called her number a fourth time.

Chapter 51: Pale Death

Santiago arrived at Abby's home panting for air. He dashed up the driveway and the empty, still porch swing shot a flutter of panic through his belly. Of course, it was too cold for her to sit outside. But the windows of her home were also all ink and emptiness. Santi glanced at the block's other homes. Yellow beams of warmth tumbled out of the window casements, a reassuring reminder that life was contently ticking toward spring.

Light from a neighbor's kitchen spilled onto Abby's driveway. Santiago could see her car in the back.

He tried to reason with his fear. Her father had likely taken her to dinner somewhere and she'd turned off her phone.

He dashed up the steps to the porch and froze to the spot. Abby's front door was slightly ajar.

Santiago's legs, which had stopped quivering back on the Metro, began to quake again, his heart banging on his breastbone.

The door creaked as he slid it fully open. With no moon, the streetlights, filtered by the low hanging tree branches, barely penetrated a few feet down the hallway.

He reached over and hit the light switch. Its click echoed uselessly through the house. The electricity was off.

Santiago stepped inside, stopped at the boundary between dim light and utter blackness slashing across the floor. "Abby! You here?"

Silence.

The house felt frigid. Without heat, dampness had snuck in, lending the front room the clamminess of a mausoleum.

Santiago's palms began to perspire. He rubbed them down his jeans.

A dull thump threaded down the staircase, followed by a rustling whisper.

He almost ran up the black stairs, but thought better of it. He would not be taken by surprise again. He rushed blindly for the kitchen, his hands outstretched to avoid slamming into a wall. If Abby had a flashlight, he'd likely find it there. Beneath his feet, he felt the wood of the hallway floor give way to the kitchen's tiles. Before he thought to slow down, Santiago's thigh thudded into a kitchen chair. He cursed in pain and spun, catching himself against the chilly, granite counter. He paused, hoping his eyes would adjust to the darkness but the sheer curtains screened the faint light trying to leap from the neighbor's house.

His panicked pulse pounded in his head. His fingers splayed across the drawers, latching onto handles. A drawer clattered to the floor. His hands read the contents: teaspoons, tablespoons, two sizes of forks, dinner knives.

Santi's fingers caught on the jagged edge of a long, serrated steak knife.

He hand-searched the other drawers and he cursed his luck. Abby had an endless collection of placemats, cloth napkins, dishtowels. Even a drawer full of batteries, cold to the touch. But no flashlight.

A double thump sounded, directly over his head: Abby's bedroom.

Santiago stifled a hopeless groan. He squeezed the polished wooden handle of the steak knife. Even back at Riggs, he didn't feel the nauseating fear that was now churning his belly, clamping a vise across his throat so he could barely breathe.

Check the car outside for a flashlight.

A heavier thump upstairs, sounding like a struggle.

There wasn't time. Santiago crouched and slid across the floor like a wild animal.

The front door was still open, casting a beam of light on the steps leading to the second floor. Santiago took the first and it groaned in protest. He grimaced, avoiding the centers of the wooden steps, bracing his weight against the banister with his left hand, keeping his feet on the four inches closest to the wall.

He climbed into the horrid, cavernous darkness. The blackness magnified everything – sound, smell, sensation.

Down the hallway, a tumult filled the air, a lamp smashed to the floor in Abby's room. Santiago squeezed the knife.

The house went silent. The bass drum of his heart boomed in his ears, his purple cheekbone pulsed painfully in time. He pressed himself against the hallway wall, found the bedroom door by touch, eased it open.

He inched inside, the knife trembled.

Santi raised his foot, slid it forward, lowered it to the floor.

The crunching of glass beneath his feet sounded like rib bones snapping. Santiago stepped back, slammed into Abby's bureau. The horrid whirring filled the air, sharp pikes dug painfully into his neck.

A terrified shout, he dropped the knife, grabbed at the thing attacking him.

Santiago threw his assailant down. He rushed to the closed curtains, crashed into Abby's desk, strewing a pile of books to the floor. He threw the curtains back to let in some feeble light.

The chicken darted in circles around the bedroom rug, clucking at him angrily.

Fear still clamped across his brain, Santiago stepped toward it to wring its neck.

He froze as a cell phone, sitting in the middle of Abby's bed, brightly glowed and rang.

One, two more times it rang before he pressed it to his ear. A hopeless tear traced across his purple cheek.

A voice like a shiver spirited through the phone. "Pale death with an impartial foot knocks at the hovels of the poor and the palaces of kings, Father Torres."

Chapter 52: A Classical Education

Santiago was too frightened to speak. The voice on the phone had deepened the chill in the dark house. "You went to a Jesuit high school and college, Father Torres. Certainly you can tell me who scratched those lines."

"Is this a test?"

There was a dry laugh like a sheet of glass cracking. "A test! After the week you've had, do you suppose you could pass one?"

Santiago waited for the man to speak again.

"It's like a shadow, isn't it?"

Santiago hopelessly spun in the pitch-black room. "What? What is like a shadow?"

"Death, of course. It's unshakeable. It stalks you, tapping on your shoulder." His words drew out. "Tap, tap, tap. Patiently biding its time. Death can be patient, Father. It knows once the game is over, both the king and the pawn find themselves in the same box."

"Is she alive?" Santiago gasped.

"Ms. Byrne?" The voice quivered like a taut bowstring. "Oh my, yes. But you're a dead man, Father Torres. There's surely no way around that." He let the words creep down Santiago's spine. "Now whether she will share your fate will depend upon how fastidiously you follow directions."

The man paused. "There is a key on the bed."

Santiago bent to the bed, his hands darting across the duvet until he seized it.

"You are going to bring us what we want, Father Torres. We do, however, have a few ground rules."

Santiago grew impatient with the time the man took between words. "I have the key! What are your rules?"

"First, do not end this call at any time. If it drops, be it your fault or not, something unfortunate will happen to Ms. Byrne."

Santiago's anger surged, edging out the fear that had kept his heart pounding. "That's out of my control!"

"Tap, tap, tap, Father Torres." The man continued. "It was Horace, the Roman poet, who wrote it." The man repeated the quote. "'Pale death with an impartial foot knocks at the hovels of the poor and the palaces of kings.' Tsk, tsk. I'm disappointed. Your resume really insisted you were classically educated."

Santiago's hands traced the wall to the hallway. His knee struck the balustrade at the top of the stairs and he cried out.

"Perhaps you'd care to try to guess another? Redeem yourself? Tell me, Father. Who wrote, 'One should die proudly when it is no longer possible to live proudly?'"

Santiago's hands trembled. Panicked the call would drop, Santiago rushed down the stairs to reach whatever car they had left outside. In his haste, Santiago missed the bottom step in the darkness. He crashed downward. With a grunt, he landed hard, his knee cracking against the wood floor. The phone flashed from his grasp, spun across the floor. He lunged for it, his fingers trembled as he pressed it to his ear. "Are you still there?" he whispered.

Silence.

"Do take greater care, Father," the voice said with a breathy laugh. "So many people manage to lose themselves in darkness."

Santiago wanted to scream in frustration. What was the point of shutting down the power in the house? He pulled himself to his feet and the reason skittered into his brain. It wasn't just a game. It kept him from scanning or copying the documents.

"Ah, but I've misled you."

Santiago stopped, his heart thumping at the words.

"You thought I was quoting another classical philosopher or poet, didn't you. Alas, it was a different philosopher. Nietzche," he said. "The nineteenth century philosopher famous for saying, 'God is dead.' I thought you might prefer him."

From his voice, Santiago could tell the man was smiling with satisfaction. "There's an important lesson here, Father. One must be careful when dabbling with nihilism. It rarely ends well. Did you know Nietzche completely lost his mind at the age of forty-four? Less than a half dozen years away for you, is it not?"

Santiago yanked the front door of the house wide and lunged down the porch steps. He glanced around the dark front yard. A sedan was parked in front of Abby's house, a car he had never seen there before. He dashed over. The key clicked open the lock.

He slid into the seat, slammed the door. "What are your other rules?"

"Let's try another, shall we? 'To die is a debt we must all pay.'" The voice paused. "Tell me you don't know that one! How shameful. Shall I offer a helpful hint? If I told you he wrote Greek tragedies, would it help?"

"Aeschylus," Santiago spat. "Or Sophocles."

"Euripedes. Start the car."

Santiago hesitated.

"Oh, come now, Father. Have some faith in me. I'm far too subtle for car bombs. No wonder you're doing so poorly on my quiz. You are either terribly foolish or fear has paralyzed your brain. Think on this, Father: don't you think we're smart enough to ensure we have all the documents Mr. Cannon stole from us before we kill you?"

Santiago turned the key. The car's GPS also turned on.

"You're far more obedient than I realized. At least one of your vows is intact."

Santiago pressed his back into the seat. "I'm not going anywhere without proof you have Abby and she is safe."

"Ah, proof of life. Consider the irony of your demand. A rather cold and calculating request for a man of the cloth. You won't obey me unless she's here and alive. But if she's dead already, do you stupidly believe you're then free to do as you wish?"

The voice turned cold, angry. "You've struck out on my quiz thus far, Father Torres. Get the next one wrong and I'll kill Ms. Byrne right now. And because I'm such a generous man, I'll even let you listen to her scream. Proof of death, if you will."

Abigail's scream jarred Santiago. "Don't!" Santiago shouted.

"'Death may be the greatest of all human blessings.'" He paused. "Tap, tap, tap. Your shadow grows impatient, Father Torres. Who said it?"

Santiago's racing, confused mind tumbled desperately.

"Tap, tap. The clock is ticking."

"For God's sake, wait!"

"Three seconds before she's forced to swallow poison."

"Socrates! It was Socrates!" Santiago cried. The Greek philosopher the Athenians killed by forcing him to drink hemlock.

The man's voice turned icy again. "Follow the GPS. We've activated the tracking app on the phone. If you stop anywhere but at an intersection, we'll know it and Ms. Byrne will die."

Santiago lurched forward, his heart raced with the car.

Faintly lit by the dashboard readout, the glowing, familiar face of his brother flashed past Nico Torres in an unfamiliar car.

"Shit!" Nico Torres slammed on the SUV's brakes. She cursed again. He nearly rolled the vehicle swerving into a driveway to turn around.

The traffic on Connecticut Avenue had been terrible. Now that Santiago was above ground again, his brother had no plans to lose him.

"Is his cell pinging again?"

"No."

"What do you mean, no?" Nico looked over his shoulder. The tracking specialist was closing her laptop.

"This op is done. Plug's been pulled."

"That's impossible! Turn that fucking thing back on!"

She shrugged, pocketed her phone. "Take it up with someone else. There's apparently a problem with your warrant, Agent Torres. We're done here."

Nico braked. He turned again in his seat, and pulled out his weapon. The barrel of his gun, pressed against the woman's back, caused her to stiffen. "No. You're done here. You're gonna slide your weapon and your cell phone onto the seat next to me. Then you're gonna open your laptop and hand it to me. And then, if it's okay with you, you're gonna politely step out into street and walk the fuck home."

She glared at him.

"Now!" he shouted.

Chapter 53: A Troublesome Business

"Do observe the speed limit. A police stop would violate our rules."

Santiago glanced at the speedometer.

"Have I mentioned, as far as classical philosophers and playwrights go, I'm partial to Seneca. Do you know his work?"

"I know who he is."

"Would you care to guess my favorite Seneca quote?"

The woman's voice on the GPS startled Santiago with its chirping friendliness. Santiago complied with her commands and headed southbound on Wisconsin Avenue.

"Ah, Father, surely you slept in Latin class. It is: 'Death is the wish of some, the relief of many, and the end of all.'"

He fell silent as Santiago drove a few miles. He was silent so long, Santiago felt panic rise in his belly. "Are you still there?"

"I promise you one thing, Father. When tonight is done, death will be a relief. Just as it was a relief for Father Breckinridge."

"And Jasper, my friend? Was it a relief for him too?"

Silence.

"And Pat Kelly? Or was that more a relief for you?"

"Of course not, Father. You killed Pat Kelly. Death was your wish for him, was it not?"

"That's not true. I've never wished anyone dead!"

"The body you left in the library this evening suggests otherwise."

A horn blared and a taxi slashed across traffic. Santiago swerved to avoid a collision. He suddenly became aware again of his surroundings. He was back in Georgetown. The GPS voice chirped again. He veered east on P Street.

"Have you figured out your destination yet, Father? Or do you need another clue?"

Nearly all of D.C. lay to his east. The Steward could be talking about a million places. "Let me guess. Your clue has something to do with death?"

"Ah, how quickly you've picked up on this evening's theme. I feared I was being too subtle for you." A pause. "Would the Eagle's Perch mean anything to you?"

Santiago's spine iced over. He was back in the confessional, absorbing Charlie Breckinridge's story: *My father and his men dragged him up to Eagle's Perch, a cliff overlooking the river. Tied him up, plied him with whiskey, forced it on him, slapping his face when he refused, until the boy was good and drunk.*

"If you're planning to toss me off a cliff in Harpers Ferry, I'm headed in the wrong direction."

The GPS chirped and he headed south on North Capitol Street. The Capitol shone brightly in the distance. The Eagle's Perch? Could he mean the eagle's helmet on Lady Liberty atop its dome?

"A final quote for you, Father. I've saved the best for last, the most poetic one of all. It speaks to me like a sweet love song, percolating through my brain as the people I've slain rattle with death. 'Dying is a troublesome business: there is pain to be suffered, and it wrings one's heart; but death is a splendid thing – a warfare accomplished, a beginning all over again, a triumph. You can always see that in their faces.'" He hissed the last sentence.

The skin on Santiago's arms prickled.

"Ah, fooled you again. It's no Greek or Roman. It's an Irishman, Father. George Bernard Shaw." A pause. "I respect the Irish. They know death well. You saw what Shaw was referring to this afternoon in the library, didn't you? You saw it in the dying man's face. It was a splendid thing, wasn't it, Father? It was *glorious*."

A wave of nausea swept Santiago. "It was horrible."

"You are a skillful liar, I'm told. You felt triumphant, just like I shall feel. There is no shame in admitting it."

Santiago suddenly realized where he was. The Eagle's Perch. He finally understood the man's plan. It was to be just like Jasper. The Steward would have a suicide note prepared, written in Santiago's own hand, signed with his own name. He reached up and clicked off the GPS.

"So certain of yourself, are you?" The man said. "Are you prepared to die?"

Santiago turned into Gonzaga High School's parking lot. The center of his body went cold as the tires crunched across the loose gravel at its entrance.

His heart thudded so hard Santiago could barely utter the words. "I have a quote for you, Steward. Perhaps you can tuck it in the special note you've had written for me."

"By all means."

Santiago spoke the quotation carefully. "'Die when I may, I want it said of me by those who knew me best that I always plucked a thistle and planted a flower where I thought a flower would grow.'"

"So very thoughtful of you to keep with the evening's theme. Is it Aristotle?"

"It was Lincoln."

"A murdered man! How apt." The man laughed. "You know where I'll be waiting."

The call went dead and Santiago dropped the Steward's phone on the car seat beside him.

Chapter 54: The Eagle's Perch

Santiago stepped out of the elevator on the third floor of Gonzaga's rectory. A single sconce fought back the hallway's shadows. All was strangely still. No utensils rang against kitchen pans, no television hummed from the common room. The eleven Jesuits housed in the brick building were at Georgetown for dinner, celebrating John DeMaio's sixtieth birthday. Even Brother Sinclair, who would normally have stayed behind to see Charlie Breckinridge to his room at night, was across town.

Near the window Breckinridge's large recliner was cold and empty, the broad, worn dimple in its seat making clear its occupant was missing.

Santiago had never before stood in the rectory when it was empty. The hum of the fluorescent bulb above the kitchen stove accentuated the silence. The common room's black, glass windows squinted at him, filling the space with a frigid gloom.

The Eagle's Perch. The roof of the Jesuit rectory, high above Buchanan Football Field and the rest of campus. Home of the Gonzaga Eagles.

Santiago's own home. The perch of its fired headmaster.

The elevator could climb no higher than the Jesuits' third floor rooms, yet Santiago knew where the Steward was waiting with Abigail. He closed the elevator's metal gate, walked around to the stairway, scaled the final story to the rectory roof. He stepped out the door. A gust of wind struggled to wrestle him back into the opening. Above him loomed the imposing iron bell tower of St.

Aloysius Church, constructed beside the rectory decades before the nation finished the Capitol's dome.

The sound of an inferno filled Santiago's head.

He stepped onto the building's vast roof, littered with enormous heating and cooling units and even Brother Sinclair's rooftop garden in the corner. All was draped in long shadows cast by the streetlights below. The roaring grew in his head like a vast crowd cheering. Santiago stepped close to the rectory's northern edge. The school's track and football field sat empty far below, where broken row houses, a half century before, housed hookers who propositioned Gonzaga seniors smoking between classes.

"You have what we want?"

Santiago turned. The voice made clear the man on the phone had sent someone else.

The Steward stepped into a shaft of light thrown across the roof by the office building on the far street corner. It glinted off the gun in his hand. With a yank, the man pulled Abby into view. Her eyes red, her face so profoundly sad. "I'm so sorry, Santi."

The killer shook her hard to silence her.

Santiago found his voice. "Let her go and I'll give you the documents." He fished in his pocket and threw the car keys at her feet. "Abby, when he lets you go, take the car I left in the lot and drive. Go far away. Just leave the country. You can afford to."

Abby began to sob.

"Unless you have a bigger gun than mine, Father, you'll see things my way. You will bring me the documents now or she will join you in a romantic jump from the Gonzaga rectory. Two misunderstood lovers, dying intertwined. What a fitting end to an English teacher's life. A modern Romeo and Juliet."

"I'm supposed to just trust you'll keep your word that you'll let her go?"

"We're not monsters. Father Breckinridge lived a very long life."

"Until he spoke the truth. What kind of freedom is that?"

"Freedom from death?" The man shrugged. "You turn up your nose at the fundamental promise of your own religion, Father? There is a far higher moral good at stake that people like you cannot comprehend. I trust Ms. Byrne will see the virtue in silence. If she does not, we'll simply kill her father."

The Steward waved the gun. "Look around. Do you perceive you're in any position to negotiate? Bring me the documents and she's free to go. But know this. If there is anything missing or if you've withheld copies of anything, she will follow you to the grave. That you can trust."

The roaring expanded in Santiago's head. He stepped forward, reached into his jacket for Cannon's papers. He began counting his own breaths, certain they would stop before he reached one hundred. He looked down at Cannon's documents and the Steward lifted them from his hand. He was smiling. Abby had her eyes pressed shut. "Please forgive me, Santiago."

A movement on the rooftop just over the Steward's left shoulder startled Santiago. Another man took a confident step forward, his gun also drawn. The light from the office building fell across his face.

Nico, his own brother.

"Goddamn you!" Santiago sputtered at him.

A look of shock slashed across Nico's face. He shook his head in horror and gestured for Santiago to stay quiet.

Regret immediately pulsed across Santiago's brain. He had misread the whole thing. Nico wasn't with the Steward. He was trying to help him.

The Steward whirled. Two guns simultaneously exploded, their flashes turned the rest of the roof pitch black. Santiago threw himself across Abby, knocked her to the roof. He rolled, scrambled to his feet, his eyes adjusting again to the dim light. The Steward lay on the roof, gurgling, his hand pressed over a hole in his neck, spraying scarlet with every heartbeat. The blood-spattered documents lay beside him on the cold roof.

"Nico!" Santiago scrambled across the rooftop where his brother lay on his back. "My God, Abby! He was trying to help me! What have I done?"

"Give me your phone! I'll call an ambulance!" Abby cried. Santiago frantically pulled his phone from his pocket, threw it to her and bent over his brother.

Santiago ran his hand over Nico's chest, probing for where the bullet had hit him. Nico's eyes were filled with terror. He repeatedly shook his head, struggling to speak. Nico arched his back, rolled on his side. "What!" Santiago leaned forward. "What is it?"

Nico arched again. Santiago pressed his hand against the back of his jacket. He slid his hand down, stopping when he felt a growing, sticky wet circle of blood. At its center, his finger found the bullet hole.

Santiago rolled his brother, searching his chest for where the entrance wound should be.

Nothing.

Nico tried to speak, arched to roll over again, and his eyes flickered white. He fell unconscious.

Shocked confusion overcame Santiago. The Steward was in front of Nico. How could he have a gunshot wound in his back?

He whirled to look at Abby, who was standing in silhouette against the lights of the far office building.

"Get down! There's another shooter on the roof!" he screamed. Santiago ducked into a crouch and began running across to her. "Get down, Abby! For God's sake, get down!"

Halfway to her, Santiago finally understood. Abby had remained standing, perfectly still. He slowed and straightened, took five steps closer. He saw then she was sobbing, his cell phone in one hand by her side. The Stewards' documents in her other.

"You didn't call for help, did you?" Santiago's body quivered with an ache he'd not felt since his father had first brought Nico to the dinner table. He gestured to her hand, holding the blood-soaked papers. "How can you do this to me? You're a woman. How can you be a Steward?"

Yet it suddenly made sense. All along, Abigail had known everything. She'd known about the package of mailed documents, knew he put them in the school's safe, knew he was officiating at Jasper's funeral during the burglary. She kept tabs, allowing them to follow him to Breckinridge and back to Lauinger Library.

She looked at him, grief-stricken. "I'm not a Steward. I had no choice, Santi."

"No choice!" Santiago shouted. He pointed to Philip Cannon's papers and Jasper's thesis, his voice turned guttural and he surged forward. "Give those to me!"

"She'll do no such thing." Abigail's father and another Steward, a gun in hand, stepped into the light from the back of the roof. "They rightfully belong to us." Abby's father held out his hand. Abby looked away from Santiago and dutifully handed her father the papers.

The menacing look on the face of the Steward with the gun caused Santiago to take a step backward.

He turned to Abby. "I was ready to give up everything for you and you betrayed me."

"No, Santi!" Abby reached her hand out to him and sobbed. "My mother made me promise."

"Promise what? That you'd protect murderers?"

"That I'd let nothing happen to him!" She held both hands out toward her father. "She was dying, Santi!" Abby's chin trembled. "What was I to do? My father is all I have left in the world."

"You had me." Santiago's voice quavered. "Or did he order you to sleep with me too?"

"This wasn't supposed to happen!" she cried, gesturing to Nico and the dead Steward at their feet. "They just wanted the documents. That's all! Oh my God!" Abigail covered her face with her hands.

"You've certainly left a trail of death in your wake, Father Torres." Abigail's father voice had taken on an icy tone.

"You're a Georgetown alumnus then. A Steward."

"And my father. And my father's father. You can therefore understand why I'm reluctant to have you destroy everything we've built." Walter Byrne turned to the Steward holding the gun and handed him the documents. "Take these. Get them out of here. Leave me to clean up this mess." He held out his hand for the man's gun. The Steward gave Byrne his weapon, took the documents and crunched across the roof, stopping only to drag his heels across its surface to scrape the sticky blood off them. Santiago moved after the documents but Abigail's father raised the gun and he stopped.

Abigail's quiet crying was punctuated by the rectory roof door slamming. Santiago turned back to face Walter Byrne.

"Put the gun down, Daddy. You have what you want. We're going to leave now."

"Don't be a fool, Abby."

"You promised no one would hurt him."

Walter Byrne gestured to the two bodies on the roof. "That would have worked before this."

Abigail's voice rose. "You promised no one would hurt him!"

"Abigail, it's time for you to leave. Just do as you're told."

Byrne raised the gun to Santiago's head. "Kneel down, Father. I will give you a moment to pray for forgiveness."

Santiago turned incredulously to Abby.

"Do it now!" Walter Byrne turned and barked at his daughter. "Abby, leave now!"

The roaring returned to Santiago's skull. He knelt slowly, staring at the gun barrel just eight feet from his head.

"Daddy, you promised!"

"Enough, Abigail!" his voice thundered.

Abby quivered, instinctively stepped toward the door.

Santiago tried to pray but the roaring in his head drowned out everything. He gave a desperate glance at Abby. She stood frozen, just beyond arm's reach, looking on in horror.

Time slowed, each fraction of a second playing out like a single page turning in a book. Byrne raised the gun. Santiago swiveled his head back toward the man. The gun tilted. The roaring in his head fell silent. Santiago's mind flooded with images, real, imagined. The look on the assassin's face in Riggs Library as Santiago flipped backward. The look on Philip Cannon's face as he stared down at Charlie Breckinridge. The look on a young black man's face as he glanced back at a little boy sprawled in the dirt.

Walter Byrne's face creased with a grimace before his finger pulled the trigger.

"Daddy!" Abby rushed forward and seized her father's hand.

"Abigail!" he shouted.

"Stop it!" Abby wrestled for the gun. In the darkness the two melded into one figure, shouting and struggling. Santiago leapt to his feet and the gun thundered. Santiago flinched. In the dim light, he watched the two stagger apart. Walter Byrne gasped and Abby collapsed to the roof and rolled upon her back.

"No!" Santiago shouted. He fell to his knees beside Abby. She blinked twice, her hands flailing outward, slapping at the body of the dead Steward beside her. A dark circle spread over her breast.

Santiago turned to Byrne. Abby's father's eyes had come alive. They flashed between Santiago and his own daughter. He took two steps backward. As the truth parted the roof's darkness, Byrne's eyes flashed with rage, drilling into Santiago. Byrne raised the gun again. With a furious, spine-tingling scream, he pointed its barrel directly at Santiago's forehead.

Chapter 55: Upon the Ledge

A flash and explosion beside Santiago's head blinded, deafened him. He fell prone to the roof, shook his head, struggled to clear the ringing in his ears.

Walter Byrne' arm grew slack, his weapon hung from his limp hand. He staggered backward two steps, almost caught himself, then wheeled backwards until the edge of the roof pressed against the back of his thighs. He sat jarringly down on the roof's ledge. He stared at Santiago, his chin quivering, his weapon sliding from his finger and clattering to the roof. His eyes flickered sadly to Abby, lying on the roof, pointing the dead Steward's gun at him. Byrne's head lolled to the side. His eyes fell back upon Santiago.

Walter Byrne's lips shuddered as if he tried to speak, and he slipped backward, over the edge of the building and fell four stories to the ground.

Santiago crawled over to Abby, his hands desperately searching the roof where she lay, gasping for air. His hand found his phone and he punched in 911. "I need help. 19 Eye Street, Northwest," he cried. "I'm on the roof of the Jesuit rectory at Gonzaga High School. People have been shot."

Abby's hand slumped to the roof and she went limp. Her grief-stricken face turned to Santiago. "I've destroyed everything I love." She exhaled a sob. "And I was just trying to find a way to save it all."

Santiago felt a hollow, angry emptiness, yet he couldn't pull away when she reached up and placed her hand, sticky with her own blood, onto his cheek. "I love you, Santi. I've always loved you. But I've ruined everything."

He reached up and took her hand and squeezed it, pressing it against his face.

"Please forgive me, Santi."

"Of course."

Abby lips trembled into a smile of gratitude that melted as a tear slid across her face. "Don't give up. Remember Jasper, how good and smart he was. Remember what he would have done."

She struggled to say something else but shuddered and her body made a deep rattling sound.

Santiago could hear sirens approaching from the east. "Hurry," he begged.

Chapter 56: Forgiveness

He blinked at the wall. After hours of the same images looping through his head, his brain had fallen numb and quiet as the sun rose. He turned to look out the window at the bright orange fire in the sky, burning off the river mist as the early morning joggers swirled through it. It promised the first brilliantly sunny day in almost two weeks. Santiago could imagine how the sun looked down at Memorial Bridge, surging above the Potomac, tiny pinpricks of light bursting and flashing as the sculls from Georgetown's crew team skittered across its surface like water bugs.

He felt like the coroner had made an incision from his navel to his chest, removed all of his internal organs and replaced them with sawdust. Nothing was left inside but an enormous thirst.

He leaned forward in his chair, rubbing his hand along the edge of the hospital bed, feeling its rough sheets, wanting to feel something.

Pearl rose and walked over. She bent and surprised him with a kiss to his cheek. He looked at her quizzically. For the first time since he had met her, Pearl looked old. "I'm so sorry for your loss, Santiago. I know Abigail meant the world to you."

"I'm the one who needs to apologize." He gestured at Nico, unconscious and still in the bed beside his chair. "Nico and Bradley. This all my fault. Had I just let Jasper's death go. What did it all accomplish?"

The documents were lost, back in the Stewards' hands. When the D.C. police had raided ACM, Inc. on K Street, they found the office completely emptied. Then the FBI agent who visited that morning mentioned the Cayman government insisted their records showed no corporation called Athenasius had ever existed.

The Stewards had erased themselves in a mere twenty-four hours.

"No," Pearl scolded but she was unable to finish. Santiago looked into her crinkled eyes. The previous night he had numbly rushed into the emergency room trailing his dying brother and Abby, who had already died in the ambulance.

The shocking sight of Pearl's ragged face had riveted him to the floor. Finding Pearl there – learning about Bradley – nearly broke him.

Two doors down, Bradley lay near death, still unconscious. Whatever he had learned that had made the Stewards try to kill him remained locked in his head. "Given the blood loss, the doctors are worried about permanent brain damage from lack of oxygen," Pearl said when she stopped by to update him. She tried to console Santiago. "But he's alive."

Her son was still breathing only because another old woman had stumbled upon the shooter and Bradley before the Steward could fire a second time.

Pearl pressed a hand on his shoulder.

Santiago squeezed it. "Pearl, you are my good friend."

She nodded, unsure of what to do with the compliment. She turned and the hospital room door sighed closed behind her. Alone now, Santiago looked at his brother. He watched his chest rising and contracting as the machine beside the bed inflated Nico like a balloon before letting the air leak out again. Nico's face was slack, his eyes closed.

Santiago turned his chair around to face him. He felt an overwhelming desire to look away, to pretend it away, but he forced himself to look at Nico.

"I am ashamed," he said out loud.

The words caught in his throat and he began to weep. "I am thoroughly ashamed. I should have stood by you. I should have defended you."

Santiago reached out and touched his brother's arm. He rested his hand over Nico's wrist, stared at his brother's light brown fingers as he spoke. "Of all the mistakes I've made in my life, and there are plenty, there is one I most wish I could go back and relive in order to make it right.

"On that night Papi brought you home for the first time, while we were sitting eating dinner. The night that changed everything for us both. That night, Mama was so enraged and I was too frightened to even breathe. When you came to the dinner table, you were just a little boy who looked terrified. A little boy who had just watched his mom buried. And instead of doing what was right, I was such a coward that I simply pretended you weren't there.

"If I could live that moment over again, I would stand up and pull out your chair for you. I would look you in the eye and say 'Welcome home.'"

Santiago choked up as he said the words. Nico's fingers slowly closed on his wrist. Santiago looked up. His brother's eyes were opened, red. His cheek trembled and a tear dropped onto his pillow.

Santiago stood. "You have been a better brother to me than I have been to you. I should have said this thirty years ago. But I'm sorry and I ask your forgiveness."

Nico blinked. With great effort, he waved a hand as if to erase the past. Santiago leaned forward and embraced him. Nico's left arm rose tentatively and then fell across Santiago's back.

For first time in his life Santiago Torres genuinely hugged his brother.

Chapter 57: Henny Penny

Santiago had no desire to return to Abigail's house. He was content to let his bag, with his extra pair of shoes and three days of clothing, collect dust in the living room corner for eternity. But one thing nagged his conscience.

So he took a cab back over to his car in Georgetown and drove back up to Cleveland Park. The wheels crunched to a stop in her driveway and he sat in his car a long time before he convinced himself to go back inside.

He cracked open the door and entered. A persistent ray of light shone through the barren trees out front, shining warmly through the front window. The dust motes floating in it whirled in protest at the disturbance. In the sunshine the home, with its light-dappled, polished wood floors, was transformed from the previous night, when it held nothing but terror.

He listened at the bottom of the steps until the hen's clucking turned him around. She eyed him from the corner, where she stood on top of his bag.

"Waiting to ambush me again?"

The hen cocked its head, plopped down and scooted down the hallway to the kitchen.

Santiago followed, opened the pantry door, grabbed a can of corn, a can opener and a bowl. He opened the back door to the fenced yard. The chicken dashed past him, squawking loudly, into the false freedom it offered.

He opened the can into the bowl and put it at the foot of the back steps. He sat, watching the bird ignore the corn and poke through the grass for bugs. He wondered why, given all that happened, he had returned here. Was it really for the chicken? Or was it to slide one last time across the kitchen floor in a pair of sweat socks, hoping to find the fleeting contentment that had left him in wonder?

Santiago rubbed his chest. He had returned to a familiar place: complete puzzlement at his feelings. After his brother's forgiveness, the sawdust inside had been scooped out, replaced by a stew of emotion. Each ingredient, each feeling, surfaced momentarily, demanding due attention, before being pulled under. A paella bubbling with profound grief, fury at betrayal, nascent hope for forgiveness, despair for Bradley, utter fear of the future.

Santiago had failed, utterly. He has set out to prove Jasper had been murdered. He had set out to bring Jasper's killers to justice.

Of course, he'd succeeded in some ways, but the victory was bittersweet, its costs profound. *Tanto nadar para ahogarse en la orilla!* The Stewards, while bloodied, had not been stopped, just shoved further underground. He had no physical proof linking them to anything, no names of their subsidiaries. No names, outside of Walter Byrne, of their members. Santiago rubbed his forehead. The circle around Israel on the map – the warning that many would die – ate at him. Something terrible was still in play. Certainly the Stewards would also want vengeance. Was Santiago to spend the rest of his days waiting to be hunted down?

He looked down at the chicken, envying the simplicity of its life. As humans evolved, they had developed far greater intelligence. Yet they had also developed unsurpassed capacity for grave evil under the deluded guise of good.

Santiago felt drained of hope. He had reached the end of the road disgraced. He simply lacked Jasper's dogged determination, his optimism. For Jasper, there was always another option.

The thought of his friend spirited him back to Abby's last words on the rectory roof. *Don't give up, Santi. Remember Jasper, how good and smart he was. Remember what he would have done.*

She had struggled to say something else.

Santiago cocked his head. *Remember what he would have done.*

What else was there to say?

Remember what he would have done.

Another Jasper memory: Jasper delaying everyone, making them late for dinner again. "Hold on, I have to save this stuff."

"You've saved it already," Santiago growled.

"I have the Holy Trinity of backups. Three backup copies of everything. All in different places. You can never be too safe."

Santiago tilted his head, counted on his hand the number of copies of Cannon's papers and Jasper's thesis he had seen.

The first copy was Jasper's computer, wiped clean. The second copy, from the Odd Fellows Society, was stolen from Vin Guilotti's safe. The third was hidden in Riggs Library.

But the papers in Riggs weren't backup copies. They were the originals.

Santiago jumped to his feet.

Jasper's third backup copy was still missing.

Startled by the Santiago's sudden movement, the chicken dashed away. Then it turned, cocked its head, and clucked three times.

Santiago stared. His mind flew back to Chinatown. Jasper laughing with its residents, chatting in Mandarin. Jasper tucking into the restaurant's kitchens, helping the undocumented workers win their green cards. Santiago later standing in the street. A wizened Chinese woman handing him a string tied around a chicken, refusing when he protested, instead patting his hand, saying something incomprehensible.

"Holy shit," he whispered.

Chapter 58: Exposé

"Is Dr. Stevens available?"

The receptionist vaguely reminded Santiago of a persnickety poodle. She spotted the chicken under his arm and her mouth formed a perfect little o. "He's currently busy with a patient. You are aware Dr. Stevens works with cats and dogs?"

"Could you tell him Father Santiago Torres is here? From Gonzaga."

The o grew bigger.

Santiago put an end to it. "Yes, I'm *that* priest and I'm carrying a chicken. Please tell him it's an emergency."

The chicken priest's voodoo ability to read minds startled her. The woman vanished into the back of the veterinary clinic.

Frank Stevens, a Gonzaga graduate, was the only veterinarian Santi knew in D.C. He'd taught him A.P. U.S. History his junior year, the second year Santiago had been teaching. He was a polite, studious kid. After a couple beers, Frank felt compelled to seek his old teacher out at Gonzaga's annual alumni smoker. Then, as Frank's wife rolled her eyes, he'd recount the exact same story about how all the Gonzaga kids let Santiago teach an entire period with the zipper of his pants wide open.

The woman's head slipped out the door and she gestured for Santiago to follow.

Frank Stevens bounced in like an excited beagle. "Sandra tells me there's an emergency."

"Yes and no. I really just wanted to ask a favor in person. I have enough people in the world already convinced I'm crazy without adding your receptionist to the lot."

"I saw the news this morning," He said soberly.

"I'm actually thinking about saving everyone a lot of trouble and buying my own network."

Stevens offered a wary smile.

"I just want you to look inside my chicken."

Now a curious expression. "Are you looking for anything in particular?"

"Actually I'm looking for anything peculiar. But I'd prefer that the chicken still be alive when you're finished."

Stevens' eyes narrowed. "And you're not at all worried I might think you're crazy."

Santiago patted his shoulder. "Frank, as one of your all-time favorite teachers who taught you wearing virtually no pants, I think it's safe to say our relationship has moved beyond crazy."

Stevens' face broke into a broad smile. "Let's try an X-ray."

Three hours later, Stevens tucked the bandaged chicken back under Santiago's arm and pressed a small plastic cylinder into his palm. "Someone forced it down its throat. It was sitting in its gizzard. In an hour, the chicken will likely wake up, good as new."

Santiago's hands trembled as he opened the cylinder.

"What is it, Father?"

Santiago held up the tiny flash drive. "Tomorrow's headline."

Santiago shifted to his other foot and the young man in the *Post's* lobby spoke into the phone. "Regina, there's a guy named Santiago Torres down here." The man cast a doubtful glance at Santiago. "Says he's a priest you know and needs to speak with you now."

Santiago offered a reassuring smile.

"Ask him what?" he sputtered. His eyebrows went up and he turned back to Santiago. "She wants to know if you're armed." He covered the mouthpiece and whispered. "But I think she might be kidding."

"She's not kidding. Just tell her I need the most aggressive, bloodthirsty reporter on the planet. And I'm going to win her a Pulitzer."

Five minutes later Regina Reynolds, the *Post* reporter who had gotten him fired, strutted like a rooster into the lobby. Reynolds was trim, mid-thirties, beautiful and she knew it. She raked Santiago with her eyes. They narrowed in appreciation and she offered a sly smile.

Santiago reached forward and pressed the flash drive into her outstretched hand. "I actually have a real story for you. Give me two hours and you'll be the most famous reporter in America."

Chapter 59: The Stewards Flee

Santiago cracked open the hospital room door. Propped up in his bed, Nico glanced over the top of the newspaper. He attempted a laugh, grimaced in pain and let the paper drop to his lap. "My brother, vindicated on the front page of the *Post*."

Santiago offered a wry smile.

"The known Stewards have vanished," Nico said. "FBI Director Sampson, the CEOs and three vice presidents of two Fortune 500 companies, and at least one regional president of the Federal Reserve have all vanished. And all leads point to Russia as the final destination."

Santiago sunk into a chair. "Makes sense. That's where it looks like they've hidden most of their liquid assets." Santiago's cell phone rang. He looked at it and rolled his eyes. He hit ignore and tossed it on the foot of his brother's bed.

The morning's newspaper had just scratched the surface. The numbers were astounding. Reynolds' initial calculations put the Stewards' net worth in the hundreds of billions. Among their American assets were Brooker Thompson, the Wall Street bank whose mortgage derivatives sparked the Great Recession, and Greystoke, a weapons conglomerate holding billions in Pentagon contracts and funding the super PACs of the top three presidential candidates.

Santiago shook his head, still feeling less optimistic than his brother. "Regina is still trying to trace all the money, tens of millions in campaign cash to dozens of Congressional campaigns.

Yet because of weak federal laws on campaign contributions, we may never know how many Congressmen they owned."

"Given the evidence on that drive you found, the FBI will eventually roll up some Stewards. Some will talk, Santi. When they're staring at serious jail time, they always talk."

"Not this group, Nico," Santiago shook his head. "And what about the Stewards' principle plan, Outremer? Before he was shot, Bradley had broken into their files. It's something terrible and still unknown. Are you sure the agency found nothing in Bradley's office?"

"His laptop was gone. All the external hard drives. Their servers – even the space they lease on a cloud-based server all of it wiped or swapped out. Bradley even came off the ambulance clean. Nothing in his pockets at all."

"Whatever it is, Outremer is their greatest threat." Santiago's voice couldn't hide his frustration. "Has the U.S. government notified Israel?"

"Of course," Nico said. "They've redoubled security and are searching everything entering that country."

"What else is the FBI doing?"

Nico held up his hands helplessly. "My information is limited right now, Santi. I've only got one clean contact at the agency. And even he's too spooked to answer my calls until he sees proof I'm cleared."

"Cleared?"

"I pulled a gun on another agent, Santi." He laughed and grimaced at the pain. "She's still pissed. And on administrative leave until it's puzzled out. Given Sampson's ties to the case and the fact that I appeared to be his lapdog, they're not taking any risks. They are combing the Bureau for Stewards."

They fell silent a moment before Nico spoke again.

"You did good, Santi. You proved your friend didn't kill himself. That was your main goal, remember? Did you call Jasper's parents to tell them?"

Santi nodded. "His mother cried the entire time, but thanked me."

Nico gave a satisfied bob of the head.

Santiago slowly stood up. "Pearl mentioned that Dean Draper called her from the school. Media trucks are already in the parking lot, waiting to see if I show up. Regina said Senator Bradwell's committee will likely issue subpoenas this week for their own investigations. I don't want to be around for that circus."

"What's your plan?"

"I'm thinking about leaving."

"What do you mean leaving?" Nico said. "The U.S.?"

"For a while, maybe. I've always wanted to go to Spain. I just need some time to think." He shrugged. "Who knows? Maybe I'll jump aboard the first boat I can find and go someplace interesting."

"Whatever you decide, when you come back, you can stay with me as long as you need."

Santiago nodded and turned to leave.

"Hey!" Nico pointed to the foot of his bed. "You forgot your phone. If you don't take it, how do you expect me to follow you and keep you safe?"

As if on cue, the phone lit up and began ringing.

Santiago smiled. "You can have that one. When I get back, I'm getting a new line."

Chapter 60: Across the Seas

Santiago just needed time to think.

You need to pray, he could imagine Roy Taylor nudging him. He shrugged the thought off. Whether out of shame or anger, it was a well he could not drag himself to yet.

He drove instead down to the Gangplank Marina in the channel just below the Lincoln Memorial, perhaps hoping he'd miraculously look up and find himself walking beside his abuelo, toting their fishing gear and a greasy paper bag filled with breakfast empanadas. The day was sunny and warm, a tempting hint at spring. The boat owners on the docks would be prepping their boats beneath the pushy gulls, all forging forward, floating above the world's hard, but thawing ground. It would still the tumult in his skull.

He needed something to calm his growing dread of the great, unknown threat still locked inside Bradley's skull.

Once on the docks, Santiago watched in envy an older man, weathered and sunburnt, prepared to cast off.

"Where you going?" Santi called out.

He raised his cap, rubbed his forehead. "Dunno." He grinned. "Where should I go?"

"Far. Somewhere far."

The man chuckled, turned to depart, then turned back. "Would you want to come along, son?" The old man looked like he'd enjoy the company.

Santiago took a deep breath, tempted. A large yacht, anchored at the far end of the marina, sounded its horn.

The old man nodded with a chuckle. "Unless, of course, you'd prefer a bigger boat. That one's definitely going farther than me."

Santiago smiled in envy.

"Some bigwig launching a tour to save the world."

"He's gonna need a bigger boat."

The old man laughed. "You're welcome to join me. But I aim to be home by supper."

Santiago nodded. "Thanks for the offer. Maybe next time."

The old man tipped his hat and Santiago continued along the waterfront, looking back at the old man as he cast off. He reconsidered twice, nearly walking back to jump on the small boat. When he neared the last dock, he glanced back a final time. The old man's boat was now twenty feet out. Santiago stopped and watched him head down channel, deeply regretting his decision not to jump aboard.

The big yacht's horn sounded again, making Santiago jump. He looked at the large yacht, his eyes landing upon the name written in black letters on its bow: *Across the Seas*.

Santiago's heart thudded. The English translation of *Outremer*. The kingdoms of the Crusades.

He reached for his missing phone and cursed his stupidity.

The door swung shut behind the departing nurse. Nico Torres shifted restlessly in his bed, sucking a breath at the jolt of pain the movement caused. With his good arm, he picked up the television remote and shifted channels.

A perky reporter was addressing the camera. "Ambassador Edward Cochran is taking an approach to the Middle East in a way that's making waves. Having been named to his new post in Israel this past December, he'll be bringing his Fifteen Point Peace Plan to the Middle East. But here's a high seas twist. He'll be drumming up support for the plan during a seven-week overseas trip on his personal yacht. His boat, *Across the Seas*, departs this morning from the Gangplank Marina here in Washington. Yet the ambassador claims this is no publicity stunt and he's certainly no Noah. To find out what makes the eccentric ambassador tick, we sat down with one of his old university professors, Father Jack Donnelly of Georgetown University's Alumni Office."

Nico cursed and reached for his phone on the nightstand.

The call quickly went to voicemail.

In a moment, he was swaying before Pearl Freeman, his hand pressed against his bleeding arm where he had pulled out his IV.

Startled, Pearl looked up from her son's bedside.

"Ms. Freeman, I need you to give me a ride."

Santiago waited as the man who had tossed off the last rope securing the yacht walked past him. Then he broke into a sprint. In a moment he was dashing alongside the side of the large boat, whose engines had begun to churn the water alongside the dock. He aimed for the break in the hand railing and flung himself off the dock.

Santiago landed with a grunt, hanging from the side of the boat, the cold water of the channel churning just feet below him. Hand over hand, he slid aft until he knew he was out of sight of the bridge. He hauled himself over the stern's railing and lay on the deck until they were far enough into the channel that the man on the docks could no longer see him.

Santi was crouching on a yacht that was at least 200 feet long. It was three decks high with the back of its second deck holding a landing pad large enough to land a helicopter.

He skittered along the lowest aft deck, keeping low and out of sight of the yacht's superstructure.

Drawing up to the far side of the stern, he peeked around the starboard side. Twenty feet towards the bow, a man dressed in black stood, smoking on deck, staring out over the railing. The shoulder holster across the man's back assuaged any doubts Santiago had that he had guessed wrong about the boat's purpose.

Santiago pulled himself back and glanced across the deck. A ten-foot long spar, used to pluck lines from the water and keep the yacht from hewing into docks, was hanging along the back wall of the superstructure. He quietly lifted it from its place and bounced it in its hand, finding its center.

Santiago glanced once more around the superstructure. His back still turned, the Steward flicked his cigarette into the water.

Santiago charged.

The slap of his shoes across the deck caused the Steward to whirl and reach for his gun. Santiago bore down, leveling the spar at the man's chest.

The gunman's face wrinkled, betraying a final indecisive moment between aiming and fending off the spar. His hand with the gun moved to bat away the spar a fraction too late and Santiago's weapon knocked the gun free. It flipped against the man's chest and the spar hit home. The startled man gave a grunt and rocketed overboard. His gun clattered to the yacht's deck.

Santi scampered after the weapon, seizing it, spinning around in case the noise of the assault brought someone running. He couldn't believe his luck.

"You look like shit."

"Tell me about it," Nico muttered into the headset. He uttered a silent prayer of thanks his parents had sent him to Colegio San Ignacio, the Jesuit high school back on the island. Captain Eduardo Triay, seated in the front of the Coast Guard chopper arcing over the Potomac, was one of the many acquaintances Nico had made there.

Triay leaned forward, pointing to the horizon and speaking to the pilot before turning to Nico. "We'll need to hail the ship. What's its name?"

Nico waved the idea off. "That will simply warn them we're coming and, if I'm guessing correctly, all we'll get is radio silence."

Nico shifted in pain. He suppressed the panic plaguing him since he saw the television news. Whenever his brother went walking to clear his mind, it was at the Gangplank.

"Ships aren't like planes." Triay interrupted the thought. "They don't file flight plans."

"It's a yacht. I saw it on the news. A huge white yacht."

Triay cocked his head, sweeping his arm across the helicopter's windscreen. "Then tell me, my friend, if we're not going to try to hail your boat, how do you suppose we're going to find your needle in this haystack?"

The chopper's nosed dipped. Across the vast and sparkling Chesapeake far below, white vessels trailed snowy wakes in every direction.

The weight of the gun in his hand shocked Santiago. The way they were flung about on television and the movies made him think they'd be as light as the plastic toys he had as a child. It was suddenly unfathomable that he was almost forty-years-old but had never held a real gun. Just point and shoot, he told himself.

He leveled the gun and moved back to the stern, where he had spotted a door leading into the superstructure.

Enough, a voice sounded in his head.

Santiago looked down at the gun, a sharp ambivalence swelling in his chest. If he tossed it into the bay, it would harmlessly sink, never to harm another soul. Yet the fear clawing at his chest kept him from complying.

He thought of Jasper, whose voice he had imagined uttering the word. He could still imagine his friend standing beside him on the deck, arms folded, patient. *Enough. Not on my account, Santi.*

Santiago muttered a curse in Spanish. He looked at the gun and moved to throw it in the water. Then he stopped. Santiago fiddled with the bottom of the gun until he triggered the magazine release. He shoved the bullets, one by one, out of the magazine until they sat in his palm, their glimmering brass cases a startling contrast to their dull, ugly, gray heads. With a sigh, he tipped his hand forward and the bullets dropped overboard. He pulled back the slide as he'd seen done in countless movies and found the chamber empty, then shoved the empty magazine back into the gun.

Santiago stepped over to the door that led into the interior of the yacht's first level. He cracked upon the door silently. Immediately before him lay the interior staircase leading to the upper two decks and down into the ship's belly. He knew someone had to be on the bridge, likely on the topmost level. Yet Santiago had leapt onto the yacht because he was sure it held the truth Bradley had discovered. Whatever that was, it was most likely in its hold.

Santiago crept down the stairs. They opened into a single, large room filled with supplies, crates and boxes lining the walls, all faintly illuminated with help from the portholes in the ship's hull.

He paused, nosed through a large toolbox by the entrance and removed a small crowbar. Most of the crates and boxes were clearly marked as food and other supplies. He bent over and quietly worked the lids off several crates that lacked any markings. Whoever the owner was, Santiago concluded, he drank a lot of wine. He straightened and his eyes shot forward to the bow. His suspicion grew. The only odd, uncluttered space in the hold surrounded a crate just larger than a file cabinet. And it happened to be the only crate secured by a strap to the floor.

He approached the wooden box, and ran his fingers over a stamped seal of the U.S. State Department. Below it was printed the words: Confidential: Diplomatic Files.

Santiago pressed the crowbar into the space at the crate's edge, prying the front of the wooden box and pulled the side free.

Inside stood an expensive wooden file cabinet. Santiago studied it. Something was clearly odd. Santiago stepped back. The cabinet's proportions seemed wrong.

He pulled one of the drawer handles and, as expected, found it locked. He gave another yank. The drawer didn't rattle or slightly give like a locked file drawer.

Santiago's fingers flew over the front surface of the fake file cabinet and felt along the sides. His heart leapt as his fingers encountered tiny hasps on the cabinet's sides. Leveraging the crowbar, he popped the three of them off.

Santiago gave the front of the file cabinet a nudge and the entire fake front swung open like door. He gasped.

Santiago was staring at a bomb. Eighteen inches wide, it stood about five feet tall. His brain reeled. A single bomb on a yacht headed for Israel? Why would the Stewards go to all this trouble to set off a single explosive device?

His brain screamed the answer. He was staring at a nuclear weapon. And the Steward carrying it had diplomatic protection, which would allow him to bring it into whatever country he wanted.

He had to get to the radio on the boat's bridge. He rushed over to the stairs, listened quietly and began climbing. He bypassed the first and second levels and stopped.

A squawking radio filtered down the stairs and Santiago finished the climb. The stairs opened to another large room, half the size of the ones below. Its closest portion contained a sitting area and a table. Its far side was filled with a large set of cabinets overlaid with a tabletop. Beyond it stood an athletic man in a tight black T-shirt, the strap of gun holster crossing his back. The man was facing away from Santiago toward the boat's port, tapping a screen just beneath the bank of windows overlooking the bay.

Santiago's heart rattled. He crept forward and pressed the muzzle of the revolver to the base of the man's skull. The man, at least a half foot taller, stiffened. "Say anything and it will be the last thought you ever have," Santiago hissed.

The man instinctively raised his hands. "Interlock your fingers and put them on your head. If you move them even slightly—"

"I get it," he muttered. The man's thick fingers came to rest on his head.

Santiago firmly pressed the gun against the base of his skull. "Who else is on the boat with you? And let's assume I know already and am just seeing if you'll tell the truth."

"Just two. O'Reilly and the ambassador."

"The ambassador?"

"Ambassador Cochran," the man said. "You picked the wrong boat to hijack, buddy. You're going to have the entire federal government crawling up your ass if you keep this up."

The man kept whispering, thinking he was persuading Santiago to give up, but Santiago's mind had skittered backwards…Santiago standing back in Carroll Parlor, with South Carolina Senator Byron Bradwell, the senator's wife, Father Jack Donnelly and one other man, a stark, gaunt one, the one who had remained oddly quiet the entire time. "Santiago!" Donnelly had said. "So good to see you! Let me introduce you to Senator and Mrs. Bradwell and Ambassador Edward Cochran."

"Are you alumni?" Santiago had asked the group.

The senator brayed a laugh "Ah, while Edward is, we are not! With the good ambassador's assistance, I'm here today to twist the arms of some of most important men in the city."

Donnelly had laughed in delight.

Santiago gave the gun a little shove of encouragement. "Edward Cochran?"

"Yeah, that's who I said."

The Stewards' plan fell into place in Santiago's mind. The only way they could sneak a nuclear weapon into a country with the tightest security on earth would be to have a U.S. ambassador do it. With his diplomatic credentials, there'd be no searches. No suspicion.

Then the Stewards in the NSA and CIA would blame some other group for its detonation. An immediate world war that would drag the U.S. in. Massive profits and the destruction of the Islamic and Jewish worlds.

"That's a nuclear weapon in the hold, isn't it?"

The man stiffened.

Santiago pushed the muzzle harder against his skull. "Isn't it?"

An awkward laugh. "I think this conversation just went way beyond my pay grade."

"You're going to walk slowly and quietly to the cabin door."

The man obeyed but began to sputter. "You don't want to do this. You don't want this on your conscience."

"I'm touched you're so concerned." On the outside deck, Santiago finally spoke again. "Now you're going to unholster your gun and throw it overboard."

When the weapon splashed into the frigid Chesapeake, Santiago pointed to the life jacket locker at their feet. Nearly seven feet long, it was his best option. He ordered the man to pull out the life jackets and lie face down in the locker. Santiago piled the life jackets on top of the guy and sat on the locker lid to close it. The man grunted as the jackets pinned him to the floor. "Hey, buddy, can you breathe?"

"Kind of," he grunted.

"One more thing." Santiago added. "There are no actual bullets in my gun." He tapped it on the locker lid.

The man groaned.

"If it's any consolation, given your pay grade, no one will be surprised you didn't see that coming."

Santiago slammed the lid and secured its two hasps.

"They must be headed to the mouth of the bay. Get lower!" Nico shouted. "Eduardo, you've got to order every Coast Guard boat you have to seal off the mouth of the Chesapeake. That yacht can't be allowed to get through."

"It's twenty-five miles wide down there. How many boats do you think I have?" said Triay.

The squawk of the helicopter radio interrupted. "Mayday! Mayday! This is the *Across the Seas*. I am in distress. And I've discovered a nuclear weapon aboard this boat. I repeat. There is an illegal nuclear weapon aboard this boat…"

"It's Santiago!" Nico shouted.

Triay returned the hail. "*Across the Seas*, this is the U.S. Coast Guard. Please give us your location, over."

"I'm in the Chesapeake," Santiago responded. "Um, somewhere."

"Jesus Christ!" Nico cursed.

Triay leaned in. "Can you activate your GPS beacon, *Across the Seas*?"

"How do I do that?" Santiago's voice hissed over the radio.

"*Across the Seas*, I'm going to walk you through this—"

Triay flinched at the explosion crackling over the radio.

The front window of the bridge had exploded outwards, its remaining shards fell to the floor where Santiago lay. He was hidden from the gunman's view by the large map table sitting atop cabinets in the middle of the bridge. Santiago reached up and touched the burning part of his shoulder, where Ambassador Edward Cochran's bullet had grazed him.

"Father Torres," the voice mocked, "you're nothing short of a superhero."

Santiago glanced around frantically. His empty gun, which he'd dropped, had spun out of reach across the floor. It was now eight feet away, hidden from Cochran's sight by three chairs and a small table. If Santiago lunged for it, he'd be shot again before he reached the useless thing. He looked up. In the far right window of the bridge, he could see the reflection of the gaunt ambassador warily standing just outside the cabin door.

"Tap! Tap! Still alive, Father? Or are you ready to make your deathbed confession?"

The ambassador's voice was haunting. It rang like a shiver, an angry, plucked bowstring.

"I have another quote for you, Father. 'The fear of death follows from the fear of life. A man who lives fully is prepared to die at any time.'" He paused. "I'm ready to die, Father. Are you?"

"Not quite yet, Cochran. You might be surprised to learn that Mark Twain also supposedly said, 'Never let school interfere with your education.' Given that Twain was such a smartass, perhaps you put too much stock in his other sayings."

Santiago felt his bleeding shoulder again, and nudged open the cabinet beside him. Hands trembling, heart thumping, he searched it, hoping for anything useful. It was empty save for an unmarked black case sitting next to some field glasses and a single old nautical map.

"Twain it was. Well done, Father!"

Santiago watched the reflection. Cochran shifted, a step inside the bridge. Another step and he'd see the gun on the floor.

His heart galloping, Santiago opened the black case. Flare gun. He glanced at the broken bridge window above him.

"Here's another, Father. 'When he shall die, take him and cut him out in little stars and he will make the face of heaven so fine that all the world will be in love with night and pay no worship to the garish sun.' Do you recognize that one?"

Santiago's fingers trembled as he opened the flare gun and inserted two flares.

"How disappointing, Father," said Cochran. "It's from Romeo and Juliet. By Shakespeare."

Santiago pointed the flare gun toward the broken window.

"You know that one, don't you, Father?" Cochran mocked. "A tragic story of taboo love that results in the death of both foolish lovers?"

A blaze of anger flashed through Santiago. He rolled to his knees and fired the flare directly at Cochran. The flare glanced off Cochran's hand and the gun discharged. Another bridge window behind Santiago shattered as the flare spiraled out the cabin door. Cochran cursed as his gun flew to the deck behind him.

Santiago leapt to his feet and fired the second flare. The fireball slammed into the wall beside Cochran, who dove outside. The flare ricocheted back into the bridge. Santiago leapt upon the control console and pulled himself out the broken window. He desperately dashed across the bridge roof to reach Cochran before he could reach his gun.

Cochran raised the weapon and Santiago leapt.

The two men crashed onto the helipad. Cochran's gun slid fifteen feet, clattering onto the deck below. Santiago landed a punch to Cochran's face before the wiry man flipped him off.

Cochran rolled to his feet and, like a wild beast, bared his teeth in rage.

"Down! Down!" Nico screamed. He pointed in the direction of a large boat from which a flare had shot horizontally across the bay. "Give me your rifle!" he commanded of the guardsman beside him. "This is my shot."

The man hesitated.

Triay nodded and the guardsman handed over the weapon. The helicopter swooped downward, swirling around the two men. Nico screamed directions. He rolled back the chopper door and leaned against his restraint. Pain shot through his chest. Nico struggled to raise the rifle. He centered Cochran in his rifle sight. He sucked in his breath and held it.

Cochran pivoted, falling behind Santiago. No clear shot.

"¡Coño pa'l carajo!"

Cochran lunged. Santiago deftly parried Cochran's fist and threw a right hook. It caught Cochran on his chin. Dazed, the man staggered backward.

"It's over, Cochran! Don't be a fool."

Cochran lips curled into a snarl. "It's over when we're both dead." Cochran charged. Santiago stepped back. *Don't look down.* Cochran's right hand shot toward Santiago's face. He ducked, parried with his left, smashing Cochran's jaw.

Cochran kept coming. He swung wildly with left, crunching against Santiago's cheekbone. Santiago reeled backward, teetering on the edge of the helipad. Cochran charged. Santiago gained his footing, rushing forward. The two men exploded together. Santiago blocked a right hook, a left and parried another right. His fist connected with Cochran's chin, sending the man staggering. Santiago threw a jarring left. Another right left Cochran stunned. Then Santiago threw the hardest punch of his life, lifting the man off the helipad and crashing him onto his own back.

Enraged, Santiago rushed over, grabbed him by the top of his shirt and shook him. Cochran's eyes fluttered open. Santiago hissed. "If you or your buddies ever manage to stand up again, I will always be here to knock you down. Always."

Santiago dropped the unconscious man to the helipad. His knees quaking with fright, he spun a jagged, unsteady circle. He glanced up into the blinding light, where Nico smiled at him out of the open bay of a red and white Coast Guard helicopter.

Santiago fell backward onto his rump, barked a brief, ragged laugh. And then he sobbed.

It was over.

Chapter 61: A Place to Stand

"You!"

Santiago wavered at Bradley's hospital room door. It was generally not a good sign when Pearl Freeman began remarks with "You!"

Bradley waved his arm to indicate it was safe to enter. "Come in," he croaked. A smile creased his face.

Now that her son was safe, Pearl let loose. She launched her lecture with gusto. "It's one thing for you to involve me in your whackadoodle misadventures, but my children and my grandchildren are strictly off limits, Santiago Torres! What makes you think, without first checking with me, that you can casually go about risking their lives? Involving them in such outrageous skullduggery?"

"Yes! Outrageous skullduggery!" Bradley was shaking with suppressed laughter and grimacing at the same time. "You tell him, Mama!"

Pearl peered over her glasses, attempting to laser-gaze her son into silence.

"And don't forget all of Father Whackadoodle's diabolical chicanery!" Bradley added. "That was even worse!"

"Keep it up and I'll ensure your next coma is more permanent." Pearl pursed her lips and looked down at the folded crossword puzzle in her lap. Finished with the fire and brimstone approach, she would now impose the silent treatment.

"Thank you for not dying." Santiago smiled at Bradley. "I would have felt terribly guilty."

"Not for long," Pearl muttered while scratching in an answer. "I would have gladly put you out of your misery."

Pearl's silent treatment phase had passed.

"In all seriousness, I apologize for getting you shot."

"Don't be ridiculous," said Bradley. "What guy doesn't want to get shot and survive? You know how many times I've had to sit at a bar and listen to my friend Warren tell his stupid story about how he rolled his father's BMW three times on the way home from King's Dominion back in high school? Now it's like, 'Yeah, Warren, you pansy-ass, I got shot saving the world.'" He looked over at his mother playfully. "All the women at the bar are gonna throw themselves at me."

She ignored him.

"Anyway," said Santiago. "I stopped by to thank you both. Of all the people involved, both of you and Nico stood by me loyally. I'll never forget that."

Pearl put her pencil down but didn't look up.

"And, Pearl, in fairness, I've also come to tell you that I've decided to go away for a bit. It means you're stuck with Dean Draper and Stan Quigley for the time being."

He had expected some wry retort but she shocked him. She reached out and grasped his fingers, shaking his hand firmly. "You're coming back."

The way she said it made it unclear if it were a question or a command.

Santiago simply bent forward and kissed her quickly on the cheek before she could pull away. "Just don't let Quigley hug you," he teased.

Santiago had two final visits to make to tie up loose ends.

He checked the Georgetown dorm room number a final time before knocking.

A young woman with a startled, freckled face topped by an explosion of burnt orange hair opened the door. She gasped. She let go of the handle and the door kept opening until it tapped against the wall.

"How did you find me?"

"Your name is Sarah, isn't it?"

A reluctant nod.

"Well, you certainly are an odd fellow."

A nervous smile.

"You are the president of the Odd Fellows Society?"

"How did you find me?"

"You didn't make it easy. After Jasper died, you were the first in his library office, weren't you?"

"The Stewards didn't know about it. They came back the next day."

"You also were in Jasper's room."

She swallowed. "After the Stewards left, before the police searched it."

"You stripped his office and his room of anything related to the Odd Fellows."

"We're a secret society, so there wasn't that much. I burned all that I could find. Every photo. And the membership list he kept on parchment. They would have tracked us down and killed us after the clues started showing up."

"You're a smart, young woman."

"How did you find me?"

Santiago reached into his pocket and pulled out the photograph Mrs. Willoughs had given him at the funeral. He held it out to her. "You won the scavenge last year. In this photo Jasper is handing you your victory medal. That made you official president of the Odd Fellows. I just had to check last year's yearbook to track down your name."

The young woman took the photo and studied it. Her face crinkled. "He looks so happy here." She looked up at Santiago. "He was one of the nicest guys I've ever met."

"And you helped him. You proved a great friend."

"He hid all that stuff the day before he was killed, thinking he was being overly cautious. All those clues were supposed to be for this year's scavenge, but he gave them to me and made me promise that I'd send them to you if something happened to him. I would have just handed them to you but he made me promise to do it anonymously to keep all the Odd Fellows safe."

"You kept your promise, Sarah. You helped me and kept a lot of other people safe. I just wanted to thank you properly."

She held up the photo. "Can I keep this?"

"Absolutely."

Santiago turned to go.

"I'm writing new clues. The Odd Fellows Society is still going to hold their scavenge this spring. In Father Willoughs' honor," she called after him.

Santiago turned. "Then make it impossible."

Sarah's laughter filled Santiago with hope.

Twenty minutes later, after a quick trip back to his car, Santiago knocked on Roy Taylor's door. Roy's voice invited him to enter. Santiago stood at the open door until Roy looked up. The old priest sat back in his chair and smiled broadly. "Come in! Come in, Santi!"

He closed the door, put the bag he was carrying down and slipped into his favorite chair in Roy's office. Roy jumped up from his desk and walked over. He fell into the one beside him and slapped his knee. "Anything exciting happen since your last confession?"

Santiago laughed. "Where do I begin?"

"I'm the one that needs to begin. I owe you an apology." Roy shook his head. "It was just all so hard to believe on the face of it—"

Santiago held up a hand. "It still is."

Roy shook his head. "I should have believed you. I'm sorry I didn't."

Santiago nodded. "Forgiven."

Roy smiled at him. "Stan Quigley and Alvin Stokes are looking for you. Alvin's even hoping for exclusive rights to your personal story."

Santiago pressed himself into the back of his seat and chuckled. Gonzaga's president and its board president would have to wait. "I think Stan was smart about putting me on sabbatical for the rest of the year. I plan to take him up on it. When I come back, I'll know."

"Know what?" Roy knew the answer to his question but had asked it anyway.

"Whether I'm committed to remaining a priest."

Roy looked at him. "You're not really here for confession, are you?"

"That's just it. I don't know that I'm sorry for any of it." Santiago pulled at a stray thread on the arm of the chair. "As horrible as so much of it was, I'm not sure I would do anything differently if even given the chance. I know that sounds wrong, but—"

"It doesn't sound wrong."

"I just wanted you to know I told the truth." Santiago nodded. "And, while Jasper was the lever, I found my place to stand. That's all. My plane leaves in three hours. It's an international flight, so I should get going."

Roy nodded.

"Could I ask a favor?"

"Name it," Roy said.

"I really don't want to go back to Gonzaga and wade through the media just to return some of my stuff to my room. Could I just leave a bag here until I get back?"

"You're not taking anything?"

"All my other stuff is still at the residence. I'd rather travel light and get what I need when I get there." Santiago stood and Roy Taylor followed. The two old friends embraced before Santiago walked over to the door. "Thanks, Roy."

Roy patted Santiago on his back and he shut his office door. He stood on the other side a moment, uttered a quick prayer for his friend and walked back around his desk. He fell into his chair and peered through his bifocals at his computer screen.

An odd sound caused him to glance back up.

Roy Taylor cocked his head, then looked back at his computer screen. Sighing, he swiveled forward and walked around his desk. He eyed the bag a moment, then bent to open its zipper.

A single white feather floated up.

And the clucking began.

Author's Note

During the mid-1990s, my brother, an undergraduate student at Georgetown University, told me that he'd been contacted by an unnamed stranger, who met him on campus and extended an invitation to join a secret society. Upon returning to his dormitory and sharing the story, a friend proclaimed, "You were tapped by the Stewards!"

While my brother declined to join the unnamed group, it planted a seed for a fictional story.

At the time I was teaching history at Gonzaga College High School in Washington, D.C., indisputably the best job I've ever had. I fell in love with the school, its rich, long history and its remarkably strong and proud community (Go Gonzaga! Beat St. John's!). My work there also added to my lifelong respect and admiration for the Maryland Province of the Society of Jesus, known as the Jesuits. As much as my parents, the Jesuits have been responsible for shaping my worldview, beginning in my high school years at Scranton Preparatory School. Since many Jesuits have proven heroes in my life, it seemed apt to make the hero of this tale also a Jesuit, however flawed he may be.

During my days poking around the capital, I learned about its former slave markets and the role that enslaved Americans had played in the construction of our nation's most significant buildings. And I was utterly surprised when a Jesuit friend told me of the Georgetown Plantation Project, which aimed to preserve and explore the Jesuits' history as slave and plantation owners. This ignominious history stood in stark contrast to the Jesuits I knew –

men committed to education and social justice. Yet the Jesuits didn't shy away from admitting this failing; in contrast, they sought to explore and preserve that truth for others.

That story of the two hundred seventy-two men, women and children sold downriver to a Louisiana planter is a fascinating yet horrifying truth. The sale even triggered outrage among Jesuits of the day. The Jesuit provincial who ordered the sale, Thomas Mulledy, later apologetically wrote that he knew history would condemn him for the act, adding, "No doubt I deserve it."

The story of the two hundred seventy-two still demands to be told in greater detail. I hope, by including it here, I have not demeaned or belittled it in any way – for I intended the opposite.

Together the two true tales, woven together in an entirely imagined way, grew into this work of fiction. In its entirety, it's intended as a metaphor for how the legacies of slavery still touch our lives in often unperceived ways.

While the geographic settings of this story will be familiar to many readers, this story is a work of fiction. The characters who interact on these pages are entirely the products of my imagination. So that there is no misunderstanding, I'd like to take a moment to tease out a few other historical truths referenced by the story's characters.

First, the story of the Jesuits' plantations and slave sale is historically accurate as told by Santiago here. It's also true that Georgetown, whose colors are the blue and gray of the soldiers' uniforms in the Civil War, did financially depend in its early years on the Jesuits' plantations and their slaves.

The university, which sat on the Potomac border between the Union and Confederacy, was also dramatically affected by the Civil War. According to the Georgetown Voice, a university publication, ninety percent of the school's students left the school to fight for the Confederacy. Yet it is also true that one of the university's most notable presidents, Patrick Healy (1874-1882), referenced within this tale, was an African-American Jesuit who "passed" as white. In his youth prior to the Civil War, Healy was a legal slave in Georgia, where he was born the son of a plantation owner and his mother, a bi-racial domestic slave named Mary Eliza. Healy was a remarkable man, sent to the North along with his brothers for his education to avoid the legal stigmas and limitations of his home state. In New York he still faced discrimination from his fellow students. Healy, however, went on to become the first African American to earn a Ph.D., the first to become a Jesuit and the first to lead a predominantly white university. His name graces the magnificent building that greets visitors to Georgetown's campus; indeed, Healy helped transform the small, nineteenth century college into the remarkable and highly respected university that Georgetown is today.

Where did the funds from the sale of the two hundred seventy-two men, women and children – a sum totaling $115,000 – really go? It wasn't stolen as this work of fiction imagines. The funds were actually used by the Jesuits to fund Georgetown buildings as well as the establishment of three other educational institutions: Xavier High School in Manhattan, St. Joseph's in Philadelphia and Fordham University in the Bronx.

Themes of race and our nation's struggles with the legacies of slavery and segregation are interwoven into the story. This brings me to the final historically accurate nugget. In Chapter 22, I included an excerpt of a February 2009 speech given by the first black U.S. Attorney General, Eric Holder, six years before this story is set. Holder uttered the words in the first speech he gave as attorney general. In addressing our national tendencies to self-segregate, Holder's words proved very controversial, as does Santiago's embrace of its challenge. The words prompted great reflection on my part and I hope their inclusion here does for my readers as well.

I also must acknowledge the writings of Franciscan Father Richard Rohr. Rohr's insights into the life arc of many adults he's encountered influenced not only my shaping of Santiago but also the metaphors Roy Taylor offers Santiago within this tale. If Roy Taylor's gentleness and insights inspire you, you may find something similar in Rohr's writings.

Last, I would be remiss if I failed to thank those who, over recent years, have helped make this story better by reading it and offering suggestions. My brother Brendan's ruthless honesty (for which I am grateful), prompted a number of rewrites that strengthened the story. Similarly Nikki Pivnichny, Carol Collins,

Ruth Smith, Cindy Diaz and Roly Diaz offered much helpful commentary and edits. I also thank Ruth Smith and her daughter, Emma Smith, for their patience and artistry in creating this book's cover. Also helping me shape Santiago into a more believable Puerto Rican were several native Puerto Ricans, including my wife, Maria, our treasured friend Dulce Roman, and my wife's childhood friend, Carmen Piñero Proctor, who also happened to attend Georgetown. A Tampa friend, Marty Hamilton, also took the time to discuss Middle Eastern geopolitics, which improved the story. Further, I would be remiss if I didn't also thank my close friend, Dave Morris, for sharing a story about an old Philadelphia hall that inspired this novel's name.

Most important, I thank you, my reader, for supporting my work. Today an author's success ultimately depends on readers' willingness to share their enthusiasm for a novel. I would be personally grateful for any support you can offer this book on social media, in online review forums and in conversations with fellow bibliophiles. Readers who wish to share their thoughts can drop me an e-mail at info@cgbarrett.com.

For more information about books I have written, I invite you to visit www.cgbarrett.com.

Book Club Discussion Topics

The author, C.G. Barrett, is available to speak to book clubs and groups. Discounts on books for book groups are available. To make arrangements, please e-mail info@cgbarrett.com.

Below are some possible topics for your book club discussion:

1. This book is very much about the failure of fathers (both priests and dads) and its impact. Consider Charlie Breckinridge and his father; Philip Cannon; Santiago and Nico's father; and Santiago himself. Which redeems himself in your mind?
2. The name "The Odd Fellows" has a history worthy of a brief Internet search. In what way does this book's Odd Fellows Society keep with the roles of Odd Fellows Societies in Europe and the U.S.?
3. Did you learn anything about U.S. history from the book? Knowledge of history and our nation's cultural heritage is essential for Santiago's success, perhaps ironic since he might be considered an "outsider" by some. Is knowledge of your country's heritage and history important for effective civic participation and success by its citizens?
4. In Chapter 22 Santiago listens to the U.S. attorney general give a speech about the racial separation that still touches American lives, particularly in their neighborhoods and friendships. Is the description fair or accurate? Do you feel

comfortable discussing matters of race with people of a different race or do you avoid the topic?
5. During a moment of frustration, Santiago observes that America is obsessed with race. Do you agree with his observation or feel it's unfair?
6. Chapter 39 is titled "Charlie's Penance." In religious tradition, a penance is an act undertaken to seek forgiveness. What do you view as Charlie's true penance?
7. Which is your favorite character and how did you connect with him or her?
8. Have you ever had experiences similar to those in the story?
9. The chicken is a reoccurring character. What is its symbolic purpose and how does it represent Santiago's own personal struggle to find his "place to stand?"
10. Why did the author make the story's main character not easily characterized as either "white" or "black?" Would it have changed the story if Santiago had been white or black instead of Latino?
11. The American Bald Eagle, the national symbol of the United States, is starkly black and white. Its name is woven into this story a number of times. How does it work as a symbol of both the U.S. – and an observation about the nation's unique racial history and divisions?
12. At what point did you figure out the mystery?
13. What choice about his future do you hope the character Santiago makes? Would you be disappointed or happy for him if he remained a priest? Is this decision, for you, an essential part of his finding a place to stand?

About the Author

    A native of Northeast Pennsylvania, C. G. Barrett received a B.A. from Johns Hopkins University and a M.A. from George Mason University.
    A former teacher and student of history, Barrett currently serves as publisher of a Tampa newsmagazine. His humor writing about life as a parent has appeared in over a dozen parenting magazines throughout the United States.
    Barrett's popular novels have included both young adult and adult fiction in the genres of fantasy and mystery. His love of mythology, fairy tales, history and politics is evident in his fiction, which frequently explores spirituality, family and identity in a rapidly changing world.
    Barrett lives with his wife, his three daughters and his two Shetland Sheepdogs in Tampa, Florida.
    For more information about his books, visit www.cgbarrett.com.